STARCHASER

R. M. GRAY

PENGUIN BOOKS

PENGUIN BOOKS

UK | USA | Canada | Ireland | Australia
India | New Zealand | South Africa

Penguin Books is part of the Penguin Random House group of companies
whose addresses can be found at global.penguinrandomhouse.com.

www.penguin.co.uk   www.puffin.co.uk   www.ladybird.co.uk

First published in the USA by Little, Brown and Company, a division of Hachette Book
Group, Inc., and in Great Britain by Penguin Books 2025
001

Text copyright © Rebekah Gray, 2025
Map by Srdjan Vidakovic
Family tree and title page art copyright © Colin Verdi, 2025
Rose ornaments © paprika/Shutterstock.com

The moral right of the author and illustrator has been asserted

No part of this book may be used or reproduced in any manner for the
purpose of training artificial intelligence technologies or systems. In accordance
with Article 4(3) of the DSM Directive 2019/790, Penguin Random House
expressly reserves this work from the text and data mining exception.

Text design by Michelle Gengaro
Printed and bound in Great Britain by Clays Ltd, Elcograf S.p.A.

The authorized representative in the EEA is Penguin Random House Ireland,
Morrison Chambers, 32 Nassau Street, Dublin D02 YH68

A CIP catalogue record for this book is available from the British Library

ISBN: 978-0-241-73509-1

All correspondence to:
Penguin Books
Penguin Random House Children's
One Embassy Gardens, 8 Viaduct Gardens, London SW11 7BW

Penguin Random House is committed to a
sustainable future for our business, our readers
and our planet. This book is made from Forest
Stewardship Council® certified paper.

For you, dear reader, for setting sail on
this journey with me

PART ONE

FURY

Chapter One

I feel his presence before I see him. His steady heartbeat never falters as he steps out of the shadows, the hood of his black cloak drawn to cover his face.

"You came," Will says, his voice dark and deep. His hood conceals his emerald eyes, but I imagine they sparkle with amusement as he draws a wicked-looking knife from his belt. "I'd begun to think you wouldn't honor our agreement."

His leather boots squelch in the mud as he makes his way down the deserted cobblestone street. He comes to a halt in a gilded puddle of lantern light, ten feet from where I stand, flurries of snow dusting his shoulders.

"And miss my chance to meet the *great* William Castor?" Captain Shade's muffled voice comes from directly behind me. He presses the muzzle of a flintlock pistol to my cheek, and I cringe at the bite of the cold metal on my skin. "Let's not waste time, shall we?"

Will tilts his head, a subtle command. Two men in full suits of bloodred armor emerge onto the street, hauling a battered woman between them, her cropped ginger hair matted in clumps. Blood steadily drips from the crudely bandaged stump that would have been her right leg only a few hours ago. I've seen Margaret amputate a limb before—I can tell the leg wasn't removed by a surgeon. If she doesn't get proper medical treatment soon, there's a chance she won't make it through the night.

"You certainly know how to treat a lady," Shade says, an edge to his light, conversational tone.

"She's alive." Will runs his gloved fingertips over the edge of his blade. "That was our agreement."

"Aye." Shade laughs as he presses the muzzle of the pistol beneath my chin. "Miss Oberon goes free, and in exchange, you return my quartermaster, Diana—safe from harm."

Click. He pulls the hammer of the flintlock back, smoothly wrapping an arm around my midsection, his hand splayed possessively over my abdomen. It's a predatory threat that would make my skin crawl—if *I* wasn't the one to suggest it.

I know Captain Shade isn't evil. His true name is Titus Anteres, the crown prince of the Eerie—the same prince who joined a secret rebellion against his own parents. But we agreed that we'd need to convince the royal Bloodknights that I was held *prisoner* aboard his ship, and so Titus's calculated hand placement is all part of that charade. I try to catch Will's eye, to reassure him that this plan will work, but he glares at Shade's hand, his jaw set.

I resist the urge to roll my eyes at him.

We agreed to all this just yesterday. I woke—having spent two weeks unconscious aboard Shade's ship, the *Starchaser*—and Will wasted no time in telling me the king's plan to appoint me as one of his Bloodknights, to make it clear to his subjects where my loyalties lie. But the king doesn't know the truth—that becoming a Bloodknight will allow me to infiltrate the royal household and get to the true depths of their evil plans for humans and Myths. And gaining access to Castle Grim will bring me one step closer to undoing the curses binding me and Will.

Once Will whisks me off to the castle, I will use my abilities to sense whether Titus is right: that his fiancée, the princess of Hellion, is possessed by Morana. Then, if what Titus believes is true, we can force the Sylk queen to take her corporeal form, use her blood to cure not only mine and Will's Underling curses, but also to free my brother, Owen, from Morana's service.

In exchange for my cooperation, Titus has agreed to give me his medallion—an heirloom that once belonged to the heir of Hildegarde, which he assures me will grant me and my family passage to the only place on this earth truly safe for humans from both the tyrannical rule of Nightweavers and Morana's Underling forces—the Red Island.

But before I leave the Eerie once and for all, I plan to take down Titus's father, the king—to make him pay for what he's done to me, to my family, and to my people.

A cure.

Freedom.

Revenge.

I catch Will's gaze at last.

And love?

I *can* have it all—I just need to hold up my end of the bargain.

Shade leans forward, his mask brushing the side of my head. "I requested the safe return of Diana to raise the morale of my crew. However, if she were to bleed out before I could bring her safely home..." He clucks his tongue. "Well, my crew would be just as pleased to know I'd robbed the king of *his prize*."

He pulls me in tighter, as if to make his point. His warm breath ghosts over the shell of my ear, and the scent of salty air that clings to his skin transports me to yesterday. To the moment when he revealed he was both pirate and prince. The moment I ran from him—horrified that a pirate I long admired was living a double life, and actually the next in line to a tyrannical dynasty of Nightweavers. I dived into the sea, my sanctuary, but Shade followed me into the water without hesitation, where he pressed his lips to mine.

Once Will pulled me from the sea and back aboard the *Starchaser*, Titus hardly spoke to me at all. And this evening he was silent again, even as we rowed to shore together. Now, as Shade, he strokes my cheek with the pistol; it sends both a shiver down my spine and a thread of guilt winding its way around my heart.

Did Titus tell Will he kissed me? Can I even call it a kiss?

And did he see what I saw under the waves, that woman made of brilliant gold dust?

Shade's voice snaps me back to reality. "Perhaps I'll allow Miss Oberon to live." I can almost hear the wicked smile in his voice. "Though, I suppose my crew might prefer that she lack the means to wield a knife, don't you?"

Shade takes a step back, dragging me with him. The Bloodknights nearly drop Diana, but Will holds up a hand, an unspoken command for them to wait. Slowly, he takes a few paces back as well, holding his knife out to his right, where the sharp edge of the blade rests on the skin of Diana's throat.

"Take one more step," Will says, his voice deathly calm, a subtle honey-gold light flaring in his eyes, "and the girl loses more than her leg."

Shade sighs. "Don't you ever get tired of making empty threats?" He removes the gun from my face, releasing his grip on my waist only to kick my legs out from under me. I land on my knees, my teeth gritted against the pain. He must aim the pistol at the back of my head, because when I look up, Will's face has gone pale. "Are you really willing to gamble with her life? I know what she means to you."

My heartbeat thunders in my chest. When we agreed on how this exchange would play out, we didn't discuss *this*. Captain Shade—*Titus*—has saved my life more than once. But can I trust a pirate not to take things too far?

Can I trust *him*?

Will never takes his eyes off me as he removes the blade from Diana's throat. The Bloodknights throw her forward, where she lands in a heap on the ground beside me.

"Your turn, pirate," Will says, fixing a glare on Shade.

I glance behind me as Shade lowers his weapon, shrugging his shoulders. "She's all yours."

I meet Will's gaze once more as I gather the strength to rise, and I see it there—the relief, the concern, the silent apology. And...something else. Something neither of us has given breath to. I brace my palms against the slick, rough cobblestones, lifting myself slowly when—

BANG.

The gunshot rattles in my chest, my ears ringing. For a split second, I think I've been shot. But it's Will who staggers to the left, sways. With his free hand, he touches his shoulder. His fingers come away wet with blood.

And then chaos.

I scramble out of the street, pressing myself flat against a building as Captain Shade's crew descend from the rooftops, swords flashing. Bloodknights stream out from the alleyways to meet them, wielding blades made of Elysian Iron. Gunshots reverberate off the brick walls, and for a moment, I lose sight of Will in the blur of bodies.

But there—there he is, locked in battle with Captain Shade.

It's all for show, I remind myself. Titus and Will don't actually hate each other. They're on the same side; they would never try to kill each other.

Still, shooting Will wasn't part of the plan. And if Shade is going off script...

With an expertly timed strike, Will uses his sword to knock the gun out of Shade's grasp, making it a fair fight. But with Will's steady loss of blood, I'm not sure how much longer he can keep this up.

I would kill for a weapon. Even though, despite the battle that rages around me, I know I'm not in any real danger. Shade's crew wouldn't dare harm me, even if they didn't fear what their captain would do to them if they did. And the Bloodknights have been ordered by the king to assist Will in bringing me safely to Castle Grim.

Nevertheless, my fingers itch for my daggers. I can't bear sitting still, watching as others shed blood in my name. Blood that pools at my feet. Blood that whispers to me in a language I feel I've forgotten, like waking from a dream...

I shut my eyes tight as the sickeningly sweet smell of copper overwhelms my senses. I can't risk anyone seeing the golden glow that now emanates from my irises—growing brighter as my affinity continues to rise within me, stronger now than it did the first time it manifested that night in the bloody fountain.

I shake my head. It's been only two weeks since Titus revealed I am half Nightweaver—a bloodletter with elemental power over water. But now is not the time for losing control. Not when I haven't even begun to discover what kind of power I can wield. Not when I can't be sure of the damage I could do if I just—

A Bloodknight slices a member of Shade's crew, and the girl crumples to the ground next to me, entrails spilling from the gash in her abdomen. I tried my best not to learn the names of Shade's crew, especially knowing what I planned for tonight, but now as the girl dies nameless beside me, shame coils in my gut.

She chokes, coughing blood onto the cobblestones, before her eyes roll to the back of her head.

I look away.

Shade's crew knew what they signed up for. They knew some of them might not leave this street alive. Still, the blood that seeps into the cracks is on my hands.

Let them believe the great Captain Shade, hero of the human rebellion, has lost, I told Will and Titus. *Then, once the king believes he's won, we'll attack from the inside. They won't suspect a thing.*

Will was reluctant, but I thought I saw a hint of pride in Titus's eyes as I detailed my plan to invade Castle Grim by using his father's own scheme against him. A brilliant plan—*if* Will doesn't succumb to the wound in his shoulder.

It has to be convincing, Will said.

It has to be a struggle, Titus agreed.

It has to look real, we decided.

Only, now I wonder if I didn't misjudge the lengths they were willing to go to stage this deception.

"Give up," Shade drawls, loud enough that I hear him over the din of clashing metal. "You're finished, Nightweaver! Run along home to your mum and dad."

Will's jaw clenches. Sparks fly as he brings his blade down hard, connecting with Shade's sword in a strike that vibrates through the street, almost as if the earth itself responded to Will's fury.

False fury, I tell myself.

But then, why does it seem so real? Why do his eyes flash with a hatred I've never seen in him before?

Why—I ask myself, even as I watch him move at an inhuman speed, too quick for my eyes to properly detect—does he deflect Shade's counterblow, lunging forward, his blade aimed at Shade's chest? Why does his sword pierce Shade's flesh with an audible squelch?

Why is all I can think as he stabs Captain Shade—stabs *Titus*, his best friend, his brother in every nature except birth—straight through the heart.

Chapter Two

This wasn't supposed to happen.

Shade—*Titus*—goes limp, skewered on Will's blade. I want to scream, but I can't seem to find my voice.

Will's chest heaves as he stares at his best friend, watching the light leave Shade's eyes. He whispers something too low for anyone to hear.

This can't be happening.

Will withdraws his sword, and Shade falls, his body toppling sideways at an awkward angle before hitting the cobblestones with a dull thump. I can't see his face—his body is turned away from me—but when he falls, his crimson tricorn is knocked from his head, his golden-blond hair now on full display.

At once, the fighting stops. Shade's crew freezes, shock apparent in their terrified expressions. Even the Bloodknights halt midswing, turning to look at Will, at his face smattered red with blood.

"Your captain is dead!" Will shouts, his voice raw—rough and ragged and all wrong. It comes out as a deep, rasping sound, as if it isn't his voice. He clears his throat, his eyes shifting from gold back to green, and when he speaks again, his voice is smooth. "Malachi Shade is dead."

He raises his foot—stomps down hard on Shade's mask. It cracks like bone beneath his weight.

I forget myself. I forget the plan. I forget everything.

I lurch forward, attempting to reach Titus's prone body, all the while telling myself that I'm doing it for the medallion—that if Shade dies, I might lose my chance to reach the Red Island, and this will have all been for nothing. But in that instant, red smoke fills the street, too thick to see Will, or Titus, or anything for that matter.

A hand covers my mouth.

And then I'm being dragged.

I bite down hard, drawing blood. The metallic fluid floods my mouth, sending a jolt of power through my veins. It gives me enough strength to nearly break my captor's hold, but, as if they expected this, they tighten their grip, crushing my arms to my sides. I kick, struggling to find my footing, but it's no use—whoever has me is much, much taller than me. With what seems like little effort, I'm pulled backward, up, through a narrow doorway and into a carriage.

Into someone's lap.

"Normally, I wouldn't be opposed to biting," comes a silky, lilting voice, his hot breath on the back of my neck sending a shiver down my spine, "but I rather benefit from having all my fingers, love."

My heart skips a beat. Restarts.

He releases his grip, and I fall forward, catching myself on the bench across from him. I whirl to find *Titus*, dressed in his princely garb—a black military jacket trimmed with scarlet thread—seated across from me in an obnoxiously luxurious carriage. He cocks his head, a strange expression of curiosity on his familiar face. Murderous rage replaces my grief as his lips tilt upward in a mischievous grin.

"You bastard!" I seethe. "I just watched you die!"

"Yes, well," he says with an infuriating shrug. "You wanted it to look real, hmm?"

My heart beats fiercely against my rib cage. I feel everything—anger, guilt, confusion, *relief*?—so acutely, so painfully, I can hardly breathe.

"Don't worry about Rook," he says with a mocking smile. "William missed his heart. My crew will have gotten him out of here by now. One of my bonewielders is probably stitching Diana and him both up as we speak."

Rook—he was one of the crew I met aboard the *Starchaser* as we planned this evening's attack. And once before, when Captain Shade saved him from the gallows, when Will saved me and my family from the hearing in the town square. Rook's impersonation of Shade—of Titus—was so believable he fooled me along with everyone else.

I swallow the lump in my throat, my voice thick when I say, "I thought you were dead."

Titus glances up at me, eyes narrowed. Instantly, his features soften.

"Aster," he murmurs, chastised. "Forgive me—"

"Don't," I grit out, my cheeks burning. "There's nothing to forgive. The plan worked. That's all that matters."

Titus frowns. His brows pull together, his blue eyes piercing.

Softly, tenderly, he says, "Please, love, don't cry."

"I'm not—" I bite my bottom lip to keep it from trembling. "It's not you, it's..."

And then, before I can stop myself, every emotion comes spilling out of me and every memory from the past few months rushes to the surface.

My father, lying dead on the kitchen floor.

My brother Owen, who tried to turn me into a monster like him.

The king, who expects me to swear allegiance to him and to fight for him against my own people.

Will, who will die if I don't succeed in forcing the Sylk queen to give us a drop of her blood—the only cure for the curse that will turn Will from a Nightweaver into a bloodthirsty Underling.

The same curse that will eventually turn me, too.

And then there's Titus. He's lied to me, manipulated me, and even now, I know he's only pretending to care about me because he intends to use my abilities for his own gain.

And yet...

As if he can sense my thoughts, he leans forward, lifting his hand to reach for me. He lets it linger in the air, his fingers inches from my face, and I have the fleeting memory of his face underwater, just before his mouth met mine beneath the waves....

It didn't mean anything, I scold myself. He was only trying to save me to save himself. If I drowned, he would have lost his only means of discovering the truth about his fiancée and curing his best friend.

The reminder douses my senses like a bucket of ice-cold water, and I clear my throat.

Titus jerks back his hand as if stung, clenches his fist in his lap. A neutral expression settles over his features as he retreats to his bench across the carriage from me, one ankle perched casually over his knee. He looks out the window as if I no longer exist.

Before I even hear the hinges creak, the door to the carriage opens.

And then Will is there, the scent of roses and damp earth enveloping me. He takes his seat beside me, his comforting warmth seeping through his cloak to my shivering skin, his hand on my cheek as his eyes—green but still glimmering with traces of gold Nightweaver light—examine me from head to toe.

I glance at his shoulder, but despite the blood that stains his shirt, it appears as if he's already healed himself.

I melt into his touch, leaning forward, my lips parting. I knew, in the instant I saw the bullet pierce his flesh, that any remainder of outrage I felt toward him and his recent revelations vanished. We did not meet on ideal terms, and our partnership may have been founded on mutual gain, but I can't deny what I feel for Will. And I can't ignore the way his fingertips graze my skin, or the longing look in his eyes as he closes the distance between us, drawing in a shaky breath....

"Later, my darling," Will hurries to whisper, sounding strained. He draws back as the door to the carriage opens once more. I cringe as a Bloodknight takes the seat beside Titus, who shifts to put as much distance as he can between himself and the soldier.

"Miss Oberon," Will says, his tone now cool, "I'd like you to meet Gabriel. He and our coachman for the evening, Flynn, will act as your private guards for the duration of our journey."

Gabriel dips his head in greeting, his face concealed by his ornate scarlet helmet.

I say nothing, my every instinct telling me to lift a blade from Will's person and drive it into one of the slits covering the Bloodknight's eyes. To be this close to one of the king's personal soldiers, knowing he's most likely slaughtered thousands of my people at the royal command, and not be able to slice him from nose to navel is almost too much to bear. The only consolation I have is that when I've completed my task, and Will has been cured, I'm free to make the Bloodknights pay.

"Fantastic," Titus drawls. "Now that we're all acquainted..." He knocks on the window, and the carriage lurches into motion. "I believe we have a train to catch."

Chapter Three

"Aster," comes Will's deep voice, coaxing me gently from sleep, "we're here."

It takes me a full moment to realize I'm no longer aboard the *Starchaser*. The lavish interior of the royal carriage comes into focus as I blink my eyes open, wondering how I could have fallen into such a slumber, and notice Will's hand resting lightly on my forearm.

The hair on the back of my neck bristles. "Did you—"

He holds a finger to his lips. We're alone in the carriage—Titus and Gabriel have made their exit—but Will urges me to silence.

"You used your magic to make me sleep!" I hiss, careful to keep my voice quiet.

He frowns. "You needed rest," he says simply.

"You don't get to decide—"

Voices from just beyond the carriage door give me pause.

Will clears his throat. "This way, Miss Oberon."

And just like that, he ends my protests before they've even truly begun. He opens the carriage door, stepping down first and then turning to offer his hand.

I grit my teeth, obliging him in front of the two Bloodknights, their scarlet armor almost jarring in contrast to the snow.

Snow. It covers the wood like a sea of white, as if my beloved ocean has come to convene with me beyond the shore. Father always said that before the Fall six hundred years ago, when Nightweavers were banished here, exiled from the heavenly realm of Elysia, winter crept slowly upon the land in late December. Some claim it's part of the curse humans brought upon the Known World, and the early arrival of winter is a sign of the True King's wrath. Others, including the Nightweavers of the Eerie, believe the sudden October winters are holy, a blessed omen from the True King, and mark the occasion with a grand celebration known as Holy Winter's Day. Under different circumstances, I might secretly be thrilled to partake in the festival—the spiced nuts, the mulled wine, the exchanging of gifts—but the celebration now marks the day that Titus will be wed to the princess of Hellion. And when I see his stark figure, a lithe silhouette of midnight fabric against the frosty backdrop of the wood, the abrupt winter feels more cursed than blessed.

It's Prince Titus who stares back at me now, his chin high, expression cold. Not the pirate captain who'd rescued me from the *Deathwail*.

"Where are we?" I ask, taking in the thick foliage that strangles the wooden loading platform where a gilded train idles, sputtering smoke into the dense white canopy. It must be midafternoon—I slept well through the morning, thanks to Will—but the scant light that filters through the leaves is gray.

"Nowhere," one of the Bloodknights answers. His helmet differs slightly from his comrade's, so I assume this is Flynn speaking, not the silent, brooding Bloodknight Gabriel who sat in the carriage beside Titus. Flynn's voice is oddly pleasant—light and friendly and somewhat disarming. "One of the king's many private boarding platforms in one of the many abandoned woods of the Eerie."

"Abandoned?" I murmur. "How could the woods be abandoned?"

Although their eyes are mostly covered, I sense Gabriel and Flynn share a look.

"Myths," Will explains, his expression neutral. "They fled these woods hundreds of years ago."

Titus surveys the woods, his mouth twisted with something akin to disgust. "Whatever creatures my ancestors failed to exterminate, anyway." He performs the role of the cruel, haughty prince with such ease; I have to remind myself it's all an act. Without so much as a glance in my direction, Titus starts toward the boarding platform, beckoning Will with a simple nod. "Wait here," he says to Gabriel and Flynn. "Watch her."

I stand between Gabriel and Flynn on the old, rotting platform, my arms wrapped tightly across my chest to keep from shivering. I was made to wear dirty rags and commanded not to bathe before the *Starchaser* made port along the Cutthroat Coast. I was supposed to look the part of a distressed prisoner. And I can tell, by the uncomfortable silence, that these Bloodknights fully believe that the king doesn't plan on knighting me because he thinks me deserving. *Me*—a weak, scared little girl who needed to be rescued. A traitorous wretch who needs to be watched carefully, lest she attempt to flee.

Good. I love to be underestimated.

"Miss—" The word has only just left Flynn's mouth when an arrow whizzes past my ear.

Gabriel pushes me behind him as the two Bloodknights draw their scarlet weapons. Flynn hefts a crossbow from his back, while Gabriel unsheathes two massive swords from bloodred scabbards at either hip.

"Get her inside!" Gabriel shouts, his rasping voice grating against my eardrums as he shoves me toward Flynn.

Flynn pulls on the same door Titus and Will used to enter the train only minutes ago, but it doesn't budge. "It's locked!"

"Damnit," Gabriel grunts. An arrow pings off his shoulder. "Cover me!"

Gabriel charges into the woods, moving with surprising speed and agility despite his armor, and a moment later, I lose sight of him in the tangle of thickets.

The barrage of arrows stops the instant Gabriel enters the woods, the eerie silence of the forest now deafening. Flynn shifts, standing in front of me. His head swivels left, right. Leaves rustle nearby, and he aims his crossbow in the direction Gabriel disappeared, but the Bloodknight never reemerges. Flynn takes a step toward the thicket, and instinctively, I watch his back, focusing on the thick, snow-covered undergrowth, where shadows seem to seep from the darkness....

"Behind—!" I start, but I'm too late.

Flynn turns to look behind him, his crossbow raised, but the dark figure has overtaken him, knocking his weapon onto the platform. The assailant straddles the Bloodknight, but I can't see its face. I can't really *see* it at all. It's as if the figure is made of shadows—a manifestation of darkness itself.

What I *can* see is the wicked-looking dagger in its blurred grasp, its blade, inscribed with ancient script, festering with green energy that almost seems...alive. The weapon itself whispers, too low for me to hear, in a voice that chills me to the bone.

My gut tells me the assailant is an Underling, but it looks different from any Sylk or Shifter I've seen. Those have always possessed a host, or transformed into a human or animal, and this creature of shadows appears like something else entirely. I can sense the evil radiating from it and instinctively understand this is *another* kind of Underling, and I watch in horror as it plunges its dagger into one of the thin grates that cover the Bloodknight's left eye.

Flynn's scream is deafening.

The Underling fixes its glowing red eyes on me. Cocks its shadowy head.

Flynn's crossbow landed at my feet, but I'm not fast enough to retrieve it, so I remain perfectly still. Take a deep breath. Attempt to calm my frenzied heart.

The blood pounding in my ears drowns out the sound of Flynn's agony.

"Has my brother sent you to collect me?" I whisper, too low for the Bloodknight to hear.

The assailant rises in one fluid motion, shedding the veil of shadows, which dissipate as if he merely removed a cloak. Before me stands a slender, masculine frame, his clothing made of what appears to be black bandages, and the same black gauze obscures his face, covering everything but his now golden eyes.

He grips the glowing dagger in his gloved fist, the green energy appearing to lap at his hand, his wrist, his forearm.

"Leave the Eerie," comes a deep, raw voice, "or meet your death."

My palms itch for the feel of metal in my grasp. *Blast Will and Titus for insisting I remain unarmed!*

"You can't harm me," I say slowly, glancing at his cursed dagger.

His eyes narrow. "Dangerous to assume," he says, his voice like gravel.

"I'm protected." I swallow hard, careful not to touch my bracelet and draw attention to the trinket—the band of braided leather that each of my family wears and Owen revealed was imbued with magic strong enough to dispel an Underling's attack. "By an enchantment. No harm can come to me by an Underling's hand."

His golden eyes flash with what looks like amusement. "Who said anything about Underlings?"

The door to the train groans, as if someone was trying to unlock it from the inside.

"Open the damned thing!" I hear Titus's muffled voice through the metal door.

"It's jammed!" comes another voice from within.

The assailant takes another step toward me, closing the gap between us.

"Leave," he rasps, "or die."

The door to the train compartment sounds as if it's been torn from its hinges. The assailant whirls, consumed by shadows once more, and before I can even register the movement, he vanishes.

Chapter Four

Titus stands in the doorway to the train compartment, his eyes wide as he surveys the platform. His gaze first lands on Flynn's writhing form and Gabriel, who reappeared moments after the assailant vanished, now calling for aid as he kneels over his fallen comrade. Then Titus spots me, his expression wild.

"Get inside," he says quickly, his voice hoarse. He grabs me by the arm and hauls me into the compartment, past the group of officers clustered there, half-dragging me down the narrow corridor. I scarcely gather my bearings enough to notice the doors lining one side, but I realize we must be in a sleeping car.

Titus doesn't stop until we enter another compartment—another sleeping car by the looks of it. He peers over his shoulder, glancing all around, before opening the door to a small, private cabin, pulling me inside.

He grabs my other arm, turning to look in my direction. His eyes inspect every inch of me. "Are you hurt?"

I shake my head, unable to meet his probing stare. "I'm fine," I say, hating the rush of heat that warms my cheeks. I shake his hands off me. "Where's Will?"

He swallows, his throat bobbing with the effort. "He's still relocating the passengers from this car to the front of the train."

"Why?"

"For privacy." Titus steps away from me, tucking his hands into his pockets, but his eyes continue to search my face, my hair. "Word has gotten out about your presence on this train. You're rather...popular." He frowns. "We shouldn't have left you alone."

"I wasn't alone," I say, quirking a brow. "You left me with two Bloodknights. You couldn't have—"

"We should have known better." He hisses a breath through his teeth as he runs his hands through his hair. Loose blond strands fall free from his grasp, framing his face. "*I* should have known better."

My stomach sours. "I can take care of myself. Besides, if something happens to me, I'm sure it's not too late for you to find another cursed pirate capable of sensing Sylks."

He glances at me, his face twisted with disgust. "What?"

"You can drop the act, Titus—*Shade*—whatever your name is."

His jaw tightens, eyes narrowing. "Act?"

"Are we speaking in only one-word sentences now?" I roll my eyes. "Yes, *Your Highness*, the *act*. I don't know who you really are, but it's hard enough to tell the difference between the pompous prince and the commiserative pirate captain. Now, we made a deal, *none* of which requires us to pretend, even for a second, that we care about the other's well-being aside from what we can offer each other. Do I make myself clear?"

He grits his teeth in a smile laced with venom. "Perfectly." He turns, as if to leave, but then he stops, his shoulders shaking with a barely contained chuckle.

Indignation burns the back of my throat like acid. "Did I say something amusing?"

He faces me again, his lips kicking into a smirk. "It's just that you seemed to care a great deal for my well-being when you thought William had driven a blade through my heart."

The tips of my ears feel as if they've caught aflame. "Yes, well, I was confused. That's all."

His tongue prods at the inside of his cheek, and he scoffs. "Confused."

"*Confused*," I repeat, squaring my shoulders at him. "I watched Will drive a blade through *Shade*'s heart. You'll excuse me if I'm still coming to terms with the fact that you're the same person, Your *Highness*."

"Oh?" His brows lift. In one swift maneuver, he pins me against the door, bracing himself with one hand over my head. He towers over me, looking every bit as menacing as the stories depict him. "So you only care if Captain Shade dies," he says, his voice low. I catch a glimpse of the wicked prince he's reputed to be as he examines me with a cruel, calculating gaze. "Not me."

Electricity charges the air, crackling all around us, ready to ignite. *Not me.* Not Titus, the prince who has haunted my nightmares since we were children. Not the prince who is rumored to drink the blood of humans, eat their hearts, and impale their heads on the castle walls. Not the prince who masquerades as Captain Shade, a hero of my people.

It dawns on me that I don't really know that I can trust either of them.

I lean in, my body trembling with rage. "Exactly."

He grins, eyes sparkling. "Now who's speaking in one-word sentences?"

His breath ghosts my face, the smell of sea brine reminding me again of that underwater kiss, and I have to fight to keep my gaze from dropping to his lips as his tongue darts out, wetting them as if he were about to speak when—

"Oh!" comes a small, girlish voice.

Our heads whip in the direction of the open doorway, where a human girl in her black-and-white uniform stands, holding heavy bags in either hand. She gapes at us, her mouth wide.

"You're lost," Titus grits out, lowering his arm and taking a deliberate step back. He turns to look at the girl, his entire being practically vibrating with annoyance, his expression dark. "Run along."

Her jaw snaps shut, but the surprise in her eyes is quickly replaced by fear. "M-my prince," she stutters. "I-I'm so—forgive me—yes, yes I'm lost—I was looking for—"

She curtsies, almost losing her balance from the weight of the bags, before taking off in the direction from which we entered the compartment.

"You don't think she'll..." My heart leaps into my throat. "You're engaged! We shouldn't be seen alone together. What if she—"

"What if she announces it to the entire Known World?" Titus snorts, rolling his eyes. He smirks, and the charged electricity between us fades to a gentle hum. "Are you worried you'll cause a scandal?"

"You're such an ass," I snap, swatting his chest. Lowering my voice, I hiss, "All of this will have been for nothing if I don't stay in your fiancée's good graces. I still need to get close enough to see if she's actually possessed by Morana, remember?"

Titus winces at the word *fiancée*. Or maybe I'm just seeing things.

"Believe me, you won't have any trouble getting close enough to the princess to detect the Sylk queen," Titus says, his words clipped. "Morana will have adopted Leo's entire personality."

"Leo?" I echo. It's the first time I've heard anyone refer to the princess of Hellion by name, and for a moment, it cuts through the cloud of rage I feel toward Titus.

His shoulders sag a bit, his mouth tight. He nods. "Leo," he says, "is a remarkably kind person. She won't be difficult to befriend. Even for you," he adds, his lips twitching—the makings of a playful grin.

Shame coils in my gut. I've been so focused on exposing Morana I've given little thought to the girl she's possessed—the girl who will have to die if we're to force Morana to take her corporeal form. "She sounds wonderful," I murmur.

Another nod. "Leo and I have known each other since we were children." He sighs. "Her ability to stir up mischief might have been more hazardous than my own." Again, traces of a smile line his eyes, but they're gone in an instant. "She had the most contagious laugh."

Had.

I don't know why, but I can't keep the words from tumbling out of my mouth. "What if the princess *isn't* possessed—"

"She is." His face hardens. "I knew from the moment she arrived. Leo is nothing more than a costume Morana has chosen to wear. The girl I knew is gone."

I note the pain in his voice, his eyes. "But *if* she wasn't possessed," I start again, "would you have..."

"Would I have felt differently about marrying her?" Titus's expression softens. He pinches his nose, takes a deep breath. "I always suspected my parents would attempt to form an alliance with Hellion—we both did—but neither of us wanted this. Leo was my friend. Nothing more. That's why I first suspected she wasn't herself." He grimaces. "*This* Leo couldn't be more excited about the wedding."

A knot forms in my throat. "Do you think," I say slowly, "that perhaps Leo feels differently than you? Maybe she's changed. Maybe—"

"No," is his swift reply. "I'm certain of this."

"But, Titus—"

"No, Aster," he says through gritted teeth. "Leo is *gone*. It's not just the wedding! It's—" He hesitates, then drops his voice to a whisper. "When Leo first arrived at Castle Grim, she asked to see the Bloodroses."

Months back, Will enlightened me on Bloodroses and how the flowers produce *Manan*, a glittering gold substance known as "the dust of creation." *Manan* offers power to both humans and Nightweavers alike, if they can get their hands on it, and the last remaining garden is purported to grow within Castle Grim, making it a scarce, highly coveted resource—even for the nobility.

"I didn't think anything of it," Titus continues. "Leo's seen the garden plenty of times, though she'd always expressed a certain...

distaste for it. She never liked the way *Manan* made her feel—hated it, even. But that night in the garden, she said something to me—something odd."

A muscle feathers in his jaw, and his mouth works, as if he was fighting to keep the words from spilling out—a final attempt to save his friend from further condemnation.

"What did she say?" I whisper, prompting him to continue—hating that I must.

Titus's nose twitches, and he clears his throat. "She said, 'Just think what we could accomplish if we no longer needed the Bloodroses for *Manan*.' She started talking about 'our rule' and seeking alternative sources of *Manan*—*human* sources." His lip curls with disgust, and as I watch his face, I remember Will's words from long ago: *Blood is the purest source of* Manan, *but human blood is the most potent*.

"The Leo I knew would never have said anything like that. It was like...like she was a completely different person." He nods, as if still trying to convince himself. "She's possessed, and the only thing I can do to help her now is give her a dignified death—to set her free from Morana's control."

A dignified death. It's the same thing Owen promised me when we were surrounded by the Nightweavers who took us from our life at sea to one on land. I knew then what he was prepared to do—that if he could not save me, he would be the one to take my life.

I'm still not certain Titus is right about Leo, but if there's even the smallest chance that he is, and that exposing Morana would mean obtaining a cure for Will and me, then I have no other choice but to hope he's onto something.

"If Leo *is* possessed..." I say quietly, "how do you know it's Morana and not just another Sylk?"

"I just..." He looks out the window, his eyes somewhat distant. "I just *feel* it. I've been around plenty of Sylks—battled them, banished them. But that night in the garden with Leo, I felt something else. Something ancient and evil and..." He shakes his head. "It's Morana, I'm certain of it. And with your ability to see Sylks, we can prove it."

I hesitate. "If it *is* Morana," I start, hurrying to add before he can correct me, "how do you plan to force her to take her corporeal form?"

He blows out a tight breath, pinching the bridge of his nose. "I'm still working on it."

My mouth gapes. "You're *working* on it?" I say. "You're telling me I've come all this way—that I'm going to take an oath to become a Bloodknight—and you don't even have a plan?"

"I have a plan," he says through gritted teeth. "The details are just...not your concern."

I huff, craning my neck to look him in the eye. "It's my job to determine whether she's possessed. And I'm able to do so only because of *my curse*—you know, the one only Morana can cure?"

His jaw clenches. "It's complicated," he says, his voice surprisingly soft. "Your people have long believed there is a ritual that can force Morana to take her corporeal form. But it requires immense power, and..."

"And?" I demand, but my voice cracks.

Titus's brows pinch. His gaze drifts, as if his mind were somewhere far away. "And I'm not yet sure I'm capable of doing what must be done to see it fulfilled."

Dread pools low in my gut. "Tell me," I say, attempting a quieter, gentler tone, but my building frustration seeps in, tainting the words. "I can help. I *want* to help."

He looks at me then, and there's such sadness in his eyes—such heartache—that I feel as if I'm seeing not Captain Shade, not Prince Titus, but someone else entirely. An instant later he clears his throat, and his expression turns harsh, his eyes now cold and empty, as if I imagined the sorrow that transformed him only moments ago.

"You *are* helping," he drawls. "*You* will use your strange, unique ability to see the big bad shadow creatures," he adds, wiggling his fingers, "and *I* will perform the ritual that forces Morana to take her corporeal form so that *I* can get a few measly drops of the Sylk queen's blood and use it to cure you and our poor friend William. Do I make myself clear?"

Before I can say anything, he straightens his jacket with a furious tug, adding, "Now, if you'll excuse me, there's someone here who has been waiting very patiently to greet you."

Without another word, he storms out of the train car.

I collapse onto the narrow cot, my mind whirling. I'm not sure how many minutes pass before a familiar voice startles me out of my daze.

"If Lewis could see you in those rags," Margaret says, "I think he'd have a stroke."

Chapter Five

My sister Margaret crushes me in her embrace.

"Oh, Marge," I say, tears stinging my eyes. I pull away, twining my fingers with hers. "What are you doing here? How—"

"Lord William had it arranged," she explains, somewhat giddy. "I'm to be your lady's maid until we reach Ink Haven."

"Ink Haven?" Just the mention of the township nestled in the valley below the Castors' estate fills me with longing. "I didn't know we were—"

"Stopping there? It was a last-minute decision. I was supposed to go all the way to Jade with you, but I suppose Lord William wanted to see his home again before you all left for Castle Grim." She gives a watery smile, and my stomach flips at the thought of the capital city—of Jade, where I'm to be knighted. "Oh, Aster, he was so distraught. He wouldn't rest until he got you back."

My stomach somersaults. Even though I know the rescue was fake, the thought of Will anxious to find me, to bring me home...

I give her hands a squeeze. "I'm so glad you're here."

Margaret squeezes back. "Me too." Her expression turns apprehensive. "Aster, what they're saying, about Captain Shade—"

"I know."

"He's really dead then?"

I hope Margaret doesn't see me hesitate when I say, "I suppose so."

Her eyes narrow. "He didn't really take you captive, though, did he?" She glances at the rags I'm wearing, no doubt assessing what anyone else would have been too distracted by the fanfare of my rescue to notice: I'm unharmed. No bruises, no cuts. And I don't look like I've been underfed. Lowering her voice, she adds, "I know he wasn't responsible for what happened at Bludgrave."

It still feels as if it were only yesterday that the Sylk who murdered our brother Owen led a troop of Underlings into Bludgrave Manor and slaughtered the guests on Reckoning Day. The image of the Castors' ballroom, bodies strewn across the bloody floor, flashes through my mind every time I close my eyes. And Owen, waiting for me in the woods, a dagger in his hand...

I peek my head into the hallway, ensuring we're alone, before shutting the door to the sleeping compartment.

"What do you mean?" I ask innocently.

"Well, I was there. I saw the Underlings with my own eyes. And—" This time, it's Margaret who hesitates. "Jack told me everything."

Jack. The Castors' stableboy and I had become fast friends during my time at Bludgrave, but he and Margaret had become something *more.* I should have known he would tell Margaret the truth about the attack, but I can't be sure what exactly that truth entails. "Told you...?"

Margaret's cheeks flush. She rolls up her shirtsleeve, where the inked lines of a winged dagger blossom on the surface of her skin.

My blood turns to ice. Margaret bears the mark of the winged dagger, an enchanted tattoo that signifies her allegiance to a dangerous cause—to the Order of Hildegarde, the centuries-old coalition between humans, Nightweavers, and Myths all fighting for justice and freedom from the Nightweavers who rule over them. The same enchanted tattoo that marks my forearm as well.

"Oh, Marge," I groan. "You didn't! *He* didn't!"

"Jack—"

"I'm going to kill him."

"He only wanted—"

"I don't care. He's dead."

"It was my choice!" she says, standing up straighter, her shoulders pulled back.

"And what about our brothers and sister?" My blood warms, heats, reaches a boiling point. "Did Jack take it upon himself to recruit them, too?"

"He didn't *recruit* me." Margaret blushes again. "And no, he didn't tell them. They don't know anything."

"Good." I unclench my fists. "It's going to stay that way."

She nods, her expression suddenly serious. "Agreed."

The weight of Margaret's revelation settles on my shoulders. But then it lifts, and I feel lighter than I have in months. If Margaret has joined the Order of Hildegarde, then I don't have to keep my involvement a secret from my sister any longer. At least I'll have one sibling I can talk to.

"I'm sorry I didn't tell you sooner," I say quietly.

She waves her hand. "You couldn't have. Before..." She lets out a low sigh, and I understand the words she hasn't said: *before Father died*. "I wouldn't have listened to you. I would have said no."

"But now?"

Her eyes flash, fire and rage and bitter grief alight in her blue gaze. "This has to end."

For a moment, all I can do is stare at her—at my sister, the warrior. And in this instant, everything feels possible. With someone like Margaret in the Order, things can be different now. We might actually have a chance.

This has to end. But when does it end? When the king and queen are dead? When Morana has been captured? Even if we succeed, could it really be that simple? Could we end six hundred years of war and hatred?

"Jack knew you'd be furious," Margaret says, a grin tugging at her lips. Mischief sparks in her eyes. "He's expecting your worst."

I snort. "He couldn't handle my worst."

We both break into laughter, the two of us falling back onto the cot beside each other. We exhale at the same time, the brief moment of reprieve gone as quickly as it came.

We sit up, leaning in as we did when we were children and we would huddle in her hammock, sharing secrets or dreaming about things we thought we could never have. I realize, with a pang in my chest, that during the time we spent living together at Bludgrave, we rarely even spoke to each other. Margaret was starting a new life, and I was holding tightly to the one we left behind.

"So," Margaret whispers, "what really happened then? Did you see him?"

"Who? Captain Shade?" I lift my shoulder and bite my bottom lip, attempting to give myself time to think of a response. "No," I say carefully, using a half-truth to mask the lie. "He never visited me onboard his ship."

"You were on his *ship*?" she nearly squeals. "What was it like?"

"Like a ship."

She rolls her eyes. "You know what I mean."

I drum my fingers on my pantleg, pretending to be contemplative. "It was..." I consider lying, but, "Oh, Marge, it was just as the legends say. His crew was rightly terrifying, and the ship... the *Starchaser* is mysterious, and fantastical, and unlike anything you've ever seen before."

Margaret's eyes widen with wonder. "That's..." She frowns. "That's terribly sad."

The word *why* almost leaves my lips before I realize what she means. "Yes," I agree, my voice cracking. I've just learned that my sister is privy to the secret I've been keeping—about my allegiance to the Order of Hildegarde, and now, her own—but already I cannot tell her the truth of Captain Shade's false identity, much less his false death. Another secret. Another lie. "It's awful."

We remain silent for a long while. Then Margaret takes my hand.

"There's something else you should know. The king sent his men to Bludgrave," she says quietly, her gaze searching mine. She bites her bottom lip, as if unsure whether to continue. "They are considering Lewis and Charlie for military service. They said they might be required to join the League of Seven."

I jump to my feet, my heart nearly leaping out of my chest at the idea of my brothers being forced to join the fight against the Underlings. Jack told me all about the League of Seven, and while the seven kingdoms of the Known World have joined together to battle Morana's forces, they see their human conscripts as little more than cannon fodder. "They can't! Will would never let—"

Margaret stands slowly, her gentle movement causing the words to catch in my throat. She gives me a sympathetic look. "Lord William thinks it might be the Crown's way of ensuring *you* act accordingly," she tells me.

I clench my teeth so hard I fear they might break. I fear *I* might break.

"This is all my fault," I say, pressing the heels of my palms to my forehead.

Margaret places a soft hand on my shoulder. "Jack said the Order asked that you keep an eye on the prince the night of the ball. How could you have said no?"

I let out a low, hollow sigh. "I had a choice," I say. "I chose to do it because I thought—at the time..."

Understanding flickers in Margaret's eyes. "You were going to try to kill the prince." She nods slowly. "I can't say I blame you."

My stomach lurches. "Why do you say that?"

She looks at me as if I'd grown a second head.

"You know what he's done," she says, dropping her voice even lower than before. "I don't care if he's part of the Order. He's still killed countless humans for the Crown. I've heard stories—"

"Not all stories are true—"

"Well, I believe them! They say he hunts humans for sport on the streets of Jade—that he kills men with his bare hands more efficiently than you could with a blade. They call him the king's beast—the Reaper." Her face blanches as a chill sweeps through the tiny cabin, as if the very name stole all warmth from the room.

"The Reaper?" I whisper.

She nods, her throat bobbing. "They say the blood sends him into a frenzy. It turns him into something...else. We've always known he was a monster." Her eyes flit between mine. "Don't tell me you've changed your mind?"

"I—" My voice suddenly sounds unnatural. "It's complicated. There's so much I want to tell you, but..." I cut a glance at the door, shake my head. "Not here."

She looks taken aback, but she must understand my hesitancy to talk about such matters when Titus could return at any moment and overhear our conversation, because she dips her head. "Whatever you say." She blows out a tight breath. "So long as no one expects me to watch his back on a battlefield."

"I don't think anyone would," I say, forcing a teasing grin to my lips even as my stomach churns. I knew Titus had a reputation for cruelty, but the Reaper...Margaret makes it sound as if he were another creature entirely. I can't help but wonder if in seeking a cure for my curse—in fighting for my freedom—I have chained myself to a beast.

Margaret spends the afternoon scrubbing, brushing, curling, applying, and blotting—all with surgical precision. I'm beginning to think she enjoys the hours it takes to transform me, because she seems most at peace when she has a series of small, tedious tasks to complete. However, despite Margaret's sense of pride in her work, now, as I step into the hall where Gabriel and Flynn wait to escort me to dinner, I feel like crawling into a deep, dark hole.

Flynn lost his eye only a few hours ago, but with the aid of bonewielder magic, the wound has healed beyond the point of pain. And from what I heard, they managed to remove the eye before the poison from the attacker's cursed dagger could spread and infect his bloodstream.

I can almost feel Flynn gawking at me from behind his helmet—can almost feel him smirking obnoxiously when he says, "How pretty."

My fist clenches around an invisible dagger. "Do you wish to keep your other eye?"

Flynn chuckles. Gabriel clears his throat.

"This way, m'lady," Flynn says in a singsong voice, making a grand gesture in the direction of the compartment door.

I wish our attacker had aimed for his vocal cords.

At the mere thought of the shadowy assassin, a shiver runs through me. His golden eyes, his cursed dagger...

Leave the Eerie or meet your death.

What I wanted to say was, *Gladly.* Either way, stay or go, I'm dying. But this isn't about just me. If the League of Seven conscripts Lewis and Charlie, then I have to act fast. I can't risk losing them in a war they were never meant to fight. No assassin, no king, no one is going to stop me from trying to make this world a safer place for my family.

"Miss Oberon?" Gabriel's gentle voice stirs me out of my thoughts.

We've reached the door to the dining car.

I take a deep breath. On the other side of this door, a cacophony of laughter and vibrant conversation hints at a life of careless ease I have never known.

I give a slight nod, and Gabriel opens the door.

The silence that greets me is so heavy and thick I feel as if I can hardly lift my foot to take another step inside.

Ornate golden candelabras adorn every table. Grand scarlet

curtains line the windows, and tables clad with black silk tablecloths and set with gilded plates line either wall. The dining car in which I met with Will when I first came to the Eerie was opulent, but I was not prepared for this height of luxury. Just one of these forks would have been considered a treasure fine enough to pay for a year's worth of food for my family and me. The jewelry in this compartment alone is enough to humble a dragon's hoard.

I don't realize I've shuffled back until I bump into Flynn's chest.

"He's waiting for you in the next compartment," he says in a low, steady voice. "Just keep walking."

I can't bring myself to look up, to look at these people on either side, all staring at me as if I were a wild animal. Like I don't belong.

I *don't* belong.

I've never belonged in this world. I don't belong on land; I don't belong with these people. I might be half Nightweaver, but I will *never* be one of them.

It is only the presence of Gabriel and Flynn behind me that keeps me from turning around. I'm grateful to them, in some strange way, because despite the helmets that hide their faces from sight, I can sense the looks they give the patrons of the dining compartment as we pass. Looks that beg to be trifled with. Looks I don't understand.

Gabriel and Flynn are Nightweavers; they should hate me, too.

We enter the private dining compartment, this one even more luxurious than the first, the single table bedecked in finery fit for a queen.

"There you are." Will's deep, smooth voice is like a salve to my frayed nerves. He stands from the table, where he sits across from two people I've never met, candlelight flickering in his green eyes, catching flecks of gold and casting them in a dazzling glow that reminds me of *Manan*, mesmerizing me, drawing me in....

"Miss Oberon, I'd like you to meet Lady Eliza Cooper." Will gestures to the dark-haired girl seated across from him, a small, bat-shaped amulet resting between her collarbones. "And her traveling companion, Ms. Winona Congreve." The meek, auburn-haired girl—*human girl*, I think, judging by the state of her plain black servant's uniform—seated next to Lady Eliza dips her head in greeting but avoids looking me in the eye, and before I look away I note the way her hands tremble in her lap. It seems my reputation as a pirate will follow me into this new life as well.

Lady Eliza smiles warmly, her whole face alight, drawing my attention away from the timid maid. "Billie just finished telling us about your daring escape from that dreadful pirate," she says, her eyes twinkling. "It's a pleasure to finally meet you."

I mean to say, *Likewise*, but, "Billie?" is all that comes out.

This earns a giggle from Winona. Eliza's smile widens, her eyes crinkling at the edges, making her appear lovely and joyful and more beautiful than any Nightweaver I've ever met.

"He's hated that name since we were children," Eliza says with a wink. "So of course it's all I've ever called him."

I glance at Will, almost afraid *not* to catch his eye—terrified to find he's watching Lady Eliza with the kind of adoration I'm sure she's no stranger to receiving. When I turn to him, Will's mouth is parted, only slightly, as if he wasn't aware it fell open. But he isn't looking at Eliza.

His gaze roves from the hem of my skirt to the high neck of my gown, my exposed shoulders, and finally, to my lips, before repeating his slow, careful inspection of my attire. Margaret chose the silky scarlet gown from the wardrobe in my sleeping compartment. She told me she wasn't sure who left the gowns—all perfectly tailored to me—in the wardrobe, only that Will mentioned they would be there. I'm assuming he arranged this, which means it's Will whom I need to...*thank* for providing me a pair of the most uncomfortable flats to wear in lieu of my boots.

"If I didn't know any better," Eliza says, a smirk tugging at the corners of her lips, "I'd think you were searching the poor girl for weapons."

Will's eyes flit to mine, as if coming out of a daze, his cheeks flushing bright pink. I can't believe what I'm seeing—Lord William Castor, the feared and the beloved, the most powerful bonewielder of his age, *blushing*.

"Rest assured, we checked her," comes Flynn's voice from close behind. *"Thoroughly."*

Will's jaw clenches. He flexes his hands, his eyes sliding past me to my guards, his entire posture shifting. His expression changes in an instant from someone boyish into someone menacing. A past image of blood on his delicate lips sends a shiver down my spine.

"That will be all," Will says darkly, dismissing my guards.

"As you wish," Flynn says, adding, "We'll be close by, m'lady," before retreating with Gabriel to the back of the compartment.

Will watches them go, his eyes narrowed.

Eliza clears her throat. "Please, sit," she says, motioning for me to join them. "Give Billie a chance to remember his manners. And forgive my brothers, who seem to have never learned any manners at all."

I follow Eliza's gaze to where the Bloodknights stand guard near the door. She pins the two of them with a warning glare, and Flynn responds with a tiny wave. Eliza rolls her eyes, but the corner of her lip kicks up in a grin. *My brothers*—if Flynn and Gabriel are Eliza's brothers, then Will must know the Bloodknights better than he's letting on.

"Small kingdom," Will whispers in my ear, almost as if he read my mind.

"Apparently so," I whisper back.

I take the seat across from Winona, who offers me a timid smile. My heart skips a beat.

I didn't recognize her before, in the dim light of the dining compartment, but—

Ms. Winona Congreve is the young maid who saw Titus and me alone in the sleeping compartment.

Her eyes widen, her skin paling.

I open my mouth, unsure what I even intend to say, but Winona gives a small shake of her head, her expression almost pleading.

"So, Aster," Eliza starts, and my attention snaps to her. She props her elbows on the table, resting her chin on her fists. "Billie tells me you've lived a rather exciting life. I've always wondered what it would be like to be a pirate."

"I—" I've never felt so unsure of myself. What am I supposed to say?

Only dinner. It's only dinner. Eat. Make conversation. Try not to panic.

Beneath the tablecloth, a warm hand closes over mine.

"*Former* pirate," Will says, his voice light, his smile pleasant. "Aster was forced to live a certain...*lifestyle* to survive. She takes no pride in the things she did before her clan's name was written on the King's Marque."

He gives my hand a squeeze. I squeeze back.

"Pity," Eliza says, waving her hand in dismissal. "I'm sure you have some thrilling stories to tell." She winks at me. "Perhaps next time we dine together," she adds, her gaze sliding to Will, "Billie won't be around to speak over you."

"Eliza," Will says, raising his glass, "you never change."

She grins. "I certainly hope not." She takes a deep draught of her wine, the berry-colored liquid darkening her red lips to a shade of burgundy I'm all too familiar with. "Well then, I suppose you're looking forward to being knighted?"

The change of subject sends me reeling. Thankfully, at that moment, our food arrives. The waitstaff, in their crisp white uniforms, place polished silver platters in front of us, removing the lids to reveal steaming dishes of steak and roasted potatoes.

My jaw must have dropped into my lap, because Will's hot breath tickles my ear as he whispers, "You look lovely when you're surprised."

Now it's my turn to blush. I'm somewhat taken aback by Will's boldness; he's always acted indifferent toward me in front of others, constantly afraid of anyone discovering the true nature of our relationship. I realize, suddenly, that inviting me to dinner must be a calculated move. That he's chosen tonight to act so...*forward* because the king has brought me into the fold, not because we've secretly been friends—or perhaps more—for the past few months. And I find that, either way, it's a relief to finally share a moment with Will without having to look over my shoulder, even if it's all for show.

Graciously, Eliza and Winona turn toward each other, having their own conversation and allowing Will and me this fleeting moment of privacy. I can't help but wonder what it would be like to have dinner with Will, just the two of us. Alone. Him whispering in my ear, his hands on my waist, his lips on mine...

The heat in my cheeks intensifies. *Damn my cursed imagination.* Thoughts of Will's lips bring with them the memories of his kiss that night in the conservatory. So much has happened since that moment we shared among the roses, but now I find myself wishing he would kiss me again—wondering when he might. *If* he might…

"Here," Will says, removing his hand from mine and taking his warmth with him. Delicately, he cuts the steak with a decorum I'm not sure I'll ever be capable of. "Try it."

I pierce the steak with my fork and pop it into my mouth. I bite down, flavor flooding my taste buds. And though I wish I could simply enjoy this divine culinary experience, my thoughts shift to the only two people in this world who I wish I could tell all about this single, glorious bite. In a past life, Father and Owen would have listened to me rant and rave about the tenderness of the meat. Father would have speculated over what seasonings the chef chose. Owen would have teased me about using the wrong fork.

Suddenly, I've lost my appetite.

"How exciting!" I hear Winona say. "It's quite an honor to be appointed by the king himself."

I realize they're talking about me—about my joining the Bloodknights—and the pit in my stomach deepens.

"Of course, I'd be terrified," she goes on, dabbing at the corner of her mouth with her napkin. She peers over my shoulder at my guards before lowering her voice to add, "The king's soldiers are all rather…"

"Violent?" Will supplements, his eyes dancing with amusement. "Not all the king's soldiers are as vicious as the papers would have you believe."

Her face blanches as she realizes her mistake. She sputters out, "I didn't mean—"

"Then again," he continues, flashing his teeth—teeth I've seen him use to rip flesh from bone—in a charming smile. "Some of us are worse."

Winona appears both petrified and dazzled by the young lord, as if she isn't sure whether to fear him or fawn over him.

"Forgive Miss Congreve," Eliza says, cutting a reassuring glance at her companion. "She merely means to say that the Bloodknights in particular have a reputation for brutality. Aside from my brothers, who have a reputation for being asinine."

"Ah, then you haven't heard." Will's lip quirks, the makings of a smirk. "I believe Aster's reputation makes the Bloodknights seem like nursemaids."

"Is that so?" Eliza cocks a perfectly manicured brow. "In that case, I'm delighted to see how the Bloodknights fare against you, Miss Oberon." She raises her glass, toasting the air. "May you crush their bones and break their spirits."

Oh, I like this woman.

I raise my glass, dipping my chin in acknowledgment. "I'll drink to that."

"And I as well," comes a familiar voice.

At first, I think I've imagined it, but he appears before I have a moment to doubt.

A Shifter stands at the end of our table.

And not just any Shifter.

"I don't believe we've officially met," Owen says, flourishing a bow in his fine purple suit. His lips curl, a wolfish smile full of vain secrets and wicked promises. "Owen Oberon, at your service."

Chapter Six

I can't breathe. Owen has seemingly appeared out of thin air, as if he has used his powers as a Shifter to transform into something small enough he could enter the dining compartment without detection.

Will stands, his hands flexing at his sides, the air thickening as he draws on his *Manan*.

Owen smiles, his demeanor unnervingly calm even as his eyes light with mischief. "Lord William Castor," he drawls, extending his hand. "You are every bit as intimidating as they claim."

"Odd," Will says, ignoring Owen's proffered hand. His voice is cool, his expression aloof, but I catch the way his jaw tightens. He shifts, shielding me with his body. "You don't seem intimidated."

Owen's eyes narrow as his smile grows, showing teeth. "Looks can be deceiving." He cocks his head slowly, his hand retreating to his jacket pocket. "I'd think you, of all people, would understand that."

45

I get to my feet, my fists clenched in a feeble attempt to hide the way my hands tremble. "This isn't the place," I say, struggling to match his poised composure, as if seeing my dead brother again doesn't completely rattle me.

The last time I saw Owen was under the violent crimson skies of Reckoning Day. That night, I learned he was the monster haunting me for the past few months. He died trying to save me from the Nightweavers who attacked us that fateful day aboard the *Lightbringer* and was reborn as an Underling. As a Shifter, a kind of Underling who can transform into any living creature, he left a trail of bodies in his wake to lure me from the safety of Bludgrave Manor, a string of vicious murders that led, ultimately, to our father's death.

I learned of Owen's allegiance to the Underling queen, Morana, just before he drove a cursed dagger through my chest. I nearly succumbed to the Shifter curse that night. And if I had, I would have been forced to join Owen in service to Morana and leave our family behind without so much as a goodbye.

Will takes a step closer to Owen, a subtle threat in the protective way he angles his body in front of mine.

"We don't have to do this," I say, my voice more even than I expected.

Because it's Owen—because he knows me better than anyone ever could—he flicks a glance at my trembling hands, amusement glittering in his eyes. "Now, now. There's no need for violence," he says, one hand raised in a placating manner. It's only now that I notice Gabriel and Flynn have crept quietly up behind me, their hands on the hilts of their swords. This seems to incite Owen, who gives a sinister grin. "Of course, if it's violence you prefer, I'm happy to oblige."

Flynn and Gabriel fall limp behind Will and me, unconscious. Their bodies hit the ground with a dull thud at the very moment Eliza grabs a steak knife from the table and Winona shrinks behind her, sobbing quietly. Eliza raises her arm as if to strike, but Owen lifts his hand, halting Eliza midmovement.

He gestures to Flynn and Gabriel. "Don't worry; they're alive—for now. I learned that trick from a friend of mine, actually. Did you know that as a windwalker, I can simply...steal the breath from their lungs?" He snaps his fingers, eyes bright with perverse merriment. "Just like that!"

"What do you want, Owen?" I say, my hands straying to my hips, only to remember that Titus has yet to return my daggers to me.

"Must I need a reason to visit my own flesh and blood?" he asks, his expression one of mock innocence. He looks even paler than he did before—as if something terrible has happened in the two weeks since I saw him on Reckoning Day—and I can't help but wonder if he was punished for failing to retrieve me.

"Fine," he says, a mischievous grin tugging at the corners of his lips. "I admit I didn't come here to chat. Believe it or not, I've come to warn you." He brings a hand to the side of his mouth and lowers his voice, leaning in as if to share a secret. "You're in grave danger."

Will forces me back a step, and my heel catches on Flynn's armor.

"What do you mean?" I ask, my heartbeat kicking into a gallop. I think of the assassin who attacked me on the train platform—his ominous warning. "What kind of danger?"

Owen watches Will with a gleeful sort of curiosity before fixing his gaze on me once more. "Some time ago, Morana sent her best general to seek out a"—he rolls his tongue in his cheek—"*lost treasure*. If the general failed, he would be forced into exile. Now, Morana has reason to believe that if he finds this *treasure*, he plans to keep it for himself—to use it against her. He is second in power only to Morana, but if he were to recover that which Morana seeks, he would become all powerful. And she can't have that."

My brow furrows, my palms slick with sweat. "What does that have to do with me?"

"More than you realize," he says, his expression suddenly serious. "All the lies Mother and Father told us—I know the truth now. And you will, too. Join me, Aster." He extends his hand, as if expecting me to take it. "Forget the Red Island. The Known World is ours for the taking. We can go anywhere—be anything. We'll go together, just like we promised."

The truth. Something within me latches onto those words, drawing me a step closer to Owen, and I find that I'm barred only by Will's solid frame.

"Aster," Will says softly, gently, his hand brushing mine. "You can't trust him."

My chest aches. Will's right—I know he's right. But as foolish as it is, some part of me believes Owen when he tells me there's more to be known than what Mother and Father revealed. After all, they lied to us about so much—about our heritage as Nightweavers, about what life was really like on land—what else didn't they tell us? And if Owen knows...

I shake my head as if to clear it. This is no different from the last time we spoke, when he tried to turn me into a Shifter. The only way to join Owen is to become like him—to become an Underling and forsake everything I'm fighting for, turning my back on my family, my people, Will.

"No," I say with renewed determination. "I won't join you. Not like this. Leave now, or—"

"Or what?" Owen challenges, flashing his teeth in a baiting smile. "You're going to kill me?" He throws his head back with laughter. "You can't save them. You can't save any of them," he says, his tone dripping with pity, as if I am still just a child grasping for something I can never reach. "You can't even save yourself."

"Maybe not," I say, raising my hands, reveling in the *Manan* that vibrates in my palms, in my chest, eager to be tapped. "But I'm going to try."

I meet Owen's gaze, trying to pull from that same well of power I accessed the night I caused blood to stream from Percy's eyes. But as I stare at my brother's face, as I study the torment that twists his features into something childlike and human and so, so fragile, my power begins to fade. It isn't his fault the Guild of Shadows turned him into a Shifter. It's mine. If I had been faster—if I hadn't distracted him that day—Owen wouldn't have died. He wouldn't have been forced to join the Underlings. Morana wouldn't have been able to use him this way. He would have never compelled Father. He would have never tried to hurt me. And now, I'm the only one who can save him.

I can still save him.

I'm lowering my hands when Owen grabs me by the throat, lifting me off the ground.

Will must move toward me, but Owen throws out his other hand, and a blast of wind sends Will careening back. The force of Owen's power pins Will to the wall, and the precise use of his ability—his control over his windwalker affinity—chills my blood.

"I'm disappointed in you, sister," Owen says, a crazed, malicious smile wiping away any trace of humanity. "You've become far too trusting for your own good." He squeezes, and I resist the urge to fight back.

He won't kill me. He can't. Not while I'm wearing my enchanted bracelet.

"You can't really believe you're going to change anything?" He cocks his head, his eyes searching mine, hungry in his pursuit of fear. "Six hundred years the Nightweavers have reigned, and one *prince*"—he spits the word, his voice taking on a dark, grating quality, reminding me of the assassin's rasping voice—"with a bleeding heart has you convinced you can turn the tides?" His grip tightens, cutting off any chance of getting oxygen to my bursting lungs. "This prince of yours is using you, just as your little lord used you. Neither are who you think them to be." I claw at his hands, my feet jerking uncontrollably as my vision fades. "Don't be a fool, Aster. There is a war coming, and soon, *when* the venom turns you, they will cast you out like a worthless toy they no longer wish to play with. You'll have no choice but to accept your place in Morana's ranks."

He releases me, and I drop to the floor, heaving for breath. Owen kneels, and for a brief second, when he looks at me, I think I see a glimmer of regret in his eyes.

"There are limitations to the protection your trinket offers," he says, his gaze hardening. "You'll do well to remember you're not invincible."

"Careful, brother," I wheeze. "I might start to think you actually care whether I live or die."

My words seem to strike him. "I care about *you*, Aster," he whispers, and the sincerity—the lack of teasing—has me second-guessing everything he's said to me since Reckoning Day. "No matter what happens, that will never change." He glances up at where Will remains pinned to the wall a few feet away and adds, almost too low for me to hear, "William Castor is lying to you. You cannot trust him."

Before I can register the movement, darkness envelops us, an oppressive, unnatural force that bears down on me with a physical weight, and I find myself unable to move.

"Don't say I didn't warn you," Owen says, his voice distorted, as if muffled by the shadows. "I'll see you soon, sister."

There's a rustling of feathers, the sound of glass breaking, and as the shadows dissipate, I catch a glimpse of a raven fleeing through the shattered window. Just like that, Owen is gone.

And I feel a piece of myself go with him.

Chapter Seven

The instant Owen's power releases Will, his arms are around me, the sweet scent of roses enveloping me as he pulls me into a warm, unyielding embrace. His fingers tangle themselves in the hair at the nape of my neck, pulling me impossibly close to him. "Are you all right?" His voice breaks. He draws back, his hands cradling my cheeks as he searches my gaze. "Aster?"

"I'm fine," I say, wincing at the hoarseness of my voice. I rub my throat, where Owen's hand felt like a noose.

Will doesn't appear satisfied by my answer, a muscle in his jaw twitching, but he nods. Finally, reluctantly, he looks away, watching as Eliza crouches over her brothers' bodies, shaking her head.

"They're still breathing," she says with a sigh, getting to her feet. "How did he get in here, anyway? Do you think he shifted into something small enough to fit under the door?"

"Perhaps," Will says as he helps me to my feet, his movements stiff. He turns to face Winona, cowering beside Eliza, his expression grim as his eyes shift from green to gold. "Forget what you've seen here tonight." He adds, his voice rough, "We had a lovely dinner, and you retired to your quarters for the evening."

Winona nods, her eyes vacant, and at once, her body stills, her breathing returning to its calm, measured pace. Her face brightens, and she whispers a quick, polite goodbye to us all before excusing herself from the dining car.

Eliza inclines her head at Will, her brows drawn. "Was that necessary?"

"No one can know that Owen Oberon is alive," Will says, and I wonder just how close the two of them are if he trusts her to keep my brother's appearance a secret.

"I trust Winona," Eliza says, crossing her arms.

He shoots her a look that would send anyone else stumbling back in fear, but Eliza levels him with a challenging look of her own. When it seems as if neither will concede this terrifying staring match, Eliza rolls her eyes. "Go," she says, her eyes softening. "Get Aster to safety."

Will dips his head to Eliza. "I'll be right back," he tells her. He nods at Flynn and Gabriel. "I'll need to check their memories—ensure no one but the three of us remembers what happened here tonight."

Eliza nods. "No need to hurry," she says, her voice dripping with morbid sarcasm as she settles back into her seat at the dining table. "I haven't even finished my dinner yet."

I follow Will down the dimly lit hallways. The winter wind howls, sending tremors through the already noisy train, and as I look out the window, at the all-consuming darkness just beyond the glass, I think of Owen, alone out there in the pitch-black night. Did Morana send him to warn me? Or did he seek me out of his own accord?

My stomach twists into knots. *William Castor is lying to you.*

"Will," I say quietly, "is there something you're not telling me?"

He turns, the flickering lanterns casting his face in a warm amber light. He frowns. "Like what?"

I roll the words around in my mouth, trying to form them into something plausible. "Owen mentioned Morana's general seeking a treasure—"

Will lets out a long, heavy sigh, scratching his jaw. "It's a bedtime story," he says softly. "Children are told the treasure the Underling general was sent out in search of is their souls, and if they don't behave, he'll steal them away to Havok."

I shiver, thinking about how easily even Owen managed to gain access to Bludgrave Manor—how easy it would have been for *him* to steal Albert or Elsie away the night I found him in their chambers. If there really were an Underling general, second only to Morana in power—if he's here, in the Eerie—how much easier would it be for him?

"I know what you're thinking," Will says, his voice gentle. He slows his pace, turning to face me in the narrow corridor. His gaze finds mine, confident, reassuring. "The assassin who attacked you at the train station was sent to scare you away from Castle Grim because Morana must know you plan to expose her. If the stories about the Underling general were true, he would have taken you right then." His teeth clench, as if the very thought might send

54

him into a fit of violent rage. He reaches out, his thumb tracing my jaw, his expression softening. "I promise you, Aster, no one will take you from me."

I melt into his touch, the panic and confusion I felt after my encounter with Owen fading to the background of my mind. "No more secrets?" I whisper, searching Will's gaze.

He leans in, his lips hovering over mine, a breath away from touching. "No more secrets," he whispers as his eyes drift shut, his hand cupping my cheek. He hesitates, his shoulders tense as his nose brushes mine, and he presses a chaste kiss to my lips.

The butterflies in my stomach take flight, taking with them my ability to move or speak. All I can think about is Will—his touch, his lips, his other hand as it snakes around my waist, splayed across the small of my back with tender reluctance, as if he was trying to be gentle but some fierce desire prompts him to pull me closer.

"No more secrets," he murmurs against my lips, his warm breath sending another shiver down my spine.

And I don't want to think anymore. I thread my hands through his hair, and Will makes a desperate, pleading noise somewhere between a purr and a growl as his mouth descends on mine like a wave crashing over the shore. My lips part as I grab hold of him, and we stumble backward until my spine is pressed against the frigid windowpane. The icy glass sends a thrill through me, tangling my stomach into knots.

Will is always so careful to hide his affections for me when someone might see us, but he kisses me dizzy, delirious, his hands frantic, chest heaving, right here in the middle of the hallway, where anyone can find us, and it's as if he doesn't care—as if, in this moment, kissing me is more important than avoiding treason.

More. I want *more.*

I deepen the kiss, my fingers tangling in the hair at the nape of his neck, pulling him closer. It's as if the cord of Will's restraint snaps, his teeth nipping at my bottom lip, my jaw, my throat....

He freezes.

Just as quickly as he lost control, he stops. Inhales. His throat bobs as he draws back, tucking a strand of hair behind my ear. For a moment, he just stares at my lips, like he might kiss me again—and I want him to. Want him to kiss away all my doubts, all my fears. But he sets his jaw, his nostrils flaring, and the memory of our last kiss—how the blood rushing from my nose nearly sent Will into a frenzy—cools the heat coursing through my veins.

He presses his forehead to mine, his heavy-lidded eyes rimmed with a thin line of honey-gold. "You can trust me, Aster," he says, still panting for breath. "I promise."

I want to believe him. But after everything that's happened, I don't know what to believe. It's as if the hallway feels a little colder, a little more...*empty*. And I remember, now, that Will knew this car would be empty—he relocated the passengers himself. No more secrets—except when it comes to how we feel about each other. Except for every furtive kiss, every stolen touch, every whispered promise.

The knots in my stomach tighten, and the butterflies drop dead. "Will, I—"

"*What*," Titus's low, sharp voice comes from my right, where he stands in the open doorway at the end of the corridor, "*happened*?"

He reminds me of a lion as he stalks toward us, as if he were attempting to restrain himself from moving too fast, and I think about what Margaret told me—about the name the people have given him as the king's beast, how they call him the Reaper. A shiver runs through me as he gives Will a once-over, his brow furrowing at the sight of Will's mussed hair, but when his gaze finds me, it's as if all the air has been sucked out of the room. A dozen emotions flash in his eyes before they harden, a look of murderous rage settling on his features when he notes the faint marks on my throat where Owen squeezed. "Who did this?"

"Owen," Will says, his jaw tightening as he and Titus share a *look*.

"Where were Flynn and Gabriel?" Titus asks, his voice a low growl.

"Unconscious," Will answers, his voice rough. "But I'm going to check their memories, just to be sure."

Titus gives a tight nod, his fists clenched at his side. "What did he want?"

Will's eyes dart to me as he runs his tongue over his bottom lip, hesitant. "The same thing he wanted last time," he answers, his eyes darkening. "He wants Aster to join the Guild of Shadows."

Titus rubs his chin, his shoulders tense. "How persistent of him." He looks as if he wants to say more as he flicks a glance at me, but then he motions for us to follow, as if the matter of my Shifter brother is inconsequential, and Will seems content to let the conversation drop.

Will's touch is light on the small of my back as he guides me down the hallway and into a large, velvet-swagged sleeping compartment. "This car belongs to Titus," he says, gesturing at the open doorway. "Your sister is staying in the compartment over. You'll both be safe here."

He moves past me, starting for the door.

"Wait!" I say, suddenly panicked. "When will you be back?"

He refuses to look at me. "I shouldn't be long, and then I'll be right outside if you need me."

I take in the luxurious compartment—the single bed with its silky scarlet sheets and plush pillows. But if this is Titus's room...

Oh Stars.

I whirl to protest, but Will is gone. Titus leans casually on the doorframe, a roguish smirk on his lips, a stark contrast to the thunderous expression he wore upon seeing the evidence of Owen's attack. He winks at me, as if the conversation we had earlier today never happened.

"Don't worry, love," Titus croons. "I won't hog the blanket."

CHAPTER EIGHT

I stare down at what could possibly be the comfiest bed I've ever laid eyes on as if it might as well be full of snakes.

"Relax," Titus says, removing his jacket and slinging it over a hook. "I have no intention of sleeping within striking distance of you." He shoots me a teasing grin, but his voice is gentle. Even his posture seems... subdued. Wary. Like he's not sure how to act.

I know, because I feel the same way.

"It was agreed that I would sleep in the chair." He clears his throat, tugs at his shirt collar. "I offered for William to share the room with you, instead, but he insisted on standing guard outside the door."

I'm not sure why Will's refusal stings, and though I try to hide the disappointment on my face, it must show, because Titus quickly looks away, pretending he didn't see my reaction. My mind insists that Will declined only because if it were discovered that we had shared a room, it would put both of us in danger, whereas Titus's indiscretions are to be expected. As sole heir to his father's kingdom, he might endure punishment, but not to the extent that Will would. But my heart whispers, *Will it always be like this?* Separated by doors that will remain closed, unable to risk our safety—our lives—for what we truly want?

Titus takes a seat in the velvet chair, his bare, tattooed hands clutching the armrests. He blows out a tight breath. "It's only a bed, Aster."

I roll my eyes, gesturing at my gown. "I can't sleep like this."

He quirks a brow. "Then take it off."

My face burns with an unholy fire, as if I might burst into flames at any moment. "Excuse me?"

The ghost of a grin touches his lips. He glances at the wooden screen across the room. "There should be something you can change into."

Oh. Right.

I blow out a tight breath as I step around the screen, hidden from view. I find a pair of red silk pajamas folded in a neat pile on a small stool, as if someone had the forethought to leave them here for me, along with a basin of water for washing up.

"The attack at the train station gave William quite the scare," Titus drawls, apparently sensing my curiosity. "He asked that I have the room prepared for you before dinner."

"And you just so happen to keep a pair of silk pajamas on hand?" The words leave my mouth before I think better of them. Of course he would have them. He's engaged to a princess. These are probably—

"I took them from your room," he says, interrupting my

spiraling thoughts. "If they're not to your liking, I can fetch another pair. You have twenty."

I halt, the gown halfway over my head. *"Twenty?"*

He's quiet for a moment. "I didn't mean to go overboard," he says, his voice stilted and rough, and for the first time since I've met him, he sounds...awkward. Like a common boy, not a prince. "I just wanted you to have everything you might need."

I'm glad he can't see me, because I'm sure the look on my face is utterly ridiculous. I scoff, but it sounds more like I've just choked on a grape. "And you thought I might need twenty pairs of silk pajamas?"

He clears his throat. "They're not all silk," he grumbles. "And besides," he adds a bit louder, some of the pomp returning to his voice, "I couldn't have you showing up at the palace looking like a proper pirate."

I'm not the least bit insulted. "So you're the one who decided on the most uncomfortable pair of shoes I've ever had to cram my feet into?"

I imagine he rolls his eyes, but I can sense the smile in his voice when he says, "Welcome to my world, love."

I pull the pajama top over my head, biting my lip to bar the sound that almost escapes me at the feel of the cool, luxuriously soft silk gliding over my skin.

Damn him *and* his pajamas.

"If you don't like the clothes," Titus says quietly, hesitantly, "I can have it arranged for you to choose some things for yourself."

Something in my chest squeezes as I pull the pants up to my waist. So the fearsome, bloodthirsty prince actually cares whether the pretty gowns he gave me are what I would have wanted.

I step around the screen to find him glaring at the wall, his fist pressed to his mouth.

"They're perfect," I say, and his attention snaps to me like a whip.

He takes in the sight of me in these silk pajamas as if I have changed out of the expensive gown into something even more revealing, rather than the opposite.

I hate that I blush.

"You look—" he starts before scrubbing a hand over his face, groaning softly. He gives a lazy grin as he settles back into his chair, his cheek cradled in his palm. "*Comfortable*," he finishes, enunciating the word as if to convince us both that was what he intended to say all along.

Now, it's my turn to roll my eyes. Still, I feel sheepish under his gaze, and whether I want to admit it or not, I'm grateful. "I've never owned a pair of pajamas," I say. "Let alone twenty."

He smirks, but his eyes soften. "Well, 'pirate' and 'comfortable' don't really go together, do they?"

I sigh, collapsing back onto the bed. "Don't tell my sister that. She already doesn't like you very much."

He laughs—a genuine laugh unlike any I've heard from him before—and I fight the urge to turn my head to look at him. "I'll wager she doesn't feel that way about Captain Shade."

He's right, but I refuse to give him the smug satisfaction of knowing Margaret is a firm believer that Malachi Shade is preternaturally handsome.

"Why weren't you at dinner?" I ask, changing the subject.

He grunts. "I despise dinner."

I prop myself up on my elbow, watching him intently. "The meal or the occasion?"

He shifts uncomfortably in his seat, his expression sour. "The company."

I quirk a brow. "I'm wounded."

"You shouldn't be. I've never had the pleasure of *your* company," he says, his gaze finding mine, his eyes devoid of any teasing. "I'd like to change that."

My stomach twists. "We'll have plenty of dinners together at the palace."

"I'd rather it be just the two of us." His stare is unrelenting, and I suddenly feel like a mouse caught in a trap. "And William, of course," he adds, as if it was an afterthought.

"You don't even know me," I say, my eyes narrowing. "And after today, I'm not sure I know anything about you, *Reaper*."

There—something in his careful mask cracks, and some raw emotion flashes in his eyes before he can repair the fissure. His features darken, a shadow passing over his shuttered gaze. "Ah, so you *have* heard of me." He cuts his eyes at the door, releasing me from his piercing stare for only a brief moment. Then he turns and looks at me even deeper than before, as if he were trying to burrow into my very soul. "All the stories are true," he says, his voice rough. "Does that scare you?"

I stand, taking advantage of the one chance I have to tower over *him* for a change. "You'd like that, wouldn't you?"

He laughs again, but there's no humor in it. "You were afraid of me, once." His gaze drifts from my eyes to my lips, lingering there for far too long before meeting my stare once more. "When we reach Castle Grim, what you see..." He grinds his teeth. "You will come to fear me again."

I shake my head, my heart pounding. "Why does it matter to you what I think?"

He gets to his feet slowly, his head cocked. "Do you know how many I've killed? How many humans? How many Myths?" His brows pinch, forming a crease between them, making him look as if he's lived lifetimes rather than only nineteen years. "The king requires that I personally perform all executions in Jade whenever the occasion presents itself. These are not *humane* executions. The king demands that I show the people the very worst of our kind, so as to cow them into submission."

My chest constricts. I am no stranger to death, but when I lived aboard the *Lightbringer*, I killed only to protect my family—to protect myself. I can't imagine being forced to take innocent lives, and I feel sick when I realize that by swearing the oath of a Bloodknight, I might be ordered to do the same.

"Why—" The words stick in my throat. "Why would your father—"

"Hatred is a curious thing," he says gently. "Remember?"

Without thinking, my gaze drifts to his chest, where I know his flesh is marked by countless scars. How could a father hate his own son? Enough to force him to act with such cruelty—such...

"I'm a monster," Titus whispers, his voice breaking.

The Reaper. This is who he's afraid I'll meet at Castle Grim—the monster his parents have forced him to become. At once, it's clear to me why he would choose to join the fight against them—why he would wish them dead. Why he would don a mask and sail the Western Sea as a pirate, saving humans like me from cannibal ships like the *Deathwail*. With all the blood on his hands, every act of rebellion has become an act of penitence.

"But you're also Captain Shade," I remind him—remind myself. "You're a hero."

His smile threatens to break me—it twists itself into something wretched and small and utterly defenseless. Right now, in this moment, he looks nothing like a nightmare. He looks, instead, like a battered dream. A long-forgotten wish. An unanswered prayer.

"I am no hero, love." His lips twitch, and the shift in his expression is so subtle I almost miss it, but I see it this time—see him switch, swapping the mask of the tragic pirate to the arrogant prince. "Besides, you made your feelings perfectly clear when, rather than accept that the *great Captain Shade* was *me*, you dived headfirst into the ocean."

I wince, but I don't back down. "Perhaps I didn't make my feelings clear enough. *You* are a lying, manipulative, spoiled—"

He takes a step toward me, crowding me until the back of my knees hit the bed frame, his brow furrowed even as he flashes his teeth in a biting smile. "Go on."

I shove against his chest, but it's like pushing against a brick wall. "You're the most confusing person I've ever met! One minute, you're kind to me, and the next, I feel like—like I'm just some pawn for you to control. You make me feel important—you save my life—and then I find out it's only because you plan to use my curse to your advantage!"

Just like Will, I think, but I don't say the words out loud.

"And I hate that I can't hate you," I whisper. "As hard as I try, I just...can't."

He glances at my lips, his voice gruff. "You should."

"I don't."

He grits his teeth. "Why are you making this so difficult for me?" His voice breaks, and he leans in, so close I can feel his warm breath on my face.

A shiver runs up my spine. "What do you mean?"

"You were never supposed to come here," he says, his eyes drifting shut. "You were supposed to stay far, far away from the Eerie."

"Why?" I ask, but I think I know the answer. After he saved me from the *Deathwail*, I was supposed to remain at sea, safe aboard my family's ship, the *Lightbringer*. I lift my hand, as if to touch his face. "Titus—"

Before my fingers can skim his cheek, his eyes go wide, and he jerks away, putting two feet of distance between us—distance that feels like a gaping chasm that's just opened up to swallow me whole.

He sighs heavily, running his hands over his face. "You should get some sleep." He turns his back to me, taking a crystal bottle from the small bar and pouring two fingers of amber liquid into a glass. He knocks it back in one gulp, pours another.

I want to argue, but at the very mention of sleep, my body yearns to curl up on this plush mattress and surrender to the obscene comfort that is Titus's bed. As I slide under the covers, I watch him turn off the lamp and settle into his chair, having traded the glass for the bottle itself.

After a little while, when my eyes have adjusted to the dark, I look toward the foot of the bed, where Titus sits in his chair like a statue, his gaze fixed on the ceiling, the empty bottle clutched to his chest.

"Titus?"

"Yes, love?"

He sounds just as tired as I feel. Sleep overtakes me, but before I go under, I manage to whisper words I'm not sure he can hear.

"Thank you for the pajamas."

It's too dark.

And I'm falling again.

I claw at the emptiness of the void, trying to gain purchase, but there's nothing to grab hold of—nothing solid I can cling to.

There's just...

Nothing.

No stars. No light. Only me. Only darkness.

Until it isn't.

A pair of glowing red eyes materializes in the void. Then another—and another, until hundreds of red eyes fill the darkness, watching me, waiting for me to hit the ground.

But there is no ground here. When I look down, all I see are teeth.

Thousands of teeth, ready to shred me to pieces.

That's when I hear it: laughter. High-pitched, guttural, grating, monstrous—it's all around me. Loud. Too loud. And then I realize...

I'm the one laughing.

Far away, someone screams. It's a broken, heartrending scream that sets my nerves on fire.

"Aster." A soft voice reaches me in the void. *"I'm here. I'm not leaving you. Not again."* And then, quieter, *"Never again."*

I wake up sobbing.

Strong arms wrap around me, but before they can pull me

close, I wrench myself free. I scramble away, blinking furiously to adjust to the darkness.

Nothing. Nothing. Nothing—

My heart leaps into my throat as I start to fall, but just as I topple over the edge of the bed, a hand seizes my ankle, tugging me back onto the mattress. I come face-to-face with Titus, his silhouette outlined by the faint silver moonlight.

In the dark, it feels as if, just for a moment, we could be underwater once more. I half-expect some force to push us apart as he wraps his arm around me, his touch hesitant, as if it takes every ounce of self-control to restrain himself from pulling me closer.

"Where's Will?" My words come out on a whimper.

Titus's forearm tenses, and he withdraws fully, moving to sit on the edge of the bed, his back to me. "He was just here," he says, his voice still rough from sleep. "He's gone to make arrangements for your departure. We don't want another repeat of last night."

I glance at the door, thinking about Will standing out there all night in the hall, keeping watch over me. But a quiet voice at the back of my mind whispers, *Why wasn't he here when I needed him?* Though I forgave him for leaving me at Bludgrave Manor those three months he went away to war, a part of me still can't help but feel as if it's always when I need him the most he's never here. He said no more secrets between us, but it's hard to build trust with someone I hardly ever see.

It's as if the moment I think this, Titus turns, his face radiant in the moonlight. "I could go and find him for you, if you'd like."

I shake my head. "No, that's quite all right; it was just a bad—" I start, attempting to stand, when my foot gets tangled up in the sheet and—

Titus seizes my wrist, pulling me to my feet. We stand there, locked in an awkward embrace, and it appears as though he can't bring himself to let me go. "You should watch where you step, love. I might not always be around to catch you."

My heart thumps once. Twice.

"Hello?" Margaret's voice sounds from the other side of the door. She knocks again. "Anyone in there?"

Titus exhales a long, low sigh. "I'm beginning to think I don't much like your sister, either."

I start to pull away, and he steps back, shaking his head slightly as he releases me from his grip, almost as if he didn't realize how tightly he held me. Before I reach the door, I turn to find him sitting on the edge of the bed, watching me, his expression neutral but his eyes tumultuous.

"You..." I gulp. "You're sure no one will find out I slept in your chambers? If anyone knew—they'll think that I—"

"If anyone has anything to say about you," he interrupts me, standing to his full height, giving me a glimpse of the wicked villain of legend as he cocks his head, "I'll make them wish they never uttered your name."

My mouth goes dry.

"I *will* pick this lock," Margaret says, louder now. "Prince or not, if you don't let me see my sister—"

Titus opens the door before I get the chance.

Margaret flinches when she sees him, but then she doubles down, her fists clenched at her sides.

"She doesn't belong to you, *Your Highness*," Margaret snarls, and I suppress a smile. Oh, how I've missed the fierce pirate I know my sister to be. "If you've hurt her in any way—"

"Your sister can take care of herself," Titus says dryly, his expression apathetic. He looks past her, to the two Bloodknights behind her in the cramped hallway. "Are you going to let this *human* speak to your future king like that?"

My blood chills at the malice dripping from his words. He can't be serious. He wouldn't put Margaret in danger.

Would he?

Would the Reaper?

"What would you have us do, my prince?" Gabriel's muffled voice sounds somewhat bored. "I could throw her from the train."

"The thought crossed my mind," Titus mutters.

"Try," Margaret says, baring her teeth.

Flynn snorts a laugh.

Titus scowls, his lean, toned muscles straining against the fabric of his shirt as he steps into the hall, towering over Margaret.

And Margaret—Stars, I almost wish she wouldn't, and yet my heart leaps at the sight—doesn't give up ground. She cranes her neck to look up at him, mirroring his glare.

"Lord William asked that I help Aster dress," she says, enunciating every syllable as if she were speaking to a toddler. "So either throw me off this train or get out of my damn way."

I think I hear Gabriel choke.

A slow, vicious grin tugs at Titus's lips. "Does the entire Oberon clan have such unruly tempers, or is it just the two of you?"

Venom laces Margaret's smile. "Harm my sister in any way and you'll find out."

Titus rolls his eyes before fixing a look on Gabriel. "Has William made all the proper arrangements?"

Gabriel dips his head. "He said he wanted to speak with you. We'll be arriving soon and—"

"Very well," Titus says with a sigh. He takes a step to the side, holding out his arm as an indication for Margaret to enter his chambers.

She takes a step, but he sticks out his other arm, barring her path.

"Miss Oberon," he says with lethal quiet, "you'll do well to remember your place. I'm not always in such a generous mood."

Thankfully, Margaret says nothing. When she closes the door to his chambers, however, she lets out a furious groan.

"I don't know how you put up with him!" She makes a vulgar gesture at the door, where Titus can probably hear everything she's saying. "He makes my skin crawl!"

"Marge," I say, careful to keep my voice low. "Just because he's in the Order doesn't mean you can disrespect him in front of the king's men like that."

"I heard you screaming!" Margaret grabs me by the shoulders. "And those two *boneheads* out there wouldn't let me through. I didn't know if—if he'd done something—"

"He wouldn't hurt me," I say, my stomach twisting. "He's... not like you think."

But even as the words leave my mouth, a chill snakes through me. How well do I actually know Titus? And from what I do know... maybe Margaret has a right to be concerned.

Her brows shoot to the top of her forehead. But she doesn't argue. "Whatever you say." She shrugs finally. "I still don't like him."

"I don't think he likes you too much, either," I say, stifling a laugh despite the unease that settles in my gut.

Margaret grins. "Good."

Chapter Nine

Margaret and I stand between Flynn and Gabriel, waiting for the door to open and let us out onto the loading platform, growing more impatient by the minute. A part of me wishes we could have continued straight on to Castle Grim, but I'm thankful for the chance to see my family before I have to leave them again. At least this time I can give them a proper goodbye.

"Wait!"

The four of us turn to look as Eliza hurries—impossibly graceful—down the corridor, smiling at me as if we've been friends our whole lives. But there's something in her eyes—worry? Fear? Whatever it is, a chill sweeps through me as she takes me by the hands.

"Take care, Aster," she says, her grip firm. After what happened last night, I can't help but feel like there's more she wants to say. "I'll save you a seat at court."

Margaret watches the exchange with narrowed eyes, her expression incredulous.

"Okay," I say, my brows quirked. "Thank you."

Eliza smiles warmly as she straightens the lapels of my tweed coat. She laughs, as if she's heard a joke meant for her ears alone, the sound clear and sweet, like silvery bells. "Billie doesn't know what he's gotten himself into with you, does he?"

Margaret makes a choking noise. "Billie?"

Eliza winks at me. "Best of luck, Aster Oberon!"

And with that, the door to the platform opens with a groan, and Gabriel ushers me out into the gray light of morning.

I'm led down the icy steps to where a black open-air carriage waits, drawn by four horses the color of midnight, their dark coats stark against the snow-covered street. Both Flynn and Gabriel are on high alert, but it's Margaret's watchful eye on my back that gives me a small fraction of peace. I allow Will to lead me to the carriage door, allow him to guide me up the steps and onto the plush bench seat, where he takes his place across from Margaret and me.

The carriage lurches forward. I take in the buildings that line the cobblestone streets of Ink Haven. Repairs have been made since the riots that happened after Percy's unlawful executions, but there are still traces of that horrible night—the occasional broken pane of glass or the bloodstains hastily painted over in shades of blue or green or pink.

Titus leads our caravan, surrounded by a troop of Bloodknights. He rides a gigantic horse the color of the night sky, its hide flecked white, reminding me of thousands of tiny stars. In his black uniform, his scarlet sash bedecked in medals, he looks every bit a prince—and every bit as terrifying as the stories portray him to be.

We pass Mrs. Carroll's bakery, the windows boarded up, a VACANT sign on the door, and my heart sinks. And there, nailed to a wooden post, is a wanted poster of Captain Shade, now marked with a red *X*.

News travels fast, I suppose.

I meet Will's eyes, and when he offers me a small, sympathetic smile, I'm reminded of the day I first arrived in Ink Haven, the way he showed me the city on horseback. It seemed so lively then, its people more jaunty, its colors more vibrant. Now, even the air tastes stale and ashen, an echo of a memory, and the people gathered in the street appear to cower in fear of Titus and the Bloodknights, either too brave or too curious for their own good.

"*The Reaper*," the people whisper, retreating to the safety of their homes.

"*Reaper*," they murmur, shuttering their windows.

I watch Titus over Will's shoulder, and though I can't be sure, I think I see his shoulders tense with every mention of the king's beast. But he never looks back at our carriage, and he doesn't acknowledge the townspeople, his posture rigid and his gaze set on the road ahead as we make our way to the outskirts of Ink Haven and the stone fortress that sits at the top of the snow-covered hill comes into view.

In the time that I've been gone, it's as if everything and yet nothing at all has changed.

Metal creaks as the guards, Gylda and Hugh, open the iron gate that leads onto the long drive. At the end of the gravel path, the half-razed structure of Bludgrave Manor looms, a monument to the dead.

For a short while, this place was home. And I didn't realize just how happy I could have been here until it was too late.

Now, as I take in the rubble that remains of the East Wing, all I see is a carcass.

The kitchen where my father and I prepared meals side by side—gone. The ballroom where my siblings and I toasted in honor of our brother—a hollow shell, marked only by a few remaining pillars. And there, in the middle of the circle drive, the cracked fountain, its basin dried up—the fountain I destroyed by the sheer force of my power as I channeled the water that extinguished the flames.

"I wish you were staying," Margaret says, squeezing my hand. She hasn't let go of me since we entered the carriage, and I don't think she plans on letting go of me anytime soon.

"Me too," I say quietly.

Will informed me we were here for only the night. Tomorrow, my family will observe Father's burial rites, having waited for Will to rescue me from "captivity." Then I'll be leaving again. This time, I'm not sure when—if ever—I'll be returning.

We come to a halt in front of the double doors as the Bloodknights take up their posts near the front gate and all along the perimeter of Bludgrave Manor, releasing Gylda and Hugh from their duties for the evening. I watch as they make their way down the long gravel path alongside Titus, who continues his slow, steady trot, headed in the direction of the stables without so much as a glance over his shoulder at what remains of our small party.

"My lady," Flynn says, holding out his hand for me to take. There's something gentle—almost sympathetic—about his voice that gives me pause. His remaining hazel eye lights with what I assume is a smirk. "Please don't make me beg."

I roll my eyes and place my hand in his metal grasp, allowing him to guide me down from the carriage. Once safely on the ground, he does a sort of half bow before retreating to stand behind me.

Margaret follows, taking her place beside me at the base of the shallow steps. "Welcome home," she says, looping her arm through mine.

Will turns to catch my eye, his lips curved in the slightest hint of a smile. "I hope you don't mind, but..." He knocks four times on the double doors. "They made quite a fuss."

"Who—" I start, but the double doors are thrown wide, and I have my answer.

Elsie, my youngest sister, comes hurtling down the steps before I've had a moment to take in the sight of my family gathered in the foyer.

"You're back!" she squeals. "You're—"

Just before she can throw her arms around me, Margaret intercepts, catching Elsie by the arm.

Elsie's face falls when she sees the bruises on my throat. When Will tried to heal them this morning, I refused. If the kingdom needs to believe Captain Shade held me captive for two weeks, then it doesn't hurt to have it *look* as if I were mistreated aboard his ship.

"What happened?" Charlie charges down the steps.

"Are you all right?" Lewis asks, shoving past Charlie to reach me first.

"I'll kill 'em," Albert says, close at their heels. As the youngest boy, he's never far behind, and though he's a third of Charlie's size, he puffs out his chest, attempting to mimic our brother's confident posture.

Margaret rolls her eyes. "She's fine," she says. "Nothing a bath won't fix."

If only a bath could fix... everything.

Charlie grunts. "I should have been there."

"You've seen the papers," Lewis points out. "The bastard, Shade, was dealt with accordingly."

"He was," Will says, his smile tight. His gaze searches the grounds, as if he expects someone to jump out from behind a bush and drive a blade through my heart. "We should get inside."

My siblings usher me up the steps in what feels like a guard formation, and Lewis places his hand on my shoulder as if to say, *I've got you*.

Once inside the manor, the knots in my shoulders loosen, if only a little.

Streamers bedeck the banisters, accompanied by a painted cloth strung above the Castors' crest that says WELCOME HOME in sloppy red paint.

A chill runs down my spine. If it wasn't for my family's obvious involvement in the décor, I'd think the cloth was painted in blood.

I flinch when Mother places a light hand on my shoulder.

Concern flashes in her eyes as she turns me to face her fully. "Go on upstairs," she says, her voice gentle. "You must be exhausted. Get cleaned up. I'll have your supper brought to your room."

I can't imagine who would have taken up cooking in Father's stead, and I almost ask, but it's as if at the very mention of supper, all the air has been sucked out of the room. I can feel my siblings tense, and I realize everyone must expect me to lose myself as I did after Owen died. Then, my grief consumed me—it blinded me, and because of it, I failed to see what was right in front of me. I failed to recognize that Owen was still alive, haunting me. If only I paid closer attention, recognized the signs, I could have stopped Owen before he compelled Father.

I could have stopped Father from taking his own life.

"Aster?" I startle at Margaret's touch on my arm. "Are you all right?" she asks.

I nod. "Fine," I say. "Just a little tired."

I look at each of my siblings then, noting their weary expressions, the dark circles that shadow their eyes. When we lost Owen—when we first came to live at Bludgrave—I struggled to cope with the idea that we were creating a life without our oldest brother. But now, as I recognize that same bitter grief that lines my siblings' faces, I realize that because of what I know—because of what I have to do—this time, I can't be clouded by my emotions.

I must become a blade forged by the hammer of grief, not shattered by it.

Someone clears their throat, and my gaze snaps to Jack as he slips his arm around Margaret's waist, pulling her close. "Aster," he says, tipping his hat to me, a sheepish grin on his face. "It's good to have you back."

I force a smile, but my eyes narrow slightly. "Jack," I say, my tone issuing its own warning.

He cuts his eyes at Margaret and shrugs as if to say, *Of course I told her about the Order.*

I want to stay angry with him—I still *am* angry with him—but seeing the two of them together...I understand. I know all too well what it feels like to keep a secret from someone you love. To have them keep a secret from you.

"We're so happy you're safe," Lady Isabelle says, gliding toward me with that graceful air that makes her seem almost ethereal. Will's mother takes my hands in hers, the crinkles around her eyes conveying all the warmth of a proud mother. "We owe you our thanks for saving Annie."

"We can never repay you," Lord Bludgrave adds. I catch a glimpse of Will's father over Lady Isabelle's shoulder—his black hair streaked with traces of silver, his neatly pressed suit, his kindly expression. His appearance is a stark contrast to the last time I saw him, tied to a tree, bleeding out from a wound in his leg.

I hold his gaze for a moment, wondering if I'll see some hint of remembrance there, but it seems Will removed any memory of that night—of his involvement with the Guild of Shadows; Owen's compulsion over Lord Bludgrave's daughter, Annie; or my curse.

Lord Bludgrave dips his head to me. "We're forever in your debt." He holds out his hand, and Annie steps out from behind the doorframe, her head bowed, black ringlets obscuring her face. "What do you have to say to Miss Oberon?"

Shyly—in a manner I've never witnessed from her before—she peers up at me, and I'm stricken by the haunted look in her eyes.

Will mentioned he wiped Annie's memories of that night as well. But while Annie may not remember what happened, it seems it scarred her somewhere even Will's magic cannot reach.

"Thank you," she says, her voice almost too quiet to hear.

"Oh, please, you don't have to thank me." I turn, meeting Lady Isabelle's adoring gaze—noting the worry there. "I was only doing what—"

"Aster?"

Henry stands frozen on the landing, gripping the banister as if it was the only thing keeping him upright.

"Henry?" I gape at Will's younger brother—at his disheveled clothes, his mussed hair, the shadows encircling his bloodshot eyes.

He barrels down the stairs—it's a wonder he doesn't tumble down them, considering the stench of liquor that reaches me before he does—and nearly tackles me, crushing me in a desperate embrace.

"Thank the Stars," he says, his hold on me tightening before he draws back, examining my face with a look of dread, his hands cupping my cheeks as his gaze dips to my throat. "You're hurt."

"I'm fine, Henry," I say softly, placing my hands over his. "Really, I'm all right."

He doesn't look convinced. His gaze snaps to Will, his lip curling with a snarl. "How could you let this happen?"

Will just shakes his head, blowing out a weary sigh. "She's fine," he says, his voice low, steady. "If you'd let go, she could get cleaned up. Then you can visit with her all you like." His expression softens. "But first you have to let go."

Henry nods slowly. "Of course," he says. "Of course. I'm sorry," he adds in a whisper, his voice breaking as if he was on the verge of tears. "I'm sorry."

"Don't apologize." I squeeze his hands before letting them fall back to his sides. "I'm happy to see you."

He sniffles, cracking a smile—a sad, subdued smile that breaks my heart. "Don't tease me, Aster."

Margaret loops her arm through mine, guiding me to the servants' passage, where Sybil waves at me from inside the dimly lit hallway.

"That went better than I expected," Margaret says as Sybil closes the door behind us.

"You can't be serious?" I follow Margaret through the winding passage, the stench of burnt wood still clinging to the walls. It makes me realize just how little time has truly passed since the attack on Bludgrave.

"Afraid so," Sybil says as we start up a narrow set of stairs. "Mr. Castor hasn't been quite right since..."

Since he lost his love, Dorothy.

"He has...episodes," Margaret adds, somewhat hesitant. "Sometimes he's violent."

I pause halfway up the steps. "With you?"

"No," she says quickly. "With...himself."

My heart sinks.

"I heard he lit himself on fire only two days ago," Sybil whispers from close behind. "Hugh said the only reason he didn't burn is because his magic protected him."

Oh Henry.

"Just now, with you," Margaret says, opening the door that leads out into the servants' quarters, "that's the most stable I've seen him in weeks."

"Certainly," Sybil agrees. "He seems to really care for you."

I think of the way Henry cradled Dorothy in his arms after she was possessed by a Sylk and I was forced to take her life. How he was unwilling to part with her, even if it meant he would die, too. After I learned that he survived the *Deathwail*—after we grew close during the months that Will was with Titus on the front lines—I developed an immense amount of respect, even admiration, for Henry.

"I care for him, too," I tell Sybil. "He means a great deal to me."

Sybil nods considerately as we step out into the upstairs hall, her brows pinched as she glances at the green baize door that separates the servants' quarters from the residential wing.

"Perhaps you could speak to Mr. Castor," she says quietly. "There are rumors he's taken to chewing a particularly vile substance. It's poison, really. Maybe, if you tried, you could persuade him to stop."

I open my mouth to ask Sybil what she means, but there's a sound, like someone turning the knob from the other side of the green baize door, and Sybil lets out a tiny squeak, hurrying back down the stairwell and out of sight before I can get an answer.

I glance at Margaret, but she doesn't seem to think the young maid's behavior is strange, her expression nettled, gaze focused on the door.

"Come on," Margaret says quietly, taking me by the arm and guiding me into my old room. She shuts the door behind us, pressing herself against it for a moment as if to listen for something. A few moments pass, and Margaret's shoulders slump. She lets out a weary sigh, rubs her eyes.

"Are you all right?" I ask, but even as the words leave my mouth, I wish I could take them back. She just asked me that very question, and I didn't answer it honestly.

Margaret doesn't answer at all. Instead, she rummages through her trunk as I take in the cramped room. Somehow, it feels even smaller than it did before, and my memories of staying here—of working as a maid in the Castors' employ—feel like someone else's life entirely. And yet, what I wouldn't give to make my way down the stairs to the kitchen and find Father waltzing about, his face warm and bright....

Margaret withdraws a small dagger made of Elysian Iron from her belongings. "Take it," she says, presenting the dagger to me. "Don't worry," she adds when I hesitate. "I have another."

"Where did you get this?" I ask, sheathing the dagger in my boot. During my time as a servant at Bludgrave, we were never supposed to keep weapons. As humans, we could face severe punishment if we were discovered to be armed in any way. "*Jack*," I say with a sigh, and Margaret nods. Well, at least if he brought Margaret into the Order, he made sure she had the means to protect herself.

There's another sound, like a door opening and closing, and Margaret unsheathes her own dagger in the blink of an eye. On the train, Margaret seemed cheerful—composed. But it's as if the moment we set foot on the estate, she's suddenly on edge, and I think again how difficult these past weeks must have been since the attack—how the somewhat normal lives my siblings created for themselves burned to the ground, reducing their hopes of a better future to nothing more than ashes.

Someone knocks, and Margaret steps in front of me, dagger raised.

"It's only me," comes Will's muffled voice from the other side of the door.

Margaret's hand trembles as she lowers the dagger. "Come in," she says.

The door creaks as Will slips inside. He glances at the dagger in Margaret's grasp, nods slowly. "I'm terribly sorry to have startled you," he says, his voice gentle. "Would it be all right if I spoke with Aster alone? It will take only a minute."

Margaret cuts a glance at me, and I give her a small nod. She offers Will a tight smile, but she speaks to me when she says, "I'll be just downstairs if you need me."

Will closes the door behind her, listening as her footsteps fade down the hall before turning to face me. His throat bobs as his gaze roves my face, and he takes a step closer to me. Tenderly, he tucks a strand of hair behind my ear, his heavy-lidded eyes focused on my lips for what feels like an eternity.

"What did you need to speak with me about?" I whisper, breathless. When I lived at Bludgrave, Will and I spent most of our time together in the conservatory; he rarely entered my bedroom. Something about his standing here now, his thumb stroking my jaw, his other hand snaking around my waist, delicate, hesitant, sends a thrill through me. For a moment, I forget why we're here—forget that we're both cursed. Forget that he's a Nightweaver, and I'm half human, and the very fact that we're alone together could be enough to warrant our executions.

"So many nights I thought about you, just on the other side of that door." He leans in, his breath ghosting my lips. "I thought about what it would be like if there were no doors to separate us."

My heart leaps into my throat, and I press my hands to his chest as if to steady myself.

"I thought about what it would be like to call you mine." The soft touch of his lips brush my own, but just before he can seal the kiss, there's another knock at the door.

Will's fist clenches at my waist, and he groans, stepping back.

"Pardon," Jack says, peeking inside.

Will and I both pin him with a glare.

I expect Jack to give a playful wink or a nervous chuckle, but his expression is uncharacteristically serious. "It's from Killian," he says to Will, taking a small piece of parchment from his pocket and passing it to him.

My heart gives a little leap at the mention of Will's uncle. During Will's absence from Bludgrave Manor, Killian dedicated his time and effort to teaching me everything I needed to know about the Underlings.

My stomach tightens. *Everything Will failed to teach me.*

Will smooths the creases of the worn parchment, and I peer over his shoulder. I recognize Killian's handwriting immediately, and I'm surprised to find it's addressed to both of us.

Aster and Will, meet me where the wolves howl. Midnight.

I didn't know Killian was here—from what Margaret told me aboard the train, he was called away in service to the Crown just after the attack on Reckoning Day.

Will folds the parchment, sticks it into his breast pocket. "Thank you, Jack. Now, if you'll excuse us—"

Jack winces, holding up a finger. "Your father wishes to see you," he says quickly. "He's asked that you check the wards...again."

Will blows out a terse breath, casting his eyes skyward as if in silent prayer. "Of course." He grinds his jaw. "I'll be right there."

Jack retreats in a flash, leaving Will and me alone once more.

"I'll see you tonight," Will says, pressing a chaste kiss to my forehead. As he draws back, he flourishes a single purple rose—a mystik, a rare bloom cultivated by only the most talented bonewielders—offering it to me as if he pulled it from thin air.

I take the flower, but my stomach sours when I realize why Will's father has called him away. If he's asked Will to check the wards that protect the manor, the Castors must be on high alert since the Underlings managed to invade on Reckoning Day.

"Owen's already been invited inside the wards," I say.

As a Shifter, my brother spent months haunting the halls of Bludgrave Manor. He killed the Hackneys, horrifically leaving their eyes for me to find. He taunted me. Toyed with me. I think about his warning on the train—*William Castor is lying to you*. Another ploy to convince me I'd be better off joining Morana's army, the Guild of Shadows, than staying with Will. It's another twisted game. Only this time, I refuse to play.

Will scowls, but his eyes soften. "It's not just Owen I'm worried about."

I grip the stem of the flower as if it were the hilt of my dagger, attempting to mask the way my hand twitches. He's referring to the ambush before we boarded the train. The attacker seemed to imply he wasn't an Underling, which eliminates the assassin being Owen.

He runs a hand through his hair, sighs. "I'm not sure who's hunting us—hunting *you*," he says, stepping out into the hall. He glances left, then right, ensuring we're alone before he adds, "But I intend to find him, whoever he is, and when I do..."

I suppress a shudder at the memory of Will's bloodlust on Reckoning Day—of the kind of violence he's capable of if he was to lose control again.

"You won't do anything," I say, and Will quirks a brow, seemingly intrigued rather than taken aback. It's as if the very thought of Will being the one to find my attacker—to be the one to make them bleed—sends a fresh wave of anger through me. My entire life, I've been forced to run and hide—to live in fear of those who sought to kill me. First, enemy pirate clans like that of the *Deathwail*, then Nightweavers, then Underlings, and now this assassin who thinks he can tell me where I can and cannot go. No longer. "I intend to find him first."

Will's eyes twinkle with amusement. "For his sake, I think it would be better if you didn't."

Chapter Ten

As I lie in my cot, listening to Margaret snore, I stare at the grate above, expecting to see Owen's watchful red eyes peering down at me. It's strange to think that only one year ago, I would have been asleep in my bunk aboard the *Lightbringer*, with my siblings all around me and Owen only a few feet away.

Every time I close my eyes, I see Owen's face warning me aboard the train. He seemed...*different* than he was on the night he attacked me on Reckoning Day—afraid almost. Desperate. What must it be like for him, forced to serve Morana, even at the cost of hurting the family he once loved? I wonder—is he still capable of love? Does he feel *anything*—guilt for Father's death, shame for all he's put us through?

Does he even wish to be saved?

The door to my room creaks open, and I bolt upright, the dagger

Margaret gifted me already in hand. There's a quiet squeak, and the scuffling of tiny feet, and when I squint in the darkness, I can just make out the little brown mouse scurrying across the room. I chuckle at myself and take a deep breath, attempting to calm my frayed nerves as the mouse squeezes through a thin crack in the wall.

Suddenly, a shadow passes over the floorboards, and my gaze snaps to a dark figure looming in my doorway.

I don't wait for the figure to enter my room, and I don't give them the chance to catch me off guard. In a few nimble movements, I slip into the hall through the crack in the door and pin the intruder against the wall, the blade of my dagger pressed to their throat.

Will's green eyes sparkle with intrigue as he flicks a glance at the dagger.

"It's me, my darling," he whispers, his voice as soothing and gentle as a lullaby. "It's just me."

I blow out a tight breath, my heart hammering against my sternum as I remove the dagger, sheathing it in my boot. "You're lucky I didn't gut you where you stand," I hiss. What I don't tell him is that I've been looking for an opportunity to let off some steam, and he almost found himself on the receiving end of a few months' worth of pent-up aggression.

But Will appears unaffected by his brush with death. Instead, he grins, his dimples on full display as he offers me his hand. "Next time, I'll announce myself."

I take his hand, threading my fingers through his, and together, we hurry along the route I took dozens of times on my way to a secret rendezvous with Will at the conservatory. It's strange having Will by my side, and I only wish it could be this way all the time—that we could always be together, never forced to hide our affections for each other.

When we reach the stables, it's nearly midnight. Moonlight filters through the skylight, dappling Caligo's dark coat silver. Caligo snorts in greeting, and I smile, stroking his face.

"I missed you, too," I say, pressing my forehead to his. He snorts again, and out of the corner of my eye I catch a glimpse of Will's expression—a mixture of shock and delight that looks almost comical.

As I set to work saddling Caligo, I'm surprised at the way the simple task feels second nature to me now, as if I've been saddling horses my whole life, and again grief seizes my heart when I think of how much things have changed—how *I've* changed.

"What have we here?" comes a voice, and my heart skips a full beat before I recognize it. Titus sits atop his stallion as he guides the horse into the stables but doesn't dismount. In the flickering lantern light, he appears starker, more battle-seasoned—like the commander of armies the legends portray. My stomach sours when I notice the blood splattering his princely garb.

"Where have you been?" I ask, and the words sound harsher than I intend.

His expression is taciturn, all but for the slight lift of his brow. "Hunting."

My gaze narrows on the smattering of crimson freckles on his cheek. "For?"

He cuts a glance at Will, a bemused smirk touching his lips. "For anyone who might intend to do you harm," he says, flashing his teeth. "*Someone* doesn't want you to reach Castle Grim, and until we can be sure of *why*, I plan to do everything in my power to ensure they understand exactly whom it is they're dealing with." He takes a bundle of parchment from his jacket pocket and passes it to Will, shooting me a pointed look. "I wasn't entirely unproductive. While I was in town, I procured traveling papers for the inhabitants of Bludgrave Manor. The entire Oberon clan and what's left of the staff will be joining us at the palace, where we can keep a close eye on them, should anyone wish to use your family against you."

I glance at the papers as Will tucks them inside his coat pocket. "Thank you," I say, relieved that I won't have to say goodbye to my family just yet.

"Of course," Titus says, his voice clipped. He removes his gloves, revealing the tattoos that ink his skin, as he looks between the two of us. "Out for a late-night ride?"

Will makes a choking noise, and my cheeks heat. He clears his throat. "Actually," Will says, wiping his hands on the front of his coat, "I received a message from Killian. He wants to meet with Aster and me at the conservatory."

Titus smirks as he takes a note from his pocket, waves it. "Aye, it appears I've been summoned as well."

I roll my eyes and before Will has the chance, I swing my leg over Caligo's saddle. "Well?" I jerk my chin in the direction of Thea, the unicorn that belongs to Lady Isabelle. "What are we waiting for?"

Will shakes his head before setting to work saddling Henry's steed, Nutmeg, instead. "Caligo is *my* horse, you know."

Caligo trots out of the stall, following Titus out of the stable, kicking up dust in Will's face as I call over my shoulder, "Tell that to Caligo."

When we emerge on the other side of the apple tree tunnel, and the towering frame of the conservatory comes into view, nestled in the snowy clearing, I can almost convince myself that the past few weeks never happened—that Will and I are meeting here for a picnic, that I might gaze at the stars while he tends the flowers of his beloved garden. But it's as if the memories of our evenings at the conservatory have all been tainted by the revelation that during the time we spent together, he kept more secrets from me than I ever could have guessed. Secrets that ultimately led to my father's death. Secrets that might have gotten Annie killed had I not been willing to trade my life for hers.

All because Will didn't trust me.

"So Killian summoned you, too," Henry says, calling out to us from where he waits near the entrance to the conservatory. Bundled in his black cloak, his cheeks rosy, he squints at us as flurries of snow catch in his dark eyelashes. "I didn't think he'd be back from his assignment so soon."

He holds out a hand for me as I dismount Caligo, his glove warm as it closes around my icy fingers, and I offer him a grateful smile as the warmth spreads from my hand through my entire body, raising my temperature a few degrees. I suppose winter isn't so bad when you're a firebreather, but it's as if the effort required to share his magic with me takes the breath out of him, and he lets go of my hand, swaying slightly.

"He's not already here, then?" Titus asks, hopping down from his horse.

Henry shakes his head. "Haven't seen him." He takes a piece of parchment from his coat pocket, and when he speaks, the sharp scent of liquor almost masks the faint smell of peppermint. "Found this on my pillow."

Will takes a key from his pocket and unlocks the door to the conservatory, ushering the three of us inside, and the moment I step foot over the threshold, the air thickens, pleasantly warm and humid, reminding me of summer. I think about how charming a simple life at Bludgrave Manor could have been without the threat of a Shifter stalking my every move, and a heavy feeling settles in my gut. Even if the Guild of Shadows didn't use my brother to attempt to recruit me, life here was never going to be simple. Not when Will planned to induct me into the Order of Hildegarde from the moment he laid eyes on me.

Out of habit, I make my way to the old oak tree toward the back of the garden, and Henry walks alongside me while Will and Titus hang back, discussing something in hushed voices. As I make my way down the garden path, between the red roses and purple mystiks, the pixies swoop down, darting all around me, their musical laughter like the tinkling of bells. I search the dozens of colorful, glowing orbs for Liv, the pixie I grew rather fond of during my time here, but she's nowhere to be found. It's not until Henry and I reach the oak tree that I hear the door to the conservatory open once more.

"Ready for another history lesson?" comes a familiar voice.

I whirl to find Killian sauntering down the pathway toward us, a cigar dangling from his lips. It's striking, the resemblance he bears to his sister, Lady Isabelle—dark hair, green eyes, and a somewhat mischievous air that might seem dangerous if it weren't so charming.

"Uncle!" Henry brightens, throwing his arms around Killian. "You weren't supposed to be back for another couple of days!"

"Yes, well," Killian says, his smile tight as he glances at me. "Something more important came up."

"Surely, this could have waited until morning," comes Lord Bludgrave's voice, and I peer over Killian's shoulder to see Will's father dressed in a robe and slippers, rubbing the sleep from his eyes as he makes his way down the path behind Titus and Will.

"I'm afraid not." Killian's expression turns grave. "I've received some rather disturbing information concerning the attack at the train station yesterday."

Lord Bludgrave's brow furrows. "From whom?"

Killian sighs, clearly impatient with his brother-in-law. "Liv flew to me," he says, and it's only then that I notice the faint pink glow in Killian's front pocket where Liv must be sleeping. "The pixies have been keeping me informed these past weeks."

Lord Bludgrave sputters furiously, "Under whose orders—"

"Mine," Will says, adjusting his scarlet cravat, not bothering to meet his father's eyes until he's satisfied with his appearance. When he finally deigns to look at Lord Bludgrave, his gaze is hard, leaving no room for arguments of any kind.

I want to cheer at the way Lord Bludgrave takes a step back, his jaw gaping slightly, as if surprised that Will would act against his authority, ordering the pixies to keep Killian informed, but a small voice whispers in the back of my mind, *Why didn't Will at least tell me?*

Killian turns to me then. "Someone in the Guild of Shadows—and I cannot be certain that they are following Morana's orders—doesn't want you anywhere near Castle Grim. Based on Liv's observations, I believe in this case, what we might be dealing with concerning this...*assassin*..." He glances at Lord Bludgrave, as if he were expecting him to disapprove before he even had the chance to finish his sentence. "I believe we're dealing with a Changeling."

Strangely, Henry's and Will's gazes both dart to their father.

"A Changeling?" I whisper.

"It's a kind of Underling," Henry says, his words somewhat slurred even as his eyes appear to focus for the first time since our arrival.

"But my attacker acted as if he wasn't an Underling," I say, shaking my head. "And his eyes were red only for a moment before they turned gold."

"Changelings often consider themselves something more than *just* Underlings—something *other*," Will explains, and it's only then that I notice the pixies are no longer laughing. "Changelings absorb the likeness—as well as the memories—of a child no more than six in order to grow up as a sort of spy, waiting to be recalled to service by Morana when she has use for them."

"They're like Shifters," Killian adds, "only they take not just the likeness of another but their power as well."

"They take their *lives*!" Lord Bludgrave clenches his fists, clearly ruffled by the subject. "They invade their victim's family like a parasite."

Killian, in a rare show of support, seems to agree with Lord Bludgrave. "It's difficult for everyone involved," he says. "Including the Changeling."

"Why?" I whisper.

"Why not?" It's Henry who answers. "They shed their powers, their entire being as an Underling, and then possess their victim's memories, their feelings toward their family. They grow up with their siblings, they love their parents—until one day…"

"They can't," Will says, glancing at his father, his expression pitying. "When their memories of their previous life are returned to them by Morana—when they once again become an Underling, fully—they're forced to turn on the people they love the most."

Lord Bludgrave tugs on his shirt collar, clearing his throat. "I've heard quite enough of this nonsense," he says, pulling his robe tighter around himself. He dips his head curtly, avoiding looking Killian in the eye as he adds, "I'll speak with you tomorrow." And without another word, Lord Bludgrave practically flees the conservatory, slamming the door behind him.

"What was that about?" I ask, staring at the powdery white footprints he left along the garden path.

Will looks at me as if whatever he's about to say will split the earth beneath us. "My father's brother was a Changeling," he says, wincing.

I can tell by the look on his face that he knows what I'm thinking, because he reaches for me almost instinctively, but I take a step back, shaking my head. "What happened to no more secrets?"

Despite the muggy air, a chill sweeps through the conservatory.

"I didn't consider it to be vital information," Will says, a muscle in his jaw twitching.

I laugh, but the sound is hollow. "There's another kind of Underling—an Underling who takes not just someone's appearance but a person's *life* for their own—and you didn't think to tell me?"

Killian clears his throat. "It was an oversight on my part, as well," he admits, scratching his mustache. "Changelings are so rare, and it's a bit of a sensitive subject for Silas."

Will looks as if he wants to apologize, but I hold up a hand, turning to Killian instead. "What happened? Why doesn't he want to talk about the possibility of a Changeling attacking me?"

Killian's throat bobs, and he tugs at his shirt collar, casting an uneasy glance at Will and Henry before saying, "When Silas was sixteen, his brother slaughtered their family—their parents, and their brother and sister. He would have killed Silas, too, but…" Killian hesitates. "Silas drove a blade through his heart."

I think about Owen. Surely, he wouldn't come after a member of our family directly. After all, he didn't actually compel Father to stab himself. Father chose to take his own life rather than to let the Underlings use him against me. But, if Owen were to attack one of us—if he were to come for our mother, our siblings—would I have the strength to do what must be done? Could I kill my own brother?

Where I felt contempt, even pity, for Lord Bludgrave after everything that happened, now all I feel is empathy. Watching your sibling slaughter your family—being the one to take their life in the end—must change a person, and I admire Lord Bludgrave now, for having the courage to start a family of his own. To fight to protect them. And how terrifying the thought of losing Annie to the Underlings must have been for him, given his past.

"There's something else," Killian says, thick rivulets of smoke unfurling from his cigar. "I've received a message." He hesitates, glancing at the door, as if he expects Lord Bludgrave to come back at any moment. "We're protected, here, because of various wards Will and his mother have placed around the conservatory, as well as the pack of wolves that patrol the area at their command. Still"—Killian lowers his voice—"I've recently learned of"—he hesitates—"*findings* that were passed through the channels of communication in an attempt to root out a spy within the Order."

My head spins. Henry, Titus, and I gape at Killian, but Will doesn't appear to react. Alarm bells ring in my head, and I whirl to face him. "You already knew, didn't you?"

Killian coughs, jumping to Will's defense once more, saying, "I spoke to Will before he came to meet you aboard the *Starchaser*. I asked him to ensure that the inhabitants of Bludgrave Manor were free of compulsion."

I glare at Will, my fists clenched at my sides. "How?"

Will meets my gaze with what appears to be great effort. "I persuaded them all to tell me the truth."

Henry scoffs, his eyes dark. "Even me?"

Will nods slowly, his teeth clenched. "For your own good, yes."

Henry runs a hand through his hair, over his face. "Can't say I'm surprised." He laughs, but there's no humor in it. "Well, that's enough intrigue for me." He shakes his head, and I think I see tears in his eyes as he turns away. "If you'll excuse me, I believe there's a bottle back at the house with my name on it."

Will reaches for him, but Henry shakes free of his grip.

"Henry, wait!" I call out, but he doesn't turn around, and Will makes no further attempt to stop his brother as the conservatory door slams shut in his wake.

An uneasy feeling slithers down my spine, and while I agree with Henry's reaction—while I think he's justified in feeling this way—Will's admission brings to mind a question I can't ignore. "So couldn't you just do that with every member of the Order until you've found the spy?" I don't know why I didn't think of it before. "And what about the princess? Couldn't you just *persuade* Leo to tell you if she's actually possessed?"

Titus snorts, his arms folded as he leans against the trunk of the old oak. "As if William's magic were any match for the queen of Underlings," he says, picking at the blood under his fingernails. "No offense, mate."

"It's true," Will says with a sigh. "My power is limited. We rely on the Order's marks—on our enchanted tattoos—to reveal dishonest intentions, but with all magic there are...loopholes. With persuasion, I cannot always guarantee that whatever Order member I interrogate isn't protected by an enchantment of some kind. Ever since the gift of persuasion started to manifest in bonewielders in the past couple of centuries, people have invented new, clever means of dispelling it." He glances at my bracelet. "Much like the one you wear on your wrist."

I touch the bracelet, running my thumb over the soft, worn leather, a fresh wave of anger rising up in me at the thought of Will using his magic to make me sleep. "But you're able to persuade me."

"That's because your bracelet protects against *Underling* compulsion," he explains with a grimace. "Not bonewielder persuasion."

A long silence stretches out between us, and I find that whatever anger I might have felt a moment ago has been replaced by a sick feeling in my gut.

"How did you find out?" I ask Killian, turning my back to Will, cutting him out of the circle completely. "About the spy?"

"An elite member of the Order passed on the information just after the king announced his plans for you," Killian answers, his brow furrowing. "They've asked me to inform you that further instructions will be given when you arrive at Castle Grim."

I blink, struggling to process what he's just said. "Who is this elite member of the Order?"

"There are only a few of them." It's Will who answers, and I turn on instinct to find him shifting in his stance. I realize I've never seen him this uncomfortable. "No one knows how many exactly, and no one knows their real names, but the elite consist mostly of humans and Myths."

He reaches for me, again, but I step toward Killian, just out of his grasp, turning my back to him once more. "Who?" I ask him, as if prompted by something deep within—as if spurred by some invisible force, though I can't begin to understand the feeling in my chest when Killian seems to notice the urgency in my voice, the way his keen eyes seem to realize something has shifted in me at the mention of this elite member of the Order.

Killian answers, his voice almost reverent, "We received our orders from a Nightweaver by the name of Dawnrender."

CHAPTER ELEVEN

The world is a black-and-white photograph. I focus on this thought as Mother recites Father's burial rites from Captain Gregory's Psalter, in the same spot where we memorialized Owen. In most of—if not all—the books Father gifted us, there would be photographs of animals, or cities, or recipes, all inked in black and white. Stark, and shaded, and lifeless. An impression of the real thing. A moment forever frozen in time.

"…may the Stars proclaim its glory!" Mother concludes, lifting her hand in the air—two fingers pointed at the sky in lieu of a pistol.

My siblings and I follow suit, and out of the corner of my eye, I notice Killian lift his hand as well. He and the Castor family insisted on joining us, along with Jack, Sybil, and Boris, the chauffeur.

Titus and his Bloodknights already began the trek to the train station, leaving behind Flynn and Gabriel, who keep a respectable distance from our small gathering, watching from afar.

Our train to Jade is scheduled to depart shortly after sunrise, and as Mother dismisses us, only a thin pink line peeks over the cliffs that encircle the valley. The sun has yet to rise as our group disperses, all headed back down the hill toward Bludgrave, where our trunks have been loaded into the convoy of motor carriages waiting to take us to the station.

Will looks as if he intends to walk with me, attempting to catch my eye from where he starts down the hill with Annie by his side, but I hang back, making my way to where Mother stands at the top of the hill, her face turned toward the horizon, smiling despite the tears that streak her weathered face.

"Out with it," she says, shooting me a sideways glance. With the wind casting her hair behind her, she looks as if she were standing at the helm of the *Lightbringer*.

I gnaw on the inside of my cheek, my hands balled into tight fists at my sides. I open my mouth—close it. Everything she and Father ever told me was a lie—who we are, what we are, where we come from. Now, Father is gone, and while I know that Owen is still alive, Mother has lost her husband and believes she's lost her son, too.

So what can I say? And how can I tell her what I know without revealing that Owen is alive—that he's working for Morana? I know I'm part Nightweaver—a bloodletter. I know that I'm cursed. I know that if I don't find a cure, I will die and she will have lost a daughter to the Underlings as well. What more can she tell me, and how will it change the fact that no matter what happens, I must face this alone?

I want to tell her that I know the truth and that while I can't bring Father back, I am going to save Owen. I'm going to save us all. I'm going to make the king and queen pay, and by the time I'm through, both Underlings and Nightweavers alike will come to fear the name Aster Oberon.

"He won't have died in vain," is what I say instead.

Mother watches the sun rise, flurries of snow catching in her eyelashes. "I know," she says quietly. She takes something from her coat pocket, and at first glance, I think that somehow Mother holds Captain Shade's medallion. But as she slips the gilded chain over my neck, my hands cup a small gold pocket watch. "It was your father's," she whispers, her eyes brimming with unshed tears. "Go ahead, open it."

My hands tremble as I run my fingers over the hand-engraved script on its face.

There is still time to chase another star.

I swallow around the ache in my throat as I recognize Father's handwriting—as I trace the words he wrote there—and open the lid to discover there's more to the pocket watch than meets the eye.

Inside is a compass on one side, a timepiece on the other.

"I've never seen this before," I manage to say, my voice thick.

Mother's smile twists, tears pooling on her chin, and I realize she's staring at me in that perceptive way only a mother can. "I thought he'd lost it years ago," she admits. "Killian said it was all they recovered from the fire." She frowns, but an odd spark of hope lights her gaze. "Strange, how the things we lose find their way back to us when we least expect it."

She reaches up, her forefinger and thumb brushing my earlobe, and my heart sinks.

"Someone must have taken them," I say, remembering the pearl earrings she gave me at the Reckoning Day ball. My stomach twists into knots, and I realize I haven't thought of them since I woke up on Shade's ship. "Before Father..." I clear my throat, try again. "Father said something odd that night. He said he gave you those earrings. But our belongings were confiscated the day we came ashore. How did you manage to bring them here with you?"

Mother tilts her head, pushing a strand of hair behind my ear as she searches my face, her expression unreadable. "Are you sure there isn't something else you'd like to ask me?"

I can feel it then. Can see it in her eyes—hear it in her voice. She wants me to ask her about everything—about my Nightweaver blood, about our enchanted trinkets, about my curse.

"There is, actually," I say quickly before I can change my mind. "What can you tell me about—"

"Mother!" Elsie cries, and I turn to see her trudging back up the hill, her cheeks flushed from the cold. Albert races after her, shouting for her to wait, but Elsie appears determined to reach us before he can catch her. "Mother, we're going to miss the train!"

Mother greets Elsie with a patient smile. "Then I suppose we'd better hurry!" she calls down to her. She turns to me then, her smile wavering. "Keep this close," she says, closing the pocket watch and covering my hands with hers. Her gaze meets mine, full of answers to questions I haven't even begun to ask. "You can do anything, Aster. Anything at all. You need only believe you can."

Elsie reaches us, panting for breath, just as Albert catches her arm.

"I told her—" Albert starts.

"It's all right," Mother says, quirking a brow. "You three go on," she adds, turning to face the horizon once more, and my chest deflates because the moment for questions and answers has passed. "I'll be right behind you."

In one hand, I take Elsie's gloved fingers in mine, and with the other, I cling to the pocket watch—the compass—as we follow Albert back down the hill.

There is still time to chase another star.

The words pierce my heart so violently I'm surprised I don't leave a trail of blood in the snow. Even if, at the end of all this, when we've found the cure and the king and queen have been brought to justice and Titus finally gives me the medallion—once my family is safe, and we are free, and I have more time... what then?

I've spent my whole life fighting. I'm not sure who I am without a foe to defeat, a war to wage, or a battle to win.

If I am who I choose to be, then what will I choose when I'm free to become... anything?

"Az?" Elsie says, drawing me out of my thoughts. "We'll come back, right? This is our home now, isn't it?"

I squeeze her hand as we make our way toward the iron gate at the end of the drive. "Would you like to come back here?"

Elsie pauses, glancing over her shoulder at Bludgrave Manor, now empty behind us. "Do I have a choice?"

I hesitate. "What if you did? What would you choose?"

Her brow furrows, lips pursing. "I think..." She turns to face the open gate, where the carriage waits to take us far, far from Bludgrave Manor, and she smiles. "I think I'd like to live on a ship again, wouldn't you?"

I hold fast to the cold metal of the compass, my father's handwriting digging into the skin of my palm, as I look down at my little sister, her face full of wishes and dreams and the promise of tomorrow. I'm doing this for my family. For my people.

For Elsie.

"I'd like that," I tell her, forcing a smile. "I'd like that very much."

Chapter Twelve

I never thought I would grow accustomed to the jostle of a train as it hurtles down the tracks, but as I pace the length of Titus's compartment, I find the cadence somewhat soothing. If I were to close my eyes, I might even think I were back on the *Lightbringer*, rocked by the cradle of the Western Sea. But the roaring blizzard that rages just outside my window and the white-capped mountains in the distance are a brutal reminder of my situation.

"Perhaps you would have rather walked to Jade," Flynn says, his voice muffled by his scarlet helmet.

I was separated from my family as we boarded the train, escorted by Flynn and Gabriel to Titus's private compartment. Albert shed a tear as the Bloodknights blocked my path, urging me in the opposite direction, but I caught Mother's eye as they led me away—noted the subtle nod of her head, the way she flicked a glance at the compass tucked safely beneath the collar of my dress.

I can't help but think she was trying to tell me something, and even now it rests heavily over my heart. But if the compass is more than just a simple trinket, I can't risk revealing it to the Bloodknights.

"I just want to see my family," I say, wishing Titus would return my daggers to me already. People seem to listen better with a blade pressed to their throats.

"We have our orders," Gabriel replies. "You're not to leave this room until this train reaches the capital."

"So I'm a prisoner."

"You're a target," Flynn says, tapping my forehead with his metal finger.

I want to rip the bloodred gauntlet from his arm and his hand along with it.

"What about my family?" I grit my teeth. "Who will protect them?"

"Your merry band of thieves and assassins can protect themselves." Titus enters the compartment carrying a tray bearing a kettle and three dainty cups. "But just in case, I've stationed four Bloodknights at the back of the train to keep an eye on them."

I ignore the tray, but he steps around me, placing it on the small, round table. The prince begins pouring tea, his brows knit with concentration, as the door opens once more, and Will slips inside, looking solemn.

I didn't say a word to either of them after we left the conservatory last night, but this morning I found a flower on the foot of my bed—a white rose, the bloom Will once told me represented contrition. For weeks, Will used flowers to communicate with me in secret, and I feel my anger melting away at the memory of the little messages he used to leave for me all around the house. Even through my grief, Will's flowers brought me joy when I felt I might never be happy again. And on a day like today, I find it much more difficult to stay angry with Will, especially when I crave the comfort of his calm, steady presence.

"You're dismissed," Titus says, and Gabriel and Flynn take up their posts on the other side of the compartment door, leaving the three of us alone.

Will clears his throat. "It's a short trip to Jade," he informs me, rubbing the nape of his neck as he takes a seat at one of the two chairs on either side of the table. "We should arrive in a couple of hours."

"There's to be a parade," Titus adds, pulling out my chair for me. "The procession will lead you to the castle, where you'll be introduced not only to the king and queen but also to the entire court. Which is why I've arranged for a true professional to prepare you for this afternoon."

"I'd rather have Margaret," I say, refusing to sit.

Titus flashes a smile. "I'd rather not argue."

"I—"

"Aster," Will interrupts me, his voice soft as he takes my hand. At his touch, a feeling of calm washes over me, dousing my anger. Unable to fight the pull of his gaze, I meet his eyes to find him looking at me with such tenderness my heart aches because I know he could never show me this kind of affection if we weren't alone.

Well, alone with Titus. I can't help but glance in his direction, my instincts crying out for me to pull my hand from Will's grasp, but Titus appears indifferent, pouring a generous amount of whiskey into his own cup of tea. Will has been so careful to hide his... *feelings* for me from everyone—including me. But not from Titus.

The first night I spent at Bludgrave Manor, Will confided in me that Titus was like a brother to him—that he would do anything for him. But when Titus revealed that Will was dying, that he would turn into a Shifter without a cure, Will was willing to face the wrath of the king to ensure that I remained aboard the *Starchaser* and far away from Morana and her Guild of Shadows. He was willing to let Titus marry the princess of Hellion—even if it meant he was giving up a portion of his power to the Sylk queen—if it meant I was safe.

Without looking at me, Titus jerks his chin at the chair opposite Will. "Sit," he says, his voice rough, "before William feels compelled to get down on his knees and beg."

I open my mouth to tell him I'll do as I please, but it's as if before the words can form, a feeling of exhaustion overtakes me, and I find myself folding onto the chair.

Will squeezes my hand before letting go. At the absence of his touch, my body feels cold, lifeless, and I suppress a chill.

"What's wrong?" he asks, offering me a cup of tea from the tray.

"My father's body couldn't be recovered from the fire," I say quietly, accepting his peace offering. The cup warms my palms, the floral aroma awakening memories of winter nights aboard the *Lightbringer*, listening to Father spin tales about the Stars as we indulged in cups of hot tea. My hands shake as I set the cup on the table once more and pull the chain of the compass free. I know it's just a trick of my eyes, but as I offer him the compass, in the swaying light of the chandelier overhead, the gold face appears to glow. "This was all that was left."

Will's brow furrows as he takes the compass, squinting to read my father's handwriting. Out of the corner of my eye, Titus goes perfectly still, his cup raised to his lips, brows lifted. Quickly, he turns his back to Will and me, facing the window, staring out at the frozen landscape, his shoulders tense.

Will dips his chin, handing the compass back to me. "I'm so sorry, Aster," he whispers, shaking his head. "I wish I could have done more."

I nod slowly, swallowing hard around the lump that forms in my throat. "You did all you could."

There was nothing to be done. One moment, Father was alive—there was still a chance he could be saved. And the next...

I clench my fists. "Whatever happens next, I'm going to make my father proud of me."

Will frowns. "Aster," he says softly, "he already was."

I shake my head. "I don't know," I say. "I didn't really know anything about him, did I? They've lied to me my whole life—he and Mother both. About who they are. About who *I* am."

Will nods considerately. "You didn't ask her?"

"I tried, but..." I blow out a tight breath. "There just wasn't time."

Will is silent for a long moment, but just when I think he won't respond, he says, "When you do get the chance to talk to her, try to be understanding, Aster. Sometimes, people keep secrets for reasons we could only understand if we found ourselves in their position."

I glance at him, but he's busied himself with pouring another cup of tea, and I realize, with a pang of clarity, that he means to justify the secrets he's kept from me. And that voice in the back of my mind whispers...

William Castor is lying to you.

Less than a half hour later, when an elderly woman in a plain gray gown and two long white braids enters the room, Titus and Will both greet her with a warm embrace and a kiss on the cheek.

"Aster, I'm pleased to introduce you to Bellaflor," Titus says, his grin full and genuine. "Feel free to call her Auntie Bella, if you like."

I offer the kindest smile I can muster. "Lovely to meet you."

"Would you look at that?" Titus brings his hand to his chest in mock surprise. "She has manners!"

"If you don't leave this cabin in the next three seconds, I'll show you just how *mannerly* I can be."

The woman barely attempts to conceal her mischievous grin.

Titus winks at Bellaflor, bringing his hand to his mouth as if to share a secret but not lowering his voice to say, "Terrible dancer, this one. My toes will never recover. Whatever you do, watch those clumsy feet of hers."

"Get out!" I shout, throwing a pillow at his face.

He catches it, holding it tightly to his chest. "She's utterly mad," he says, backing away slowly toward the door. "William, come quickly. We can't have her throwing a vase and ruining that pretty face of yours."

Will smirks, following Titus out into the hall, his hands in his pockets. "At least I'd still have my charm," he finishes, closing the door behind him.

"They never change." The woman sighs fondly. "At least they haven't set anything on fire—yet."

I rub my arms awkwardly, unsure of what to do with my hands as the woman turns her attention on me.

"Sit." She gives me a once-over that makes me wince. "This won't take long."

One hour later, I've been plucked, brushed, painted, and dressed. Bellaflor stands behind me as I examine myself in the mirror, her face beaming with pride. She didn't speak much as she poked and prodded at my face and hair, but after spending what little time I have with her, I can see why the boys regard "Auntie Bella" with such adoration.

"Well, dear?" Bellaflor asks. "What do you think?"

I twirl, admiring my gown—admiring, perhaps for the first time in a long time, my own reflection, the scar on my throat laid bare for everyone to see. For everyone to know that I have survived before, and I will survive this, too.

"I feel…"

Bellaflor grins. "Magical?"

I can't help but smile. "Powerful," I say, running my hands down the front of the satin gown. A rich shade of eggplant purple, the tight bodice of the strapless dress stops at my waist, and yards of skirt cascade over my hips. Draped across my shoulders, a gossamer cloak flows over my arms in two pieces and down my back, longer still than the train of my gown. The glittering purple fabric reflects the light like thousands of tiny stars as I turn, and I marvel at the similarities between my cloak and a pixie's wings.

Bellaflor applied just enough rouge and powders to "draw out my natural beauty," as she put it, and I'm thankful that when I meet my own gaze in the mirror, I feel as if I'm looking at myself, not a doll.

"Glide, my dear," Bellaflor reminds me, "like you're walking on a cloud."

I want to tell her these shoes—their heels as sharp as knives—feel more like I'm walking on glass.

"And remember," she adds, adjusting a stray hair with what has to be the hundredth pin that secures my unruly brown waves. She fashioned my hair in a braided updo that gives me the appearance of wearing a small crown atop my head. "Do your best to stay out of trouble." She helps me into my white elbow-length gloves before presenting me with a heavy bundle of fabric. "But just in case you find that trouble can't be avoided, Titus asked that I give you these."

The instant I take the bundle from her, every cell in my body seems to come alive.

"My daggers," I breathe, unwrapping the fabric to reveal the gilded weaponry, their hilts encrusted with citrine jewels. "But you—"

"Have a vested interest in your success, dear," Bellaflor says, rolling up her sleeve to reveal the tattoo of a winged dagger. For an instant, her irises appear to glow with silver light, but I blink, and her eyes are brown again. "Now, go on then, let's see if they fit."

I slide a dagger into either pocket, where Bellaflor revealed sheaths were sewn into the fabric of the skirt, allowing me to hide not only the compass Mother entrusted to me but my weapons as well, giving me easy access if the need arises.

"Won't I see you again?" I ask.

Bellaflor shakes her head, her smile somber. "Titus has arranged for your sister to attend to you while you're at the palace." She adds, a spark in her eyes, "Besides, it's best I keep far away from Castle Grim. Staying out of trouble is easier said than done for an old woman like me."

She winks, and a grin tugs at my lips despite the strange sadness I feel at the thought of never seeing Bellaflor again.

"Ready?" she asks, and I commit her kind face to memory, knowing that as soon as I enter Castle Grim, I will have entered a den of vipers, their teeth bared, poised to strike.

And they will know me not as someone who is majestic or magical or even kind.

They will know me as a monster.

Chapter Thirteen

"A float?" I ask Flynn as he leads me down the corridor. "Is that like some kind of jolly boat?"

He laughs, the sound muffled by his helmet. "You could say that."

"What about my family? How will they get to the palace?"

"That's not your concern," Gabriel says, cutting off Flynn before he gets the chance to speak.

"My family is very much my concern," I say, slipping my hands into my pockets, the mere touch of metal at my fingertips enough to calm my nerves.

"If that's true," Gabriel responds, his voice a deep rasp, "then I would suggest that from this point forward, you act as though you don't even know them."

As we step onto the small platform, his warning rings in my

head. I'm relieved my family will be with me at Castle Grim, but now that they're going to be within reach of the king and queen, I'll have to adjust my strategy. Because whatever I do, from here on out, it will affect Elsie and Albert and the rest of them. And I won't be responsible for another sibling's blood on my hands.

Barricades shield the platform from the public, but the roar of the crowd vibrates in my chest, louder than any cannon. I can't see beyond the wooden barriers, and for the first time since I decided to join Will and Titus here in Jade, I realize I know nothing about a city of this magnitude.

The crisp, briny air and the overwhelming presence of water nearby slams into me with such force I almost lose my footing.

"Aster," Flynn says gently, his touch light on my shoulder. "They're ready for you."

"Right," I say, my heart pounding in my throat as Flynn leads me to the doorway carved into the barricade, and I step through it, feeling at once as if I've set foot in a different realm entirely.

The city of Jade sprawls across the landscape, more beautiful than I could have ever imagined. Thousands—if not millions—of people have flooded the streets, pushing and shoving to get to the front of the crowd, where League soldiers in olive uniforms form a barricade between the floats and the horde of citizens. To my left, off in the distance, the ocean stretches out as far as the eye can see, and to my right, the mountainous border between the Eerie and Fell looms over the city like a wave. Ahead, the dark stone turrets of Castle Grim tower above even the highest rooftops, and despite knowing the horror that resides within those walls, I can't deny that the palace is a breathtaking work of art.

Dangerous, deadly things are often the most beautiful, I remember

Will said. And Castle Grim is the most dangerous, deadliest thing I've ever seen.

Flynn and Gabriel join me on the float—which I discover is like an elaborately decorated ship that sails on roads rather than water. Dozens of these *floats* glide along the brick-paved streets, all bedecked with the various colors and heraldry of the noble houses of the Eerie. Just ahead, I spot Will and his family standing atop a float that gives them the appearance of flying on the back of a gilded dragon. Will and Lord Bludgrave don scarlet military jackets, Henry a fine scarlet suit, and Lady Isabelle and Annie wear luxurious scarlet gowns, giving them the appearance of having just stepped out of one of the many family portraits I saw during my time at Bludgrave Manor.

Following the Castors, Killian stands alone atop a green-and-silver float, wearing his full military dress, surrounded by a pack of five silver wolves—*real* wolves, all standing as still as the statues that decorate the other floats. The ghost of a smile touches my lips when one of the wolves nuzzles into Killian's side. He might be known as the Lion of the Eerie, but I can't help but think he should have been known as the Wolf.

A few floats in front of Killian, leading the parade, Titus sits, his legs spread wide, on a makeshift throne between two giant swan statues in midflight. The black swan to his left carries a rose in its beak, and the white swan to his right carries a sword in its clutches. I recognize this now as the heraldry of House Anteres, the royal family of the Eerie—Titus's family.

My gut twists when I realize just how much I don't know about him—about his life at Castle Grim, about the king and queen and the nobility that make up their court.

Our float jostles as we join the route, and Gabriel grabs my arm to steady me—the movement so quick I doubt anyone could have noticed.

The float on which I stand between Gabriel and Flynn is designed to look like a puny imitation of a galleon ship. In front of me, the helm is cracked in half, the sails shredded to ribbons.

"Subtle," I say under my breath.

"You have no idea," Flynn whispers.

I don't know when I began to feel at ease around these two Bloodknights, but at the very least, as our float joins the cavalcade, I don't feel as if I'm completely alone.

"Chin up," Flynn reminds me. "And hands out of your pockets."

I do as he says, my stomach churning as the clamor of the crowd thunders all around us.

I grind my teeth, bracing for someone to throw something at me—to hurl insults in my direction, at the very least. But the people seem to have unanimously agreed to welcome me to their city with fervent praise, and while I know it isn't something I should enjoy, I find that the sound of their cheers gives me the same rush I experience after a great victory in battle.

I've never felt more like a traitor.

After what feels like a lifetime, the cavalcade reaches the long stone bridge that leads to Castle Grim, and I get my first real look at the palace.

Surrounded by water, the castle rises from an island as if it merely floats atop the surface of the sea. Dark spires and stone pinnacles tower above the clouds and give the palace such depth and dimension it's hard to focus on any distinct feature of the structure. The walls that surround the base of the fortress are ornamented not only with the black banners of House Anteres and those bearing the scarlet sun of the Eerie but...

"Are those—"

"Yes," Gabriel answers. "Try not to look surprised."

I close my mouth, swallowing around the knot that forms in my throat.

Skulls line the castle walls—skulls that, as the legends say, were put there by the prince himself.

"Steel yourself," Flynn says. "You'll want to make a good impression."

He doesn't have to point at the dozens of Bloodknights patrolling the battlements for me to know what he means. The king's personal soldiers won't be eager to accept a pirate into their ranks—especially when they know I'm merely a pawn, meant to manipulate the humans into submission—and if they think, even for a second, that I'm weak...

"And what about the two of you?" I say, still trying—and somewhat succeeding—to throw my voice the way Father used to, my mouth opening only slightly. "Have I made a good impression?"

Gabriel shifts his weight, his hands resting on the bloodred hilts of a massive sword on either hip. "You're alive, aren't you?"

I snort. "As if you've done such a wonderful job of protecting me."

Flynn chuckles, the sound so low I barely hear it. "I think you misunderstood him," he says. "You're alive because we haven't put a knife in your back ourselves."

"And disobey orders from the king? You wouldn't."

"If you actually believe that, then you don't know much about Bloodknights."

The parade slows as Titus exits his float. I catch the word

Reaper whispered more than once, with awe and reverence but mostly fear as he makes his way up the steps that lead to the grand entrance of the castle.

The king and queen wait for him there, atop the stone landing, along with a handful of Bloodknights. I don't know what I expected them to look like—monsters, I suppose. Despite knowing what I know of Nightweavers, I've clung to the imagery of sharp teeth and sallow skin whenever I picture the king and queen. Because how could they look human when they do such monstrous things?

And yet the king has a strong but fair face, his golden hair cut to the same shoulder length as his son's, while the queen's long flaxen hair wraps around her head and flows down her back in various braids. Her smile is almost warm as she surveys her son ascending the palace steps, her eyes crinkling at the edges, but something about her expression feels...false.

To her left stands a girl with ebony braids that spiral to her waist, a modest tiara atop her head. Where the king wears black trimmed with scarlet, and the queen wears a gown made entirely of black fur, the girl wears a pale pink gown, simple and understated, a stark contrast to the queen. As Titus approaches, the girl's face brightens, and though I can see only his back, I note the way his shoulders tense.

The people erupt with applause, roaring their praises as Titus takes his place at the girl's side—*Princess Leo*'s side, I realize. And when Titus takes her hand in his, pressing a kiss to her knuckles, I'm seized by the sudden urge to vomit.

I don't know if I expected to see signs of Morana's possession at first glance, but when Leo looks up at Titus with a sweet, subdued smile, I'm struck by the sudden fear that Titus is wrong—that Morana isn't here, and therefore, we'll be unable to obtain a cure.

But even worse, if he's right...the princess must die. And I will be the one to sentence her to death.

The next noble house follows Titus, then another, all taking their place at the top of the palace steps, until the float in front of me departs, and I'm exposed, finally, at the front of the procession.

If I thought I would have a moment to reconsider, that moment has come and gone.

The instant the king and queen set their eyes on me, the games begin, but rather than feel like I have a card tucked up my sleeve, I feel, with startling clarity, that I am a mouse caught in a trap.

Flynn and Gabriel follow as I make my way down the narrow, winding steps, onto the cobblestone street. Their presence at my back is infinitely more comforting than I could have expected. When we reach the base of the steps, and they bow to their rulers before departing, joining a faction of Bloodknights to my right, I've never felt more alone.

I attempt to take a step, but before I've conquered the first tread, my shoe catches the fabric of my gown, and I lurch forward. The world seems to slow as I fall, face-first toward the stone steps.

A hand catches my arm, pulling me upright with fluid grace.

"Really, Aster," Will whispers as he flashes a dashing grin at the crowd, "you can survive a dagger to the heart, but you're bested by a flight of stairs?"

He tightens his grip on my arm, guiding me up the steps. When we reach the landing, he bows deeply, and I do the same, dipping low in a curtsy just as Bellaflor showed me earlier today.

The king raises his hands, and the crowd falls silent. Will gives my arm a squeeze before releasing me and taking his place with the rest of the nobility.

My chest constricts as the king and queen step forward.

"Welcome," the king's voice carries over the assembly, and I'm shocked to find that he sounds not at all monstrous, but rather... kind. He smiles at the people. "Queen Calantha and I are pleased that so many of you have decided to join us on this very special occasion."

The crowd breaks into deafening applause, quieted only by the mere nod of the king.

"The human you see before you defied the rebel pirate, Malachi Shade, during an attack on the noble House Castor, risking her own life to save that of Lady Annie Castor," he continues. "When I first heard the tales of her bravery and loyalty to the Crown, I insisted she not only be rescued from the clutches of the vile criminal—who has since met his fate at the hands of Lord Castor—"

He pauses as the applause swells, and out of the corner of my eye, I note Will bowing graciously, smiling at the people as if *he* were their prince rather than Titus.

"But that," the king goes on, "she be brought here, to Castle Grim, so that I could bestow on her the illustrious honor of knighthood." He raises his hands once more to attempt to quiet the crowd, but they can no longer be contained, their excitement reaching a dizzying crescendo. "A reformed pirate and servant to the Crown, Lady Aster Oberon will serve the kingdom of the Eerie with dignity and courage, fighting for justice, peace, and prosperity. But first," he adds, motioning toward the group of Bloodknights gathered at the base of the steps.

Flynn and Gabriel emerge, dragging between them a boy about my own age—no more than seventeen—his chained body so broken and bloodied I can hardly determine his features.

"Upon Lady Aster's rescue, she had only one request," the

king goes on, cutting a glance at me, his deceptively kind smile now nothing more than a sardonic smirk. "Acting as a spy for the Crown, even without having been given orders to do so, she discovered that Shade and his rebels planned to overtake the township of Thorn. I've been told that Lady Aster wasted no time after her rescue, informing my soldiers of this plot just in time for my Bloodknights to intervene. I must admit, I found her request to be rather self-indulgent, but when Lady Aster asked that she be the one to execute one of these rebels upon her arrival here at Castle Grim, my wife urged me to oblige. After all, what better way to get my son's wedding festivities under way than with a proper beheading?"

Gabriel draws one of his swords, presenting it to me without hesitation.

If I thought the crowd was ecstatic before, I couldn't have realized just how frenzied they would become at the proposition of an execution.

Their delight roils my stomach even as I take the sword from Gabriel. The weapon is heavier than the cutlass I favored during my life at sea, and with the months of disuse, my muscles strain to lift the blade.

My heart sinks as I read the words inscribed on the metal surface.

The True King Sees. Rage threatens to overwhelm me, and the words that used to bring me peace now boil my blood. The True King watched my father drive a blade through his own heart. He watched as Dorothy died in Henry's arms. Or did he look away? Has he ever looked down on me? Does he see me now, a sword in my grasp, ready to spill blood? Or has he abandoned me, just as he abandoned my people six hundred years ago?

"Please," the boy sputters, "I have a family—a little sister who needs me—"

Flynn's boot connects with his spine with a sickening crack, and he sprawls at my feet. The two Bloodknights lift him back onto his knees, holding him upright. If he's still conscious, he's too battered to utter another plea for mercy, his head hanging limp.

I cannot bring myself to look at Henry, or Killian, or even Lady Isabelle, but I risk a glance at Will, who watches the exchange with idle interest. *I can't do this*, I will my eyes to say. If I do, and the spray of his blood on my face brings my power to the surface... there'll be no denying my Nightweaver heritage when the entire kingdom sees my golden eyes glow.

I can't refuse the king. If I don't do this, what will happen to my family? But if I *do*... what happens then?

I lift the sword, my shoulders crying out in pain, my heart crying out in defiance—

At a speed my eyes can hardly detect, Titus stands behind the boy, the rebel's still-beating heart in his black-gloved hand. Before I can even lower the sword, Titus brings the heart to his mouth and—and—

Bile rushes into my throat as Titus takes a bite.

No—not Titus.

This beast standing before me, blood dripping from his chin, is not the same man who gifted me a wardrobe full of pajamas. This is the legendary prince of the Eerie—the creature from my darkest nightmares.

The Reaper.

Chapter Fourteen

Titus's gold eyes never leave mine as he chews—swallows.

Bile burns the back of my throat like acid. *Everything about my life is an act*, he said. All this time, I wanted to believe that the wicked prince of legend was his true mask and that beneath it was the kind, selfless pirate who risks his life to save children from cannibal ships—the pirate who saved me from certain death. But what if I'm wrong? What if *this*—what if the Reaper—is who he truly is, and Captain Shade is the facade?

I try to find some trace of the heroic pirate captain in his cold, cruel stare, but when his tongue swipes out, licking the blood from his lips, I see only a monster.

"It was a long journey," Titus says with an indolent shrug, tossing the heart to the ground where the rebel's body lies at my feet, a gaping hole in his back. "I was starving."

Horror sluices through my veins as he smiles, his lips, coated in innocent blood, like two sadistic slashes of crimson. My whole life, I heard tales of the ruthless prince of the Eerie, but after finding out he was Captain Shade, some part of me wanted to believe there was little truth to the stories—that the Titus I know couldn't be capable of something this depraved.

Owen's warning rings in my ears. *This prince of yours is using you, just as your little lord used you. Neither are who you think them to be.*

The king lets out a hearty, boisterous laugh, and only then does the crowd follow suit, the sound of their laughter even more monstrous than a Gore's. Only the princess—only *Leo*—shows no visible reaction, her expression neutral, but in the split second our eyes meet, I think I see something else in her gaze—the slightest hint of sympathy, too brief to properly detect.

"My son, ever eager to enact his own personal brand of justice!" the king says. "No matter, there's plenty where that came from, and it seems I owe Lady Aster a head. But alas, beyond the palace doors, the festivities have already begun. Join me inside," he says, turning to face the assembled court. "Tonight, we feast in honor of my heir and his betrothed!"

The nobility follow the king and queen through the towering steel doors that lead into the palace. I try to catch Titus's eye one final time, but he turns his back to me, joining the assembly inside. I want to follow, but I can't move. The boy's blood pools at my feet, crying out to me in a thousand furious whispers, urging me to kneel, to reach out, to taste....

"Aster." Will's voice reaches me from somewhere far away, stirring me from a daze.

Thankfully, I'm still standing upright, having controlled my impulse enough to resist the vision that still plays over and over in my head—kneeling, drinking....

"Shall we?" Will asks, extending his arm to me.

Flynn clears his throat, and I latch onto Will's arm as the two Bloodknights collect the rebel's corpse. I allow Will to guide me through the double doors, into the cool, crisp air of the castle's great hall, where the nobility have dispersed, following their guards to the residential wing. The king and queen have gone as well, along with Princess Leo and Titus.

Titus—the thought of him causes my heart to twist.

I've barely had a moment to take in the dark, enchanted interior of the castle when two familiar faces greet me.

"What are you—" I start, thankful for Will's arm remaining locked in mine, or else I might have thrown myself at the two of them. "How—"

"How do you think?" Charlie grins, tapping the pommel of the sword sheathed at his hip. "The prince had it arranged for us to be your private guards."

"Fancy, huh?" Lewis dusts the breast pocket of his jacket—the black-and-scarlet uniform of a palace guard. "Our quarters, however, are much less so."

Charlie rolls his eyes. "At least we're all together."

Hope flares to life in my chest. I remember Gabriel's warning, and I look around, ensuring that we're alone before I whisper, "You're all okay, then?"

"We're *together*, Az." Lewis places a hand on my shoulder. "Are *you* okay?"

I try to respond, but the words get tangled up in my throat, forming knots I can't seem to untie no matter how many times I blink or nod or—

"Perhaps it would be best if you show us to Aster's room," Will says.

Charlie gives him a once-over. "Don't you have somewhere else to be?"

Will doesn't even acknowledge Charlie's question, simply motioning with his hand for them to lead the way.

Lewis straightens dramatically, lowering his voice when he says, "Right this way, your lordship."

How, in the short amount of time they were here, my two brothers managed to memorize such a confusing layout of stairwells and hallways, I'll never know. I could spend the rest of my life in this castle and still not understand where I am or where I'm going. When we finally reach my room—somewhere on the twelfth floor, maybe—I realize I'm in way over my head. How am I to accomplish anything when I have no idea how to navigate my surroundings? There are no stars to follow, no compass to tell me which turns to take or steps to climb.

My compass. I'm tempted to reach for it as Charlie unlocks my room and holds open the door for me to enter, but as my fingers skim the cool metal, a little brown mouse darts between my feet, followed by a blur of scraggly black fur.

I recognize the six stubby legs and eight insectoid eyes of the Myth—an atroxis—as it chases the mouse around the corner and out of sight. The day we first arrived at Bludgrave Manor, Lady Isabelle told us the queen kept an atroxis as a pet, as they were one of the few Myths protected by the king's law. Of all creatures, I can't imagine why anyone would choose such a hideous, beastly thing, but Annie adored her atroxis, Dearest—until Owen compelled her to gut the poor thing.

The hair on the back of my neck prickles as the strange sensation of being watched crawls up my spine. I look over my shoulder, but the four of us are alone in the hall. Still, I can't help but wonder... what keeps Owen from finding me here? He made it past the wards at Bludgrave Manor. Surely, he's clever enough to persuade someone to let him into the castle....

"Az?" Lewis prompts. "Hello?"

I cough, attempting to hide the slight tremble of my voice. "Did you say something?"

Please don't ask me if I'm okay, I think. For some reason, I feel that in this moment, if he were to ask, I might find it difficult to lie—to myself and to him.

And I can't fall apart. Not now.

Thankfully, Will must sense something is amiss. "Why don't we get you settled? I'll take it from here, gentlemen," he says, guiding me past my brothers and shutting the door behind us before either one of them can argue.

The instant we're alone, I feel the parts of me I've barely held together begin to unravel. I close my eyes, take a deep breath, and begin to stitch myself back together.

I can do this. I have to do this.

My hand trembles as I take the compass, slipping the chain over my head. I grab hold of the small golden disc, now tucked safely between my collarbones, and hold it tightly in my fist—an anchor, a vow.

I will make my father proud. No matter what I must endure, no matter what I'm forced to withstand, I will not leave Castle Grim until I get what I've come for—a cure, justice, and freedom for my people. I *can* do this. I'm going to do this.

I try to picture my father's face—his kind eyes—but as I form the image of him in my mind, his eyes, like two wells of black ink, are not kind. Thick scarlet tears stream down his cheeks, but when I try to open my eyes, to dispel the distorted visage of my father, it's as if my eyelids are glued shut.

My heart rages violently in my chest, and I let go of the compass, reaching for Will's sleeve, grasping at him wildly when—

"Breathe, Aster," he says softly, his hands cupping my cheeks. Warmth flows from his touch, and my eyes fling wide to find his gaze, calm and tender, his brow furrowed as he studies my face. "Breathe for me."

I try to slow my breathing, but a flood of emotions I haven't allowed myself to feel since Father's death overtakes me, and suddenly I'm drowning in them.

"Will—" My voice breaks on a sob.

He draws me into his arms with such abandon I forget myself. I bury my face in his chest, allowing every cracked piece of me to shatter. And he holds me, even when I can no longer hold myself upright, even when he has to guide me to the edge of my bed, even when I grab a fistful of his shirt because I need something—anything—to keep me here, where I can *feel* rather than fade away.

Titus was right—I was never meant to step foot on land.

Will says, his voice like a deep hum, "Just say the word, and we'll leave this place."

I burrow deeper into his arms, wanting to forget that there

has ever been space between us—that our lives are comprised of moments in which it is forbidden to touch each other, to hold each other. "We can't," I cry—hiccup. "You'll die."

He strokes the back of my head, combing his fingers gently through my hair. "Watching you suffer is a fate worse than death."

I sniff, craning my neck to look up at him. "You can't mean that," I croak. "Your family—*Henry* needs you. And Annie...you can't—"

"Aster," he interrupts, his gaze softening. "I have known for a very, very long time that one day, I would have to leave my family behind."

His words pierce me like a dagger to the heart. "I never asked—" I start, my throat painfully dry. "Your curse..."

He grins, his eyes glassy. "It's...complicated." His thumb grazes my cheek, wiping away my tears. "I wasn't bitten—not like you."

"But, how—"

Will draws away enough to remove his jacket. He lifts the hem of his shirt just slightly to reveal a rotting black wound on his left side, just above the waistline of his pants. Green veins branch off from the lesion, pulsing like leeches.

"Will!" I gasp.

His only response is a broken, half-hearted laugh. "Does it look that bad?"

I try to school my expression into something other than shock but fail miserably. Gently, I ask, "Does it hurt?"

His lips form a tight smile. "It's nothing I can't manage."

"For now."

Will casts his eyes skyward as I turn to find Titus leaning casually against the doorframe that leads into my suite.

My suite!

I look around for the first time, my eyes wide as I take in the enormous space, its lofty ceilings decorated with trusses cut from expertly hewn oak, their pattern reminding me of the sails of a ship. To my left, a wall of steel-leaded windows opens onto a balcony that looks out over the city, offering me breathtaking views of the sea beyond. The polished mahogany four-poster on which we now sit is twice the size of any bed I've ever seen, overflowing with blue pillows and blue blankets, its blue silk sheets like a cool stream of water as I run my hands over the fabric. I quickly notice a theme—a blue canopy for the bed, blue drapes, blue wallpaper, blue upholstery. And not just any shade of blue—sapphire blue. Like the ocean. Like my eyes.

I meet Titus's gaze to find that he's watching me intently, his face perhaps a bit more open and vulnerable than he may realize, because the instant our eyes meet, he looks away, adjusting his sleeves with uncharacteristic piety. He's changed into an all-black ensemble, his jacket trimmed with shimmering ruby-red thread, glistening like fresh blood. I study his face, searching for any signs of the gore that coated his chin, but to my relief, I find none. The only evidence of the vicious display at the parade are the few strands of wet hair that cling to his face from where he attempted to wash away the attack, and a speck of dried blood just below his jaw.

When he meets my gaze again, his blue eyes are hard—resigned—and my gut twists when I realize that whatever my reaction was to the Reaper's violence, it revealed the deep distrust I intended to keep hidden, and now, there is no going back.

Titus clears his throat. "William has little time," he says, his expression taciturn. "And there's no way for us to know how long the enchantment around your heart can fight off your own curse. As long as you're on land, you'll continue to grow weak."

My eyes narrow, my stomach lurching. "How much time does he have?"

Will inhales sharply. "Don't—"

"Four days," Titus says, pushing off from the doorframe. "William has until sunset on Holy Winter's Day before the curse takes root."

Chapter Fifteen

"Four days?" I echo, looking up at Will once more. His arms tighten around me, pulling me so close I'm practically in his lap. "Why Holy Winter's Day?"

Will's jaw tightens. "As I said, it's complicated."

Out of the corner of my gaze, Titus rolls his eyes, removing his jacket to reveal a simple black shirt. He tugs at the sleeves, revealing a plethora of ink tattooing his skin. I fight to keep my eyes locked on Will's, but my curiosity to know what ornaments Titus's forearms is a battle I fear I'm in danger of losing.

"It's not that complicated," Titus says dryly, plopping down in a velvet armchair near the stone hearth across from us. "Many years ago, during William's first year of service with the League, he was stabbed by a cursed dagger—much like the one your dear brother attempted to use on you. This curse, however, came with certain stipulations. A time limit, for one." I note the way he winces when he leans back in his seat, his forearms tensing as he grips the armrests. "The Shifter who cursed him said he would have until his nineteenth birthday on Holy Winter's Day to turn himself over to the Guild of Shadows or he would descend into madness, bringing death to all those he dearly loves before ultimately turning into a Shifter with no choice but to join Morana's ranks."

My mouth gapes as I stare up at Will, but his eyes are glittering, searching mine with a desire so raw I feel as if he might kiss me right here, right now.

"Why didn't you tell me?" I demand, my voice trembling with anger—with the hurt I feel knowing that he's kept yet another secret from me. During all the weeks we spent together at Bludgrave, he never once thought it important to share with me that he was cursed—*dying*—and that he would become a Shifter before the year was out? "No more secrets—you promised!"

Will's eyes brim with tears. "I wanted to tell you, but...I always hoped I wouldn't have to. You have enough to worry about," he says, his hand cradling my jaw. "This is my burden to carry, not yours."

A tear slips onto his cheek, at once cooling the simmering rage bubbling up inside me.

I take his hand in mine, perhaps a bit more fiercely than I intend. "You're wrong," I tell him. "You need this cure more than I do."

"Touching." Titus leans forward to rest his elbows on his knees. "Should I leave the two of you to your petting, or would you like to discuss what happens next?"

I shift out of Will's arms, turning to face Titus, but Will doesn't let go of me, threading his fingers through mine.

"What now?" I ask, feeling strangely self-conscious at the way Titus's gaze flits to our hands.

"My father's demonstration with that rebel prisoner is only the beginning," Titus says, his jaw clenched. His gaze drops to my throat for the briefest moment—so swift I think I've imagined it. "Tomorrow, you'll be knighted, and he'll make good on that promise of a head."

My heart pounds against my sternum. "The blood," I say, feeling as if I'm going to be sick. "My eyes...I can't hide what I am."

"There are ways to control your power—the bloodlust," Titus says, his expression softening only for a second before his face hardens once more. "Which is why you and I will meet here, every night, so that I can teach you how."

My eyes widen, and I don't have time to think about the warmth in my cheeks before I argue, "But my *eyes*—"

"Are not an issue." Titus waves his hand dismissively. "Bellaflor placed an enchantment on you so that your eyes will appear blue even when you're exposed to *Manan*."

I gape at them both, their expressions equally mischievous for once. "Are you saying she's a—"

"Sorceress?" Will says, his eyes glittering with amusement.

A Sorceress—a human who possesses magic, just like the Sorceress who enchanted my bracelet to protect me from Underlings. I should be furious they had an enchantment placed on me without my permission, but considering what happened at the parade, I'm thankful they had the foresight to ensure my Nightweaver heritage remains a secret.

"Yes, but, Aster," Titus says, suddenly serious, "the enchantment only works if you don't consume blood."

I nod slowly. "Don't drink anyone's blood," I say somewhat sarcastically. "Got it."

"Good girl." Titus winks as he stands, rolling his shirtsleeves back down to cover his tattoos, and I spot the winged dagger inked into his forearm just before it vanishes.

"What about Dawnrender?" I ask. "Killian said we should expect to hear more about the Order's plans from this *elite* member of theirs upon our arrival."

Titus and Will exchange a loaded glance.

Will offers me a tight smile. "And I'm sure we will," he says, avoiding my gaze as he inspects my balcony doors, checking the locks. "Until then, we move forward with our plan. You should have an opportunity to speak with the princess tonight. After that—"

"One step at a time," Titus says, fiddling with the collar of his shirt, and I notice the bronze chain of his medallion peeking out from beneath the black fabric. He shoots Will a pointed look. "Once Aster has confirmed Morana's possession, I'll take it from there." His gaze slides to me, his voice firm as he adds, "Understood?"

I open my mouth, but before I can reply, there's a knock at the servant's door behind me.

"That will be your lady's maid," Titus says, clapping his hands together. He quirks a brow at me, his teasing smirk at odds with the subtle warning that flashes in his eyes. "Try to behave tonight."

Will follows him to the salon that leads into my suite, looking back at me over his shoulder, his smile sympathetic in a way that makes me want to crawl under the mountain of pillows and never show my face again. "You *can* do this, Aster."

I want to take his hand, to ask him to stay, but then Margaret appears in the doorway, silhouetted by the flickering lamplight that illuminates the dark passageway, and Will is gone.

"Well then," she says, taking in the sight of me as if I were a slab of marble and she a trained sculptor. "Let's make them wish you never stepped foot in Castle Grim."

Chapter Sixteen

"And just when I'd begun to think Margaret would never find her talent," Lewis whispers as he and Charlie escort me down the stairwell.

"You thread fabric, Lew." Charlie snorts. "Marge was threading *skin* before you sewed your first patch. I wouldn't think cosmetics would be a challenge for someone with her skill set."

Lewis lifts a shoulder. "I'm just saying, I might not have recognized our sister had it not been for the way her eye twitches when she wants me to stop talking. Ah"—he jabs a finger toward my eye—"like that!"

I swat his hand away, but I can't help the grin that tugs at my lips. "Quiet!" I whisper. "Someone might—"

We round the corner, and I run right into the back of a woman in a silver gown.

"I'm so—" I start, but the woman turns to face me, and my shoulders sag with relief.

"Aster?" Lady Eliza beams up at me from the step below. "Oh, how delightful!" She takes my hands, her mouth gaping as she appraises the gown I changed into for the evening. "You look positively stunning!"

I smile, and I'm pleased when it doesn't feel forced. "So do you," I say, gesturing at the silver gown that cuts low, drawing attention to the bat-shaped amulet between her collarbones.

"I'll say," Lewis agrees under his breath.

"Coming from you, Mr. Oberon, I'm flattered." Eliza's lips curve playfully. "Perhaps in the future, you might fashion me something to wear, if you find that you have the time. Billie tells me you're a fine tailor."

I think Lewis has stopped breathing.

I elbow him in the ribs. "It would be his honor."

"The honor would be entirely my own," Eliza practically purrs, extending her arm to me. "Now, Aster, you must tell me what I've missed."

My stomach sours as we loop arms and descend the steps. Quietly, I ask, "You weren't at the parade?"

She pats my black-gloved hand. "No," she says with a wince. "Though, I can't say I regret my decision not to join."

I wish I was given that option.

Eliza halts just before we reach the base of the stairwell, unhooking her arm from mine and standing directly in front of me. "Keep your wits about you," she instructs, fussing with a few strands of my hair, framing them around my face. "And remember," she adds in a whisper, "you are infinitely braver than you believe, Aster Oberon."

She offers me a genuine smile before turning and stepping out into the hallway.

I hesitate, perched on the last step before I round the corner and join the rest of the nobility. Their voices seem to echo in the stairwell, loud enough that I stumble backward, caught only by Charlie's quick reflexes.

I want nothing more than to turn back—to ask my brothers to take me to where the rest of my family is staying, persuade them to leave with me, and to try to escape.

If I don't have much time left under this curse, then at least I'll be with my family. At least I'll be free.

But they'd spend the rest of their lives on the run, avoiding capture, fearing for their safety at every turn. Staying here is about more than just finding a cure. Even if Morana isn't at Castle Grim—even if Titus can't force her to take her corporeal form—then before I leave this world, I want to do as much damage to the Crown as I possibly can.

If I'm going down, then so is anyone who dares threaten my family.

"We're with you, Az," Charlie says, his voice low. "Whatever you're doing here—whatever you're not telling us—we're with you."

Lewis reaches out to place a hand on my shoulder but apparently thinks better of it, and I suppress a smile when I think about the gown Titus arranged for me to wear tonight.

The neckline of the black velvet gown cuts into a deep V, the skirt flaring out at my hips, wide enough to conceal the daggers sheathed in either pocket. Alone, the dress is nothing spectacular, but paired with the armored pads chained to my shoulders, their spikes sharp enough to cut through bone, I look like the weapon the Order wants me to be.

I look like a warrior.

Charlie's words give me the strength I need to take a deep breath and step out into the hall.

I don't know if I'll ever get used to entering a crowded room and feeling as if every head turns to find me. At sea, I never questioned myself—never doubted my stride as I leaped headfirst into battle, my cutlass in hand. *Let them see me*, I would have thought as my enemies realized I had entered their midst. *Let them fear me.*

But now, embarrassment heats my cheeks at the way my pulse races as I search for a familiar, friendly face. *Pull yourself together, Aster*, I chide myself. Though this might not be a battle, though I might not carry a cutlass, I am still Aster Oberon, fearsome pirate of the Western Sea. I know who I am, and that is enough.

Charlie and Lewis remain close, and their presence fuels my courage, but with the looks the fifty or so nobility give my brothers, I fight the urge to put a dagger to their throats right here, right now. We might not survive it, but between the three of us, there would be quite a few empty chairs at the dinner table tonight.

"There she is!" Henry says, toasting me with a half-drunk glass of wine. By the looks of it, it isn't his first.

"Aster!" Lady Isabelle waves me over to where they stand near the doors to the banquet hall. The Castors all wear their House colors—scarlet trimmed with gold—with the exception of Will, who is nowhere to be seen. "You look magnificent."

"Thank you. As do you." I dip my head, the panic fading as Lady Isabelle stands at my side, surveying the room with a sweet smile and a subtle warning in her eyes.

With the Castors encircling me, I'm emboldened to take in my surroundings. Iron lanterns give light to the dark castle, illuminating portraits that I think could be as ancient as the stones themselves. I can't help but wonder if this is the seat from which Hildegarde ruled when she wore the crown. What have these hallways seen? What stories could these portraits tell were they able to speak?

My gaze flits about the room, searching for Eliza, or Titus, or—

Obnoxious laughter bounces off the walls, and a moment later, Will rounds a corner, making his way down a set of stone steps with a raven-haired lady on either arm.

I've taken bullets that hurt less than this.

"If looks could kill," Killian says, and I turn back to find him standing in front of me, dressed in his formal military uniform. The medals on his chest catch the light, reflecting it with a dazzling golden glow that gives his aged face a warmth that makes me think of sunsets on open waters. His kind eyes remind me, for just a moment, of my father. And even as the heavy weight of grief settles in my stomach, I find that the thought soothes me like a salve to my aching soul.

"Should I be afraid?" Killian says, cutting a glance at my shoulders.

"Should you?"

The ghost of a smirk touches his lips. "I fear for my nephew, yes."

The doors to the banquet hall open, and Will and the two women pass us as if we aren't even here—as if *I'm* not even here.

"After you," Killian says, urging me forward into the flow of traffic as the nobility swarm the banquet hall, taking their seats around the dining table. Enormous windows line the wall, the amber lights of Jade reflected in the dark water surrounding the castle like thousands of tiny, flickering candles, but the nobility don't seem to care for the view. They focus instead on the jewel-encrusted finery—plates carved from obsidian, candelabras hewn from ruby—and the black goblets marked by the scarlet sun of the Eerie.

I find myself looking up at the vaulted ceiling, which appears to have been painted over long ago, because where the paint has chipped and cracked, the image of a hand or a wing or a cup seems to tell a story—seems to whisper, *I was here*.

I stumble a few steps, unsure of myself and where it is I'm supposed to go, when Henry loops his arm through mine. "You're to sit by me," he says.

I notice it then—notice the way he chews, ever so subtly. The substance Henry chooses to poison himself with smells like honey and peppermint. It smells *familiar*, but I can't quite place it.

I'm grateful for Henry as he slides my chair back and takes the seat to my left, and I feel—for the first time since setting foot inside Castle Grim—as if I'm not totally alone here. Even though, as Will takes his seat across the gilded table and the two women take their places on either side of him, that familiar tang of bitterness coats my tongue. Because while sporting a Nightweaver girl on either arm is perceived by the nobility as charming, if Will were to simply take my hand—if he were to kiss my cheek—it would be our skewered heads decorating the castle walls.

This is all a game, I remind myself. Will has his part to play, and I have mine.

I'm going to be okay, I tell myself. I *believe* I'm going to be okay.

Until I see him.

Titus prowls toward the dinner table with a sort of feline grace that puts every member of the nobility on notice. I'm reminded of the first time I saw him—of the crowd's reaction when he entered Bludgrave Manor. How they couldn't help but stare—couldn't help but look at him with awe.

And on his arm, her dark hair unbound, her lavender gown simple and modest and effortlessly elegant, Princess Leo appears to glide across the floor. I know that looks can be deceiving, especially when it comes to Underlings. But as the chandeliers cast a warm amber radiance over the surface of her deep brown skin, giving her the appearance of glowing from within, I see no trace of a shadow—no corona of smoke around her head, no wisp of darkness looming over her with eyes like blood and teeth like blades. I missed the signs before, when Trudy Birtwistle was possessed, but I wasn't looking for them—dismissed any hint of a Sylk, too preoccupied with Will's return to even consider that Trudy might not be herself.

But not tonight. Tonight, I'm determined to see what I didn't before—to expose Morana before it's too late and Will falls victim to the Shifter curse.

The familiar scent of sea brine causes my breath to catch as Titus pulls out the chair to my right for the princess, and he takes his seat between Leo and the queen, whose atroxis sits primly at her feet, licking one of its six claw-tipped paws. At once, every nerve in my body feels electrified, as if whatever cursed magic inside me comes alive, attempting to sense Morana's presence in the smiling, beautiful girl seated beside me.

Leo studies me out of the corner of her eye, her expression unreadable as she leans in, whispering, "I surrender."

My heart skips a beat, my stomach clenching. I try to catch Will's eye, but he's too preoccupied with his new companions to notice the sheen of sweat that slicks my brow. It couldn't be this easy, could it? Does Morana know I've come for her, and rather than hide, she's decided to toy with me by exposing herself?

"Pardon me?" I manage to say, desperate to conceal the panic in my voice.

The hint of a smirk graces the princess's lips, and she cuts a glance at the spiked armor covering my shoulders. "If I had known it was *that* kind of dinner, I would have brought a few more weapons myself."

It takes me a second too long to realize she's teasing me, but then she laughs, sticking out her hand for me to shake.

"I'm Leo," she says, her eyes bright, hopeful. "I was delighted when Titus arranged for us to sit beside each other. I've heard so much about you."

I take her hand, expecting to feel something—*anything*—to indicate she's possessed by the Sylk queen, except I feel nothing but her smooth skin in my grasp. An odd mixture of relief, guilt, and anxiety wrestles for dominance in my gut. Could it be that the princess isn't possessed after all? Or is it that Morana is too powerful—her magic too strong—for me to properly detect? What if, since Owen attacked me on Reckoning Day, something has changed within me and my curse will no longer allow me to see Sylks? What if I never truly had any power to begin with, and I only saw the Sylks because they *wanted* me to see them?

Over her shoulder, Titus chances a look in our direction, his furrowed brow the only crack in his otherwise taciturn face. Leo's eyes narrow, and it feels as if she might withdraw her hand, turning slightly to glance behind her, but I tighten my grip, forcing a smile to hold her attention a moment longer—to give myself a final opportunity to sense the presence of a Sylk.

I say, with as much charm as I can muster, "Nothing good, I hope."

Her eyes twinkle mischievously. "Oh, dreadful, terrible things." She places her free hand over her heart, her expression one of mock seriousness. "The rumors don't do you justice."

"Rumors?" I don't mean to, but I let go of her hand, my heartbeat kicking into a gallop. I think of the day on the train when Winona Congreve saw Titus and me alone in that compartment. Did she tell someone? How can I expect to befriend Leo—to spend enough time with her to sense the ancient, evil presence Titus claims he felt when he was near her—if she suspects there's something between her fiancé and me?

"Why, of course!" Leo whispers, a conspiratorial grin setting her face alight. "Aster Oberon, the fearsome pirate. You've become quite the hero throughout the Eerie. I believe that by the time word reaches Hellion, you'll have become a legend."

My eyes dart to the king and queen, worried they might have somehow heard our conversation over the deafening chatter of the nobility, but they appear rapt with interest as Will entertains them with a story from his time on the front lines.

"I'm flattered," I say, wiping my palms on my gown. "But I'm afraid I'm much less terrifying than the stories portray me to be."

Leo's eyes crinkle with a smirk. "I highly doubt that."

I mean to say something else, to try to keep her talking, as if I could detect Morana's presence with a simple misspoken word, but the sharp tinkling of glass rings out, and our conversation abruptly ends as the king stands at the head of the table.

"I'm pleased you all could join us," the king says, his voice carrying over the dining table, bringing every conversation to a halt. "Never in the history of my reign as king has there been more to celebrate in one single evening—or one season, for that matter." He lifts his glass, red wine sloshing over the side. "When my son first proposed to the princess of Hellion, he mentioned that he wanted to be married on Holy Winter's Day. Of course, I told him—I said, 'My dear boy, you do realize your wedding celebration will last nearly an entire week—the same week that the Holy Winter's Festival will take place?' And he said to me—"

"I told him that I was well aware," Titus drawls, "and that I expect to receive twice the gifts."

Everyone at the dinner table erupts with laughter, and I wonder if I'm perhaps the only person in the room who can see the hatred in Titus's smile as he takes a sip of his wine.

"Yes, yes, of course," the king says with a wink. "I considered saying no—telling him to wait until after the festival—but my wife—"

"When else will you have the opportunity to host your son's wedding festivities during the same week of Holy Winter?" Queen Calantha speaks up, placing a hand on Titus's arm.

I tell myself I imagine the way Titus tenses—the way his jaw twitches—at his mother's touch, because he smiles at her like an adoring son.

Calantha returns his smile, continuing, "Just think of the parties—"

"*'Yes, think of the parties, Calix,'*" the king finishes, mocking his wife's voice with a playful lilt. "Calantha adores parties."

"Who doesn't?" The queen raises her glass, toasting to Will.

"After all, I happen to be seated across from the kingdom's favorite party guest."

Will lifts his glass in response, and the women on either side of him coo like doves, batting their eyelashes in such a feverish manner I hope they might simply fly away. "It is my honor to attend such fine parties, Your Grace," Will replies, his charming grin seeming to enchant the entire court.

"You make us proud, William," the king says, bowing his head just slightly. "Lord Bludgrave, Lady Isabelle," he adds, addressing Will's parents, "you've done a fine job with this one. We're positively thrilled you've chosen to stay with us during this time of celebration."

"We're most grateful," Lord Bludgrave says, lifting his glass. "To the king and queen!"

The nobility chime in, "To the king and queen!"

I quickly raise my glass, joining their toast, but the words leave a bitter taste in my mouth. Thankfully, I seem to have been granted my wish, because as the conversation picks up, and the first course is served, I feel blissfully invisible. So much so, that, halfway through my soup, the tension in my chest eases and my appetite recovers enough that I'm able to eat more than I've managed since the night Father died.

I think of Father all throughout the second and third course, wondering what he would have chosen to serve, were he the king's head chef. I even find myself thinking of Owen and what he would have to say about each dish. At the thought of my brother, anger and grief take my heart in their cruel hands, squeezing tight. White-hot shame burns my cheeks. If I *can* save Owen—if I can free him from his service to the Guild—what would that look like? Could our siblings forgive him for what he did to Father?

Could I?

"Sorry I'm late," a man says, taking the empty seat to the right of one of Will's companions, next to Eliza. I feel at once as if I know him, but he doesn't look at all familiar, with olive skin, tousled dark hair, a smile that could charm vipers, and—

A freshly healed scar over his missing hazel eye.

"Sir Cooper," the king says, offering another hearty toast. "You honor us with your presence."

"Please, Your Highness," Flynn says, bringing a hand to his chest, and I note his House crest—the bat in midflight—embroidered on his black jacket in silver thread. With his other hand, he lifts his glass. "I am ever at your service."

Excited murmurs pass between the nobility, and Henry leans over to whisper, "Eliza's brothers are the only members of the nobility who have chosen to serve as Bloodknights."

I wonder, then, why Gabriel is absent, but now hardly seems like the time to ask.

"You serve your kingdom well, Sir Cooper," the king says, sipping his wine—wine that stains his teeth like blood. "I've been well assured that the rebels have been dealt with and that they no longer pose a threat, all thanks to you."

Flynn dips his head graciously. "I cannot claim all the credit, Your Majesty," he says, his voice smooth. "There were five Bloodknights with me who enacted justice on behalf of the Crown. One gave her life to secure your kingdom."

The king frowns as the atmosphere shifts, his expression solemn.

"And she will be honored." He turns his attention, then, fully to me, and I feel as if I'm going to vomit. "Lady Aster," he begins, rubbing his chin. "You know how these people think. You were once a pirate, were you not?"

I forget how to breathe—forget how to speak. "Yes, Your Highness," I manage to say. "Before you so generously offered me a chance at reformation."

Out of the corner of my eye, I think I see Titus's lip quirk, the makings of a smirk.

"Do you believe these rebels deserve the same chance?" Queen Calantha asks innocently, but I know she means to entrap me.

If Will and Titus—if the entire Castor family—can play their parts, then I'll put on my own show for the king and queen.

I sit up straighter in my seat. "I could not help that I was born into ignorance, Your Majesties," I say, my voice stronger now than it was before. "These rebels, however, willingly oppose the Crown. I believe, truly, they know of your kindness and generosity, and yet they choose to defy you, therefore already having denied your offer for redemption."

The king's eyes narrow. "So you would agree, they should face the consequences of their actions?"

The nobility abandon their forks and knives, watching our exchange play out with rapt interest.

I've never hated myself more than when the words leave my mouth, damning me with every syllable, "Yes, Your Majesty."

His eyes are lit with an all-consuming fire as he flashes his teeth in a challenging smile. "And what, might you suggest, should these consequences be? Should they hang?"

Challenge accepted.

I steel myself even as my heartbeat kicks into a gallop and force myself to smile a bit when I answer, "A rope is much too quick." I note the way the king's eyes dart to my neck—to the scar there—and know, in an instant, that I've won this round. "If you want them to pay, bleed them out like the animals they are. A knife to the throat is slow—it's punishing. And it sends a much clearer message to anyone else who might believe they can act against the Crown and endure only a swift death at the mercy of the hangman's noose."

The king doesn't break my stare for what feels like an eternity, and I wait, praying to the Stars that I appear confident, calm, and collected under his scrutiny.

He slams his fist down on the table, and I flinch as his hearty bellow breaks the tension, the nobility erupting with riotous laughter.

"A knife to the throat!" he cries, pointing his finger at me with a gleam of approval in his eyes—approval that marks me, forevermore, as a traitor to my people. "With that attitude, you're going to make a fine Bloodknight."

Beside me, Leo claps like a giddy child, and I can't help but notice that while the king and his court seem entranced with the princess's enthusiasm, Queen Calantha's smile is laced with venom.

"So, Lady Aster—" Calantha starts, attempting to talk over the clamor of laughter, but Leo cuts across her as if she didn't hear the queen speak.

"Speaking of Bloodknights," Leo says, her chin resting on her primly knit hands as she bats her eyelashes at Flynn, and the table falls silent, hanging on to the princess's every word. "Sir Cooper, you must tell us more about your time in Thorn—"

I take a few steadying breaths as Leo willingly becomes the focus of the king and the rest of the nobility's attention. As Flynn begins to regale Leo with a story about defeating a rebel leader, I chance a look at Titus only to find he's already watching me. His twisted frown, his narrowed eyes, would lead anyone to believe the prince isn't impressed with his father's shiny new toy, but I see the question in his eyes—see the fear, there, too.

I attempt to swallow the knot in my throat as I shake my head, ever so subtly.

His jaw tightens, and he looks away, taking a generous sip of his wine.

I wonder, for a moment, if I tell him that I can't sense Morana...will he still go through with his plans to kill Leo, if only to be sure?

As I tear my gaze from Titus, I catch Leo's eye, and she smiles at me, pure and genuine, and suddenly I've lost my appetite.

I think of the compass, tucked safely in my pocket alongside one of my daggers, and it's as if I can feel the staccato *tick tick tick* of the timepiece inside.

I thought I would have at least a few days to discover the truth about Leo, but the look on Titus's face leads me to believe he doesn't intend to wait much longer for an answer.

CHAPTER SEVENTEEN

After dinner, I take Henry's arm, allowing him to escort me from the table as the nobility disperse. But, since he polished off an entire bottle of wine during the feast, Henry leans heavily on my side, and it feels more as if I'm escorting *him*. He brings me as far as the doors to the banquet hall, where I expect Charlie and Lewis wait to take me back to my chambers for the evening. Instead, I'm met by Gabriel, still dressed in his full bloodred armor, and though I can't see his face, his brooding demeanor conveys a look of impatience—perhaps even annoyance.

"Where are my brothers?" I ask as we approach the Bloodknight.

"Taking a late supper," Gabriel answers, his voice dull. He turns slightly, as if expecting me to follow him, but Henry pulls his arm closer to his body, tucking me tightly into his side. Gabriel's eyes narrow on my hand, still gripping Henry's arm, and he tilts his head. He adds, his voice a deep rasp, "I've been sent to ensure Lady Aster makes it back to her room safely."

"By whom?" Henry demands, his words slurred.

Gabriel sighs, as if bored. "Whom do you think?"

I assume he means Titus or Will asked him to collect me, but as I scan the crowd, searching for any sign of them, they're nowhere to be seen. Still, I get the feeling Gabriel isn't going to take no for an answer, and Henry seems to be looking for a fight.

Slowly, I remove my hand from Henry's arm and take a step toward Gabriel, putting myself between the two of them.

"Shall we?" I say, motioning for Gabriel to lead the way.

But as Gabriel turns, and I move to follow, Henry grasps at my arm, his touch like a brand of fire. When I meet his gaze, his glossy eyes are somewhat distant.

"Aster—" Henry grinds his jaw. "Be careful."

I peel his hand from my arm, squeezing it once before letting it drop. "And miss out on a little fun?" I smirk, winking at him.

A small spark of Henry's usual playfulness lights in his eyes as he shakes his head, chuckling to himself. But as I leave with Gabriel, and Henry is swallowed up by the lingering crowd, I can't shake the uneasy feeling that perhaps I should have stayed with him.

And when Gabriel leads me down an unfamiliar hallway, that feeling quickly turns to panic. My stomach twists into knots as I slip my hands into my pockets, my fists clenched around the hilts of my daggers. I've withdrawn them halfway, my shoulders tense, when we come to a halt at the end of a long, dark passage.

"Through here," Gabriel says, pushing open the heavy iron door. A gust of cold air nips at my face as I lean forward, attempting to see what lies on the other side of the doorway without taking my eyes off the Bloodknight.

I'm convinced he's led me into a trap when—

"That will be all, Gabriel," comes Titus's voice from close by, and the knot in my stomach unravels.

I cut a glance at the Bloodknight as I slip outside, and he dips his head at me, eyes unreadable, before shutting the door in my face. The cold night air drags its frigid claws down my spine, and I clutch my arms to my chest, shivering as I turn to face Titus.

He leans indolently against an icy statue, a long black coat draped over his shoulders, his stark silhouette surrounded by a vast, ancient graveyard that spans out in every direction. The heavy blanket of white covering every tombstone and tree muffles all sound; it's so quiet I almost feel as if I'm somewhere far, far away from Castle Grim, even though, if I squint through the flurries of snow, the warm amber lights of the dark, stone spires surround us on all sides. And yet, despite the towering fortress separating me from the sea, the gentle hum of water prompts me to venture deeper into the graveyard, toward Titus.

For a long moment, he just watches me, half obscured by shadows, half radiant in the moonlight, his eyes hard, his jaw wound tight before he pushes off from the statue and jerks his head as if beckoning me to follow.

Snow crunches underfoot as we pick our way over gnarled roots, wending between the gravestones. My heart throbs painfully in my chest when I think about how Titus might react to my discovery—or lack of it, rather—at dinner. But instead of giving too much thought to Titus's unnerving silence, I focus on the snow. The moisture beneath my feet, every flurry that swirls about my head, melting on the warmth of my cheeks—there is water all around me, even now. And farther still, beyond the walls of Castle Grim, where the ocean rages, distantly, calling out to me...

We pass a massive stone structure, framed by two winged figures—one holding a chalice, another a sword—and my heart skips a beat, my steps stuttering. Between them, a raven perches atop an iron gate. My hand plunges into my skirt pocket, my fist closing around the hilt of my dagger, but before I can unsheathe it, I realize the bird isn't real—it isn't Owen, watching over me in the form of a raven, just as he did all those months at Bludgrave.

Titus must mistake my fear for curiosity. "A mausoleum," he explains quietly, his voice almost jarring after the long stretch of silence.

I mean to ask him what a mausoleum is, but I never get the chance. At the heart of the courtyard, a dark pond reflects the sky above, a shimmering pool of starlight. Two swans sit serenely atop the water, one black, one white—just like the Anteres crest. Another shiver passes through me, but an instant later, Titus drapes his coat over my shoulders, the heavy material still warm from the heat of his body.

"I'm not that cold," I insist, slipping the coat from my shoulders, but Titus is too quick, turning me to face him. He grabs the lapels of the coat, wrapping it tighter around me.

"Can't have you falling ill," he says, flashing his teeth in a biting smile, even though his hands are gentle as he secures the top button of the coat. His hands linger a little too long, his gaze drifting....

I clear my throat, and he takes a step back, putting distance between us. He runs his hands through his hair, dappled silver beneath the light of the stars, and I note the tattoos on the backs of his hands—the matching sparrows in midflight.

"Well?" His throat bobs. "What did you see?"

My mouth works, my breath like a puff of white smoke. I know I have to tell him the truth—that I didn't see anything. But the way he's looking at me—the desperation in his gaze... I can't bring myself to say the words.

"Aster," he says softly, hesitantly, "you can tell me."

My heart aches. He expects me to tell him he'll have to kill his childhood friend, not that I couldn't sense Morana, which means he won't be able to cure Will's curse. Either way, someone he loves must die.

"Titus, I—"

"Apologies," Will says, and I whirl to find him jogging toward us, his expression somewhat pained. He stops a few feet away, his hands on his knees as he pants for breath. "I'm not sure how long I have before they find me again." He looks over his shoulder, as if the two girls from dinner might appear at any moment. Apparently satisfied that no one followed him, Will closes the distance between us. His gaze flits to Titus's coat, and I almost expect him to scowl, but his eyes soften when he looks at my face. "Are you all right, my darling?"

I shake my head, my lips pressed tight as a rush of emotions rises within me—disappointment, fear, guilt, all lodged like lumps in my throat. "I—my ability—I didn't see anything tonight. Leo was right beside me, and I couldn't sense that she was possessed. There were no signs of a Sylk. What if something's wrong with me?"

What if I missed it, as I did before? I already lost Father because I failed—what if Will is next, and it's all my fault?

"Nonsense," Titus says, waving his hand in dismissal, and though I should feel relieved that he appears calm, it only serves to unsettle me. "I expected you might have trouble. Morana is powerful—more powerful than you can imagine. It won't be as easy to detect her as it has been with other Sylks." He meets my eyes, his voice level, confident. "You'll try again tomorrow."

"Brother," Will says gently, his voice strained. He clutches at his abdomen, a muscle in his jaw feathering. "It could be time to accept that Morana isn't here. You can't force Aster to—"

"I'm not forcing her to do anything!" Titus's eyes go wide, his frozen breath punctuating every word. "She's cursed, too, William!" He points at me, nostrils flaring, and suddenly the swans take flight, disappearing behind the mausoleum. "She's *dying*, too. You can't run from this! You say you want her safe? She needs the cure. Don't you want this? If not for yourself, then for her?"

"Of course I do!" Will snaps, spit flying, voice cracking. He squares off against Titus, but he winces, fist clenched at his side. "I wouldn't be here if it weren't for her—if I didn't have hope that there was even the slightest chance she could be saved from this fate. But I don't have much time left, and there's no one I trust more than you."

Titus opens his mouth as if to argue, but Will doesn't stop.

"No, listen to me!" Will insists, his voice rough. "I need you to keep searching for a cure even after I've turned. But you can't do that if you won't let go of this—this unfounded belief that Leo is possessed!"

Will staggers a step to the left. Titus reaches for his arm as if to steady him, but Will brushes him off, half-sitting, half-collapsing onto the base of a large, winged statue. The carved face of the woman looks down at Will, her expression mournful, as he buries his face in his hands.

Gingerly, I kneel beside him, my touch light on his arm.

Will captures my hand in both of his. "It's nothing." It looks as if he attempts to hide his grimace with a reassuring grin. "It comes and goes in waves."

That's when I see it—the dark green veins peeking out from underneath his collar.

I gasp. "It's spreading?"

"Please, Aster—" Will starts.

I shake my head, whirling to look at Titus. "Can't you help him? Slow the spread, like you did with the venom in my veins?"

He glares at the veins as Will adjusts his shirt collar, covering them once more.

"It doesn't work like that," Titus says, his brow furrowed. "There's nothing I can do for William, save for the cure. Tomorrow you'll see Leo again and then—"

"And then what?" Will presses, his teeth gritted. "Say the princess *is* possessed. You still have to force Morana to take her corporeal form. You're not strong enough to perform the ritual, not without—"

"I've already told you." Titus cuts him off with a look that threatens violence. "I have a plan."

I look between the two of them, my heart racing. "Without *what?*"

Titus grinds his jaw, pacing. Will blows out a tight breath.

"Without human blood," Will says, pinning Titus with a glare.

I stand, closing the gap between Titus and me, but he refuses to meet my gaze. "Where are you going to get human blood?" I demand, but an image of Titus with a human heart between his teeth roils my stomach, and I regret asking. As the Reaper, it wouldn't be difficult for Titus to consume enough human blood to obtain the power he claims it will require to perform the ritual, but at what cost?

He snorts a laugh, cutting a glance at the exposed column of my throat. His lips curl into a cruel smirk. "Are you offering?"

Will gets to his feet, then, stepping between Titus and me. "This isn't a joke. You know what will happen if you feed. I won't let you lose yourself to bloodlust. Not again."

My blood turns to ice. *Not again.*

Titus rolls his eyes, nodding slowly, but when he takes a step toward Will, his expression turns cold—sinister. "I will do what I must to save you, even if you disapprove of my methods."

This time, I push between the two of them, forcing Will back a few paces, but Titus doesn't budge, towering over me like one of the stone statues. "Will's right," I say, chin raised in defiance as I crane my neck to look up at Titus. "If my ability doesn't work—if I can't sense that Leo is possessed—"

"You will," he cuts in.

"If I *can't*," I push through, teeth clenched, "will you kill Leo anyway? Just to be sure?"

The spiteful mask of the heartless prince slips, if only for a moment, and Titus appears conflicted. But his expression hardens once more, and when he speaks, his low voice is lethally calm. "There is nothing I wouldn't do for the chance that William might be saved."

Will. We're both doing this for Will.

"Lord Castor?" comes the trill of a woman's voice.

Before I can react, at a preternatural speed I can hardly comprehend, Titus and Will move as if they were of one mind. Will practically shoves me into Titus's arms before emerging from behind the statue, jogging a few paces toward the direction of the two approaching courtiers. Titus spins me around, pinning me to the back of the statue, shielding us from view, his hand covering my mouth.

I bite his middle finger, if only out of instinct, but I wish I didn't.

Titus smirks, his gaze intent on my mouth, and I suppress a shiver as he brings his lips to my ear and whispers, "I'm going to need that finger, love."

I bite down harder, earning a quiet hiss of surprise as Titus jerks his hand back.

The courtiers' voices have already begun to fade as Will escorts them away from the pond. I peek around the side of the statue as Will's voice is lost to the night, ensuring the coast is clear before taking off in the opposite direction. Titus follows, close at my heels, and I swear I hear him mutter a curse under his breath.

"Aster, wait," he says with a sigh. "My coat—you can't—"

Just before I reach the door from which I entered the graveyard, I turn, unbuttoning his coat and holding it out for him to take.

He reaches for it but seizes my wrist instead, pulling me toward him. He searches my gaze, and I'm surprised to find no trace of the haughty prince, the debonair pirate, or the villainous Reaper staring down at me—just blue eyes, as deep and dark as my beloved ocean.

"If you truly believe that Morana hasn't possessed Leo, then, no, I won't lay a finger on her. You have my word." His brows pinch, his mouth pressed tight. "But please," he whispers, "promise me you'll try again? Just to be sure?"

I throw off his grip and shove his coat against his chest.

"I'm doing this for Will," I say. "Of course I'm going to try."

I open the door to find Charlie and Lewis standing guard, whispering to each other, their faces rosy in the lantern light. When they see the prince behind me, they straighten, schooling their boyish grins into what I'm sure they believe to be serious expressions, and though I can't smell the liquor on their breaths, I've seen my brothers tipsy enough times to know they've had one too many cups.

I shut the door in Titus's face, leaving him out in the cold, and start past my brothers.

"Boy," Charlie says, pretending to whisper to Lewis, "if I didn't know any better, I'd think our sister had just stabbed that poor bloke through the heart."

Chapter Eighteen

I fall from one nightmare to the next. Without the wards Killian placed at Bludgrave Manor to protect against unwanted dreams, I fall prey to visions of gnashing teeth and blood-soaked hands, trails of eyes that lead to crimson ballrooms and fires that burn and burn and burn—

I wake with a gasp. Cold sweat beads on my forehead, and I sit up, blinking as I attempt to force my eyes to adjust to the dark.

Something you can smell, something you can touch, something you can see.

In the past, when I would wake from a nightmare, Mother was always there to gently guide me through that mantra. But even though we might be within the same castle walls, she feels farther away from me than she ever has.

I run my hands over the velvet blanket, taking a deep breath. The air smells of sea brine, and I realize the doors leading onto my balcony are wide open, my curtains billowing like phantoms in the night.

I slide off the mattress and make my way to the balcony, wondering how the doors could have swung open on their own, when I realize I'm not alone. A dark figure stands silhouetted by the dazzling lights of Jade, their hands resting on the balcony railing as they overlook the city beyond.

I don't move—don't breathe. My daggers are hidden under my pillow, but I'm afraid if I take a step, I might alert my uninvited guest.

The figure hums, low enough that I can barely hear it over the crash of the waves lapping at the shores of Castle Grim. But the melody sounds so familiar, like a tune my father used to whistle.

And then it stops.

My heart leaps into my throat as the figure whirls, drawing a dagger from their belt.

"Titus?"

He lowers his dagger, squinting at the open doorway. "Aster, love," he says, sheathing the dagger. "You should know better than to sneak up on someone with a knife."

"Oh?" I say, taking a step out onto the balcony. "I don't think I'm the one doing any sneaking here."

His lip twitches, as if his mouth can't remember how to smile. "You should go back to sleep."

I roll my eyes. "You should take your own advice."

He sighs, turning his back to me, looking out at the city once more. "Do you ever just do as you're told?"

"Never," I say, resting my elbows on the railing next to him. I close my eyes, inhaling the fresh, salty air, and when I open them again, a gentle snow has begun to fall. Even here, even with everything that's happened, the sound of the waves is like a balm to my spirit, repairing something vital within me.

"Forgive me for intruding," Titus says, his gaze fixed on the sea. "I just wanted to make sure that you..." He bites his lip.

"That I what?" I press, my brow quirked.

His hands curl into fists. "That you hadn't run off."

I want to curse him, but a strange choking noise is all I can manage. "Do you really think I would do that? That I would just leave Will to his fate?"

A dark shadow passes over his face. "No," he says, his eyes lit with a subtle red glow, so faint I feel as if I'm seeing things. "But you should."

Before I can react, he grabs me, his teeth as sharp as daggers as he rips into my throat, holding me so tightly I can't move, can't fight back—

I jolt awake.

But the relief that my exchange with Titus on the balcony was just another nightmare is swiftly overturned...by the panic of realizing I'm only conscious now because I'm losing oxygen. And fast.

The hands around my throat squeeze, but my attempts to grab the hands, to pry them off, are futile.

Gold eyes light the assassin's wrapped face. Fear grips me—if this assailant made it to my bedside, then they must have fought their way past Charlie and Lewis, because my brothers locked the door to the servants' passage before I went to sleep. And if my brothers were still alive, they would be here now. As black spots edge my vision, I'm seized by the overwhelming guilt that not only will Mother lose a daughter tonight, but she'll have lost two more sons as well.

All my fault. All my fault. All my—

"You're meddling in matters you don't understand," my assailant says, his voice a deep rasp. "This is your final warning. Leave Castle Grim, and your family will be spared."

Charlie, Lewis—they could still be alive.

I attempt to nod, and my assailant's grip loosens, just enough that I can inhale my first breath.

"Swear it to me," he growls. "Swear an oath."

I cough as the air rushes back to my lungs. "I swear—" I wheeze, slowly reaching behind my head. "I swear…" My hands close around the hilts of my daggers, igniting some kind of primal fury—a power buzzing in my veins, begging for release. "To make you wish you'd never threatened my family."

I draw my daggers, slashing at my assailant's arms, but he dodges swiftly. He curses as he stumbles backward, his eyes shifting from gold to red. Shadows seep from his body, pulsing in the air all around him like a great, dark cloud.

"You lied," I say, leaping to my feet, my daggers poised to strike. "You *are* an Underling!"

My assailant laughs, the sound gritty and cruel, as he stalks toward me. "Your parents are the ones who have lied to you, fledgling." He draws his dagger, the green energy crackling like lightning around the blade. "You know so little of the world and your place in it. It's pathetic."

I take a step back, bumping into my wardrobe. "Why are you doing this?" I ask, stalling for time. "What do you gain if I leave?"

My assailant cocks his head, his gilded eyes lit with amusement. "You still haven't figured it out?" He runs a fingertip over the sharp edge of his dagger, and despite the gauze covering his face, I know he's smiling as he steps closer to me. "Don't fight it, Aster," he rasps, extending his hand. "I know what you feel. I feel it, too. Our...*connection*."

Shadows cloak his palm, and I'm gripped by the sudden urge to reach out, to thread my fingers with his.

"You really don't remember me?" he asks, gaining ground, towering over me with every step. I have nowhere to go as he closes the distance between us, placing his hand on the wardrobe, caging me in. He points the tip of the dagger at my shoulder, where an Underling's teeth pierced my flesh, before sheathing it. "And here I thought I'd made a lasting impression."

My blood runs cold. "You? *You're* the Shifter who cursed me?"

He bows his head, looking up through thick, dark lashes to meet my gaze. "I marked you so that no one else can have you," he rasps, leaning in, his muffled breath hot on my neck as his nose brushes my throat. "You're mine, Aster Oberon."

My grip tightens around my daggers, my heart racing.

"I have been away for quite some time," he says, drawing back, his glowing eyes boring into mine with such intensity I feel as if he can see right through me. "The others seem to have forgotten who you belong to, but Queen Morana promised me." He grabs the hilt of his dagger, but he doesn't unsheathe it again—not yet. "She promised I would get to be the one to kill you."

He gives me just enough space that I'm able to kick, my foot colliding with his stomach, sending him stumbling backward.

He laughs again, the sound low and gritty, as he rolls his shoulders, drawing the dagger, its green light illuminating the dark bedroom with an ominous glow.

"Then why are you still tormenting me?" I stall, pivoting so that the backs of my knees hit the edge of my bed. "I know she's here. This is what she's always wanted, right? She has access to me, now. And when my curse finally takes me, there'll be no reason for you to kill me. I'm already dying—I'm dying from a bite *you* inflicted."

He tsks, shaking his head. "No," he rasps. "You're not."

It feels as if the ground has shifted beneath me. "But the venom—"

"The venom, if it were able to reach your heart, would weaken you to the point of death." He stalks toward me at a languid pace. "But you would not die." He twirls the dagger, the electric green energy crackling, climbing up his forearm. "Not unless I will it. Because my venom courses through your veins, I can make you feel however I want. If I want you to feel sick—near death, even—I can."

"My bracelet—the enchantment—it protects me from Underlings. You can't do me any fatal harm." I think about the way Owen could grab me by the throat, and even though I know the level of harm an Underling can cause me is somewhat undefined, I'm confident he cannot kill me. Even Owen had to wait until the enchantment was weakened on Reckoning Day to stab me with that cursed dagger.

As he draws closer, I make to climb onto my bed, ready to launch myself to the other side, putting distance between us again, but... panic closes around my heart like a fist. I can't move. I can hardly breathe.

He stands over me, lifting his hand to grip my chin. "Your little enchantment protects you from lesser Underlings," he whispers. "Not from Queen Morana. And certainly not from me."

Horror snakes down my spine. "What *are* you?" I know I'm

able to speak only because he releases my tongue from his power—power that radiates from him like darkness incarnate, his shadows filling the space so that his golden eyes and the green glow of his dagger barely cut through the gloom.

"I have been many things." His deep, smoky voice seems to come from everywhere, as if it emanates from the shadows themselves. "Lived many lives." He raises the dagger with what appears to be concerted effort, holding it close enough to my throat that the proximity of the cursed magic corrodes the collar of my shirt. "In this life, I am what the Fallen call a bonewielder."

I sip at whatever air he'll allow my lungs to hold. *Of course*—Killian suspected the assassin was a Changeling. This one has stolen the life of a Nightweaver—a noble with an affinity for bonewielding. *That's because your bracelet protects against* Underling *compulsion*, Will had said. *Not bonewielder persuasion.*

There are limitations to the protection your trinket offers, Owen told me. Did he know about this Changeling, too? Was he trying to warn me?

"What are you waiting for?" I grind out.

He tilts his head. "All in due time. I have my own plans for you, fledgling. Morana had the opportunity to turn you on Reckoning Day, and she failed. Sending your brother to break your enchantment was a mistake. But now," he croons, the gravelly sound grating against my senses, "I'm going to do things my way. And your presence here complicates things for me. I've asked you politely, but"—he leans in, whispering in my ear—"if you refuse to listen, I could be more *persuasive*."

"Then why go through the trouble of threatening me?" Sweat beads on my forehead from the effort it takes to speak. "Just persuade me to leave—if you can." I pray to the Stars that he doesn't call my bluff. That he *can't* call my bluff.

A smirk crinkles the corners of his eyes. "Watching you wrestle with that pitiful morality of yours is infinitely more satisfying." His grip on my chin becomes painful. "You will choose to leave Castle Grim of your own accord before Holy Winter's Day. Of this I have no doubt."

He takes a step back, and I feel his hold on me relax, the weight of his magic lifting from my bones.

"I am trying to be merciful." He sighs. "I would hate for your family to suffer the consequences of your disobedience."

My lip curls, and I strain against his magic, but it's no use. "If you touch them—"

"You'll what?" He chuckles darkly. "You're out of your depth, fledgling. Go now, and when I come to collect you, perhaps I'll teach you how to defend yourself against the petty magic of the Fallen. Until then," he says, bowing at the waist, "I'll be keeping a close eye on you."

In the blink of an eye, he transforms, taking on the form of a bat that darts out my open balcony doors, over the banister, and into the night.

For what feels like too long, I don't move, staring out at the city, feeling as if I might still be caught between asleep and awake.

You're mine, Aster Oberon.

Chapter Nineteen

Pain laces through my shoulder, startling me out of my daze, and I whirl, stumbling through the dark, my daggers still in hand as I throw the door to my suite wide.

Charlie and Lewis sit slumped against the stone wall on either side of my doorway, their heads hung.

Flynn, still dressed in his finery from dinner, crouches over Lewis, his fingers pressed to my brother's neck.

"They're alive," he says, as if by way of greeting. "Someone poisoned their food, but the dose wasn't lethal. They'll wake soon." He looks up at me then, his expression dull as he notes my daggers. "Do you mind putting those away? I don't feel like explaining to the others why you've earned yourself a one-way trip to the dungeons."

"Others?" I pant, somewhat dizzy from the heady spike of

adrenaline. I look left, right, willing my eyes to adjust to the dim torchlight of the hall. From what I can tell, we're alone. Still, I don't lower my daggers, my heart racing.

Flynn rolls his eyes, getting to his feet. "Your brothers are safe with me. Go back inside," he says. "I'll keep watch until they wake."

My eyes narrow. "I only just met you a few days ago. Why should I trust you?"

"That's an excellent question," comes a deep, dark voice. Will steps briskly out of the shadows, his fists clenched at his sides. His hair is mussed, his clothes disheveled, and in the flicker of candlelight his cheeks appear flushed. He looks as if he's just hurried off from somewhere, and my stomach tightens at the thought of him just having left the two courtiers from dinner.

Will appraises Flynn with a cold, lethal stare. "What are you doing roaming the halls at this hour?"

Flynn snorts. "I'm a bit of a nocturnal creature," he says, performing a mock bow. "And thank the Stars, because I heard a commotion coming from Lady Aster's room. That's when I found these two." He gestures at my brothers' limp bodies, and I note the subtle rise and fall of their chests. Relief floods my veins, and I lower my daggers.

Flynn jerks his chin at Will, his forehead creasing. "Suppose I could ask you the same thing."

Will takes a step toward Flynn, a muscle in his temple feathering. But he ignores Flynn's question, turning sharply to me, his eyes narrowed as he inspects me. "Commotion?"

I look between the two of them, my mouth babbling. I struggle to put into words what just transpired in my room, and Will must sense my hesitation to divulge the truth in front of Flynn, because he quickly nods, motioning at the door to my room.

"I'll take a look," he says, his voice soft. He faces Flynn once more, his tone a thinly veiled threat when he adds, "Stand guard. If anything happens to the Oberon brothers, you'll have me to answer to."

Flynn flashes his teeth at Will in a biting smile, his eyes darkening. "I would expect nothing less."

A moment later, Will closes the door to my salon. Alone, he places his hand on the small of my back, his touch warm as he guides me into my bedroom. I hesitate in the doorway, but he urges me forward, his tense shoulders the only indication of his wariness as we enter the suite.

My mouth goes dry at the sight of my balcony doors, the lock latched tight, and my daggers slip from my grasp. Frantically, I move about the room, searching for evidence of the attack, but my wardrobe has been straightened, my bedding unrumpled.

"He was—he was here in my room," I say, stumbling around in the dark, whirling to face Will, his back to me as he kneels in front of the fireplace, his silhouette like a looming shadow. "He attacked me—the Changeling from the train station! He turned into a *bat*. He flew from my balcony! The doors were open and... Will?"

Calmly, Will strikes a match, tossing it into the hearth. He turns then, brows knit as he surveys the room. Fire illuminates the locked doors that lead to my balcony as he runs his lithe fingers over the handle.

"I'll have Killian place an enchantment on your suite to ward off nightmares," he says gently, finally meeting my gaze. He takes a step toward me, his hand outstretched as if to cup my cheek. "It's been a long day, Aster—"

I take a step back, just out of his reach. "You don't believe me?"

Will's mouth twists as his hand falls back to his side, his expression pained. "The doors are locked from the inside."

I gape at him, horror creeping up my spine like a thousand tiny spiders. "He tried to strangle me!" I make my way to the fireplace, casting my hair over my shoulder to give him a clear view of the fresh bruises that are sure to mark my skin.

Will approaches me carefully, his touch light as his fingertips skim the exposed column of my throat. He drags his thumb over my pulse point, and I think I see a hint of gold rimming his green eyes but decide it must be the reflection of the flames. Still, he clears his throat, putting space between us again, and shakes his head. "I'm sorry, but..." he says quietly, running a hand through his mussed hair.

I stagger to the full-length mirror in the corner of the room, and my heart drops into my stomach.

There are no marks on my skin—no bruises, not even those that Owen's attack left behind. Nothing.

"He was here," I say, tears blurring my vision. "I know what I saw."

Will wraps his arms around me, the scent of roses and damp earth soothing the ache in my chest. "You're safe now," he croons, stroking my hair. He draws back, his gaze intense. "I swear to you, Aster, this Changeling will pay for what he's done. I will see to it personally."

My lips part, my breath quickening at the way his gaze drops to my mouth, the buttery light of the fire illuminating the constellations of freckles that scatter across the bridge of his nose.

"I thought you didn't believe me?" I whisper, a single tear slipping onto my cheek.

Slowly, delicately, he leans in, his warm breath ghosting over my jaw as he presses a kiss to my skin, capturing the tear with his lips. "I never said that," he whispers against my cheek, his hand snaking around my neck, his fingers tangling in my hair.

I inhale a shaky breath as his nose brushes mine, his lips hovering just over my lips, when an unfamiliar floral perfume assaults my senses, and I pull free from his grasp.

"What *were* you doing out so late?" I ask, stumbling backward. I fish the compass from where I hid it in the seat of the armchair. I flip open the lid, squinting at the timepiece in the scant firelight. "It's the middle of the night! Were you..." I hesitate, heat flaring in my cheeks. "Were you with those girls?"

This time, his mouth babbles. His brows lift, a brief look of confusion passing over his face before he barks a deep, husky laugh, scrubbing a hand over his jaw. "Did you think—" He chuckles, eyes glittering with amusement, and my face is suddenly hot for an entirely different reason. Forget curses, I think I might die of humiliation.

Just as I'm about to order him to leave, he cups my jaw, urging me to meet his eyes, now soft and unguarded.

"I was following orders," he says, his gaze locked on mine. "Clemson and Davina are the daughters of a very powerful woman from Fell by the name of Eva Mercer. Dawnrender sent a message through Killian, asking me to gather information on Eva. I was doing my duty to the Order. That's all."

I ball my fist around the compass, the tiny etchings of my father's handwriting digging into the skin of my palm. "Why?"

He shakes his head, strands of dark hair falling over his forehead. "I'm not sure, but it could have something to do with the fact that Eva controls over half of the trade routes that transport goods to Castle Grim."

I struggle to maintain eye contact when I know I don't look as unaffected as I'd like to project. "Maybe if you weren't such a good spy, the Order wouldn't expect so much from you," I say, trying to sound indifferent. Trying not to think about those women clinging to his side. Trying not to wish it had been me, instead.

"Maybe." He grins, but it doesn't reach his eyes. "I almost forgot," he says, reaching into his jacket pocket and withdrawing a sprig of blue salvia. "I came to find you shortly after we spoke in the graveyard, but your brothers said you already retired for the evening. But I couldn't stop thinking about you and, well, the Crystal Atrium is unlike anything you've ever seen. The gardens are magnificent and…" He tucks the sprig behind my ear, and my heart soars when I remember what he once told me the flower meant.

This one means I'm thinking of you.

The gesture is almost enough to make me forget where I am—who I am. But a gust of wind rattles the doors to my balcony, and I flinch. Beyond my window, a storm rages, thick flurries of snow blotting out the lights of Jade.

"I can help you sleep," Will says, his voice low as he follows my gaze to the locked doors. His fingertips graze my cheek, leaving a trail of warmth in their wake. "If you want."

I seize his wrist, lowering his hand. "No," I say, my voice firm. "No magic."

He dips his head, clears his throat, takes a step back. "Of course," he says. "It's your choice."

He turns as if to leave, but I tighten my grip on his hand. I think, hazily, that I mean to tell him I worry my ability to detect the Sylks might not return, and how I still fear that Titus might act against Leo regardless of what I discover. But the words never materialize, melting on my tongue like snowflakes. "You could stay," I say instead, breathless. The instant the words leave my mouth, I wonder why I said them.

Will's body goes rigid, his throat bobbing as he inspects me with a curious look. "If that's what you want," he says, his deep voice like the distant roll of thunder.

I nod, threading my fingers with his. "I do."

He tugs at his shirt collar, clears his throat. "Then I'll stay."

I mean to let go of his hand as I move toward the end of my bed, but it's his fingers that slip from mine as he takes a step in the opposite direction. He smiles, soft and subdued, as he plops down in the armchair, his elbows resting on his knees.

He inclines his head, eyes glittering. "Sweet dreams, Aster."

I don't know what came over me, asking him to stay, but I'm relieved he understood I didn't intend for him to sleep in my bed. As I crawl under my blankets, listening to the crackle of the hearth and Will's steady breathing, all thoughts of Underlings feel distant, like a dream that fades upon waking. But the compass, still safe in my grasp, heats my palm. Fiery. Insistent.

The last thought that crosses my mind is not one of flowers or would-be kisses, and though I can't remember why, as I drift off to sleep, the feeling that wraps itself around my beating heart isn't one of bliss.

It's one of dread.

Chapter Twenty

Will is gone when I wake, but the sprig of blue salvia remains.

And while the feeling of dread lingers, I'm finally able to give it a name.

Homesickness.

When Margaret helps me into my gown, when my brothers escort me to the main hall, as I stand outside the doors to the throne room—all I want is to go home. Home, where my family is safe aboard the *Lightbringer*. Home, where my purpose was clear. I want to go home so fiercely it manifests as an illness for which there is no treatment. A dull ache forms in my temples, and there's a pang in my chest with every breath I take.

Once, when I was about Elsie's age, I asked Father if he had always lived aboard the *Lightbringer*. He laughed then, the sound so full and rich it almost masked the sadness in his eyes. *No*, he told me, *I had a different home, once.*

Why did you leave? I remember asking.

His smile faltered as he looked out at the Western Sea, as if he was searching for something he could never find. *We aren't always given a choice.* He turned to me then, crouching down so we were eye to eye. *Someday, you might have to leave* your *home. And you might miss it very much—so much it makes you feel sick. But wherever your family is—wherever we're all together—that is home, Aster. Home is not a place—not a ship.* He pointed at my heart, his kind eyes like the warmest, safest hug I've ever felt. *It's here.*

He patted me on the head, rising to his full height once more, but even then, I could recognize the longing in his gaze as he surveyed the horizon.

Do you ever feel sick when you miss your *home?*

I thought, just for a moment, that a tear slipped onto his cheek, but he grinned, swiping at his eyes before I could see.

Every day.

Today, even as my brothers flank me, homesickness twists my stomach into knots.

This morning, as Margaret set to work on my hair, she took my hands in hers, meeting my gaze with the kind of intensity I saw from her only in battle.

Today, you become something more than Aster Oberon, she told me as the sun rose over the rooftops of Jade, illuminating my room with a golden glow, a stark contrast to the shadows that filled the space just hours before. *From here on out, when the people look at you, they will not see the rouge on your cheeks or the braids in your hair.*

They will see vengeance and fury. They will see power. It's my job to make them see that you are more than just a courtier—more than just a pirate—with the stroke of a brush. But only you *can make them believe it in the way that you carry yourself in that throne room today.*

I almost forgot that it was Margaret who would often rally us to arms. And it's because of Margaret that, despite the homesickness I feel, when the doors to the throne room open, and my brothers depart to take their posts on either side of the entrance, I walk over the threshold and into my new life with my shoulders back and my head held high.

Because today, I am more than just Aster Oberon. I am every mother who has ever sent her child to war. I am every daughter who has ever lost her parent to the sting of a blade. I am every sister who has ever watched her sibling suffer under a burden they should never have been forced to carry. I am every human who has ever endured the cruelty of Nightweavers and Underlings alike. I am every Myth who has been driven from their home, forced into hiding. I am every Nightweaver who has met their fate at the hangman's noose for daring to rebel against the Crown.

I am the judgment that was foretold.

I am vengeance. Fury. Power.

And I will not be silenced.

Bloodknights line the pathway on either side, and I fight the urge to search for Flynn and Gabriel, focusing my gaze on the dais before me even as murmurs trickle through the crowd of nobility and foreign dignitaries, but I struggle to conceal the smirk on my lips when someone gasps, "Her gown!"

Composed entirely of scarlet metal, my gown is surprisingly—if not supernaturally—lightweight, and it fits unlike any other in my arsenal, hugging my hips and trailing behind me in a bloodred train. The armored dress resembles a Bloodknight's armor, with a red long-sleeved gambeson adorned with a top layer fashioned from chain mail, but the shoulders, bodice, and skirt consist of hundreds of plated pieces all fitting together to create the appearance of dragon scales.

I might not carry my daggers today, but I feel like a weapon as whispers erupt, and for the first time since I learned that Titus curated my wardrobe, I feel I owe him genuine thanks.

Out of the corner of my eye, I spot the entire Castor family, along with Killian and Eliza. My head turns of its own accord, and I lock eyes with Will. It looks as if he's trying to say something to me, trying to convey something without words, but a moment later I've reached the edge of the dais, with only a few shallow steps between me and the Nightweaver responsible for countless widows and orphans. The king responsible for hundreds of mass graves. The man who has fed rivers of bloodshed so deep he should be drowning in his sins.

I meet Calix Anteres's stare—note the glint of challenge in his eyes—as I take the last three steps, rising to join him on the dais. Today, I will not falter. I will not stumble. Titus ensured this when he had a pair of flat-soled boots crafted to match my gown rather than heels, as if he knew these three steps could either give me a chance to prove my decorum or rob me of my dignity.

It takes everything in me not to seek out Titus as I halt in front of the king and queen's thrones and sink to one knee, even though I feel him there, standing at the right hand of his father. And just behind him, Princess Leo wears a gown of lilac chiffon—ever the demure fiancée. All soft, smooth edges in a way I will never be.

"Your Majesties," I say, my gaze fixed on the floor.

It feels like a lifetime passes before the king gets to his feet.

"Aster Oberon, daughter of Philip and Grace Oberon, servant to the Crown of the Eerie..." The king's voice carries throughout the throne room, full and rich, and if I didn't know who he was or what he's done, I might even think he sounds like someone I would follow into battle. Someone who, perhaps in another life, could have led his kingdom with fairness and humility. "Do you this day solemnly swear an oath to your king to uphold the laws of this kingdom with honor, integrity, and courage, fighting for justice, peace, and prosperity throughout the land?"

I knew this was coming. I knew I would have to swear an oath to be knighted. But now that the moment has arrived, cold sweat beads on the back of my neck. To defeat the evil that seeks to destroy everyone I love—to abolish everything I believe in—I will have to become the very thing I hate the most. And I realize, now, with my knee pressed to the dais of a king's throne room, with my head bowed in surrender and an oath on my lips, that after this is over, no matter the outcome, if I am to create a home for my family—if I'm to give them any hope for a future—I must give up on the idea of having a home to return to.

I close my eyes, remembering home one last time. I picture Father, his arms around my mother at the helm as he hummed along to the song she was singing. I hear my siblings—hear their laughter as they chased one another about the deck, wild and carefree. It's as if I can feel the spray of the sea on my face—taste the briny air, see the sun glinting on the open waves—and I smile then, because no matter what, in my heart, I will carry *this* home with me forever.

And when I stand before a broken throne with a crown of bones beneath my heel, I will have given someone, somewhere, a chance at a lifetime of happiness that I will never know.

"Do you swear to serve your king and country in whatever capacity you might be called upon, even if it costs you your life?"

The image of my family—of my home—crumbles to dust, and I let go, casting it to the wind.

"I do," I say, even if the words taste like ash in my mouth.

Iron scrapes iron as the king unsheathes his sword.

My teeth clench. Could this have been a trap all along? Does the king plan to send a message to the rebel factions and murder me in front of the entire court?

Fine, I think, even as I brace myself. *Make me your martyr.*

The blade comes to rest on my right shoulder, a heavy, lingering weight.

"Today, Aster Oberon, you join your brothers and sisters in arms, a Bloodknight chosen and appointed by the Crown to serve your kingdom until death." The king removes the blade, sheathing his sword. "Now, rise, Bloodknight, and receive your king's blessing."

I stand, my legs shaking as a servant presents the king with a chalice of blood. He dips his thumb into the cup, his eyes glowing gold as he presses the bloody digit to my forehead.

"Before you join your brothers and sisters in arms," the king says, the glow of his eyes subsiding as his lips curl into a wicked smile, "I believe I owe you a head, and what better day to present such a gift than on the second day of the Holy Winter's Festival."

My stomach sours, and I swallow bile as the doors to the throne room open once more. I glance over my shoulder to see Flynn and

Gabriel drag a woman down the aisle. Even though a cloth sack covers her face, and chains bind her hands and feet, she struggles like a tempest given flesh, her screams sending the nobility scattering. They back against the walls as if she were about to break loose and slaughter them all.

The woman lets out a violent screech, sending a chill down my spine. Gabriel and Flynn carry her emaciated form between them as if she weighed as much as an anchor, dragging her down the aisle at a snail's pace.

Titus must decide that he lacks the patience to wait, stepping down from the dais and starting toward them with purposeful strides. He rips the sack from the woman's head with a snarl before grabbing a fistful of her sparse, auburn hair and hauling her toward the dais with little effort.

He deposits her at my feet like nothing more than a bag of potatoes, placing his foot on her back to impede her writhing form.

I wish I felt some comfort in the way he stands at my side, facing his father with a look of apathy cold enough to turn fire to ice, but this isn't Titus. This is a monster starved for blood. A cruel, vile beast set free from his cage.

The Reaper grunts, digging his shoe so deep into the woman's spine, a loud crack echoes throughout the throne room. Inwardly, I wince, but I manage to maintain an indifferent composure that I hope exudes confidence.

I have taken a life to protect my family before. This will be no different.

A Bloodknight steps up to present me with a sword, the dark, Elysian Iron shimmering with hues of purple, green, and blue.

"In keeping with the celebration of my son and his bride-to-be, I had this blade commissioned especially for you, Dame Oberon," the king says, gesturing at the sword. He runs his hand over the metal. "But it was my future daughter-in-law, Princess Leonora Boucher, who arranged for a new shipment of Elysian Iron to arrive just in time for the work to be completed."

I glance at Princess Leo, but her expression is neutral—almost dreamlike—as if she were wholly unaware that the king mentioned her name. But when I catch her eye, she gives a slight smile, and it could be a twitch, but it looks as if she winks at me.

"Let this blade represent a new era. Our alliance with the kingdom of Hellion will bring new shipments of *Manan* to their shores, and in return, their Council of Merchants has agreed to increase shipments of Elysian Iron to the Eerie, enabling us to arm our soldiers bravely fighting against the Underling hordes in the League of Seven."

He pauses as the nobility break into deafening applause, and I realize just how little I truly know of the politics between the kingdoms of the Known World.

"And now," the king continues, "today you shall witness a reformed pirate—the first human to serve as a Bloodknight—christen this blade, having vowed her allegiance to the Crown."

The smattering of applause is notably weaker. The nobility—the Bloodknights—have been forced to accept my presence here, but that doesn't mean they have to overturn a lifetime of hatred for me and my kind.

I take the sword, weigh it in my grasp. I consider the space between myself and the king—consider the damage I could do before this Bloodknight could even draw his weapon. I could drive this blade through Calix Anteres's throat in the blink of an eye, and some sinister, hungry thing inside of me seems to come awake at the thought. *Do it*, it whispers. *Kill him*.

"Thank you, Sir Cooper," the king says to the Bloodknight who gave me the sword, and it's only then that I realize Flynn was the one to present me with the weapon.

"My king." Flynn dips his head respectfully, crouching at Titus's feet, where the woman has gone limp. I send a silent prayer to the Stars that she might already be dead, but she lets out a weak moan as Titus peels his shoe back, allowing Flynn to grab the woman by her shoulders and lift her to her knees.

I see her face for the first time, and my stomach turns to water. Somewhere beneath the swollen, bloodied wreckage, I recognize Winona Congreve—Eliza's traveling companion from the train to Ink Haven.

The young maid was quiet—timid—that night in Will's private dining compartment. Since meeting Eliza, I suspected Flynn and Gabriel's sister of siding with the Order, though I can't be sure to what extent. But I could never imagine Winona to be a rebel soldier.

Still, where then she appeared to be a shy human girl, the battered prisoner before me looks as if her spine were made of steel, her lip trembling with barely contained rage. And yet, it's as if she's resigned herself to her fate as Titus and Flynn step away and I take my stance at her left side, my palms slick as I adjust my grip on the hilt of the sword.

I take a deep, steadying breath, but it does nothing to calm my thunderous heartbeat, loud enough that any bloodletter in this throne room—the king and queen included—can surely hear it.

An ache splits my chest when I think about what Winona could have done to have ended up here today—who might mourn for her—but I force myself to push the thought away. To focus on my mission: to protect my family, no matter the cost.

I lift the blade, hoping I'm strong enough to make it clean. I know my blow will strike true, but I practice my swing just once, aligning the sharp edge with the base of her skull if only to stall. I draw the moment out, memorizing the face of the true martyr—the woman whose life I trade for my own.

Matted clumps of hair cover her face, her head bowed as she whispers something under her breath. At first, I think it might be a prayer, but then I catch the words, "...lurks in shadows, devouring the light," and my blood runs cold.

I worried I might no longer possess the ability to see Sylks when I spoke to Leo at dinner, but I know now that I was wrong. I can clearly see the faint corona of smoke around Winona's head, the shadows seeping from her flesh.

Winona is possessed. And right now, I'm the only one who can see it.

In the instant I hesitate, her neck snaps, craning at an unnatural angle as she looks up at me, her eyes like wells of ink. *"We know why you're here."*

A spider crawls out of her open mouth as her jaw unhinges in an animalistic smile, and only then do the Bloodknights surround the king and queen, blades drawn. The crowd begins to scream.

"She's possessed!" a woman cries.

"An Underling—in the palace!" a man shouts.

King Calix orders his Bloodknights to let him through, unsheathing his own blade as if he were prepared to cut Winona down himself. But the queen cries, begging her husband to come back, and the Bloodknights encircle the king once more.

Winona's shriek of laughter causes a nobleman near the dais to faint. She licks her lips, her voice low and gravelly as she hisses, *"Aster Oberon, the cursed daughter, the queen's bane, the destroyer of kingdoms—"*

There's a dull thud when the woman's head lands at the king's feet, followed by the keening wail of the Sylk as it's expelled from its host, fading like vapor.

Inky black blood drips from my blade onto the dais, and a heavy silence blankets the throne room.

I pant from the effort it took to slice through bone, but I stand up straight, my gaze level as I meet Calix's inquisitive stare. He pushes past his Bloodknights, his expression hard as he sheathes his sword. He meant to rattle me by making me perform this execution, but by the flicker of surprise in his stare as he glances at the blood pooling around his feet, I feel as if I've done more than just unsettle him.

"A gift for *you*," I say, pointing the blade at Winona's severed head, *"my king."*

Chapter Twenty-One

The king dismisses the assembly with a lighthearted air, but murmurs slither throughout the throne room like an overturned basket of venomous snakes. And when Calix fixes his attention on me once more, I no longer feel as if I've won.

I hold the sword level, ready to defend myself, but with preternatural speed, Titus rips the hilt of the blade from my grasp. He pushes me backward a step as he angles his body in front of mine, forming a barrier between the king and me.

"Escort Dame Oberon to her chambers at once," he hisses, his shoulders rigid.

A few Bloodknights shift, closing ranks around the king and queen, but Flynn and Gabriel don't hesitate to flank me. I'm ushered back down the aisle as the feverish nobility press in on all sides. I try to find Will in the crowd, but every time I turn to look for him, Gabriel urges me forward.

"Keep walking," he says, his voice a deep rasp in my ear. "Don't look back."

My blood beats like a drum in my ears, my mind racing. Surely, no one thinks it's my fault an Underling was brought into the castle? The king chose the prisoner—not me. I couldn't have known she was possessed. I couldn't have planned for Winona to be chosen. And I was the one to kill her.

A gift for you. Will the king use my own words against me, to make it seem as if I'm responsible? All he has to do is say the word, and it will be my neck beneath the blade.

Will he make Titus carry out my execution?

My stomach clenches when I think of my family, but the instant I pivot, as if to break free from the throng of people that flood the palace halls, Flynn seizes my arm.

"I wouldn't do that," he says, his tone sharp, grip tightening.

Horror numbs my hands and face as Gabriel gathers the train of my dress and Flynn practically drags me up flights of steps. "What's going on—" I start, but as we round the corner and the door to my suite comes into view, relief overwhelms me, and it's only Flynn's hold on my arm that keeps me upright.

Margaret, stationed between Charlie and Lewis, starts toward me, but Lewis grabs her wrist, pulling her back a step.

"Inside," Flynn says, gesturing for my brothers and Margaret to follow me into my chambers. Without another word, he shuts the door to my suite.

I can barely bring myself to look at the faces of my siblings and tell them I've doomed us all, but when Margaret takes my hands, prompting me to meet her gaze, her eyes are bright, a smile tugging at the corners of her lips.

"You have to find Mother," I say quickly, certain that panic must be distorting my vision, because how could Margaret look so happy? "Find a way out of here while you still can—"

"What are you talking about?" Charlie asks, laughter crinkling his eyes.

"She doesn't know," Lewis says, elbowing him. "How could she know? We've only just heard."

"Heard what?" I struggle to form words around the lump in my throat.

Margaret beams at me, squeezing my hands. "Word is spreading. Everyone saw what you did—how you saved the king and queen from that Underling."

"Saved them?" My voice sounds strange, as if I were listening to myself speaking from far away.

Lewis grins, propping an arm on Charlie's shoulder as my siblings all share a mischievous look.

"They're saying you're a hero," Margaret tells me, her smile broadening. "They're calling you the Shadowslayer."

PART TWO

RUIN

PART TWO

RUIN

Chapter Twenty-Two

Tonight, the second night of the Holy Winter's Festival, is marked by a revel not unlike the ball the Castors host every year for Reckoning Day. Only, when Margaret receives word that I'm not to change out of my red armored gown—despite the inky black blood that stains it—I learn that the king has made a new proclamation.

The Holy Winter's Gala is to be held in honor of the Shadowslayer.

The great hall buzzes with an energy I can't comprehend as Charlie and Lewis escort me to the entrance of the grand ballroom, where hundreds of nobles from across the Known World assemble in all-white finery, dressed in alabaster ball gowns and ivory tuxedos. After what took place at my knighting ceremony, I expected a solemn gathering—hateful, suspicious glances cast my way; cruel whispers; and scornful glares. But it seems as if the nobility have come alive, their skin bright, their eyes flecked with gold, too preoccupied with their revelry to notice me as I make my way through the crowd.

"What's going on?" I say, focusing on keeping my lips from moving—determined to learn my father's trick, even if it takes a lifetime of practice. Even if he's no longer here to teach me himself. "Why is everyone so...giddy?"

"The nobility were given their allowance of *Manan* this afternoon," Charlie explains, his voice low.

I look up at him, noting his rigid posture, the way his hand hovers near his hip. I realize, then, that my brothers no longer carry swords. At once, I know this is the king's doing—that he's sending me a message. My brothers cannot defend themselves, and they cannot defend me. And in a crowd of Nightweavers, buzzing with their allotment of magic, as humans, we are not safe. A subtle warning, but effective enough.

"Dame Oberon," comes Flynn's familiar, muffled voice, and I'm almost relieved to see him dressed in his scarlet armor, weapons strapped to his body. He and Gabriel flank me, dismissing my brothers with little more than a nod.

Charlie and Lewis both look as if they don't want to leave me, but I give them a nod of my own, and they retreat into the crowd—hopefully far, far from the party and its bloodthirsty guests.

"Maker of All!"

I jump at the sound of Eliza's voice. I've only just turned, catching a glimpse of her bloodshot eyes, her contradictory smile, before she pulls me into a hug.

My heart drops into my stomach.

"Smile," Eliza whispers, her voice raw. "We're being watched."

I try to force a smile, but my lips quiver. "Eliza," I whisper back. "I—" My voice catches. What can I say? I'm sorry for beheading your friend?

She hugs me tighter, and for a moment, I'm not sure which one of us needs this more—her or me. "Winona was possessed," she says. "You set her free."

Eliza draws back, taking my hands as she prompts me to meet her tearful gaze. No words pass between us, but I understand Eliza's intentions all the same—to absolve me of my guilt. Winona *was* possessed. I may be forced to do many horrible things now that I am bound to the oath of a Bloodknight. But though I spilled Winona's blood, the Sylk that claimed her for a host is the monster who truly took her life. And whether or not I blame myself, Eliza has rendered me innocent.

My shoulders sag, tears welling in my throat.

"Show no mercy," Eliza says with a wink, squeezing my hands before disappearing into the crowd.

I barely have a moment to collect myself when Gabriel says, "They're ready for you." And with that, we make our way to the tall, elaborately carved doors that lead to the ballroom.

"Chin up," Flynn whispers. "Deep breath."

I hear voices on the other side of the thick wooden barrier, the blare of a trumpet. A moment later, the double doors swing wide, and I'm ushered onto a gilded landing overlooking the ballroom. At once, I'm blinded by the dazzling glow of the dozens of crystal chandeliers. All around me are clusters of tall trees bedecked with candles and shiny scarlet ornaments that reflect the light, making it difficult to focus on what's right in front of me. But with the plush white carpet underfoot and my ruby-red train trailing behind me, my gown gives me the appearance of fresh blood on snow, and it sends its own message.

I am not like the rest of you.

"Dame Oberon," someone announces, and the assembly draws in a collective breath. "The Shadowslayer."

I'm disoriented by the deafening applause, and when I manage a smile at the crowd, I hope it doesn't look as forced as it feels. Because across the ballroom, the king sits on his throne atop the opposite landing, his golden crown askew, watching me with narrowed eyes.

The king must have thought himself clever, forcing me to wear this gown—parading me in front of the court, tainted with the blood of an Underling. But by the slight curl of his lip, and the way the queen, standing to his right, places a calming hand on his shoulder, he must have realized his mistake.

As a human, I *am* different. As a pirate, I *don't* belong here. And the nobility can't seem to get enough of me.

Titus is nowhere to be seen, but as Flynn and Gabriel escort me down one of the twin staircases, the crowd clears just enough that I spot Will standing in the center of the dance floor, his ivory jacket trimmed with scarlet thread that glitters like gold dust in the candlelight, as if it were imbued with *Manan*.

A few nearby partygoers sigh as Will extends his hand to me, teeth bared in a rare, brilliant smile that reveals dimples in either cheek.

I hesitate as the orchestra begins to play. I try to look up, in the direction of the king, but I can't see past the gilded banister. Still, I know he's watching me. I know this is another test I can't afford to fail.

I take Will's hand, and he pulls me close, his warm fingers gripping my waist with such desperation I have the fleeting thought that he might never let me go again. And as the nobility converge on the dance floor, the music competing with their indulgent laughter, I don't want him to. My fingers grasp his shoulder, clinging to him as if I've been swept away in a flood and he is my only means of staying afloat.

Will's lips brush my ear, his hair tickling my cheek. "The king never intended for you to gain favor with the nobility," he whispers. "You were meant to be a symbol of submission to the humans—nothing more."

I think about Charlie and Lewis—how the king wanted me to see how easy it would be to get to my family, and my gut twists. "What can I do?"

Will exhales, his hot breath on my neck sending shivers down my spine. "Perhaps I can talk Titus into giving you the medallion now. We can arrange passage for you and your family—"

I try to pull away from him, to look him in the eye, but his grip on my waist tightens, almost painfully. A moment later, we reach the edge of the dance floor, and he seizes my wrist, glancing over his shoulder to make sure no one sees us as we dart behind a cluster of potted trees and outside, onto a small balcony overlooking the city beyond.

Will releases me, and I whirl to face him, ready to argue his plan to send me away before we've found a cure, but the soft *tut tut tut* to my right gives me pause.

"*The Shadowslayer*," Titus drawls, pushing off the balcony railing with fluid grace. "I must admit, it has a nice ring to it."

Gentle flurries of snow drift down from the starless sky and land on his golden hair, tousled from the crisp ocean air. Behind him, just beyond the ship-laden waters that separate Castle Grim from the city, the towering spires of Jade sparkle like a glittering tapestry of gilded light, silhouetting him, dressed in all black, in a faint haze of amber radiance.

"Shouldn't you be inside?" I ask.

"Shouldn't you?" he counters, toasting me with the half-drunk bottle in his hands before taking a swig. Red wine stains his lips crimson as he flashes me a teasing smirk. "Guest of honor and all that."

Will clears his throat, shivering against the cold. "We were wrong to bring her here," he says as he moves in front of me, blocking my view of Titus. "It's too risky. The king—"

"Stop!" I step out from behind him, my back to the banister, facing the two of them. "Stop talking about this like it's your decision to make! Stop talking about me as if I'm not right here! Both of you!"

Will's brows lift, as if surprised, but Titus's lip quirks as he takes in the sight of me, my cheeks flushed from the cold, eyes blazing with defiance. My breath catches as his gaze roves the bloodstains on my gown, his expression hardening. Still, I don't back down, my spine straight, teeth clenched.

Chin up, I imagine Flynn would tell me. I lift my head, meeting both of their stares with a measured look that I hope conveys all the determination I feel.

"Even if I wanted to, I can't leave." I hesitate when Titus's jaw tightens, and he looks as if he's bracing himself for what he must know I'm about to say.

"Leo isn't possessed," I declare, and as the words leave me, it's as if a weight lifts from my shoulders, only to settle in my gut.

Titus takes a step back, his brow furrowed as he rubs his bottom lip, eyes glossy with unshed tears. "No," he says softly, and then again, with such conviction his body trembles with the word. "*No*. She has to be. That's *not* Leo. It's—"

"I told you that my ability to see the Sylks might not work," I hurry to add, my chest aching as Titus runs his hands over his face, shaking his head. "But today at the execution, I sensed that Winona was possessed before the Sylk made itself known. I saw the shadow, just as I have before." Gingerly, I step toward him, my voice gentle. "Leo isn't possessed," I repeat.

He laughs, but the sound is cold and cruel, and he turns away from me to face the city, his fists pressed to his eyes. Will places a hand on his shoulder, but Titus shrugs him off.

"Listen to me!" I say quickly, urgently. "I do believe Morana is here. The Changeling, the one from the train station—he attacked me last night. He said—"

Titus whirls, his eyes wild as he looks at me then, emotions flashing in his gaze that I can't even begin to name. His expression turns murderous as he meets Will's stare. "Did you know?"

Will lets out a harsh breath, but before he can say anything, Titus must already have his answer, because he advances another step, within striking distance of Will. And I think, for a moment, that he might plunge his fist through Will's rib cage and pull out his still-beating heart.

"Why didn't you tell me?" he asks, his voice lethally calm.

A muscle in Will's jaw feathers. "I was going to."

Titus's lip curls, and he barks out a sharp laugh. "I'm sure."

For what feels like forever, the two of them remain locked in a tense stare, and I get the feeling Titus wants to say more—that this is about more than just this one secret.

"What did he say?" Titus finally asks, tearing his gaze from Will to look at me, his expression softening, if only a little.

"He's not just any Underling," I tell him, wincing at the sudden ache in my skull. "He's the Shifter who bit me when I was a child." At this, Will's eyes go wide, but I don't stop, afraid I'll never get the chance to say this again. "He told me I won't die from the venom—not unless he wills it." Searing heat stitches across my forehead, but I keep going. "He wants me to leave Castle Grim. I think he knows Morana is here. I think—" I grit my teeth as the pain intensifies, cleaving my head in two. "I think he's the general from the stories, and that he's trying to use me against her for some reason. Don't you see?" I brace my head between my hands, shirking Will's grasp as he reaches for me, backing up until my spine is flush against the cool stone banister. "It's how we find Morana. We use me as bait."

"Absolutely not," Will says with a violent shake of his head. "Look at what's happened today!" He gestures at the ballroom behind us, the music muffled by the thick panes of glass. "You will not put yourself in any more danger."

"It's my life!" I shout, and it's as if the words echo over the waves below, as if the ocean amplifies my voice. I turn to Titus, my jaw set. "We'll keep trying, right? We still have three days until the wedding."

His nostrils flare as he looks at Will, almost apologetic. "I told you she would figure it out on her own."

If it weren't for the banister at my back, I would think I was tumbling, free-falling, plummeting hundreds of feet toward the water below. "What are you talking about?"

"Your ability should allow you to sense Morana," Titus says slowly, carefully. "But your blood..."

Will shoves him, the vein in his forehead bulging. "Don't you dare—"

"Your blood is the only way to draw Morana out," Titus says, not bothering to look at Will as he regains his balance. "A halfling with Shifter venom in her veins—there's a reason Morana sent your brother to collect you. Your blood is valuable to Morana, I'm sure of it. I believe we can persuade her to reveal herself if she thinks she'll have access to it."

Will's hands ball into fists at his sides as he glares at Titus.

"You already knew?" I ask, my voice quiet.

Titus frowns, sorrow creasing his brow. "I hoped Morana would be tempted."

Will huffs, outraged. "If she wants to leave—"

"I'm staying," I say, my gaze never leaving Titus's. "I'm not done here." I turn to Will then, his face falling with defeat. "And neither are you."

I take his face in my hands, and he presses his forehead to mine as his hands come to rest on my hips, holding us both steady. "Please," I whisper. "Let me carry this with you."

A tear slips onto Will's cheek, and without thinking, I press a chaste kiss to Will's skin. At the brief contact, his shoulders slump, his breath catching.

Titus clears his throat.

"Looks like the two of you have some things to sort out," he says, taking another swig from his bottle. "I'll leave you to it."

He slips inside the ballroom without another word, and as I watch him go from over Will's shoulder, an uncomfortable heat singes my cheeks.

I draw back, my hands cupping Will's jaw, imploring him to meet my gaze. "I know you don't like this plan, but I do. He's not giving up," I say, cutting a glance in the direction of the ballroom, where Titus disappeared into the crowd. "Please, don't give up."

Will takes my hands in his, his fingers trembling as he blinks away another tear. "I've known Titus since we were children," he says, the ghost of a smile touching his lips. "He fought for me when I didn't want to fight for myself. He always has, and I'm sure, even after I've turned...he'll keep fighting. It's just who he is."

The raw, tender emotion in his gaze as he tucks a loose strand of hair behind my ear almost cools some of the rage I feel. "Even if you turn—which you *won't*—we can still cure you—"

"You don't understand," Will says. "I'm not like your brother. As a Nightweaver, I've done things—unforgivable things." He worries his bottom lip, looking over my shoulder toward the city beyond. A chill snakes down my spine as his features darken. "If I can't control the bloodlust now..."

My stomach churns at the thought of what Will is capable of—the damage he can inflict if he so chooses. "But you *do* have it under control," I say quietly. "We could—"

"No, I don't," he admits, a frown twisting his features. "Every moment I'm awake, I have to fight the urge to kill. To"—his throat bobs—"to consume."

I don't miss the way he glances at my lips—my neck.

"Even with me?" My words come out on a breath. I don't know why I ask. I don't think I want to know the answer.

His frown deepens. "Especially with you." He takes a step back, creating space between us, and runs a hand through his disheveled hair. "When I turn..."

"You *won't*," I insist, trying to close the gap between us, but he continues his retreat. Some of that rage, just sizzling beneath the surface, comes to a boil. Hot, angry tears well in my eyes. "Why don't you think I can do this?"

"It's not you," he says, looking as if he were about to jump out of his skin. He refuses to look at me. "I believe in you, Aster. More than I've ever believed in anyone. But I don't have much time left, and I don't want you anywhere near me when it happens."

"Don't say things like that," I say, trying—and failing—to keep my voice below a whisper. "You have time. *We* have time. We're going to get the cure—"

"Aster," he breathes, reaching for me.

"No!" I cast off his hand. "It's like…like you've already accepted it! But I can't accept it. I won't. Don't ask me to."

Instantly, I regret pushing him away, because all I want is for him to hold me—to tell me he'll fight until the end. And for a moment, I think he will—think he'll wrap me up in his arms and whisper promises in my ear. But he lowers his hand. Takes another step back. Straightens his lapels.

"I'm not asking you to give up on finding the cure for yourself," he says, his jaw set. "But I never asked for you to save me."

Each word feels like a death blow. *I never asked for you to save me.* He might as well have told me that I *can't* save him.

And I don't like to be told what I can and cannot do.

I don't need to be saved—I never have. Will knows that. But we were supposed to do this together. Only, there never truly has been a "together" for Will and me. This whole time, he's known he would die. Every moment we've spent together—every night spent beneath the stars in the conservatory. He knew. He always knew. And even if we manage to find the cure—even if I can still save him—what kind of life could we have together? Surely, he can't see a future with me when the law forbids us to love—to marry.…

Unless I kill the king and abolish the law that prevents our kind from being together, it won't matter if Will is cured. He will still be a Nightweaver of noble birth.

And I will always be a pirate.

Inside, trumpets blare, signaling the start of the feast. Will breathes a heavy sigh as he takes one last look at the lights of Jade and extends his hand to me.

"I don't want to fight with you," he says, his voice rough. "Come, before we're missed."

I take his hand, but as he leads me back inside, for the first time since our paths crossed all those months ago, his touch is cold.

CHAPTER TWENTY-THREE

Tick. Tick. Tick. I feel the seconds slipping through my fingers like water as Will escorts me to one of the tables along the outskirts of the dance floor, where Killian and the Castor family have taken their seats. He pulls out the chair to his right, between him and Annie, who seems to shrink in her seat, glum and reserved and nothing like the cheerful, outgoing little girl I met all those months ago. And while Will immediately strikes up a conversation with Killian, as if our argument on the balcony never happened, I decide to show him I'm not the least bit affected by turning to Annie, who could use a friendly chat more than even I could.

"Oh, good," I say, offering her a conspiratorial smile as I cut a glance at Henry, drinking lazily across the table. "I thought they were going to put me next to Henry, again."

This seems to get Henry's attention, but he must see what I'm trying to do, because he carries on as if he didn't hear me mention him.

Annie peeks up at me through a curtain of dark curls. "I thought you were friends?" she asks, somewhat sleepily.

"Oh, sure." I wink at Henry, lowering my voice to a whisper as I lean in toward Annie. "But he chews awfully loud."

Annie giggles. "He does, doesn't he?"

Henry's eyes narrow, but then he sticks his tongue out at Annie, and the three of us share a brief moment of simple joy before the trumpets blare once more and the king raises his glass from where he stands on the landing above.

My heart twists when I glance at Annie to find she's staring down at her lap, her posture rigid. I think of my sister Elsie when I take her hand, giving it a gentle squeeze—the kind of reassurance that says *I'm here, you're not alone* without having to say anything at all.

Annie squeezes back, tight enough that I don't let go.

King Calix welcomes the assembly to the feast as Titus and Leo take their seats on either side of Queen Calantha at their table overlooking the ballroom. I struggle to see Titus's face from where I sit, but I note the bottle in his grasp.

He knew this entire time he planned to use my blood to draw Morana out—planned to use me as bait. And rather than feel angry at him for it, I'm more frustrated that I didn't think of it first.

"...the Shadowslayer," the king says, and the sudden uproar of applause snaps me out of my thoughts. "Stand, Dame Oberon, and accept this great honor."

Great honor?

This time, Annie squeezes *my* hand, as if to reassure me that I'm not alone, either. Still, as I get to my feet, my heart throbbing in my chest, I stand alone. I stare up at the king, looking down on me from above, alone. It's as if everyone else has simply vanished and the king and I are the only two people in this room. Him, on his gilded dais. Me, in my bloodstained armor.

"I had planned to wait, but after your heroic display of bravery in the throne room today, the queen has urged me to act now, on this very night," the king says smoothly. He smiles, but it doesn't reach his bleak, lifeless eyes. "Following the wedding on Holy Winter's Day, I have arranged for you to lead a troop of soldiers to the border of Hellion, where you will represent the Eerie within the League of Seven in the ongoing fight against the Underlings."

I feel the ghost of a dagger pierce my heart. Feel it twist.

The nobility cheer for the Shadowslayer, but their voices, distorted and warbling in my ears as the blood rushes to my head, sound like the macabre toll of a death knell. And because the king has just called for my execution, he thinks he's won this round. But for an Oberon, death is the only defeat. And I'm not dead yet.

"Thank you, Your Majesty," I say, my voice clear and strong, because I know something the king does not.

I have rendered my own judgment. On Holy Winter's Day, I will claim *his* head.

And so my hands do not tremble as I'm swarmed by the nobility, and I smile when Nightweavers, clad in finery as pure as snow, pledge to support me from abroad, as children Elsie's and Albert's age push and shove their way through the crowd for a chance to speak with the Shadowslayer, the king's new prized soldier.

It's only when the king and queen have said their farewells for the evening, and we're dismissed from the ballroom, that I feel Will's familiar touch at the small of my back.

"That's enough," he says, his deep voice rich with laughter as he dismisses a group of children that encircled me all throughout dinner. "You'll have plenty more chances to speak with Dame Oberon before she begins her journey."

The moment he pulls me away from the crowd, my body begins to shake, and I tell myself to hold it together long enough to make it back to my suite. He must sense my overwhelm, because he rubs little circles into my spine, tucking me close to his side. He politely declines every bid for conversation, from dignitaries and courtiers and high-ranking officers, and gratitude for Will swells in my chest. Despite our disagreement on the balcony, I hold on to the promise of his arms around me, the thought of whispered apologies and sprigs of blue salvia and stolen moments under the stars as he leads me through the ballroom.

We've almost made it to the doors when the two girls from the night before—Clemson and Davina Mercer—practically throw themselves at Will, clearly having had one too many glasses of wine during the feast.

"Oh, Lord Castor!" one shrieks. "You simply must show us the gardens—"

"Please!" the other chortles, talking over her sister. "Mummy won't let us explore the castle on our own."

"We'll be forever in your debt," her sister adds, batting her eyelashes.

There's a brief moment where Will appears conflicted, the muscles in his arm tensing. *He's going to say no*, I think. He wouldn't leave me alone at a time like this—would he? But the way he transforms—his grin, the playful quirk of his brows—leaves me wondering how many times he's put on an act with *me*.

"If you'll excuse me," he says, effectively dismissing me as he removes my hand from his arm and instead offers himself as escort to the two giggling courtiers.

It feels as if the floor gives way beneath me.

I'm almost too stunned to move, to speak, when a familiar, lilting voice says, "Just the girl I was looking for."

Titus offers his arm to me, and I don't hesitate to take it, allowing him to lead me out of the ballroom, away from Will and those two obnoxious courtiers.

"I must admit," Titus says as he leads me up the winding staircase, away from the great hall and the rest of the nobility. His breath reeks of liquor, but beneath it, clinging to his jacket, his hair, the warm, familiar scent of sea brine calms my breathing, settles my racing heart. And his rhythmic voice, albeit slurred from one too many drinks, reminds me of hushed lullabies hummed on moonlit nights at sea. "I haven't felt this jealous of Will since we were children and his parents bought him a pet rabbit for his birthday."

I try to picture Will as a child, celebrating with his family, but all I can think is that if we can't find the cure, in three days, Will's birthday is the day he is doomed to turn into a Shifter. The thought causes my chest to ache, but not only because of Will's curse. Even if things were different, it's hard to imagine standing beside Will on his birthday. Would his family throw him a party? Would I be forced to watch as giggling courtiers draped themselves on his arm while I planned a secret rendezvous with him in the conservatory?

"Ah, well," I say, taking the lead as we emerge onto my floor. I find my pace quickening as my door comes into view, wishing I could simply lock myself inside and hide from the world until I'm forced to rejoin it tomorrow morning. I find it strange that the hall is empty—Charlie and Lewis are supposed to be here, standing guard, waiting for me to return from dinner—but all I can think about is Will's arms around someone who isn't me—the way he abandoned me with such ease. "Clemson and Davina *are* rather beautiful."

Titus laughs, shaking his head. He sounds just as bitter as I feel. "I don't envy the things he does for the sake of the Order," he says, and suddenly his expression is serious, his gaze capturing mine as he takes a step toward me, backing me against my door. "And you should know—William only has eyes for you."

It's as if the butterflies in my stomach can't seem to find it in themselves to take flight. I should be thrilled, but shouldn't Will have told me that himself?

Titus places a hand on the doorframe, crouching so that he's almost eye level with me. His teeth work at his bottom lip, and his eyes narrow on the space just above my head before drifting down, landing briefly on my mouth, only to find my gaze once more. "I'm jealous because I'd give anything to have you by my side at every ball."

The admission hangs in the air between us, encroaching on the oxygen until every breath I take is heady with an emotion I can't define.

"You're drunk," I breathe.

"And wicked." He hums, his lips hovering near mine. "After all, what kind of vile, despicable monster says something like that to his best friend's girl, hmm?"

I think, for a moment, that this is the least of his crimes. The image of blood running down his chin, a human heart in his clutches, turns my stomach. But if Titus is a monster because he's been forced to commit unspeakable acts of violence, then what does that make me? As a pirate, I've done whatever it takes to protect my family—killed without mercy to ensure their safety. It's the reason I'm here, the reason I have submitted myself to the same cruel king whom Titus is obligated by birth to serve—the reason I was prepared to kill Winona, even before I knew she was possessed by a Sylk. And I don't regret my choices. I know who I am—what I'm willing to do for the people I love.

Everything I've seen of Titus since my arrival here—everything he's done as the Reaper—has been an act. But this—the way he's looking at me, his blue eyes sparkling with hope—feels real... right. Even though I know it's wrong. Even though I know he wouldn't have said any of this if he were sober.

"Well," I whisper, "now I know what to get you for your birthday."

He leans in, lips so close to mine. "And that is?"

"A pet rabbit."

His lip quirks. "If only wars were fought and won by humor alone." He pushes off the doorframe, but he doesn't take a step back. He lifts his hand once more, as if to touch the scar that cuts across my throat, before letting it fall back to his side, his expression one of barely contained fury. "Tomorrow night," he says, his voice dropping to a whisper, "after dinner, I'll meet you here. We've already lost one evening to a...*disagreement*," he adds with a pointed look, "and the sooner you learn to control your affinity, the better. Once we've cured your curses, we'll need your power to turn the tides in the Order's favor."

Two evenings have come and gone, and we're no closer to finding a cure than we were before we came here.

"Why not tonight, then? Why not now?" I don't want him to go, but I can't say that, and I know it's probably best he go now, while I'm still angry with Will and clearly unable to think rationally.

His jaw tightens, and he looks away. "I'm needed elsewhere."

I think about Leo, and I wonder if whatever he has to do involves the princess of Hellion. I know how he feels about their engagement, but after tonight—knowing that she isn't possessed by Morana—will his feelings for her change? It shouldn't make me feel sick to my stomach to think of the two of them together, taking a midnight stroll in the gardens or venturing into the city on horseback. Maybe, I tell myself, it's because I wish I could do those things with Will.

That must be it.

"Good night, Titus," I say, turning the knob and taking a step inside my room.

He doesn't make a move to leave, standing as still as a statue, as if he was debating something that robbed him of any proper ability to reason. A crease forms between his brows, his expression pained—sad, even. "Good night, love."

I shut the door, resting my forehead against it, waiting for what feels like hours before his footsteps fade down the hall.

"I don't know what you've gotten yourself into," Margaret says, her voice stirring me from my daze, "but you need to come with me."

I turn, then, noting the urgency in her voice. Immediately, I search her face, her arms, her body for any sign of injury, but she looks fine, other than the pleading expression that twists her mouth into a frown.

"What is it?" I ask. "Is someone hurt?"

Margaret hesitates, and my heart leaps into my throat. "Everyone's fine." She sighs. "It's Mother," she says. "She's called a family meeting."

CHAPTER TWENTY-FOUR

I follow Margaret through the servants' passageways—dark stone tunnels that make the dimly lit corridors of Bludgrave Manor seem warm and inviting. My thoughts spiral, and I brace myself for what's waiting for me at the end of this maze, but I don't dare ask Margaret any questions for fear that someone could be waiting just around every corner, listening to our conversation.

If Mother has called a family meeting—if she sent Margaret to retrieve me—something must be seriously wrong. She wouldn't risk casting suspicion on Charlie, Lewis, and me for no reason. Because if someone were to pass by my room and notice my guards aren't at their post, and worse, if they were to knock and find that I'm wandering the castle unattended, without permission...

I walk faster, nearly racing Margaret toward an unknown destination.

After half an hour of descending staircases, abrupt turns, and long stretches of hallway, Margaret comes to a halt in front of a stone door. She turns to face me then, though I struggle to make out her face in the darkness. She looks as if she wants to say something, but she shakes her head, apparently thinking better of it, and pushes open the door.

Margaret leads me out into the abandoned kitchens, and I have to fight the urge to stop and look around, following my sister to the wooden door at the far side of the room. She checks over her shoulder before waving me inside a massive storeroom and closes the door behind us.

"Well?" I ask, feeling my way through the dark.

"This way," Margaret says, and I follow the sound of her voice. She tugs at my gown, pulling me down to my knees beside her. She moves a barrel of potatoes to the side and pushes on a loose piece of stone. The wall gives way to a tunnel barely big enough to crawl through.

"You first," she says.

I gape at the hidden passageway. "How—"

"Ask me again when we're not hiding in the king's pantry."

"Right," I mutter, starting down the tunnel, "just hiding somewhere in the castle walls, apparently."

In the dark, it seems as if the passageway goes on forever. Margaret stays close behind, our labored breathing and the scuff of stone the only sounds in the dank crawl space, until—

"Mouse!" Margaret squeaks, and an instant later, a tiny brown mouse squeezes past me, disappearing farther down the tunnel.

I chuckle as Margaret curses under her breath. Finally, somewhere in the distance, muffled voices break up the silence.

"...door, Jack," someone says.

A few feet in front of me, the pitch blackness gives way to a circle of warm amber light. Jack appears, framed by the stone, Albert and Elsie pushing against him on either side as if vying to get a glimpse of us.

My heart squeezes at the sight of my youngest siblings' bright, cheerful faces. Jack helps me to my feet as I emerge from the tunnel, and before I've gained my balance, Elsie and Albert throw their arms around me, chattering endlessly about everything they've seen since their arrival. I'm thankful that from their perspective, this seems like a grand adventure.

I want it to stay that way.

"I don't think I realized how tall you've gotten!" I say, mussing Albert's dirty-blond hair. I always thought Albert looked the most like Owen—like our father—and the resemblance makes my heart ache.

"Don't tell him that," Charlie says, his back against the stone wall of what appears to be a small study. "He already thinks he can take me in a fight."

Albert snorts. "Because I can."

Jack mediates the inevitable arm wrestling match between Albert and Charlie as I take in my surroundings. Maps decorate the torchlit walls and clutter the long wooden table at the center of the cramped space. Mother stands at the head of the table, dressed in the black-and-white-striped apron of a laundress, stray curls sticking to her sweat-slicked face. She points at a region of a map while Lewis nods intently, the two of them so engulfed in their conversation that it's as if they didn't notice our arrival.

In the corner of the room, Killian stands over a crate, holding a raggedy stuffed lion.

"Killian?"

His gaze snaps to me, as if I jarred him from a memory. "Oh, good." His shoulders sag a little. "The others should be along any minute now."

At that moment, Lord and Lady Bludgrave emerge from the passageway, followed by Henry, who looks as if he were trampled by a horse—and smells like it, too.

"Lovely to see you," Henry says, planting a kiss on my cheek, his honeyed, peppermint breath like a jolt to my senses. He offers an exaggerated bow to Margaret. "Miss Oberon."

Margaret rolls her eyes.

"Welcome," Mother says, finally looking up from her maps to greet the new arrivals. "We're just waiting on a few more."

A crease forms between Lord Bludgrave's brows as he takes in his surroundings, brushing the dust from his suit. "Bless the Maker!" he says. "Killian? What is the meaning of this?"

Lady Isabelle places a hand on her husband's arm, her gaze calculating as she meets my mother's eyes from the opposite end of the table. "My apologies, Grace," she says. "My brother didn't tell us you'd be joining our meeting."

"Not *our* meeting," Killian says, the ghost of a smirk playing on his lips. "*Her* meeting."

Lord Bludgrave's face reddens as he looks between Killian and Mother. "But—you—how—"

I look at Charlie's and Lewis's faces, too—note the surprise and confusion there. So they have no idea why Mother's called us here, either.

"Yes," Mother answers, smiling slightly. "Killian and I decided you would be more willing to meet if he invited you, rather than I."

When it seems that Lord Bludgrave may finally form a complete sentence, the passageway opens once more and Flynn and Eliza Cooper emerge. I hardly have a moment to process their arrival as Tollith—the bespectacled badger I last saw in the kitchen of Bludgrave Manor—tumbles into the room after them, followed by Sybil, who looks even younger and more timid than she ever did at Bludgrave. Not far behind, a pink orb of light flies past Sybil and darts straight for me.

"Liv!" I giggle as the pixie presses her forehead to mine.

She perches on my shoulder, kicking her legs as we all pause, listening to the scuffle of clothing as one final guest makes their way through the tunnel. My stomach flips when the flickering light reflects off Will's dark hair.

Earlier this evening, all I wanted was to be alone with Will, but now, as he crawls out of the passageway and rises to his full height, acting as if I'm not standing two feet away as he surveys the inhabitants of the room, I'm thankful for Margaret, standing by my side, and the stable presence of my family.

Will smooths his lapels. There's something about the way he closes the door behind him, the sureness of his surroundings—no keen perusal of the map-laden walls, no curious glance at the crates stacked in the corner—that leads me to believe he's been here before. "I don't suppose we're gathered here for after-dinner drinks?"

"I'm afraid not," Killian says, dropping the stuffed lion on the crate and taking his place at the end of the table beside Mother, who looks every bit a captain, her chin raised high as she meets the gaze of each individual gathered around the table with a measured look.

"We don't have much time," Mother says, her eyes softening when her gaze lands on Charlie, Lewis, Elsie, and Albert gathered to her right. "I should have told you sooner, but the time wasn't right." She cuts a glance at me, where I stand between Margaret and Henry, the latter leaning on me for support. "Long before you were born, your father and I joined an organization known by many as the Order of Hildegarde."

Charlie's eyes narrow. "An *organization*?"

Lewis nods slowly as he looks about the room. "You're all rebels, aren't you?"

Eliza winks at him. "Pirate, rebel—I'd say we're one and the same, honey."

Lord Bludgrave scoffs, which earns a laugh from Flynn.

"After everything," the Bloodknight says, "you still don't like to think of yourself as a rebel, do you?"

Killian clears his throat before Lord Bludgrave can argue. "Gentlemen, please," he says. "You're going to want to pay attention."

Lewis eyes me suspiciously. "You knew," he says, jerking his chin at Margaret. "Both of you."

Margaret shakes her head. "I didn't know about Mother and Father."

"Neither did I," I say, imploring Mother to meet my stare, but she watches Albert and Elsie, her mouth pressed in a tight line. "Our parents kept plenty of secrets from us all, it would seem."

Mother smiles sadly. "We did what we had to do to protect you," she says, finally meeting my eyes, and instantly I feel as if this is far too private a moment to be had in the presence of so many outsiders.

"I don't understand," Elsie says. "Why is everyone so upset?" Her quiet voice sounds so young, so fragile, and a sudden rush of anger overcomes me as I realize what Mother intends to do.

"No," I say, slamming a hand down on the table. Mother and I stand on opposite ends of the room, and for the first time in my life, I feel as if we're on opposing sides of a battlefield. "You will not recruit them. This isn't their fight."

"It most certainly is," Mother says, her demeanor as calm as ever—which in this moment only serves to infuriate me. "It always has been."

"Why now?" I ask, my throat painfully tight. "Why wait until Father is dead to finally *do* something?" Tears streak my face, but the rage within me will not be sated. "You knew—you knew about all of this—and you let me face it alone!"

Mother frowns. "Oh, Aster," she says, fixing me with a look that makes me feel childish and weak. "You've never been alone. Not even for a moment."

Lord Bludgrave huffs. "This is absurd," he says, adjusting his cravat. "As a senior member of the Order, if Philip and Grace Oberon were sympathetic to the cause, surely we would have been made aware."

"Silas, I wouldn't—" Killian starts, but Mother raises a hand, and he falls silent.

"It's all right," she says to him before squaring her shoulders at Lord Bludgrave. "The Elite have always thought it best to keep my and Philip's identities a secret. Your clearance didn't warrant this level of disclosure."

Lord Bludgrave's face reddens. "My clearance? I beg your pardon, ma'am, but I find it hard to believe that the Elite would keep the identities of two pirates a secret from the senior members of the Order, especially when you were living under *our* roof!"

Lady Isabelle's eyes crinkle as if she were laughing, but her voice comes out on a breath. "Killian, your message said you'd received new information from Dawnrender." She cocks her head at Mother. "Maker of All," she whispers. "How did I not see it before?"

I've only ever seen Mother smirk on certain occasions—when she knew she was about to win at cards, when an enemy was seconds away from surrender, or when she knew she proved Father wrong in a petty argument. Now, her lips twitch, the makings of a wry grin, and I feel as if she's about to strike a match to ignite a flame that will consume us all.

"Each of you were called here tonight because the Order considers your cooperation vitally important to our cause moving forward," Mother says, rolling up her sleeve to reveal the tattoo of a winged dagger; only, hers is slightly different. Inked down the center of the blade is a single word—a name. "You have known me as Grace Oberon." She sticks her hand out in Lord Bludgrave's direction, as if waiting for him to shake it. "But you may call me Dawnrender."

CHAPTER TWENTY-FIVE

Dawnrender. My mother is Dawnrender.

I watch Will, attempt to gauge his expression. The only hint of surprise I detect is the slight widening of his eyes. But any shock he may feel quickly gives way to a look of amusement, his gaze narrowed with that calculating intelligence that he and his uncle seem to share—as if he's already one step ahead of everyone else in the room or knows something he shouldn't. It's both captivating and unnerving, and at this very moment, it feels almost...dangerous.

"Dawnrender," Will says, squeezing between Henry and me, placing himself a half step in front of me.

He fixes Killian with an inquisitive look. "How long have you known?"

Killian's expression is part exhaustion, part relief. "I've known—" He sighs, pinching the bridge of his nose between his forefinger and thumb. "I *knew* Philip Oberon since we were young. About your age, actually."

The somewhat civil conversation gives way to chaos, everyone speaking at once. Sybil shifts uncomfortably—I almost forgot she was in the room, but I notice her now, scratching at her arm where the tattoo of the winged dagger peeks out from beneath her sleeve. Eliza stands to the right of Sybil, and I try to focus on whatever it is she says to Lord Bludgrave, but her voice fades beneath the pounding of a thousand drums in my ears.

Mother isn't just a member of the Order—she's an *Elite* member. She must have known when I joined, but she never said anything. She never tried to help me. Surely, it wasn't a coincidence we ended up at Bludgrave Manor. Did Mother know Will would offer us employment? Did she plan for us to be captured? Was Owen's death an accident—collateral damage she didn't account for? Or did she know about the Sylks—know I would hunt down my brother's killer, and that everything would lead us here, to this moment?

Father's compass weighs heavily in my pocket, like an anchor threatening to drag me to the depths of the sea.

Lie after lie after lie—all from the person I trusted the most. And now she's right in front of me—she's finally revealed herself, but she's done it in a room full of people, and in such a way that it's as if she expects me to just...accept it. As if I can accept that everything I've ever known about her is a lie. And worse— everything I ever knew about Father is a lie, too.

Because I know, now, what I only suspected before. Mother is the reason I have Nightweaver blood in my veins. And though Owen claimed our siblings didn't possess an affinity, because I'm a bloodletter and Owen a windwalker, I can only assume that somewhere in our family tree, we came from a line of nobility.

The information feels as if it opens a chasm within me too wide to cross. Especially not here. Especially not now.

Because Mother isn't the only guilty party in this room.

Charlie looks between Mother and Killian, his hand clutching his chest as if he were physically wounded. "All this time?" he says. "You've known each other all this time, and you pretended—you never—"

"I don't believe this!" Lord Bludgrave huffs, looking to his wife as if she could give him an answer that would satisfy him, but she merely shakes her head.

"I didn't know," Lady Isabelle says, but her eyes glitter with something akin to admiration as she turns to Mother. "My brother has always been a rather talented actor."

"Might have had a future in the theater, too," Killian says dryly, curling his mustache, "if it weren't for the war."

The pressure in my head builds, and I push past Will, bracing both hands on the edge of the table, a map crinkling beneath my palms. "Enough! How is anyone supposed to believe anything you say? Even now, you won't tell them the truth! You won't tell *me* the truth!"

"Aster," Will whispers, the warmth of his hand on my lower back seeping through the fabric of my gown, melting like butter down my spine. It's as if I lose my will to be angry with him when he's this close, even though my frustration with him lingers somewhere at the back of my mind, nagging at me despite the calm that floods my veins. "Now's not the time."

"The time for what?" Margaret asks, crossing her arms. She looks at me, then at Mother. "What else haven't you told us?"

Mother shakes her head. "William is right," she says, her tone firm. "I didn't call you here to discuss private family matters." I feel the admonishment in her words like a slap to the face, but her gaze is soft, almost apologetic when she looks at me. "There are sinister forces at work, and we have little time."

She turns to my siblings then, her expression patient. At once, I feel as if I'm a child, listening to her spin stories about the Stars of legend on the moon-washed deck of our family's ship. "You all know the tales of Hildegarde, a powerful Sorceress who possessed the power of the Lightbringer—dominion over all creation, gifted to her from the True King himself."

Dominion over all creation. During my lessons with Killian, I asked time and again what the power of the Lightbringer entailed, but he was never forthcoming with his answers. Now, it's as if the moment Mother says the words, something deep within me cranes forward, listening....

"Morana, driven by jealousy, killed Hildegarde and took the power of the Lightbringer," Mother continues. "But it has long been believed that before Hildegarde was slain, she passed a portion of the Lightbringer's power on to her first heir, hindering Morana from having the means to use the full power of the Lightbringer. For years, the Order has bided its time, waiting for Morana to leave her throne in Havok to slay the heir of Hildegarde, taking the full power for herself. I've spent the past few months gathering information that has led me to believe that time has come." She straightens, and I can almost picture her standing behind the helm of the *Lightbringer*, bathed in sunlight. "Morana is here."

"Here?" Lord Bludgrave sputters. "In the Eerie?"

"Not just the Eerie," Killian says, pointing at the map—at Jade. "Here, as in Castle Grim."

I feel Will tense beside me.

"Why now?" I ask, blood pounding in my ears. "And why here?"

I can't help but wonder if Titus's suspicions are correct—that Morana has come here for me, for my blood. My eyes narrow on Mother, but her expression gives nothing away.

"We believe Morana is searching for something," Mother says. "Something she believes will give her the strength she needs to slay the heir."

My heart beats faster. "Like what?"

Mother grimaces, lifting her chin. "Everyone who needs to know already does."

I stagger backward a step, feeling as if I've been punched in the gut. Heat creeps into my cheeks when I realize no one will look at me, not even Killian. I clench my fists. After everything I've done—joining the Bloodknights, risking my life by putting myself in the king's sights—I'm not important enough to know a crucial piece of the Order's plans? My *mother's* plans?

Tollith coughs, and Killian retrieves a crate from the corner, placing it beside him at the table. The badger climbs onto the crate, trembling slightly. "It hasn't been confirmed," he says, his voice shaking. "But we have reason to suspect Morana has chosen a member of the nobility as a vessel."

I knew it! It takes everything in me to fight the overwhelming urge to find Titus and tell him there's still hope—that he might have been wrong about Leo, but there's still a chance, and the Order is now working toward the same goal of exposing Morana.

Lord Bludgrave looks as if his head might explode. "Where did you receive this information? I demand to know who—"

Flynn clears his throat. "My brother and I have overheard some things," he says, "through some old... *sources*."

"This is outrageous!" Lord Bludgrave points a finger in Flynn's direction, his eyes wild as he looks at Killian. "The Cooper family are known Underling sympathizers! You know what he did to his family—to his own parents!" He looks at Mother then, his expression almost pleading. "Grace, please. I implore you to see reason. Whatever this man has told you, he's—"

"I *did* work for the Guild of Shadows," Flynn says, his teeth gritted. "But only because my parents offered me up in exchange for protection from the Underling regime."

Lord Bludgrave's fists clench at his sides. "How do we know you aren't spying for the Underlings at this very moment?" He takes a step toward Flynn, who stands his ground, looking wholly unbothered by the interrogation. "Do you really expect me to believe you're working against the Underlings?"

The Bloodknight's jaw tightens, the only indication of his annoyance. "And what about you?" Flynn says, staring Lord Bludgrave down. "How do we know you're not a spy?"

"Enough," Mother interrupts, her tone firm. "Each of you has something to contribute to the Order's efforts moving forward, and we will all have to cooperate if we're to have any chance at turning the tides of this war." She turns to my siblings then. "Your father would have wanted to be here—he would have wanted to ask you himself." She smiles, her eyes glistening with tears. "I know that I have asked you to fight your entire lives. But this time, the choice is yours. Will you stand with us? Will you fight for freedom not only for yourselves and for your family, but for all those who cannot fight for themselves?"

Charlie straightens, and Albert follows suit, rolling his shoulders and trying to make himself as tall as he possibly can. Elsie skirts in front of Lewis, standing at attention. Lewis glances at me, his eyes narrowed, as if waiting for me to give him any sort of indication that he should walk away.

But how can I expect any of them to walk away when I've done just the opposite?

He must see the answer in my eyes, because he nods. "Whatever it takes," Lewis says, offering his arm to Mother.

Mother takes a deep, shuddering breath, and I note the tremble of her chin even as she stands a bit straighter, her look of approval enough to inspire me to battle at this very moment.

A reverent silence falls over the room as Killian administers the enchantment, marking each of their arms—first Charlie, then Lewis, then Albert, and finally, Elsie. My jaw clenches when the ink appears on Elsie's forearm.

"Now that that's settled," Mother says, strictly business once again—as if she didn't just recruit her own children to be soldiers in a violent war. "We've much to discuss, and it's only a matter of time before someone comes looking for any one of you."

Elsie leans forward, her chin barely at the height of the table, eager to listen to whatever secrets Mother is about to share, and even though I hate that she's here at all, I can't help but feel pride for the way she's adjusting to this new information so quickly.

A pirate, I think. *Through and through.*

"Silas, Isabelle," Mother says, the torchlight flickering in her fierce gaze. "Many of your kind are sympathetic to the cause—we just need to give them the push they require to make the switch. Your sway with the nobility will be invaluable in the coming days." She turns to Eliza then. "You as well, Miss Cooper."

Eliza does a sort of mock curtsy. "It would be my pleasure."

Lord Bludgrave clears his throat. "I mean no disrespect," he says to Mother, appearing, for the first time, genuinely dutiful. "I have fought for this cause since I was merely sixteen years old. I have served the Order faithfully and will continue to do so until my dying breath. However," he adds, cutting a glance at the Coopers, "before I agree to do anything, I'd be interested to know exactly what it is the Elite have planned for all of us."

Mother dips her head. "Of course." She points at the map—at the waters surrounding Castle Grim. "Three days from now, on Holy Winter's Day, a fleet of a thousand ships will invade the Eerie's naval territory, launching an attack on Castle Grim the likes of which hasn't been seen in over six hundred years."

Lord Bludgrave's face goes slack. "A thousand ships? But how—"

"Pirates!" Eliza gasps. She giggles at Mother's nod of approval. "Finally, some action!"

"Yes," Mother says. "One thousand pirating crews will band together to reign fire down on this castle, creating chaos in the wake of Prince Titus's wedding and ensuring a swift surrender of power from Calix Anteres."

I shake my head, staring at the dark structure on the map. "Why Holy Winter's Day? And why now? If the Elite has access to a fleet of a thousand ships—if that many of our people have agreed to join the cause and fight—then why wait?"

Mother cocks her head, and I know that look in her eye—the same look she got when she quizzed us on battle strategy aboard the *Lightbringer*. "When we strike—when this kingdom falls—the Known World will look at the Eerie. Kingdoms like Fell and Nera will wait for the opportunity to invade. We have to be strategic about how we handle the transfer of power, don't you agree?"

All eyes find me, but I don't shrink away from their scrutiny, because I think I finally know what Mother has planned. "And by the transfer of power, you mean Titus and Leo will assume the throne."

"But the alliance with Hellion—" Will starts.

"Not with Hellion," Mother interrupts. "With its princess."

Will's jaw twitches. "We were told—"

"You were told only what you needed to know at the time," Mother says, and I can't help that small part of me that thinks, *Doesn't feel good to be left in the dark, does it?* "We have reason to believe Princess Leonora could be sympathetic to our cause."

"Says who?" Lord Bludgrave asks, his eyes narrowing.

Killian sighs. "Members of the Order in Hellion say the princess has been known to aid humans. A maid of hers says she overheard the princess expressing her discontent with the way humans and Myths have been treated."

Lord Bludgrave scoffs. "We're supposed to risk everything because of something some maid thinks she heard?"

Mother quirks a brow at Lord Bludgrave, but she doesn't acknowledge him further. Instead, she turns to me. "You'll have access to the princess in the gathering Prince Titus has arranged for you to attend in the Queen's Court. Befriend her. Gain her trust. It's crucial that you sway her to our side before the festival ends."

I don't tell Mother I was already instructed to befriend the princess, but for a very different reason. Instead, I nod—ever loyal, ever obedient, despite everything.

Mother gives a slight nod of approval. "Once Princess Leonora and Prince Titus are wed, and they have access to the wards surrounding Castle Grim, together—with their combined magic—they will have the power to bring those wards down. In the aftermath of the battle, Prince Titus and Princess Leonora will assume the throne, and the Eerie will become the first kingdom in six hundred years to liberate humans and Myths."

"It will also become a civil war zone," I add, glancing at Killian, who stares at the map before him, his brow furrowed. "What of the nobility who refuse to fall in line? What of the soldiers who remain loyal to the League of Seven?"

Flynn folds his arms over his chest. "The rebels outnumber them. Any unrest will be short lived. After the initial battle, we'll bring the insurgency into submission in under a week."

I study Killian's expression—his eyes lost in thought as he strokes his mustache. "Is that true?" I ask.

The wrinkle in Killian's forehead deepens, but he nods. "Once we've liberated the Eerie, rebels throughout the Known World will see that it's possible to fight back." He meets my gaze then, his eyes ablaze with an emotion I can't put into words, but that I feel even now—rage, determination, hope, boiled down into something raw and vicious and all-consuming. "It's only a matter of time until Morana grows in strength, enabling her to find the heir of Hildegarde and seize the power she lacks. Right now, we have a rare opportunity to find Morana first and stop her. But, if we fail, and Nightweavers, humans, and Myths refuse to unite, we don't stand a chance against the Underlings. The world as we know it will cease to exist, and everything in it will fall under Morana's dominion."

A chill skitters down my spine, and for a moment, no one speaks.

"So what now?" It's Jack who finally breaks the tension, clutching his cap to his chest. "Whatever you need me to do, I'll do it gladly, ma'am."

Mother smiles softly. "Thank you, Jack." She smooths her hands over the map, and I feel the same flourish of excitement I used to get when Mother would assign my siblings and me "duties" for our next battle. My feelings of hurt and betrayal aside, it's a relief to know I'm not on my own here. That there *is* a plan, and that in three days, all this will have been worth it.

Unless Leo really *is* the noble possessed by Morana.

I almost speak up—almost say something to that effect—when Will takes my hand in his, giving it a gentle squeeze, and a feeling of calm settles over me. As Mother explains the details of Lord and Lady Bludgrave's roles over the next few days, Will bends down, his lips brushing my ear. "Not here."

Next to Eliza, Flynn watches me uneasily, his gaze narrowing on Will, and I'm struck with a realization that ties my stomach into knots.

What if the spy Killian and Will have been looking for is in this room?

Surely, if it was Dawnrender who fed the Order false information to root them out, she wouldn't choose to share such confidential information with a group like this. Now, if the spy *is* present, they'll know of the Order's plan to attack on Holy Winter's Day.

They'll know of our plan to sway Leo to our cause. They'll know that my little brother and sister are rebels—easy targets to be used for ransom, or bargaining chips, or worse.

"Sybil," Mother addresses the timid maid. Again, Sybil was so quiet, so impassive, that I might have thought she already left the room. "I'm trusting you to watch over Elsie while the two of you complete your chores around the castle."

Elsie groans. "I can take care of myself!"

"And *you* will watch over Sybil," Mother adds, running a hand through Elsie's blond hair. "The two of you will have perhaps one of the most important jobs—and also the most dangerous."

My mouth opens at the very moment Will gives my hand another gentle squeeze, and the words die out on my tongue.

"Sybil, Elsie," Mother says, "you're to be my eyes and ears in this castle. Listen while you sweep, observe the nobility while you tend hearths and empty wastebaskets. At the end of the day, you'll report everything you hear and see to me."

Sybil nods vigorously. "Yes, ma'am!"

Eliza glances at Sybil, her eyes narrowing slightly, but it's as if she notices me staring, because a moment later she smiles at the young maid, even offering to aid the two girls in any way she can.

"Henry?" Mother asks, attempting to look at something over my shoulder.

I turn to find Henry slumped against the wall in the corner, snoring softly.

Splotches of red blossom on Lord Bludgrave's cheeks, and Lady Isabelle brings a hand to her forehead, letting out a weary sigh.

"I've got him," Jack says. "Albert, mind giving me a hand?"

But as Jack bends down, Henry comes awake with a start, his

fist flying before he's even gained his footing. His knuckles connect with Jack's jaw, a loud *pop* echoing throughout the cramped room.

I recognize the terror in Henry's bleary eyes as he takes in his surroundings—as he looks down at Jack, struggling to pick himself up off the floor.

Margaret rushes to Jack's side. "You idiot!" she huffs at Henry, examining Jack's face. "You've dislocated his jaw!"

Will exhales sharply through his nose, crouching beside Margaret. "This will hurt," he tells Jack before placing a hand on his jaw.

Another loud *pop* causes me to wince, and Jack lets out a string of curses.

"Better?" Will asks.

Jack nods, rubbing his jaw. "Good as new."

Will stands to face his brother, his anger melting into something soft and pitying the instant he sees his face. The glaze over Henry's eyes gives me the impression he's not fully here, that whatever nightmare he's been suffering through has followed him into his waking life. "Perhaps it's best if you turned in for the night."

"Perhaps it's best you all did," Mother says, looking down at her maps once more. "I'll discuss your appointments with the rest of you in private tomorrow. Until then"—she glances up at each of us in turn, her gaze landing, finally, on me—"stay vigilant. If Morana is here, at Castle Grim, we cannot be sure when she'll act, but we must be ready if she does." Mother's gaze drifts back to her maps, and she gives a dismissive wave that I'm sure sets Lord Bludgrave's teeth on edge. "Get some sleep."

Sleep. *As if I can sleep now*, I think, even as the others mumble their agreement, yawning as they make their way for the small, round door.

I wait as the others exit through the tunnel, until only Mother, Will, Killian, and I remain, my hands gripping the edge of the table, tethering myself to this moment.

"Gentlemen," Mother says, dipping her head curtly to Killian and Will. "I need to speak with my daughter."

Killian touches Mother's elbow, as if to show his support, before meeting my gaze. He frowns slightly, looking as if he wants to say something, but he must decide against it. He lingers at the entrance to the tunnel, however, as Will laces his fingers with mine, refusing to leave my side. My heart swells with gratitude, and while I appreciate that Will has chosen this moment to stand with me, I know I need to do this alone.

"It's all right," I tell him, squeezing his hand. "I'll just be a minute."

His shoulders tense, but he nods, and a minute later, Mother shuts the door that leads to the passageway, sealing the two of us in the dimly lit room.

There's so much I want to say to her. I intend to say something about Father, about the Order, but, "You're a Nightweaver" are the first words out of my mouth.

She nods, her expression carefully neutral. "Yes."

"And Father was human," I say, my voice shaking. "But you come from nobility."

A noble Nightweaver and a human pirate, forbidden to be together, forced to spend their lives at sea.

"When do you plan to tell my brothers and sisters they're half Nightweaver, too?" I demand.

"It's not that simple," she says, her tired eyes crinkling around the edges as she offers me a small smile. "There is a reason I didn't reveal my true heritage tonight. Only Killian is aware of our family's secret, and until our mission here is complete, it isn't safe for the others to know. Your siblings will need time to process—to understand the callings they've felt their entire lives are tied to their affinities." She approaches me slowly, her hand outstretched as if to reach for me. "I never meant for you to find out this way."

I take a step back, shaking my head. I think about everything I've learned about life on land, about all the things Mother and Father never told us. I realize, with a sharp pang of grief, that if Killian knew the Red Island was real, if he actually saw it with his own eyes… "You lied to me," I say. "To all of us! You let Owen—" I swallow around the lump in my throat as hot, angry tears burn my cheeks. "You let him believe the Red Island wasn't real, but it is!"

She winces, as if I've struck her. "Aster, you don't understand—"

"No, I *don't* understand!" Rage burns like fire in my veins. "I don't understand how you could have let us believe we were safe," I seethe, holding up my arm and tugging at my leather bracelet, "when you were the one who had our bracelets enchanted! You knew the Guild of Shadows would come for me, and you didn't think it was important to tell me? You knew," the words come out on a sob, and it only fuels my anger, "that I was cursed. That I'd been bitten! And you never—you didn't—"

"I made a mistake," Mother says, her voice soft, and this time, when she reaches out, I let her place her hand on my cheek. My vision swims with tears, but I make out the blurry shape of her frown. "I'm only trying to protect you."

I laugh sharply, gesturing at the stone walls. "Protect me?" I hear my own shrill voice as if from somewhere far away. "Look at where we are! Look at what I'm doing! For the Order—for *you*—"

"For me?" Her gentle expression hardens, and I remember, a moment too late, that she isn't just my mother, but the fiercest captain to have ever sailed the Western Sea. "You're here because the True King has a plan for your life. A purpose."

"The True King?" My voice cracks as my rage gives way to trepidation, but I don't back down. "*I* have a plan! Me. Not some—some *king* who turned his back on us when we needed him most."

"Oh, really?" Mother's brows lift. "And what *is* that plan exactly? Did you really think you were just going to waltz in here and wait for the perfect moment to cut off the heads of two of the most powerful Nightweavers in the Known World? Then what?" She gestures at the maps. "You said it yourself, it will be a civil war zone. Who will rule?"

I open my mouth, but I can't seem to find my voice. Mother notices my hesitation, like a shark scenting blood in the water.

"You don't know what it takes to lead," Mother says, and I feel every word like a punch to the gut. "You can't even begin to fathom the sacrifices I've made for this family, for this cause—*for you*," she adds, throwing my own words back at me.

"And you think your plan is perfect?" I challenge, my heart pounding against my sternum. "What happens if Princess Leo is the noble you suspect is possessed by Morana? Even if Titus manages to bring down the wards on his own, do you really think the king and queen are going to surrender? Just like that?" I snap my fingers. "What if they fight back? What then, *Dawnrender*?"

I brace myself for Mother's fury, but her face pales. "Why would you say that?"

My brow furrows. "Why would I say—"

"Why would you think Princess Leo is possessed?" she asks,

moving toward me now, her expression a mixture of fear and urgency that sends a shiver down my spine. "Who told you that?"

"I—" I don't know what compels me to keep my former suspicions about the princess a secret, though I can't help thinking Titus wouldn't want me sharing his doubts with my mother, and therefore the entire Order. "It was just a question. It could be anyone. Why *not* her?"

Mother's gaze searches mine, her mouth pressed tight. Finally, she nods. "Of course," she says, her features smoothing out, as composed as she was when I first arrived here tonight. "But Princess Leo is not a suspect."

I blink, stunned. Apprehension twists my gut. "How can you be sure?"

Mother glances at the maps, her brows drawn. "There have been...signs." She hesitates. "We're monitoring a few suspects closely. We believe we're close to discovering who Morana has chosen for a host."

Hope swells in my chest. If the Order reveals Morana's host, we'll be one step closer to the cure. "Who—"

"I can't tell you that," Mother says swiftly, cutting me off with a dismissive wave of her hand. "Now, can you befriend the princess, or are you going to let your emotions get in the way of what I've asked you to do?"

I feel as if my legs have been kicked out from underneath me. The tips of my ears heat, a lump rising in my throat. Mother has lied to me my whole life—I should have known she wouldn't pick tonight to start telling the truth. To tell me anything. I realize, now, that it wouldn't matter if I told her about the cure. She cares more about the Order—about the rebellion—than she's ever cared about me. Even now, she's only concerned with my ability to fulfill my duties.

Fine, I think. Let her keep her secrets, and I will keep my own. I didn't need Mother when I defeated the Sylk that killed Owen, and I don't need her to obtain the cure.

I move toward the exit, my steps nearly as heavy as my heart. Before I crouch to enter the tunnel, I turn to find her staring at the stuffed lion Killian left on one of the crates in the corner of the room, her expression nettled. "You can count on me, *captain*," I say, but for the first time in my life, I hate that word. Hate that she's my captain, rather than just my mother.

As I make my way down the dark tunnel, grief pierces my chest like a shard of ice, and I can't help but wonder if, were Father here, he would have told me the truth.

I think of Owen and his promises that all would be revealed to me, if only I would join him. And some twisted part of me thinks, if he made me that offer tonight...

Would I take his hand?

Chapter Twenty-Six

As Charlie and Lewis escort me through the castle, my stomach twists and turns with every step we take down the spiraling staircase. Before, meeting Princess Leo was strictly a matter of identifying whether she could be possessed by the queen of the Underlings. Once I did that, Titus made it clear that what happens next is out of my hands. But after my conversation with Mother last night—after *Dawnrender* revealed the Order's plans to form an alliance with the princess of Hellion—the pressure of striking up a friendship with Titus's fiancée sits heavily on my chest, a crushing weight.

"Thank the Maker," Eliza says as we approach the doors to the queen's drawing room, where she waits alone. "I didn't want to go in there unarmed." She loops her arm through mine and winks at Lewis. "I'll take it from here, boys."

Lewis blushes, bowing slightly at the waist. "By all means."

Eliza clears her throat, and the two guards posted at the doors announce our arrival to the women inside. I match Eliza's stride as we enter the large, domed room, mimicking her upright posture as best I can. Floor-to-ceiling windows line the outer wall of the Queen's Court, at least twenty feet tall, looking out over the place where the Western Sea meets the unknown expanse of ocean beyond. Sunlight glitters on the waves—water so blue it reminds me of Titus's eyes.

I blush, glancing at the ceiling to avoid the looks from the other courtiers, their expressions ranging from curiosity to outright contempt. Above, an elaborate work of art decorates the domed surface, depicting winged figures scattered throughout a garden of white roses, covering their eyes with either their hands or their feathered appendages. In the center of the image, a woman kneels, clothed in white, at the foot of a king who appears to glow golden—his aura so bright it's almost impossible to make out his frame or the crown of stars atop his head.

"Beautiful," I murmur, allowing Eliza to guide me to our designated seats.

"Tragic," Eliza whispers. "The woman who painted it, I mean."

"What happened to her?" I whisper back, aware that Clemson and Davina, seated across the room from us, have begun to whisper, too, cutting their eyes at us as we take our place near the window.

"She was human," Eliza tells me. "She'd been sold into service here when she was merely thirteen. The rumors say she and the king—who was still only a prince then—had been friends. He was the one who discovered her talent for art." She glances at the ceiling, her smile sad, and says, almost to herself, "Perhaps it would have been better if she'd had no talent at all."

We're approached by a young servant girl carrying a tray bearing two goblets of wine and a plate filled with tiny cakes. Eliza takes a goblet of wine but declines the cake, and though her smile appears genuine, her lip twitches as she shakes her head.

"You can leave them on the table. Thank you," she says, and the girl grins slightly at the acknowledgment, placing the tray on the small table between us before scurrying away.

"So? What happened to the artist?" I ask, inspecting one of the cakes before taking a bite. Raspberry filling drips from the warm, vanilla sponge, plummeting toward my lap.

Lightning quick, Eliza's hand darts out. She catches the drop of jam, almost as if she couldn't stop herself.

"She disappeared," Eliza says, wiping her hand on a crisp white linen napkin, staining it red. "Shortly after she painted this room. No one knows what happened to her, and she was never seen again."

Disappeared. I think about my family—how easy it would be for the king and queen to make any one of them vanish from existence, as if they were never here at all.

I take another bite, this time careful to catch the crumbs with my other hand. "What was her name?"

"Mina," says a clear, gentle voice.

I follow the beam of Eliza's kind, welcoming smile to the right of my chair. There, clothed in a blue gown the color of the morning mist, Princess Leo stands, impossibly regal, like the living statue of a goddess.

Margaret mentioned that the queen rarely attended these gatherings, but that Leo often joined them, though she preferred to sit alone near the window, looking out over the city. *The servants say she always looks sad*, my sister told me this morning. *She's probably homesick.*

I'm glad I no longer have a reason to be wary of her, because she might be the only person in this entire palace to whom I can truly relate.

"Mina Avery," Leo says, turning her gaze to the sea. She's so still that for a moment, it's as if she really *is* a statue—a girl cut from marble, her eyes forever mesmerized by the waves and the far-off memory of what lies beyond. "I'm told the queen painted over most of her murals. But the king refused to let her paint over this one."

"My," Eliza says, taking a sip from her goblet, "you've learned quite a lot during your stay here."

Leo's lip quirks then, the ghost of a smirk. "The servants love to gossip almost as much as the nobility."

Denying the help of one of the guards, Leo drags her chair from its lonely spot a few feet away to sit directly beside me.

"Do you mind?" she says, already plopping down in her chair. Her expression—her round eyes, her soft cheeks, her dimpled chin—projects a sort of lightness that compels me to nod without a second thought. She grins, reaching for the plate of tiny cakes, taking one in each hand. Her eyes roll to the back of her head as she takes a bite of the first, not the least bit concerned as the jam drips down her chin and splatters her dress.

This is what I'm here for, I remind myself. From the beginning, my priority has been to get close to her. First, to discover if Morana is in there, somewhere, pulling the strings. And now that I know she's not possessed, it's my duty to find out if Leo is sympathetic to our cause and persuade her to join forces with Titus to bring down the wards on Holy Winter's Day.

Leo's smile broadens, revealing one slightly crooked canine, and I see, then, what I wish I never noticed. The sunlight pales in comparison with the warmth of her face—the smattering of freckles across the bridge of her nose, the gossamer radiance of her dark eyelashes—beautifully imperfect in a place where men and women go to great lengths to conceal their natural features. She exudes laughter, as if joy were woven into the very fiber of her being, and her long, ebony braids seem to glow, as if every strand of hair has been spun by the hands of the Stars.

Relief courses through me when I realize that I know with certainty that my ability to see Sylks still works, and now that I'm this close to the princess, I can't detect even the faintest *hint* of a shadow. There was a small part of me that thought being near her again, I would at least *feel* some indication of the Sylk queen, but the only thing I feel in Leo's presence is awe.

I want to be her friend.

"I dread these tea parties," Leo says through a mouthful of cake, loudly enough for all fifteen women scattered about the room to hear her. "I'd rather *actually* spend the afternoon with my future mother-in-law, and that's saying a lot."

I *really* want to be her friend.

"You're not the only one," Eliza agrees, taking another draught of wine.

"Why don't we get out of here? Do something fun before we're needed elsewhere," Leo says. She turns to me, her eyes sparkling with mischief. "We've made an appearance, haven't we? Besides," she adds, raising her voice, even though the room fell silent the moment she entered, "everyone seems far too interested in what we're saying to make any sort of entertaining conversation. It doesn't matter, anyway. The servants will tell me anything they say that's worth hearing once we've left."

I glance at Clemson and Davina, their mouths gaping, their cheeks the color of raspberry jam, and a grin tugs at my lips.

"What did you have in mind?"

"Are you sure we're allowed to be here?" I ask.

Leo has led Eliza and me to an inner courtyard of the castle—a garden that spans out before us like the ocean itself, overflowing with robust roses the deep scarlet color of freshly spilled blood. Tall stone walls surround the garden, but not a single window overlooks the courtyard, sealed up by a domed roof made entirely of green stained glass. I inhale deeply, my senses electrified by the overwhelming tang of metal that seems to overpower the perfume of the flowers.

"Oh, we're definitely not allowed to be here," Leo says with a wink. "That's what makes it fun."

I remember what Titus said about her ability to stir up mischief—and the hazards of that particular talent.

"Maker of All," Eliza whispers, her mouth agape as we step out of the servants' passageway and onto the garden path.

The path, paved with opalescent bricks that appear to be made of some kind of glass or crystal, shimmers as the bricks catch the light of the pale, wintery sun overhead. I fold my arms against the chill, thankful that Leo sent for three coats before sneaking away from our guards through a servants' corridor in one of the castle's many powder rooms.

"Are they..." My gaze flits between the dozens of servants carrying baskets as they weave through the garden like ghosts, gathering the roses. "Is this how the *Manan* is harvested?"

Leo glances over her shoulder. "This is where it begins," she says quietly. "They'll ship what they gather by train to a secret location, where the *Manan* will be harvested by the king's private league of bonewielders."

I watch as one of the servant boys plucks a rose from its stem, and it's as if the petals appear to bleed, the liquid staining his fingertips dark red. All around, the servants' fingertips are marked by this same shade of crimson.

Bloodroses, I realize. These are Bloodroses.

I think about what Titus told me that day on the train—how after Leo first arrived at Castle Grim, it was here, in this garden, that he first suspected she was possessed by Morana.

"We shouldn't be here," Eliza says, taking me by the arm. Even through the heavy fur coat, I can feel her hand clutching me with urgency—panic, even.

"But we—" I just begin to protest when I turn to look at Eliza and find her gilded eyes staring back at me, glowing so brightly they're somewhat blinding.

"Oh, dear!" Leo says, her eyes wide. "I didn't realize—"

"I must go," Eliza says, tugging at my arm. She looks over her shoulder at the servants' passage. "You should, too."

"We'll all go," Leo says, sounding somewhat disappointed.

"No." I give Eliza's hand a squeeze, saying, "I'd very much like to stay and hear more about these bonewielders." I give her a look, attempting to convey my purpose while absolving Eliza of any guilt she might feel for leaving. "I'll see you tonight at dinner."

Eliza gives a tight nod, withdrawing from me and hurrying back through the passage by which we came.

"Poor dear," Leo says, her frown seemingly genuine. "I forget how different things are in this kingdom."

"What do you mean?" I ask, sticking close to Leo's side as she leads us down the center path.

"It's just that..." She shakes her head, smiles a little. "Where I come from, my people—" She glances at me, lowers her voice. "We're not quite as bloodthirsty as the Nightweavers you've come to know."

"I don't think of Eliza as bloodthirsty," I say, somewhat shocked by my own defensiveness of a Nightweaver I barely know.

"No, no, of course not," Leo adds quickly, her round eyes innocent and pleading. "I don't mean to insult your friend. I only mean to say that in Hellion, Nightweavers do not struggle with their... impulses. Not like they do here."

The servants don't seem to notice Leo as she passes, as if they don't know who she is, and she doesn't seem to mind. In fact, her stride lengthens, until I feel I'm jogging to keep up with her. I look at the servants then—*really* look at them—and note that their complexions are ashen and dull, their cheeks hollow. They wear black uniforms that conceal almost every inch of their skin, except for their faces and hands, their fingertips stained red from plucking.

None of them speak. Not even to one another.

"Have you been here before?" I ask.

"A few times," she admits, her light tone now hushed as we

hasten to the end of the path, to what appears to be another servants' passage. "Hurry," she says, opening the door to the passageway. "In here."

I follow her into the narrow stone hall, and she shuts the door, sealing us in pitch blackness.

My heart plummets.

"What is this place?" I slip my hands into my pockets and grab hold of the hilts of my daggers. Have I been wrong about Leo? "Why did you bring me here?"

A flame ignites from Leo's gilded lighter, illuminating her face, and I withdraw my blades an inch before she lights a torch along the wall.

Leo sags against the stones, sighing deeply. She retrieves a long silver pipe from her coat pocket, lights it. After a deep drag, she exhales, the clove-scented smoke easing the tension in my shoulders.

"Titus trusts you," Leo says.

I open my mouth to respond, but she cuts me off.

"Don't argue. I've known him all my life. It's plain to see that he confides in you." Her lip kicks up in a slight grin. "He used to confide in me. Before…" She exhales a cloud of smoke, holding up her ring finger, the diamond-encrusted band glittering in the torchlight. "Before this."

My stomach twists, and suddenly the hallway feels entirely too cramped.

"I know when I'm being used, Aster," she says, making a fist and letting it fall to her side.

Panic forms a knot in my throat, and I tighten my grip on my daggers once more.

"Every day of my life from the moment I was born has been manipulated by my parents and their advisers." She glances at the door, as if she can still see the rose garden that lies beyond. "My kingdom depends on the Eerie for *Manan*, weapons, and soldiers to fight at our borders. But the Eerie depends on us for the Elysian Iron needed to make those weapons and supply those soldiers. This marriage is a strong alliance between our kingdoms—only a fool couldn't see that. And Titus is no fool. A pain in my ass, on occasion, but not a fool."

I'm somewhat taken aback by her bluntness, and perhaps it shows on my face, because she chuckles.

"I doubt I've said anything that could make a pirate blush."

"It's not that," I say quickly. "It's just...I don't understand why you're telling me this."

She takes another long drag off her pipe, her face pulled tight in a frown. "There is no one here I can trust. I thought perhaps you and Miss Cooper might be able to help me."

Slowly, I withdraw my hands from my pockets. "Why us?"

"You're outsiders here as well, aren't you?"

My eyes narrow. "Eliza is a member of the nobility."

Leo nods. "And yet there are rumors that she and her brothers work for the Guild of Shadows." She cocks her head. "You didn't know?"

I can't admit that Lord Bludgrave accused Eliza's brother of exactly that just last night, so I shake my head. "Don't have much time for gossip."

Leo grins. "I like you." She sticks out her free hand. "Let's be friends, shall we?"

I hesitate. "You don't even know me."

"I know you well enough," she says. "I know you're here because you had no other choice. So am I." She wiggles her fingers, quirks a brow. "Care to form an alliance?"

The ghost of a smile tugs at my lips. If the princess is this trusting with someone she's only just met—this eager for my friendship, for my help—then it shouldn't prove difficult to persuade her to join the fight.

I take her hand, shake it once. "You're going to get me into trouble."

Leo smiles broadly. "And you're going to have a grand time, I guarantee it." She extinguishes her pipe, tucking it back inside her coat pocket. "So," she says, suddenly serious. "You didn't know about the Coopers?"

I know I must choose my words carefully. "What about them?"

"Let's walk and talk." She opens the lighter, sparking a flame. "There's something I want you to see."

I can't see down the passage but for a few feet beyond Leo's flickering light. She could be taking me anywhere—she could be leading me into a trap. But this is what I came here to do, and if Leo is offering to share her secrets with me, I have no choice but to follow.

"I've heard rumors that Flynn Cooper is a Changeling," Leo says. "It's said that when they turned sixteen, he persuaded his brother to join the Guild of Shadows and help him kill their mother and father. They massacred the entire household, but it was Eliza, their little sister, who covered it up. To protect her brothers, she made it look like they were attacked by a local gang. It's said that Eliza made a deal with the Guild of Shadows to free them from service to Morana, but some believe the three of them still work for the Sylk queen. Spies, the lot of them, trading information for their freedom."

An uneasy feeling prickles the hair at the nape of my neck as the passageway ends and we begin our descent down what appears to be an ancient, spiraling staircase.

Killian mentioned there was a spy in the Order, and I know now that my assailant is a Changeling.

Flynn could be both.

"Of course, I don't believe a word of it," Leo says, "but the rumors alone have made others wary of befriending Eliza."

The staircase seems to go on forever, but we take our time, careful to avoid broken steps. Stone crumbles beneath my foot, but Leo catches my arm just in time to steady me, and I watch as the pieces tumble into the vast, unknown darkness below.

"If you need help, why not ask Titus? He told me the two of you were best friends."

"*Were*," she echoes. "Not anymore. Not since our parents decided we were to be wed. Ever since I arrived, he's acted...strange. It's like I don't even know him. Like...like he's been *influenced*, somehow."

I bite my lip to keep from speaking, waiting for her to elaborate.

"I sound crazy, don't I?" She half-laughs, half-sighs. "I didn't expect him to be happy about it. The True King knows I'm not thrilled about the prospect of producing heirs with the boy I used to tease for wetting the bed."

I wipe the sweat from my palms on my gown and chalk up the weird feeling in my stomach to the fear of falling to my death in this hidden stairwell.

"But he said you were excited about the wedding," I press. "He said you seemed like you couldn't wait to be married."

"As opposed to what?" she asks. "If Titus had even an inkling of how miserable I am about the whole thing, he'd do something reckless, and I can't let him tear our two kingdoms apart just because I'm unhappy."

My chest aches, my heart breaking for this girl I've only just met. In this moment, I know her. I know her better than anyone might ever know her. Because if there's one thing I understand, it's making an impossible choice to help the ones you love, even if it destroys you in the process.

"So you're going to go through with the wedding anyway?"

"I will do what I have to do to serve my kingdom," she says, and I recognize the determination in her voice, firm and steady and believable.

I pity her, but I respect her even more. And I think now might be the perfect opportunity to share what the Order has planned. It could be so easy. After only a few minutes of speaking with Leo, I'm convinced she would gladly assist in the Order's scheme.

"But, Aster," she whispers, halting abruptly. "That's not why I need your help." She closes the lighter, extinguishing the flame and plunging us into darkness once more. "I think the Guild might be using Titus. I don't know how, but…I think he might have been compelled."

My heart skips a beat.

I whisper, "Because he doesn't want to marry you?"

She stifles a laugh with her hand, the muffled sound bouncing off the stone walls like the tinkling of tiny bells. "I don't think so highly of myself, Aster, but I can always appreciate an opportunity to be humbled."

Warmth bleeds into my cheeks. "That's not what I meant."

"I'm only teasing," she says, her voice warm and soothing. "I know what you meant. And no, not because he doesn't want to marry me. I wouldn't expect him to want that. I never have. But he always knew it was a possibility, as did I. We discussed it. We even agreed to be strategic about it when the time came. Only, now that the time *has* come, he's barely said a word to me. He's cold and cruel—as if it were *my* fault. And perhaps it *is* my fault for not showing him just how miserable I truly am, but if he knew..." She pauses, the heaviness of what she's just said stifling the air. "It's not that simple, though. I wish this was just about securing an alliance between our kingdoms. If it were, eventually, I could persuade Titus to see reason. To be my friend again. But something else is going on. Something I fear Titus has no control over."

Leo takes me by the arm, guiding me down the last few steps and into another dark hallway.

"Years ago, when Calix became king, he established a law that forbids the taking of human blood," she whispers. "He wasn't the first to do so—Hellion and the other kingdoms have had similar laws for centuries, set in place by the True King upon our banishment here. But the Nightweavers of the Eerie were particularly outraged. They think the king has abandoned their traditions—rituals that involved feeding on humans that were considered sacred to their way of life. They believe that this was their right, and with the Bloodroses dwindling out of existence, many are convinced the Crown only created the law so that they could further control the nobility by forcing them to rely on the king for *Manan*."

"What are you saying?"

I can barely make out her features in the darkness, but she seems to hesitate. "The law has two exceptions. The Crown is not bound by the decree," she says slowly, and I think about Titus taking a bite of a human heart in front of a whole host of Nightweavers—something that should be forbidden, but that the king openly condones. "And neither are the noble families that control the distribution of *Manan*."

My stomach twists into knots.

I nod. "Like the Castors." A noble family with notable bone-wielders. I knew the Castors were in charge of allocating *Manan* to the nobility, but I never asked exactly what that entailed. "But they don't consume human blood," I say, realizing only after the words have left my mouth that I saw Will feed firsthand.

Leo nods. "Of course," she says politely, but she doesn't sound convinced. "As long as the Bloodroses are plentiful, they don't have to. And if the nobility receives their portion of *Manan*, they're satisfied—they don't ask too many questions, and they don't oppose the law. But what happens if the Bloodroses die out completely?"

The knots in my stomach tighten. "Chaos."

"War," Leo agrees. "And not just within the Eerie—between this kingdom and the kingdoms like Hellion who depend on the *Manan* the Eerie provides. It's not a perfect system, but without the Bloodroses—without a dedicated supply of *Manan* to keep the population at bay—my kind will slaughter every human on the face of the earth before day's end."

"But the garden," I say. "It doesn't look like the Bloodroses are dying out."

"For now," she says, starting down the long hallway. "But each year, the supply dwindles, and no one knows why."

I place my hand on the stone wall, following her voice down the corridor.

"I'd heard rumors of facilities," she says. "Farms where humans are kept, their blood harvested so that the *Manan* can be extracted and shipped off to the other kingdoms. A direct violation of the law." She lowers her voice, so quiet I can hardly hear her whisper. "It's affecting my people—Nightweavers who have never consumed *Manan* from human blood are turning feral. Many are defecting to the Underling regime to feed their addiction. My father believes that it's because of these facilities that the Bloodroses have dwindled—that the True King is punishing us. But King Calix denies what's really going on. He says the facilities are for reeducating rebels before releasing them back into service, nothing more."

My stomach roils. *Reeducating rebels*. Even if it were true, and the king wasn't harvesting their blood, what he's done—locking up innocent people, forcing them to submit to his tyrannical rule...

He would silence anyone who dares speak out against him, just as he intends to silence me. I clench my jaw, steeling myself as the overwhelming desire to tear Calix's head from his shoulders threatens to cloud my judgment. I promised myself I wouldn't be reckless—that I wouldn't let my emotions control me. And when I drive my blade through the king's heart, I will not be blinded by my rage. I will render my judgment with a clear mind.

"How can I help?" I ask. "You said it yourself—I'm an outsider here, too."

We halt a few feet from the end of the hallway, where a heavy wooden door muffles a low, keening wail.

Leo grabs me by both arms, the silhouette of her face stark, her eyes desperate in the pitch blackness. "Titus trusts you," she says. "No matter what compulsion he might be under—no matter what's influencing him—he'll listen to you. I can feel it, Aster.

You can get through to him. You can persuade him to stop all this before it's too late."

"Me?" I balk, even as an unfamiliar sensation writhes in my gut. "Why me?"

Something akin to sympathy flickers in Leo's gaze. "He's never looked at anyone the way he looks at you." She squeezes my arms. "Underlings draw their power from fear and hate. There is only one thing powerful enough to defeat their magic."

I remember what Will told me once—that the only thing more powerful than fear is love.

"But I don't—" My cheeks heat, my neck slick with sweat. *Love? Titus?* I might have laughed if it weren't for the earnest, pleading look on Leo's face. "He doesn't—"

"Of course," Leo says, not pretending to be convinced. Still, she doesn't press the issue.

She guides me to the door, and it creaks open just a fraction, letting in a narrow band of amber torchlight. The stench of rot and decay hits me like a punch to the jaw, and my eyes water, blurring my view of the dungeons—divided by a narrow canal—and the Bloodknights patrolling the rows of cells. Two soldiers drag a young human man down the block, his skin nearly translucent, as if every drop of blood were drained from his body.

"Not again." One of the Bloodknights curses under his breath. "They took too much. He's already dead."

The other Bloodknight groans, dropping the corpse. "They always take too much."

The first Bloodknight kicks the man's limp body. "What a waste."

They haul the man out of sight, and Leo closes the door just as another tortured moan echoes from down the row of cells.

A fresh wave of anger rises up in me, and I have to fight the urge to burst through the door and cut the two Bloodknights down where they stand. But to act now would mean I blow my cover and expose myself—and the Order—before the time is right.

Again, I take a deep breath and push my emotions aside, burying my grief, my rage, deep down. I will not be shaken. I *cannot* be shaken.

Leo, however, appears overcome with emotion, tears spilling onto her cheeks. I'm not sure what I find more shocking—the fact that the rumors are true or Leo's reaction to seeing the king's atrocities with her own eyes.

"It's worse than I thought," Leo says, taking my hands. "Please, you have to find a way to make him stop this. Break the compulsion, by whatever means necessary."

"But these are the king's facilities," I say. "Surely, if Titus knew what was going on—"

"He knows what's going on," she insists, her voice hoarse. "Why do you think they call him the Reaper?"

I think about how Will described the ritual, that Titus would need to feed on human blood. These facilities would give him exactly that—with access to enough *Manan*, he would have the strength needed to force Morana into her corporeal form. But I can't exactly tell Leo about our plans, and even if I did, I'm not sure she would believe me. Still, I shake my head, but before I can tell Leo that Titus has been forced to act as the Reaper, she interrupts.

"My parents think the king has made a deal with the Guild of Shadows," she says. "They think he's allowed Titus to be compelled by Morana herself so that when we're married, and we're given access to each other's magic, Titus will be able to bring down the wards that surround Hellion's fortresses. Their soldiers outnumber ours ten to one, and they feed on human blood, making them stronger, deadlier. Hellion would fall to the Eerie. It won't even be a fair fight."

My heart drops into my stomach. Leo believes Titus is compelled, not just by any Underling, but by Morana herself. Which means the Order is right—Morana *is* here. And worse, she's possessed someone close to Titus, someone who would have access to him to compel him. But why would Morana need Titus to overthrow Hellion? "I don't understand—"

"The mines, Aster," Leo hurries to add. "The Elysian Iron. If the Guild of Shadows destroy the mines in Hellion, there'll be no weapons to hold the front. The Underlings will take control—not just of the Eerie, but the entire Known World. My parents believe King Calix has secured a place for himself in Morana's new empire. And he's using Titus—he's using this marriage—to bring it to pass."

My head spins. "And the facilities," I say, starting to make sense of it all. "The *Manan* from human blood. It's all part of Morana's new empire. A way to keep the Nightweavers and the humans in check."

Livestock, I think. We'll be nothing more than livestock in Morana's empire of nightmares.

"That's why I'm here." Bile burns my throat, and I swallow hard. "To help keep the humans in check."

She nods, offering what feels like an apologetic squeeze as she takes my hands in hers. "I can't be certain," she says, "but I'm willing to bet the Crown plans to make an example of you. To show Nightweavers that no matter what, humans can't be trusted. That your kind belong in the facilities he's building."

"They're going to frame me for something terrible." Once I've said it out loud, I realize now that is the only way this was ever going to end. Everyone I love is in danger, and there's nothing I can do to save them. Nothing, except… "What now? Tell me. Whatever it is you need me to do, I'll do it."

It seems as if she might break down, her chin wobbling even as she lifts it in defiance. "You have to break the compulsion on Titus before we say our vows on Holy Winter's Day and he kills me."

"Or what?" I ask, although I fear I already know the answer.

It's as if she attempts to blink away her tears, but they streak her face, nonetheless. "Or I have to kill him first."

Chapter Twenty-Seven

I rest my elbows on the stone railing, the gentle breeze carrying with it the scent of heady spices, vanilla, and sea brine from the sparkling city across the water. The golden glow of Jade spans almost as far as the ocean beyond Castle Grim, pulsing and flowing with an intoxicating energy akin to the Western Sea, speaking in its own voice—not as familiar to me as the soothing lullaby of the waves, but familiar still, as if I knew it well, once, in a long-forgotten dream.

In the privacy of my chambers, I tilt my head back, my eyes closed, savoring the soft kiss of the wind on my face as it casts my unbound hair behind me. During my time at Bludgrave, I used to dream of being near my beloved ocean once more. But now that I'm here, it's a different kind of torture to be surrounded by the sea on all sides and yet unable to set sail, to go where the current takes me....

"Beautiful."

I fight the urge to turn around at the sound of Titus's voice. Shivers skitter down my spine at the memory of the nightmare in which he sank his teeth into my neck on this very balcony, and as if on instinct, I slip my hand into my pocket, closing my fist around the hilt of my dagger.

Beautiful. Surely, he meant the view.

"You're late," I say, attempting to sound cold and detached—praying to the Stars he can't detect the subtle hint of disappointment in my voice. Truthfully, when he told me last night that he would teach me to control my bloodletter affinity, we never decided on a time to meet, but I can't seem to think of anything better to say. Especially not after what Leo said this afternoon—after she shared her suspicions that Titus could be compelled, working for Morana against his will.

"I apologize," he says quietly. "I was"—he hesitates—"detained."

My mouth goes dry at the image of Titus patrolling the dungeons, overseeing the capture and torture of humans and Myths, his hands stained red with innocent blood.

"Aster?"

I flinch at his touch as his fingertips graze my shoulder, and I meet his gaze at the exact moment he jerks his hand away as if he were stung, his mouth twisted in a frown.

Shame and regret form a knot in my gut. Titus can't be compelled. Leo must be mistaken, just as Titus was wrong about Morana having possessed Leo.

I find myself wanting to reach for him, wanting to touch his skin, to see if it might be possible to *feel* the magic pulsing in his veins, magic that would force him to act against his will—

He clears his throat, his princely mask settling into place once more. He looks past me, at the dark, frothing waters of the Western Sea. "Follow me," he says, turning his back to the balcony.

I shuffle into my chambers behind him, the cloying heat of embarrassment prickling my neck as I lock my balcony doors behind me.

"What I'm about to show you is never to be shared with anyone," he says, kicking the edge of the blue carpet aside and kneeling in the center of the room. "Not even William."

I hold his stare, feeling as if all the air were siphoned out of the room. I don't know everything about Will and Titus's friendship, only that they consider their bond to be like that of true brothers—that they would go to war for each other, risk their lives for each other. If Titus has kept a secret from Will, I have to believe he has a reason, even if he doesn't seem willing to share it with me.

"You have my word," I say.

He dips his head, his mouth pressed tight. "Stand back."

He removes the glove from his right hand, revealing the tattoo of a sparrow, and places his bare palm on the stone floor.

"Adonoc verash melor," he whispers, his voice like a deep, gentle hum.

Thunk. The stone paver sinks a fraction beneath the rest.

Titus rises, taking a few steps back as two more stones sink, then another and—

He grabs my elbow, yanking me backward as the stones beneath my feet give way, and my heel lands on his big toe.

"Ouch," he mutters under his breath. "Every damn time."

Laughter dies in my throat as I gape at the square opening in the floor and the stone staircase that descends into utter darkness.

"How did you…"

He brings a finger to his lips, curved in a wicked smirk. He holds out his other hand to gesture at the staircase, cutting a glance at the hole in the floor. "After you."

I hesitate, thinking back to everything Leo said about the possibility of Titus being compelled—about the facilities, including the one below this very castle....

As if he senses my hesitation, his mouth twists, a subtle scowl. "What's wrong?"

I search his gaze, trying to reconcile what Leo told me with what I know of the Order's plans to unite Leo and Titus and use them to bring down the wards on Holy Winter's Day. And then it hits me, as electrifying as a bolt of lightning.

Of course! The Order suspects there is a spy in their midst, one who's passing their plans along to Morana. If Morana's forces are on to us, maybe their *spy* is sowing seeds of deceit between the prince and princess. If each of them believes the other is subject to an Underling's control, that would prevent the marriage and, in turn, prevent the wards from coming down.

Relief and determination flood my body in equal measure. The Guild of Shadows thought they could manipulate Leo and Titus—thought they could manipulate *me*. But I've been down this path before, during the months Owen haunted me at Bludgrave. I refuse to be misled, distracted from what I came here to do: cure Will and overthrow the king of the Eerie. And though I never intended to play matchmaker, the Order's plans now hinge on my ability to convince Leo that Titus isn't compelled—and to convince Titus that Leo is not possessed.

Titus *must* marry Leo, and I have to ensure that he does. Perhaps, once they've said their vows, he might even find that he truly loves Leo. Perhaps, when all this is said and done, they can be happy together.

I wet my lips, suddenly parched. "What if I trip?"

He quirks a brow. "I suppose that *is* a genuine concern for you." He presents his hand to me with a flourish, a kind smile lighting his eyes—so pure and genuine I feel as if I'm seeing him for the first time. "If you fall, I fall."

I take his hand, the warmth from his calloused palms sending a jolt of electricity through my veins, bright and dizzying. I press my lips together to stifle a gasp.

Stars, this isn't the first time I've held someone's hand. But that *feeling*...

His throat bobs. "Ready?"

"Ready."

Together, we descend into the darkness. The moment we're clear of the opening, Titus places his hand on the stone wall and whispers, "*Granitum zeruuk shanol.*"

I grit my teeth as the stones scrape, closing in overhead, sealing us in the pitch blackness. Another secret staircase—another secret room. How many secrets can one castle conceal?

"I might need that hand someday," Titus murmurs, and it feels as if he's much closer than he was before.

I don't realize I tightened my grip until I force myself to loosen my hold on him.

"Sorry," I mutter, thankful he can't see me blush.

I allow him to lead us down the stone steps. It feels like an eternity before the cool, dusty air warms, tinged with the unmistakable scent of a damp room and the faintest whiff of sea brine.

"Almost there," Titus assures me.

We descend twenty, maybe thirty, more steps before we emerge from the stairwell into—

"*Maker of All*," I whisper, my eyes wide.

Water divides the torchlit cavern, the canal flowing in from the mouth of the cave and forming a tiny channel that flows through a narrow space in the back wall.

I drag Titus along behind me as I rush for the mouth of the cave to gaze out at the black midnight waters of the Western Sea. Unimpeded by the city, the ocean spans for miles, mirroring the starlit sky, the silver path of moonlight interrupted only by the horizon.

He gives my hand a squeeze. "What do you think?"

I look up at him, my throat clogged with emotion. "What is this place?"

He flashes a dazzling grin at me before dropping my hand, crouching to remove his boots. "This," he says, "is my best kept secret." He tosses one boot aside, then the other. "Although," he adds, wading backward into the pool of water that separates either side of the cavern, "it isn't really my secret so much as it was hers."

"*Hers?*" I echo.

He smiles then, his face nearly as radiant as the stars. "A long, long time ago, when this castle was first built, it was much smaller than it is now. Then, your room belonged to a queen." He lowers his voice, his expression suddenly mystified with the same reverence and awe that overtook him that night at Hildegarde's Folly.

"To Hildegarde," I say, a heaviness weighing in my chest. "And this—"

"This was one of Hildegarde's many secret hideaways. She had a fondness for them. Much like the one you visited in the pantry," he adds with a wink.

I crouch beside the canal, running my fingers over the cool surface of the water. "You knew about the meeting?"

"I volunteered the space," he says, his posture stiffening. "When we were children, and William's family would come to stay at the palace, the two of us called it our *war room*. We spent hours planning imaginary battles there. Stole quite a few maps from the royal cartographer, too." The ghost of a grin touches his lips. "I thought the Order could make use of it."

"How did you find it?" I ask. "Wouldn't the king and queen know about these secret rooms?"

He flashes me a smirk. "I've always been far too curious for my own good."

"But just now," I press, "that was sorcery, wasn't it? You used sorcery to open the passageway." My eyes narrow. "Sorcery only Hildegarde would have known."

Titus runs his hands through his hair. "Take off your shoes," he says, "and if you can manage to focus long enough to learn a bit of control over your own powers, I might just tell you a little something about *my* unusual talents, hmm?"

I roll my eyes, but I don't waste any time removing my shoes. "Isn't it freezing?" I ask, gesturing at the water.

"Not to a bloodletter," he says with a wry grin, as if that were explanation enough.

But he's right. As I wade into the canal up to my hips, the temperature of the water warms, completely at odds with the winter winds that howl just beyond the cave entrance. With every step I take, my heart beats faster—stronger—as if coming fully alive, and my eyelids drift shut. The water welcomes me into its embrace, whispering *welcome home* with every gentle pull and push of the tide. When I open my eyes, Titus watches me, his lips parted slightly on a breath. He doesn't look away, not even after I catch him staring.

"There's nothing like it, is there?" he asks, his voice barely above a whisper.

I run my fingers along the surface of the water, savoring the feel of the ocean on my skin. At once, I am whole. Awake. Free.

Powerful.

"Does it—" I hesitate. "Does it ever speak to you? Not even in words, but—"

"The language of the sea." He nods, a smile touching his lips. "It speaks to all bloodletters—in different ways, at different times in our lives. But yes, I can hear it." He chuckles softly, shaking his head as he wades closer to me. "Louder when you're around, actually. Like it's..." He trails off, his head cocked, his expression suddenly serious. "Like it's trying to tell me something."

I swallow hard. "What do you think it's trying to say?"

Something in his gaze shifts, and his lip quirks, almost playful. "Maybe"—he leans in, the ghost of his breath on my face, his voice barely a whisper—"it's saying, *'Don't do this.'*"

My heart hammers against my rib cage. "Do what?" I ask, breathless.

He smirks. "This."

A wave of water crashes over the top of my head, soaking me to the bone.

I splash him, a trill of laughter slipping past my lips. "Bastard!"

He flourishes a mock bow. "Now," he says, raising his hands. Two streams of water rise up to mimic the flow of his movement, hovering in the air like two vipers poised to strike. "Focus. How do you feel?"

"Wet."

His expression cracks, and he barks a laugh before schooling his features once more. "Yes, but how do you *feel*?"

I huff. "I don't know. There's this... buzzing."

"Close your eyes," he instructs. "Breathe deep. Listen to that voice—what does it sound like?"

I do as he says, squinting my eyes shut, attempting to focus on the quiet voice that hums in the water all around me. "Like music," I answer. My heart twists as I realize the melody feels familiar—tugging at my chest, a bittersweet reminder of days spent on the *Lightbringer*. I recognize the song—recognize the melody—as the tune my father used to hum. "Like a song."

Water caresses my hands as they hover just above the surface, encircling my wrists, spiraling up to my elbows. I gasp, opening my eyes to find Titus's hands outstretched, commanding the two tendrils of water that dance in the air around my arms.

"The buzzing," he says, "can you still feel it?"

I nod slowly, latching onto the hum of the water he commands, feeling it vibrate in the air around me, until I'm not sure where my limbs end and the water begins. "Yes."

"Good." He lowers his hands. "Now," he tells me, "let it *sing*."

So I do.

I let the blood thrumming in my veins become its own force—let it sing its own melody—commanding the tendrils of water as if they were merely extensions of me.

Me. I find myself in the water, in the moisture that clings to the air, in the steady beat of Titus's heart. I am there, in every drop of blood. In every wave. In the depths of the ocean and the firmament of the sky.

I am so much more than Aster Oberon. More than what they forced me to become. More than I could ever hope to be.

"Aster?"

Titus's muffled voice seems to come from below, buried somewhere in the dark.

I open my eyes—I'm not sure when I closed them again—to see him looking up at me from dry ground. The cyclone of water that encapsulates me distorts his worried expression, but there's no mistaking the glint of awe in his eyes.

Fear grips me. This isn't control. This force—this power—came from somewhere within.

And it *terrifies* me.

I blink, feeling my connection to the water break—feeling the tentative hold on my magic snap—and I fall as the cyclone transforms into a wave that crashes over Titus, dragging us both beneath the surface of a deeper pool than the one we were standing in before.

For a moment, I'm lost, frantically kicking as I attempt to swim for the surface. But then his arms close around me, pulling me close to his chest, and in seconds, we breach the interface, gasping for air. Above, the stars twinkle against the backdrop of night. The current pulled us out into the sea, depositing us a few strokes from the mouth of the cave.

"You clearly have no issue with shows of force," Titus says, laughter dancing in his eyes. His wet hair sticks to his forehead, water dripping from his eyelashes, but he makes no move to release me. "Perhaps we should start with something simple, like stirring a cup of tea."

I almost laugh, but the voice of the water seems even louder than before, shouting at me—at the part of me that petitions me to surrender to the force of the waves. To let my power rise up and drown all of Castle Grim beneath its crushing weight.

I twist Titus's shirt in my fists, my teeth clenched. "Don't let me go," I plead, my eyes shut tight.

His grip on me tenses, pulling me closer than I was before, our bodies flush as the waves toss us back and forth. "Never," he whispers, pressing his forehead to mine. "Not ever again."

At the feel of his skin on my skin, the voice quiets, the waves relenting as the surface of the water smooths out, peaceful once more. In its place, the soothing beat of Titus's heart lulls me half to sleep.

I'm not sure how long we remain this way, but finally, Titus stirs.

"Can you swim?" he asks.

"Can you breathe?"

He chuckles, releasing me slowly from his grasp, but he doesn't allow me to drift out of arm's reach. I kick, swimming toward the mouth of the cave, a knot forming in my stomach.

I haul myself onto the bank, my ribs sore, and a moment later, Titus flops onto the stone floor beside me, staring at the ceiling.

"I can't control it," I say quietly. "It...it controls *me*."

"You'll learn," he says, standing to offer me his hand. "You've been suppressing your magic your entire life, and now you have to figure out how to live with it. It's going to take time."

"I don't have time," I mutter, taking his hand. "What happens if I lose control in front of the wrong person? What if I hurt someone?"

"You won't," Titus says, his thumb brushing my knuckles as his other hand comes up to tuck a strand of hair behind my ear. "I believe in you, Aster."

A shiver passes through me, and he mistakes it for a chill.

"You're freezing," he says, guiding me toward the staircase. "A hot bath should fix you."

We emerge from the staircase, and Titus kneels, whispering the words to seal the passageway once more. Before the last stone has risen back into place, Titus has excused himself to my bath, and I listen to the sound of the water filling the tub with a gnawing sense of dread.

I step into the chamber to find him sitting on the edge of the massive, opalescent tub, his hand under the faucet as if to check the temperature. Surrounded by the glittering finery of the bath chamber—the sparkling gold faucets, the white marble floors—he appears so... out of place.

"Titus," I murmur, lingering in the doorway.

"Yes, love?"

I bite my bottom lip, afraid to say the words that taste like poison on my tongue. "Did you know?" I ask, my voice trembling. "When you volunteered your war room for the Order's meeting... did you know who my mother was?"

He frowns, but he meets my gaze, his brow furrowed. "Did I know she was Dawnrender, you mean?"

I forget how to breathe. Forget how to speak.

"Yes," he says softly, getting to his feet. He takes a step toward me, his movements careful, as if he were approaching a wild animal. "I knew."

I want to back away, but I can't move.

"How?" is all I manage to say.

He looks up at the ceiling, as if uttering a silent prayer to the Stars, before meeting my gaze once more, his expression somewhat pained. "I have known your mother since long before you were ever taken captive by the *Deathwail*, Aster."

Chapter Twenty-Eight

Everything—the sound of the water flowing from the faucet, the rapid beat of Titus's heart, my own thoughts—fades beneath the shrill, deafening ring of silence in my ears.

"What—what are you saying?"

He attempts to take me by the hand, but I step back, out of his reach.

"Aster, please," he begs. "Let me explain."

"Explain?" My voice is hoarse. "You lied to me. You've been lying to me all this time!" A small, broken sound escapes me. "Why?" I advance on him now, ready to grab him by the shoulders and force him to look at me—demand that he tell me everything. Every secret. Every lie. But even as I ask the question, a part of me already knows the answer—I keep my own fair share of secrets from the people I love.

Titus sinks to the floor, resting his back against the wall, as if he no longer has the strength to stand under the weight of his words.

"I was a child when I met Grace," he tells me. "She had infiltrated Castle Grim on behalf of the Order. She discovered something...." He grimaces, a crease between his brows. "Something about my father. She wanted to take me with her then. Against all Order directives, she was going to help me escape this awful place. But once I realized what your parents were doing—how they were fighting back—I wanted to help. I knew I would be of better use to the cause from inside the castle walls. So I stole away in the middle of the night—took a jolly boat and made my way back here."

He falls silent for a long moment, staring at his hands—at the tattoos there—with a look so haunted I know, instantly, that he now relives whatever dark memories followed his return.

"They came back for me—your parents. Many times. Your father found ways to reach me—visited me often in the years to come. He was kind to me." His throat bobs, his mouth twisting into a frown. "He was a good man."

My own legs give way beneath me, and I slide down the front of the vanity, sitting opposite Titus. My grief splits me in two like a fresh, gaping wound in my chest—the pain so visceral I almost expect blood to pour onto the tiles.

"He's the reason Captain Shade exists," he says slowly, quietly. "The reason I became a pirate."

A pirate. Sometimes, it's easy to forget that Titus is a pirate, too. Even if he is a prince, as well.

"When you were taken captive aboard the *Deathwail*, Grace asked me to track them down. To bring you home." He sighs, running his hands through his hair. "Seeing you again...seeing what they'd done to you..."

"Again?" The word comes on a whispered breath, so low I wonder if he's even heard me.

He smiles—a warm, tender smile full of regret. "Again," he confirms. "Of course, the first time we met you nearly took a chunk out of my arm. You have always been quite fond of using your teeth." He rolls up his sleeve to reveal a small scar hidden beneath a tattoo of a moth.

Just like the moth inked into my spine—my only tattoo. It has been so long since I saw it myself, sometimes I forget it's even there. Or why I asked Lewis for that specific tattoo the year I turned thirteen. But now...

"Why don't I remember meeting you?" I ask, attempting to sift through fragments of memories from my childhood. The more I try to remember, the more I'm met with blank stretches of time. Dark spots in my memory. Vague, blurry images I can't seem to grasp.

And then I realize, with a jolt of panic—I don't remember being bitten by the Shifter, either. I reasoned it was the traumatic nature of the event—that I somehow blocked it out—but no. Someone tampered with my memories, just as I saw Will do to his father and Annie. I'm sure of it.

"I suppose I don't have a memorable face," Titus says, flashing me a lopsided grin. It fades as his gaze roves my expression. "They didn't tell you about me because they were trying to protect you," he says. "They were—"

"Please," I say, raising my hand. "Don't make excuses for them."

"Aster, listen to me," he goes on, somewhat pleading. "There are things at work—things that, if you knew, would put you in even more danger than you're already in. You have to trust—"

"Trust?" My laughter is as sharp as any blade. "Who am I supposed to trust? Everyone I've ever trusted has lied to me. I don't trust my mother, and I certainly don't trust you."

His teeth clench. "Aster—"

"Just leave!" I shout, hot, angry tears already spilling onto my cheeks. He shifts forward, his hand outstretched, but I swat it away. "Leave me alone!"

He winces, his jaw set. "Fine," he says softly, getting to his feet. "I'll go."

I bury my face in my hands, listening as his footsteps halt by the door.

"You should know," he says, his voice firm. "No matter what happens"—he fishes something out of his pocket and tosses it to me—"the thing I want most in this world is your and Will's happiness."

I catch the medallion in my hands. Look up at him through teary eyes.

This medallion—an heirloom that once belonged to the heir of Hildegarde—could secure my family and me safe passage to the Red Island. I could leave Castle Grim. I could run far, far away from the king and queen and Morana and the Shifter who bit me as a child. I could be free.

But at what cost?

Now that I know my mother is Dawnrender—now that my siblings have joined the Order of Hildegarde—and that the Order has planned an attack for Holy Winter's Day, they would never agree to go, and I can't leave them behind.

"I thought if you saw who I've been forced to become, that it might make it easier, somehow," he says, his brows pinched. "That if you hated me, I might feel justified keeping this secret from you. That I might be able to drive you away and spare you from the horrors of this place." He meets my gaze, his eyes brimming with an emotion I can't place. "I was wrong."

I wait for the door to my suite to close behind him before I break, but once I do, the tears don't stop.

I clutch the medallion to my chest and cry myself to sleep.

"Aster?"

Something prods my face.

"Aster? Wake up!" Leo pokes my cheek. "This can't be comfortable."

I blink up at her, feeling as if I've tumbled into some strange dream. She wears a tattered brown cloak, a satchel slung over her shoulder. Her appearance alone might convince me I *am* dreaming, but the icy sting of the cold tile against my cheek and the crick in my neck prove otherwise.

"Goodness, you're a mess!" Leo says, taking me by the arm and lifting me upright with surprising strength for someone of her stature. "A few more steps and you might have drowned in your own bathwater."

I groan, rubbing my eyes. "Who let you in my room?"

"About that," she says, biting her bottom lip. "I came through the window. The doors to your balcony were unlocked, and I didn't see you in your bed...."

"The window?" I was certain I locked my balcony doors behind me, but I suppose I was distracted by Titus and the hidden passageway in my flooring. Maybe I should have checked them again. I straighten, suddenly wide awake, searching for the medallion. The tension in my shoulders loosens when I find it in my pocket. At least I had the good sense to store it there before the exhaustion finally overtook me.

"I was out for a little climb—to clear my mind, get some fresh air," Leo says, as if what she's saying isn't totally insane. "Windwalkers are particularly fond of heights." She shrugs. "Well, most of us are anyway."

This is the first I've heard of it. Then again, other than Annie, I haven't met very many windwalkers.

Except for Owen.

"Here," Leo says, fishing something out of her satchel. She tosses me another cloak. "Put this on. We have plans."

"Plans?"

She nods eagerly, her eyes lit with mischief. "The Holy Winter's market in Jade. It's magnificent."

I get to my feet, shaking out the cloak. "You climbed hundreds of feet in the air just to ask me to sneak out so we could go *shopping*?"

Her easygoing expression falters. "I overheard something," she admits. "A shipment of humans is being brought in tonight—to the castle. I thought we might be able to intercept them at the harbor in the city."

I search her face—scanning for any sign that she might be lying—but if she isn't telling the truth, I can't detect any insincerity. And if she's right, and we can save these people from the terror that awaits them in these dungeons…

I drape the cloak over my shoulders and pull the hood over my head. "Lead the way."

Scaling down the ancient stone facade of Castle Grim is nothing like climbing the rigging of the *Lightbringer*.

"Isn't this grand?" Leo shouts, her voice nearly swept away on the wind.

She insisted she could carry me, but I didn't believe her until she hoisted me onto her back with such ease even Charlie would have been envious of her strength.

"You do this for fun?" I ask, clinging tighter to Leo than I've ever clung to anyone or anything in my life. I made the mistake of looking down a few stories up, and I nearly lost my dinner.

"I thought you'd be more reckless," Leo shoots back, her playfulness evident in her voice.

"I thought you'd be more...sensible!"

Leo laughs, and my heart squeezes as I realize Titus was right—her laughter *is* contagious. Despite the ache in my chest, I find myself laughing alongside her, and soon enough, we reach the narrow, rocky shore that rims the base of the castle.

For the first time in all my years, I'm tempted to kiss the dirt beneath my feet.

"Now what?" I ask, somewhat breathless as I adjust my cloak.

Leo smiles impishly, clapping her hands. "Your turn!"

I stare at her, feeling as if I've just missed something vitally important.

She knits her hands together, somewhat nervously. "I"—she

bites her bottom lip—"I know about your..." She makes a vague gesture at me, then the water—huffs a sigh. "I know your secret."

I know your secret. Those four words send me reeling.

I take a step back, my spine pressed to the stone wall, and reach for my dagger.

"No, Aster, don't," she hurries to add, her eyes wide with panic—*and hurt*, I think. "Tonight, when I came into your room—your clothes were dry, but I could still smell the sea on you. And when you woke, the bathwater..." She winces. "Well, it sort of..." She motions with her hands, waving them around like two tendrils of water. "I've been around bloodletters my whole life. I put it all together, and, well..." Her face breaks out in a grin. "You're a Nightweaver!"

My heart beats wildly in my chest. I'm supposed to uncover Leo's secrets—not the other way around. And if she was able to figure it out, how soon until someone else sees something they're not supposed to?

"Leo, you can't—"

"I wouldn't dare!" She places her hand over her heart, her expression gravely serious. "Your secret's safe with me," she says, holding out her little finger. "Promise."

I flick a glance at her outstretched digit. "What are you doing?"

She doesn't budge. "You're supposed to give me yours," she says, nodding encouragingly. "We lock fingers, and it represents a solemn, unbreakable vow of trust between us."

Trust. Why must everyone insist on asking me to trust them?

I think of the humans Leo told me about—think of the dungeons awaiting them if we don't rescue them first—and realize I don't have much of a choice.

I twine my little finger with hers, and Leo grins again.

"Right," she says, releasing my hand to gesture at the water once more. "Shall we?"

I blink once—twice. "You expect me to *swim* us across?" I balk, motioning at the length of water between the island of Castle Grim and the shores of Jade.

"Of course not!" Leo giggles. "Follow me," she adds with a mischievous grin. "You're going to love this."

Entering Castle Grim's private indoor harbor feels like stepping into another world entirely.

"Keep your head down," Leo says, her hood casting shadows over her face as we climb up from the rocky shore and onto one of the long wooden piers that leads into the massive mouth of the cavern. Inside, illuminated by thousands of gilded lanterns, ships from all over the Known World rock idly as hundreds of dockworkers, servants, and soldiers bustle to and fro, loading and unloading crates. "Look like you belong," she adds, picking up a small barrel of fruit, and I do the same, towing a basket of fragrant spices from Kane.

When we reach the end of a long pier, Leo throws her barrel into the water, checking over my shoulder before grabbing my arm and dragging me a few steps to the left, where I'm concealed by the aft of an empty galleon.

"Wait here," she says, then disappears around the other side of the ship.

I pretend to inspect the contents of my basket as a group of four

Bloodknights pass, but my shoulders ease at the sound of their raucous laughter. When I realize they're more concerned with whatever drunken song they're attempting to sing, my casual perusal of ingredients turns into something more.

I recognize a few of the spices, but most have names I've never heard of—*ground Kalmarian root, Yog pepper, smoked Romilly, Tarron sprigs*—and I'm struck with the sudden urge to stash them away in my pockets at the chance I might get to cook with them one day. But it's as if the moment the thought crosses my mind, a sour taste coats my mouth, and I drop the basket, the spices spilling onto the dock and disappearing through the gaps in the wooden planks.

I think of Father's compass, hidden safely in my room, and the words he wrote on its face. *There is still time to chase another star.* I would like to believe I have all the time in the world—that there'll be more dishes to cook, more adventures to be had. But time is slipping through my fingers like the spices sifting into the water below.

I look over my shoulder, searching the docks for any sign of Leo, when a sparkle of gold catches my eye and I stumble back a step, my stomach twisting.

MERRYWAY is written in gold letters along the side of a ship. It's the same one that attacked my family's vessel, the *Lightbringer*. It's the same ship that brought us to the Eerie. The name I swore to remember should I ever get the chance to seek justice for what was done to Owen, my family, and me. I thought the next time I saw this ship I would be here to kill the Nightweaver who took me from the sea, not because I came to Castle Grim to save his life.

A whistle cuts through the chaos of the harbor, and my head spins as I attempt to locate the source of the sound, as if it came from directly beneath me. I peer over the side of the dock to find

Leo rowing a small, strange-looking skiff with a single crimson sail and barely enough room for two people to stand.

She waves at me as she steers the skiff parallel to the lower pier that runs below the dock, and I don't hesitate to jump down. The planks creak underfoot as I jog a few paces and hop onto the skiff beside her.

"Now what?" I ask, my breath fogging the air. "What even is this thing?"

She grins, her face bright. "It's called a skipper," she says. "Bloodletters use them to get across the water quickly. And we'll move much faster if you..." She gestures at the sail, then at the entrance of the harbor, where, in the distance, the lights of Jade glitter like fireflies.

"But I don't know how—"

"Nonsense," she says with a dismissive wave. "Just think about where you want the water to take you, and the skipper will do the rest."

We stare at each other for a long moment. My brow creases, but she just nods encouragingly.

"Go on, give it a try!" she says.

I remember what Titus taught me earlier this evening—the language of the sea. A rush of emotion rises up at the thought of him, but I push down the feeling and focus on the waves lapping at the sides of the skiff. After what feels like too long to be drifting at the docks, I almost tell Leo the truth—that I don't yet know how to control my affinity—but then I hear it.

A faint, melodic hum that tells a story of joy, and thrills, and unbridled excitement. Only this time the song comes from within, and it's as if the waves calm for the span of a heartbeat, listening....

The skipper takes off at a dizzying speed, bouncing over the surface of the water, and I barely have time to grab hold of the sail.

"Like that!" Leo says as I steer the skipper, weaving between Eerie naval ships and foreign schooners, flying toward the mouth of the cave, out of the harbor, and across the moonlit waves. "There you go!"

She laughs as we take off, gliding across the surface of the water, and I find my own laughter coming more easily than I ever would have thought.

I know your secret. It should terrify me that Leo knows about my affinity—it *did* terrify me at first. But now, those words have somehow eased the heaviness in my chest.

Still, I find it replaced by something else—something I've worked my entire life to push aside. The only other person who ever made me hope for a better life—a different life—was Owen. The stories he told me of the Red Island and the freedom that awaited us there filled me with such longing that some nights I grieved for a life I never knew. For a world that didn't exist. For a version of myself I knew I'd never get to meet. And every time I began to hope for more, I had to bury those dreams somewhere deep; otherwise I might not have been able to survive the pain of knowing it could never be true. But tonight, sailing across the sea on a stolen skipper with someone who, in another life, might have been my very best friend, I find that all those feelings have rushed to the surface—a dream demanding to be dreamed once more.

There is still time to chase another star.

I have to believe, if everything goes wrong and I don't leave Castle Grim alive, that the things I've done—the things I'm doing—will give my family more time to dream the dreams they once thought were impossible.

"We're nearly there," Leo calls to me. "Up ahead, see? Under the docks."

The skipper seems to understand where my thoughts have gone, and the water carries us to our destination, gently depositing us on the shore beneath the first wooden pier.

I step off the skiff onto the rocks, lightheaded, my heart racing, but feeling more alive than I've felt in a long time, and I gesture for Leo to lead the way. "Your turn."

Wooden stalls line the streets of Jade for miles, the small booths emanating warm golden light as the bustling crowd browses their goods, filling the city with the scent of baked treats and mulled wine. We emerged from beneath the docks of the North Harbor and into the bustling market, our cloaks still soaking wet. Leo coached me through drying our clothes, and I think with a small tug of annoyance that in less than an hour, Leo taught me more about using my own magic than Titus.

"Here," Leo says, her hood casting shadows on her face as she cocks her head in the direction of a nearby alleyway. "This should lead us to the East Harbor."

I hesitate before following Leo down the dark, narrow passage, the cobblestone streets reminding me of the night I watched Captain Shade's blood spill onto the street. The look in Will's eyes as he drove the blade through his chest—wild with fury. Even though it turned out to be one of the *Starchaser*'s crew pretending to be Shade—even though he survived—so many members of his crew lost their lives that night. All because of me.

"Leo," I say quietly. "Why are you doing this?"

"Doing what?" She glances at me sidelong, her expression innocently blithe. "Risking a death sentence to free a couple of humans?"

"Yes, that."

Her brows knit, her eyes blazing with familiar determination even as she casually lifts a shoulder. "I don't care what the laws say. It's not right—Nightweavers ruling over humans. Humans being drained of their blood just so we can maintain power." She looks at me, and I'm struck by the sincerity in her gaze. "If I can do something—anything—to change even a small part of the world my ancestors have built, I'm going to do it. No matter the cost."

My pace slows as I process the weight of Leo's declaration. If there were ever a moment to persuade the princess to join our cause—to fight alongside the Order—it's now.

"Leo—" I start, but she holds up a hand, silencing me as we approach the end of the alleyway.

She peeks around the corner before motioning for me to follow, her finger pressed to her lips, urging me to be quiet as we step out onto the empty street. The symphony of music and laughter carries over the rooftops, but here, we're alone.

"There," Leo whispers, pointing at the docks up ahead, the cream-colored sails of a galleon reflecting the amber glow of the gas lamps lining the streets. "That's the ship."

The silhouettes of a group of soldiers moving about the ship, down the gangplank and onto the pier, are all I can make out, but aside from their presence, all appears relatively calm. Near the end of the dock, two Bloodknights wait beside a carriage that is rigged to pull a wooden compartment.

A cage, I realize, my fists tightening around the hilts of my daggers.

Even worse, when the Bloodknights turn to speak to each other, I recognize one's helmet—recognize the weapons he carries.

Gabriel.

"What's the plan?" I ask, my palms slick. We haven't been noticed—*yet*. We're about two blocks away, but all it will take is for Gabriel or his companion to look over their shoulders and spot two cloaked figures and we'll be caught. When Leo doesn't answer, I glance at her, staring straight ahead at the two Bloodknights. "You *do* have a plan, right?"

She cocks her head slightly, her gaze fixed on Gabriel and the other Bloodknight.

Thump. The Bloodknights' bodies hit the ground in unison, the sound inconspicuous enough that the soldiers don't look their way.

I think of the way Owen stole the breath from Flynn's and Gabriel's lungs that night on the train, and a chill runs down my spine. "Did you just—"

Leo shakes her head. "They're alive," she says simply, her gaze focused now on the soldiers. Including those that crewed the ship, there's too many to count.

"And the rest?"

She flicks a glance at my hands in my pockets. "You know how to use those, *right*?"

I unsheathe the daggers, twirl them. "Do you even have to ask?"

Leo's smile is purely deviant. "Shall we?"

Her strides lengthen, and I match her pace, sticking to the shadows and out of the lamplight as much as possible as we near the docks. We just pass Gabriel's limp body, lying unconscious in the mud, when—

"Aster, stop," says a familiar voice that sounds at once close to my ear and yet far away. *"He's here. It's a trap."*

"Who's here?" I whisper, my pulse hammering in my throat, but I think I already know the answer.

"Hey, you there!" One of the soldiers calls out, storming down the dock to meet us. "Harbor's closed! Best be on your—"

His eyes go impossibly wide, and he makes a gurgling noise as blood squirts from the dagger in his throat.

There's a wet noise as the blade retreats through flesh, and the soldier falls to the ground, revealing the Changeling assassin behind him, his eyes glowing gold.

The Changeling cocks his head at me, takes a step in my direction.

Leo angles herself in front of me, hands raised in warning.

"Am I supposed to be afraid?" The Changeling chuckles, his deep, raspy voice so low I almost don't hear. His gaze slides to me, his eyes crinkled in what I can only imagine is a smirk. He tsks. "I told you there would be consequences if you stayed," he says, shaking his head. "This is your fault, Aster. Remember that."

Behind him, the soldiers have gone rigid, their swords drawn. As if awaiting his unspoken command, they point their weapons at one another.

There were never any prisoners, I realize. And the voice that tried to warn me just now... *It's a trap*, the voice said. Had the Changeling planted the rumors of the prisoners to draw Leo and me out of Castle Grim, or could it be I'm wrong about Leo—just not the way I thought? Is she working *with* the Changeling, and I've walked right into their trap?

I lurch forward as the soldiers swiftly dispatch one another, but Leo grabs my arm with such force I'm yanked backward, narrowly avoiding a blade I hadn't seen flash through the air—a blade that would have cut me down had Leo not intervened. The choked gasps of the soldiers drone on as their blood spills onto the dock, and all I can think about is Charlie and Lewis and how this could have just as easily been my brothers, forced to fight in a war they don't believe in for a king who will never know their names.

I don't waste another second. One moment, I break free from Leo's grasp, a sharp pain flaring in my shoulder, and the next, I plunge my dagger into the Changeling's chest.

CHAPTER TWENTY-NINE

Bone cracks as I thrust the blade deeper. I miss the Changeling's heart, but the blade pierces his flesh with little effort—*flesh*, not shadow.

The only indication I've struck him at all is his slow intake of breath. Slowly, calmly, he holds my hand in place, hindering me from withdrawing the dagger, as his free arm wraps around me, pulling me close in a morbid embrace and effectively stopping me from plunging my second dagger into his eye.

Leo's footsteps are cut short as he seizes control of her bones, holding her in place, too.

His head dips low, his breath caressing the top of my ear. "Do you feel better, Aster?" he purrs, deep and dark.

I look up at him, meeting his stare, praying to the Stars that he feels every ounce of my fury. "Let go of me, and I might," I say through gritted teeth.

He chuckles again, amusement flickering in his gilded eyes. "Your little daggers have no effect on me. Or did you think you could banish me?" he adds, his voice mocking. "Can't you feel it, Aster?" he whispers as he eyes the soldiers' blood pooling at our feet. "I know you want a taste."

I push the dagger as deep as it will go, but it only seems to incite him, his eyes flaring with untamed desire. "The only blood I wish to taste is yours," I hiss.

His eyes crinkle with wicked glee. "If that's what you truly wish," he rasps, "I won't stop you."

His grip on my hand loosens just enough that I'm able to pull my dagger free but tightens again when I thrust it toward his face. He guides my hand to clean my dagger in slow, controlled movements, wiping his dark red blood on his shoulder.

"But first," he says, his voice low and sinister, "I left you a little gift back at the castle. I think you're going to find it... *motivating*." He draws back, his stare capturing mine with such authority I can't physically bring myself to look away. "Return to Castle Grim," he whispers, both to me and to my traitorous body. "When you've made your decision, meet me underneath the bridge to Jade tomorrow night, just after sunset. Make it quick—I won't wait long. Oh, and Aster," he adds, "come alone."

When he releases me, I find I'm unable to do anything but heed his command. My feet turn of their own accord, my hands moving to sheathe my daggers against my will.

There's a sound like a *whoosh* of wind, and a bat flies overhead. Only when the Changeling has fled, the bat disappearing over a rooftop, does Leo regain control of her own body.

"What was that?" she asks, grasping at my arm. "*Who* was that?"

I shrug her off, unable to keep myself from moving toward the castle. Despite his compulsion that set me on this path, I know now that I make my way there of my own free will. I need to know what he's done. I need to stop whatever he's planning before—

Leo lets out a muffled sob, her hand over her mouth, as she looks over her shoulder at the carnage on the docks. "Why?" is all she can say, over and over again, following me back down the street, toward the alleyway that leads to the market.

"Because of me," I tell her. "Because I'm still here."

"What do you mean?" she asks, sniffling. She straightens, pulling her hood tighter as I hurry down the alley, attempting to get her emotions under control, it would seem.

"I mean—"

I halt, squinting at the two figures at the end of the alleyway. A boy with curly black hair gives a frail-looking man a burlap pouch, and the man hands him a small velvet sachet in return. Just as quickly, the man slips back into the crowded market, but the boy lingers, staring down at the sachet, the lines of his face hard.

"Henry?" I call out.

His head whips in my direction, a hand straying to his hip. But in an instant, he recognizes me, his eyes wide with panic.

"Aster?" He nearly throws himself at me, his hands on my shoulders, my face. "What are you doing here?" he asks. "Why—" He spots Leo over my shoulder, and although he doesn't withdraw from me, he eyes her suspiciously. "Have you come to visit the market?"

"It's a long story," I tell him quickly. "What are *you* doing?" I glance at the sachet, still clasped between his fingers. "What is that?"

He closes his fist around the sachet—tucks it into his coat pocket. Up close, I note the dark circles under his eyes, the sheen of sweat above his brow, the faint scent of peppermint on his breath.

"It's nothing." His throat bobs as he takes my hand and places it under his arm. "You shouldn't be here. It's not safe. Come," he says, leading me out onto the busy street, Leo in tow. "You can take my carriage back to the castle. No one will stop you."

Taller than most of the shoppers, he motions in the air, and a moment later, a horse-drawn carriage parts the crowd.

"Only if you come with us," I tell him. "I'm not leaving you out here alone."

He laughs nervously, his lip kicking into a half-hearted smirk. "I think I can manage to stay out of trouble."

"Well, I don't." I clench the fabric of his sleeve like a lifeline—for him or for me, I'm not entirely certain. "Please, Henry. How else can you be sure I've made it back to my room safe and sound?"

A muscle ticks in his jaw, and he rolls his eyes. "I don't doubt you'll make it there just fine on your own," he says, opening the carriage door. "But if you insist..."

"I do."

He assists Leo up into the carriage before offering his hand to me. It's then that he looks at me—*really* looks at me—his eyes narrowing. "What happened?" he asks, searching the crowd over my shoulder as if an Underling might materialize at any moment. "Are you all right?"

I pat his cheek, just once, where his scar reflects the light with a soft pink glow. "Ask me that again once we've reached Castle Grim, and I might be able to give you an answer."

I learn that, much like Will, no one questions Henry Castor.

When the carriage crosses the bridge, we're stopped only momentarily by the guards, but before they can search the carriage, Henry sticks his head out the window, his expression severe.

"Is there a problem?" he asks petulantly. "I don't like to be kept waiting."

"Of—of course not," the guard stammers. "Welcome back, sir."

Henry nods once, his jaw clenched, and the carriage makes its way through the gates and toward the stables.

"Thank you, Boris, old chap," Henry says as he hops out of the carriage.

I didn't even notice it was the Castors' chauffeur who was seated on the bench of the carriage until Henry hands me down and Boris tips his hat at me.

"I refuse to use the main entrance," Henry tells me as he leads Leo and me to a servants' passage. "Too many nobles waiting around, just itching to make small talk with Lord Bludgrave's spawn."

If it wasn't for the ominous warning the Underling issued a little over an hour ago, I might have laughed.

"I can find my way from here," Leo says when we reach a fork in the passageway. "Make sure she locks her doors," she adds to Henry. She pulls me into a hug, then whispers, "It's not your fault, Aster," before turning swiftly on her heels and taking off down the passageway.

Henry stares after her, his brow quirked. "What was that all about?"

I sigh, starting down the opposite corridor. "Long—"

"Yes, I know," he says, following close at my side. "It's a long story. We have a long walk back to your chambers. Care to tell me what you were doing in the city? Late at night? With the princess of Hellion? Wearing...*this*?" He tugs at my cloak, shooting me a pointed look.

"You first," I shoot back. "Why won't you tell me what's in that sachet?"

His nostrils flare. "Because it's none of your business."

"None of my business?" I scoff, coming to a halt. "Henry, look at me."

He keeps walking.

"Henry, please."

He stops. Turns.

"*What?*" he snaps. "What do you want me to say? That I can't sleep unless I have *this*?" He fishes the sachet out of his coat, opens it for me to see. The fragrant pink petals have been crushed into a fine pulp, the scent of peppermint nearly overwhelming.

Sorrowsnaps, I realize.

"I see her—every time I close my eyes—" His voice breaks on a sob. "I see Dorothy, dead in my arms. And I'm tired, Aster. Of all of it. I just want to sleep. I just want to...to hold her again. To see her smile. To hear her voice. I'm useless without her. It makes me sick." His lip curls as tears stream down his porcelain cheeks. "I don't—" He rubs furiously at his eyes, and the words crack, splinter, shatter as he says, "I don't think I will ever love again."

"Henry, don't say—"

"How can I?" He touches his scar where it cuts a jagged line over his jaw, his fingers trembling. "There were no secrets between

Dorothy and me. She knew me—all of me. The good and the bad—she loved—" He presses the heels of his palms into his eyes, shakes his head. "She loved the broken parts of me so much that I felt if only when I was with her that I could be whole again."

My heart sinks, and where Henry's laughter has always given me hope that we escaped the *Deathwail*, his tears leave me feeling as if I'm still trapped in the dark hull of the cannibals' ship, overwhelmed with despair. And I realize, then, that for all the grief I've felt—for my brother, for my father—I do not know the pain of losing a lover. I have not felt the cleaving of my soul the way Henry did the night Dorothy lay dead in his arms.

"Please." The word comes out on a whisper, and I reach for his hand. "Don't say that."

He steps away from me, out of reach. "I think everyone would be better off if I had stayed behind," he says, his face hardening. "I'm no use to anyone here."

"You—" I start to argue, but he holds up a hand, cutting me off.

"I've made up my mind," he says, his voice hollow as he looks off down the dark passageway. "When all this is over, I'm going to go somewhere I can be alone, where I can't cause my family any more embarrassment."

I open my mouth, but before I can say a word, Henry turns his back to me, stalking off down the passageway, and as I watch him go, the corridor feels colder than it did before.

When I finally make my way back to my room, my feet are sore and my muscles ache, but I ensure that my balcony doors are locked. I check them once, twice, three times before peeking my head out of my front door to make certain that Charlie and Lewis are all right.

"Char—"

I stop short when I'm met with strange looks from two guards I don't recognize.

"Is something wrong, my lady?" one of the soldiers asks, his expression neutral.

"Oh," I say, my pulse hammering in my throat. "No, I just… do you know where my guards have gone? Their names are Charlie and Lewis Oberon. They're here every night. They—"

The guards share a look, and my stomach twists into knots.

"They've been reassigned," the second guard says.

"Where are they now?" I demand, clutching the doorframe so hard I fear it might splinter in my grasp.

The guards share another look, sweat glistening on their brows. *Good*, I think, *two people with enough sense to be afraid of me*.

The first guard clears his throat. "They'll be staying in the barracks until after Holy Winter's Day," he answers. "It's unusual for new recruits to ship out so quickly, but the king—"

I slam the door, my knees suddenly weak. I move toward the entrance to the servants' passage, intent on finding Mother or Margaret or Will, but as I turn, I notice the white piece of paper lying face up on my bed.

Scrawled elegantly in red ink—at least, I think it's ink—are the words:

You can still save them.

I crumple the paper in my fist, wishing I could set it on fire with merely a thought.

The gift the Changeling promised me—he somehow found a

way to influence the king to conscript my brothers despite my service to the Crown. He told me to make my decision and meet him on the bridge tomorrow night. Stay here, and if the Order fails to overthrow the king on Holy Winter's Day, my brothers will be sent to war. Leave, and they might still have a chance at freedom. I could give them the medallion—Titus could call for the *Starchaser* to collect them.

They could make it to the Red Island, where they could be safe. Free.

All I've done is make things worse. I'm no hero. And I'm tired, too. Tired of pretending. Tired of trying. Tired of losing people I love.

Tomorrow night, I tell myself as I curl onto my side, wrapped in a blanket of midnight blue. Tomorrow night, I'm going to do what I should have done when all this began.

CHAPTER THIRTY

Since my arrival at Castle Grim, I've heard talk of the Crystal Atrium, but nothing could have prepared me for the lush expanse of gardens that occupies a third of the outer court, dappled with a soft orange light as the sun sinks toward the horizon. Glass encloses the various landings dispersed among the hundreds of species of flowers and trees, shielding us from the elements, with the aid of firebreather magic to warm the enclosure. The plaza appears transformed by opulent candelabras and tables dressed in white silk, and as servants hustle throughout the crowd, serving tiny dishes and fizzy drinks, I get the strangest feeling this is all an elaborate display for the Nightweavers in their pastel finery.

I stand at the top of the curved staircase, concealed by a shrub, struggling to breathe—from nerves or the corset of my elaborate green gown; I'm finding it increasingly difficult to tell the difference. For the Nightweavers in attendance, Holy Winter's Eve marks the closing of their festival and represents the victory of some king I've never heard of. This year, it is the eve of Titus and Leo's wedding day. But for Will, it's his last night before his curse turns him into a Shifter, and for me...tonight is the night I have to choose: my family or Will. My freedom or my family's. The Order's mission or my own vow to protect my mother and siblings no matter the cost.

The conversation lulls as every head turns to watch as I descend the staircase. I spot the king and queen, clothed in black and red, a stark contrast to the flowery atmosphere of the atrium, their expressions pleasantly neutral. Beside them, Leo looks as if she belongs in the garden, her petal-pink gown sparkling in the soft glow of the candlelight. The Castors stand nearby, Lord Bludgrave diligent to keep his eyes on Annie, who sits at their round banquet table, picking at her food with a vacant stare, while Lady Isabelle watches me with a look I know only as motherly pride. Eliza, dressed in a black lace gown and purple elbow-length gloves, matches Flynn's black suit, a purple flower pinned to his breast pocket.

The two Cooper siblings talk among themselves, seemingly unaware of the party taking place around them. Flynn clenches his jaw as Eliza whispers something in his ear, and a moment later she draws back, covering her nose with a handkerchief, her lip curling as if she were disgusted. But when they catch my eye, they offer warm smiles, toasting me with their drinks. Immediately, I search for my own family dispersed among the crowd, but the moment my eyes wander, I'm trapped.

Clemson and Davina Mercer cling to Will's either arm, glaring at me, and I realize why when Will starts forward, if only a fraction of a step, his jaw clenched, as if he truly cannot contain himself. Our eyes meet, his gaze pleading—imploring me to make my way toward him.

But I look away.

I look for *him*.

I *hate* that I look for him. But after everything Titus confessed to me last night—after he gave me the medallion—I need to see him. I want to see him. And I don't know how to feel about that, especially when Will is looking at me in the way I've wished for him to all these months.

With every step, I scan the faces of the crowd, expecting to see Titus, but he's nowhere to be found. My search grows somewhat frantic as I near the bottom. Just last night, I told him to leave me alone—but I didn't really want that, did I? Maybe I wanted him to stay. Maybe I hate him more than I realize. Maybe I don't hate him at all. Maybe...

Maybe I don't know how I feel.

As I descend the final step, a thread of panic winds around my heart, gets tangled up in my rib cage, making it difficult to breathe.

Damn this corset.

"Aster?"

I whirl, my gown twirling, and come face-to-face with Titus, half cloaked in shadows in the alcove beneath the staircase.

"Aster?" he breathes, his gaze roving my gown to my face once more, lingering a moment too long on the place over my heart, where he must know the medallion rests, hidden beneath the fabric of my dress, before meeting my eyes. "Last night—"

"There you are!" Killian's voice sends Titus and me careening back a step. He hesitates, looking between the two of us, and I don't know why guilt gnaws at my stomach, but it's as if Killian knows more about what was just happening—what might have happened—between Titus and me than we do. He clears his throat somewhat awkwardly, tapping his foot. "Might I speak with Aster alone?"

Titus dips his head, and in the glow of the lanterns, I swear I see a faint blossom of pink on his cheeks. "Of course. I'm afraid I must be going soon, anyway."

"But this is *your* party?" The words escape me before I can hold them back.

"Duty calls." He shifts in his stance, seeming uncomfortable as he tugs at his shirt collar. He looks to me then, his gaze hopeful—pitiful—and the world seems to slow, the clamor of the party fading until all I hear is his heartbeat, wild and unpredictable. "Will I see you tonight?" He leans in, whispering, "One last swim?"

One last swim, I know, is his way of offering to teach me how to control my affinity one final time before his wedding tomorrow, and something about his voice, rough and soft and achingly tender, sends the butterflies in my stomach into a fit. I almost nod, but instead I school my expression into something neutral—or at least I hope it looks that way. "Perhaps."

He casts his eyes skyward, as if petitioning the Stars, but I note the ghost of a grin on his lips. He scratches his jaw, chuckles under his breath. "Perhaps," he echoes, clapping Killian on the shoulder as he passes.

Killian offers him a polite shrug and a quick farewell, but the moment we're alone, he turns to me, urgent.

"I've spoken to your brothers," he whispers, his gaze flitting over my shoulders every few moments. "They're all right—you needn't worry."

"Do you know why the king conscripted them?" I ask warily. "They were supposed to be safe so long as I swore my allegiance to the Crown."

Killian's mustache twitches, his expression grave. "They volunteered, I'm afraid." He cracks his knuckles uneasily, glancing all around before adding, "They were compelled, Aster. I suspect the Changeling—the one who attacked you at the train station."

I open my mouth to tell him about the way the Underling made himself known to me in my room or the attack at the docks last night, but he's already looked away, surveying the alcove before continuing. "I know about the other attacks, as well." He shoots me a pointed look then, his brow cocked. "I have my sources."

I almost ask who, but then I remember what Killian told us in the conservatory—how the pixies were keeping him abreast of things. "*Liv*," I mutter, shaking my head, even as the ghost of a grin touches my lips.

He continues, "Although in the future, it would be helpful if you'd keep me apprised of these situations. Might be useful to know you're being haunted. Perhaps I could have offered my assistance—I'm somewhat of an expert at hunting Underlings, you know."

I cringe with shame, opening my mouth and closing it again at least a dozen times, but nothing I think to say seems to fit.

"It's quite all right," he adds, his demeanor gentle. "I know you want to do everything on your own, but I'd be foolish if I didn't remind you that there are people who care about you. People who want to help." He inclines his head, understanding twinkling in his eyes. "You're so much like your father in that way—fiercely independent." He laughs, shaking his head. "I never knew what was going on in that head of his until it was too late to stop him."

My heart twists. "I think you might have known him better than I did."

"Oh, I very much doubt that," Killian says, smiling wistfully. "But someday soon, I'd like to tell you what I *did* know, if you'd like to hear it."

I return his smile, my throat thick with emotion. I know now that the only way to break the Underling's compulsion over Charlie and Lewis is to give myself over to him. But it's a nice thought, all the same—hearing Killian's stories of my father when they were young. "That would be lovely."

"Of course, of course." Killian takes a cigar from his breast pocket. He flicks open his lighter, the tip of the cigar glowing red. "Now," he says, puffing smoke, "back to the matter at hand—"

A trumpet sounds, and the king and queen step onto a makeshift dais near the edge of the garden, followed by Leo and Titus. Behind them, the ocean sparkles as the last tangerine rays of sunlight scatter across the waves.

"Damn it, that's my cue," Killian hisses, ushering me toward the gathering crowd. "I would love to stay and chat, but I must take care of something before the ceremony ends. Until we meet again, trust no one. Do you understand?" I nod, and he smiles. "Excellent. Oh, and you do look rather lovely in Bancroft green, if I say so myself."

And just like that, the crowd swallows him up, and I find myself standing alone.

"Welcome all," the king says, toasting the air with his glass. "Tonight, as we gather for Holy Winter's Eve, we remember the victory of my ancestor, the great king Marcellus Anteres, on a night very much like tonight."

I watch Leo, her head bowed, hands knit together, attempting to catch her eye, but she never looks up.

"...why we light the lanterns," the king goes on. "To remember that in our darkest hour, Marcellus used his affinity to light the torches that surrounded this castle, rallying the people of this mighty city to arms."

Calantha places her hand on Titus's arm, and I note the way his jaw clenches. And it appears I'm not the only one who notices.

When Leo takes his hand, the tension in his shoulders seems to loosen.

I can't help but stare at their clasped hands—can't ignore the pang of jealousy in my chest—even if I know he doesn't have feelings for her. Even if I know that in Leo's heart, she believes Titus has been compelled, and come tomorrow, she'll be forced to end his life. In this moment, I see what could have been—what might have been—if it weren't for the secrets that have forced two best friends to become enemies.

"And so tonight we ignite the lanterns not only in celebration of Marcellus's victory but also for the love that burns brighter than any fire—the love that will unite our two kingdoms. To Prince Titus and Princess Leonora!"

The crowd lifts their glasses, blocking Titus and Leo from my view as they echo, "To Prince Titus and Princess Leonora!"

I feel his presence before I see him, standing there at the edge of the crowd near the dais, watching me. Will makes a subtle movement—jerks his head to the left slightly—as if beckoning me to follow.

When I look back at the dais, Titus gazes at Leo with such adoration that despite everything he's said about the princess—despite him still holding fast to the idea that she's possessed—I almost believe he might feel differently. That maybe his feelings for her—or lack of them—are just another lie. After all, he meant to drive me away. Perhaps all this was just because he couldn't confront the change in his relationship with Leo.

Or perhaps Leo *is* right about his compulsion, and all of it was truly an act—just not for the reasons he's led me to believe.

I weave through the crowd as the music starts up again, signaling the conclusion of the king's speech. I find an opening and head straight for Will when—

"We found you!" Clemson giggles, latching onto Will's arm.

"Why'd you run off like that?" Davina pouts, tugging at his shirtsleeve like an insufferable child.

My eyes meet Will's for only a moment before I turn, nearly bumping into the tall, broad-shouldered woman behind me.

"Pardon me," I say, hardly sparing her a glance as I make to move past her.

"Aster Oberon?" she asks, her voice clear and calm. "Ah, it *is* you, isn't it?" Her eyes brim with warmth, but her smile is merely polite, as if it were an afterthought. "I've heard so much about you. It's a pleasure to finally meet." She extends her hand to me, and I shake it, noting her strong grip. "My name is Eva Mercer."

I glance at her daughters, fawning over Will.

Oh.

"Lovely to meet you," I say, my smile feeling out of place on my lips.

She follows the direction my eyes darted, nodding slowly. "I assume you've already met my daughters?"

"Briefly."

She offers a coy smile. "I see." She taps her nails on her wineglass. "Well, surely you must understand how important it is for a girl to marry well. I believe Lord Castor will make a fine husband for one of them—if only he'd hurry up and choose."

I feel as if I just took a cannonball to the face.

Choose? Marry?

Will?

I wet my lips to speak, to say something—*what*, I can't possibly begin to know—when Eliza appears at my side. She looks as if she'd rather be anywhere else, her eye twitching, lip slightly curled, but her expression shifts as she plasters on a wide, charming grin, the portrait of geniality.

"Eva, darling!" Eliza kisses the air on either side of Eva's face. "You're here! How marvelous. You know, a few people have been just dying to make your acquaintance, and who am I to deny them? Come, come," she says, ushering Eva toward the banquet tables. "Oh, and your lovely daughters, too!" she adds, smiling sweetly.

Eva glances at me, then Will, her eyes narrowing before she calls out, "Girls! Girls! Come along, leave Lord Castor be."

Clemson and Davina groan in unison before blowing Will a barrage of kisses as they trail after their mother. When their backs are turned, Eliza glances over her shoulder at me, jerking her head in Will's direction.

Thank you, I mouth.

She winks at me, leading the group of women away.

"We'll have to be quick," Will says, his voice low and deep. He closes the gap between us in seconds, taking me by the hand and leading me out a door in the glass wall that lines the plaza and down a crumbling set of steps near the balcony railing. "The ceremony will start soon, and if I'm not already out on the water, I'll be forced to share a boat with those two."

The waves lap at the stone staircase, water spraying my arms, my face. When we reach the bottom, Will helps me into an ornate wooden rowboat, the seats littered with both rose petals and the purple petals of his beloved mystiks. The moment I'm seated, Will takes the oars, rowing us out to sea. Not too far off, party guests have begun to depart from the dock there at the castle harbor, dozens of rowboats making their way into the bay, but Will makes a point to row us in the opposite direction, keeping a reasonable distance between us and them.

The sun slips below the horizon, and for a moment, the world seems to hold its breath. Slowly, the stars twinkle into being, silver beams of moonlight penetrating a wispy cloud overhead. And the water...deep sapphire blue.

I reach out, my fingertips gliding across the surface of the water, as soft and as cool as silk. The sensation stirs something within me, and a feeling of contentment seems to settle in my chest, soothing my aching heart.

"I met Eva," I say, unwilling to look at him, although I feel his gaze on me. I watch as lanterns float above the surface of the water, drifting up from the dozens of rowboats littering the bay, their golden light illuminating the darkness. "If Titus were to obtain the cure...you would marry one of her daughters, wouldn't you?"

I take his silence to mean guilt, but when I look at him, his mouth gapes with open shock.

"You can't honestly believe that?"

I mirror his surprise, my brows raised. "Why wouldn't I? In all the time we've been here, you've done nothing but *entertain* them.

You're a Nightweaver, Will! And I'm—" I half-laugh, half-groan. "I'm a human—a halfling! We both know this was never meant to be. Regardless of the law, I will always be a pirate, and you will always be the great Lord Castor. But these Mercer girls...suppose the Order asked you to marry one of them—would you do it?"

Indignation and laughter war in his features, his brow furrowing, lips twitching, before he finally gives in to the latter. "Aster, your mother asked that I get close to the Mercer girls to ensure Eva Mercer follows through with the bargain she's made with the Order."

I struggle to take a breath, the tight band around my stomach hindering my every attempt. "And I'm supposed to take your word for it?"

He drops the oars, running his hands over his face. "Of course not," he says, gaining some measure of control over his composure. "Ask your mother—ask Killian, he knows! Eva Mercer has agreed to allow the Order's naval forces through her trade route, enabling the attack set to take place tomorrow, on the day of the wedding. I just need Eva to believe for one more day that one of her daughters is set to enter a beneficial marriage proposal, and then I will never, *ever* have to speak to them again. Ever."

I want to believe him, but...he promised he wouldn't keep any more secrets from me, and yet that's all he's done. What if this is who he is, and of all the secrets he keeps, I am his biggest secret of all?

He leans forward, taking me by the hand, suddenly serious. "It has been the worst form of torture having to remain apart from you—having to pretend as if I'm not going out of my mind every minute of every day that you're not by my side." His thumb strokes my knuckles, his other hand coming up to brush my cheek, and I think I see tiny dark green veins peeking out from his sleeve, as if the curse were trailing up his arm, into his fingers. "There is only one girl I wish to spend the rest of my days with—that I wish to spend my final hours with, however few they may be, and she's sitting right here, in this boat, looking more beautiful than the stars themselves. And you're right," he adds quickly, wincing as if in pain, "I can't give up. I won't. Even if I turn, I'll keep fighting for us. For our future together." Our gazes meet, his green eyes ablaze with emotions so intense I almost look away. "I love you, Aster."

The air whooshes from my chest at his admission. He's going to fight for us—for our future.

We can have a future together.

He loves me. He's finally said it—finally confessed his feelings for me. So then why don't the butterflies in my stomach take flight?

"I—" I clutch my abdomen, my head light. "I can't breathe."

Will smiles, squeezing my hand. "I understand it's a lot to take in—"

"No," I gasp, "I can't—*breathe*."

Will's eyes widen as realization dawns on his face. He cuts a glance at my corset before taking hold of the oars once more, rowing us back toward the narrow sliver of rock from which we departed.

"Just"—Will grunts, rowing us back to Castle Grim with surprising speed—"hang on."

My head spins, dark spots edging my vision. I stare at him, almost dreamlike, attempting to piece together what he said. It sounded a lot like...

"Were you..." I wheeze for breath. "Asking me..."

He barks a wild laugh, the creases in his forehead deepening as he fights against the current. "Maker of All, Aster, *yes*."

In minutes, he ties the boat off and grabs me beneath my arms, dragging me, half-conscious, onto the stone landing. He reaches for the front of my gown—hesitates.

"May I?"

It takes everything in me to nod, my head as heavy as a ball of lead.

Will rips the gown open with what feels like little effort, sliding it from my shoulders. I watch through a haze as he opens his pocketknife, slicing through the bindings of my corset.

The medallion clatters to the ground, and I gasp at the influx of air as breath floods my lungs.

Will rubs little circles on the small of my back. "Breathe. Just breathe."

At his touch, my frenzied heartbeat slows, the fog in my head clearing as my breathing regulates. But as Will retrieves the medallion from where it fell, my pulse quickens once more.

His brows knit. "I see," he murmurs.

I cross my arms over my chest, feeling as if my thick cotton slip might as well be made of lace. "Will—"

"Please, Aster, don't give me your answer just yet," he says softly, his expression somewhat pained as he slips the chain over my neck, letting the medallion fall to rest between my collarbones. "Wait here. I'll go fetch you something to cover up with."

Without waiting for me to protest, he hurries up the stairs, disappearing around the corner.

I allow myself a minute—one minute—of self-pity. If it weren't for the Underling—if it weren't for the Order, or the war, or six hundred years of hatred between Nightweavers and humans—what would my answer be? It doesn't matter, now. Without Morana's blood, Will is cursed to turn into a Shifter. Even if we could find a way to cure him before tomorrow, I'll never escape the Underling who's marked me for death. No matter what, he'll keep coming for me. I can't continue to put everyone I love in danger.

One minute of self-pity. One minute of grief. One minute of hope. When the minute has passed, I bury those feelings along with my fear and fish my daggers from my gown.

With one last look at the staircase above, where in a few moments, I imagine Will appearing to find me gone, I make my way along the narrow ledge of rock, moving as quickly as I can toward the bridge to Jade.

Chapter Thirty-One

I tighten my grip on the hilt of my daggers, my teeth chattering as a gust of cool air blows through the underside of the bridge where I wait. In the distance, fireworks bloom over the rooftops of Jade, each shrill whistle followed by a crackle that sounds far too much like gunfire, causing my muscles to tighten with every eruption. I look to my right, where the boats appear like swans on the surface of the water. By now, Will has surely returned to find me gone. Will he come looking for me? Will he alert Killian and the others that I've gone missing?

I grit my teeth at the sound of gravel crunching underfoot.

"What took you so long?" I ask, injecting as much venom into my tone as I can muster as I turn to find the Underling leaning casually against a stone pillar.

His gilded eyes twinkle with amusement. "Oh, I've been here," he drawls. "I just wanted to watch you contemplate your decision a minute longer. I thought you might still change your mind."

My lip curls. "Break the compulsion." My knuckles turn white as I clench my daggers in my fists. For the first time in my life, I know I've been physically outmatched. My daggers have no effect on him, my bracelet offers me no protection against his compulsion. He's already in my head—in my blood. He can make me do whatever he wishes with merely a thought.

But he doesn't. And I think I've figured out why.

"Oh, Aster," he chides, tilting his head. "It's too late for your brothers. They've already volunteered—there's no going back on that commitment. I thought, as a Bloodknight, you'd understand that. You're bound by your oath—they're bound by theirs."

My arms tremble with rage, my nails biting into my palms. "Your note said I could still save them."

He nods slowly, considering. "Yes, yes," he says. "You can still save the rest of your family. I had rather devious plans for them should you have decided not to come tonight."

I fight the urge to lunge at him—to thrust my blades into his chest. But I know that won't do me any good. I'm not fast enough, and he's practically invincible.

But I'm not.

I drop one dagger, letting it clatter to the stone, and point the other at my chest—directly over my heart.

He rolls his eyes. "A touch dramatic, don't you think?"

I let the tip of my dagger bite, drawing blood.

His pupils dilate, the gold of his eyes thinning. "Aster," he says slowly, breathlessly, "we need not play this game."

"You marked me for death." I hiss through the stinging pain of the blade pressing into my skin, sweat forming on my brow. "But you don't want me dead yet, do you?"

His eyes narrow, his fingers twitching at his side. I feel his magic take hold of me, seizing my hands in its unyielding grip. He forces the blade deeper, breaking flesh. "If I didn't want you dead, I could stop you," he rasps, his voice dark, as deep as the depths of the ocean and as gritty as smoke. "Come along, before I change my mind about your family. You wouldn't want them to suffer for your petulance, hmm?"

"No," I say firmly, my hands shaking as I fight to resist his magic. "You need me to come willingly; otherwise, we wouldn't still be here, would we?"

He laughs, the sound almost as violent and grating as a Gore, only far more sinister, like the distant roll of thunder.

My knees collide with the stone as his magic forces me to kneel.

He strides forward to stand over me, tall and menacing. "Why do you insist on fighting me?" He crouches down so that he's eye level with me, his head cocked. "Don't you realize," he says, grasping my chin with his gloved hand, "I'm only trying to give you what you so desperately desire?" He leans in, his eyes searching mine as he dabs a finger in the blood pooling at the front of my dress. "*Power*, Aster." He smears the blood over my lips, his eyes wild. "Can't you taste it?"

I spit at his face, the blood spraying his bandaged mouth.

A low growl vibrates in the back of his throat as he straightens once more, the shadows encircling his towering form seeming to grow darker, denser.

"*On your feet*," he commands, the rich, sonorous sound needling itself so deep in my mind, I withdraw the dagger from my chest and stand, the metal clanging as my weapon falls to the ground beside the other.

"*Decide*," he barks, throwing out his hand. An invisible grip tightens around my throat, crushing my windpipe. "Or I will decide for you."

My eyes feel as if they're going to pop out of my skull. I attempt to make a sound, and he releases his magic hold on me just long enough for me to say, "Fine!"

He lets go, and I fall to the stone beside my daggers, heaving for breath.

"I'll go willingly," I pant, picking myself off the ground. "Under one condition."

He chuckles, his demeanor once again cool and collected. "And what is that?"

I meet his gaze, searching his gilded eyes for something, anything that might give me an answer. "Tell me who you really are."

Bang. Bang. Bang. A series of fireworks spray their colorful, glittering light over the rooftops, the golden shimmer reminding me of *Manan*.

He tilts his head again, eyes lit with curiosity. "You mean you haven't figured it out yet?" His shadows begin to fade as he reaches for the bandages that cover his face, slowly unwinding the first strip, revealing his lips, his nose.... "I—"

BANG.

At first, I think it's just another firework, but it sounded so close—the shot still ringing in my ears, the crackle of the fireworks now muffled and distant.

The Underling's golden eyes narrow—widen.

He opens his mouth as if to say something, and blood dribbles over his lips, onto his chin.

He falls forward, grabbing me by the shoulders, the full force of his weight taking us both to the ground.

And there, stepping out of the shadows no more than ten feet away, holding a flintlock pistol—the Howler gifted to me by Killian so long ago, on the hillside of Bludgrave Manor...

"Will?"

"Aster!" Will rushes to my side, the flintlock still pointed at my assailant, sprawled out on the stone beside me, laboring for breath as he chokes on his own blood. "Get up," Will says, extending his hand to me. "Quickly, now."

I reach for Will's hand just as the Underling grabs my wrist, his grip weak but desperate.

He tries to say something, but all that comes out is a wet, gurgling noise. He claws at his bandaged face with his free hand, as if attempting to remove the wrappings, his cloak of shadows now faint, barely a dark wreath of vapor around his bound form.

"Aster," Will says again, but I ignore him.

I remove the first bandage from the Underling's face. Then another, and another, until...

"Flynn?" I gasp, staring down at the Bloodknight's familiar features.

He tries to speak again, but blood coats his teeth, the sound of his voice thick in his throat. He tries one more time, clutching his chest, where the bullet blew a hole through his heart. I see the moment he realizes it's futile, see the determination there in his eyes as something shifts, as if he were coming awake.

He lifts his trembling hand and points.

Right at Will.

CHAPTER THIRTY-TWO

Flynn's hand falls as his body goes limp.

"Aster."

I hear Will's voice from far away as I stare at Flynn's face, at his rigid finger, still pointed in Will's direction.

William Castor is lying to you.

"Aster?" Will pleads, gripping my arm and hauling me to my feet. "Aster, listen to me, we have to go—we have to—"

I stumble as he pulls me along, unable to take my eyes off Flynn. For the first time in months, the constant ache in my shoulder dissipates. I may still have Underling venom in my veins, but it's as if I felt his connection to my curse severed the moment he drew his last breath.

"He was the spy," I say, my own voice distant, muffled by the ringing in my ears. But even as I say the words, something nags at me.

Flynn attacked me tonight, but the day on the train platform...the Shifter attacked *Flynn*, just after Gabriel ran off. I think of what Leo told me—how the two of them killed their parents together—and my stomach sours. "There's two of them." I nod, putting the pieces together. "Flynn *and* Gabriel Cooper. They're working together."

But who could have shot the arrow that day when Flynn was attacked?

"Aster, we don't have time!" Will grabs me, urgently spinning me around to face him. He holds me in his unrelenting gaze. "Eva Mercer's been killed."

"What?" I shake my head, attempting to clear the fog that descended in the moments following Flynn's death. "By whom?"

I see it, then—the look of pure grief on Will's face, his expression twisting, contorting into something I don't recognize. Something raw and human and utterly defeated.

"Eliza," he chokes out, his voice breaking. "Eliza Cooper."

I follow Will through the servants' passages, distantly aware of the twists and turns, his grip on my hand my only anchor to the present moment.

"Eliza's on the run," he explains, nearly breathless as he leads me up a narrow staircase. "The king has guards searching the city for her. They believe she's been working for Morana, for the Guild of Shadows."

My head swims, and I think of what Leo told me—of the rumors that Eliza covered up Flynn and Gabriel's crimes, and I realize it could have been Eliza who shot the arrow that day on the train platform. "But—Eliza wasn't—" I want to argue, want to petition on Eliza's behalf, but...Flynn just tried to *kill* me. "I don't understand. Eliza is your friend!"

"And Owen is your brother," Will shoots back, his teeth clenched. He runs a hand through his hair, and softer, he says, "You of all people should know you can't always trust those closest to you."

He drops my hand as he shoves through the servant's door and into my bedroom, immediately going to the balcony doors to ensure they're locked, then to the door to my suite. He checks my wardrobe, my bath chambers, even under my bed. Apparently satisfied, he takes me by the shoulders, forcing me to meet his eye.

"Lock this door behind me," he says, pointing to the servant's door. He takes my daggers from his belt—thankfully he retrieved them from beneath the bridge while I was distracted with Flynn—and gives them back to me. "I'm going to find Killian."

"I want to go with you!" I say, my fists tightening around the hilts of my daggers.

A muscle in his jaw ripples. "It's not safe."

"Safe?" I scoff, attempting to shove past him, but he blocks the doorway. "My family is somewhere in this castle. If Gabriel is—"

"I know!" Will shouts, clearly losing his tentative grip on his composure. "I will do everything I can to ensure your family's safety, but I need you to *stay put*."

He doesn't give me a chance to argue, sweeping through the door and shutting it behind him. I reach for the knob, but it won't budge. On the other side of the door, I hear the scrape of stone, and I realize what he's done.

He used his abilities as a bonewielder to block the door with a rock, locking it from inside the passageway.

Teeth gritted, I plunge my daggers into my mattress, savoring the feeling of stabbing something—anything. I open the doors to my balcony, a gust of wind casting my hair back as I lean over the railing, attempting to hear the commotion from the party, but on this side of the castle, all I hear is the crash of the waves as they beat against the ancient fortress.

I slam the balcony doors shut, headed straight for the door that leads out into the castle, where the guards remain at their posts all hours of the day and night. I'm prepared to demand they take me to the kitchens, where I might find my family, but my foot catches on the rug, and my heart skips a beat.

I tear the rug aside, placing my hand on the stone floor.

"Adonoc verash melor," I whisper.

Nothing.

I slam my fist against the stone. Take a deep breath.

I try again, this time attempting to mimic the deep, gentle hum of Titus's voice when he spoke the words before.

"Adonoc verash melor."

Thunk. The stone paver sinks.

I wait until the passageway has revealed itself, take the first couple of steps, and when I've descended far enough that I'm clear of the opening, I place my hand on the stone wall and whisper, *"Granitum zeruuk shanol,"* sealing myself in the darkness.

I race down the steps, blood pounding in my ears. Titus implied he would meet me here tonight. Surely, he's waiting for me. Surely—

I emerge into the cavern, his name already on my lips, but it's empty.

My heart squeezes in my chest.

He didn't come.

"Titus?" I call out, hating the way my voice breaks. Hating how small it sounds. Hating how badly I wish to see him in this moment. "Titus!"

Follow me.

The voice is clear, and yet I can't be sure if I've heard it or if the words have come from my own mind. Still, I know it instantly.

This way.

The water that divides the cavern seems to undulate, and it appears as if a hand forms, waving me toward the crack in the wall to my right, where the pool filters into a stream.

I make my way to the gap in the stone, finding that it's just wide enough for me to wedge my body into the narrow passage sideways. A subtle blue glow emanates from the stream, as if guiding me forward.

Hurry.

The water laps urgently at the passage, encouraging me to venture farther into the dark, cramped space. A few feet in, the path widens slightly, enough that my shoulders scrape the stone wall, ankle deep in the stream as I follow the blue light.

Quiet, the sea commands.

I attempt to slow my breath, straining to hear beyond the steady trickle of the water as it filters through the cave. Ahead, the gap narrows once more, and the blue glow vanishes, plunging me into darkness.

An animal screams, the sound ragged and violent, sending a shudder through me.

I peek through the gap in the stone, and my vision narrows on the bloody form chained from the ceiling, head hung, a cruel gash carved into his chest, two more across both shoulder blades.

He cries again, weaker this time, and I cover my mouth to silence a scream of my own.

Not an animal.

Titus.

Queen Calantha's eyes glow gold as she brings a curved dagger to her lips, collecting the blood on her tongue.

"*Shh*," she croons, bringing a bloodstained hand to Titus's cheek, brushing his sweat-soaked hair from his face. "Behave."

She places the knife on a nearby table, the rough-hewn wood covered with an array of weaponry, crude tools, and various jars of dark red liquid—*blood*, I think. The passage led me to a small cave in the dungeons, the stream widening to cut through the stone floor and feed into the canals that separate the cells.

Calantha takes a goblet from the table and presses it to the fresh, gaping wound in Titus's chest. Blood pours from the cut, slowly filling the goblet, all while Calantha fusses with Titus's hair, stroking his cheek, whispering softly.

"That wasn't so bad, was it?" She tuts. "I told you I'd be quick. Have I ever lied to you?"

I think he must be unconscious from either pain or loss of blood or both, but when Calantha draws back, smacking him hard across the face, he makes a rough, quick noise, like a grunt.

She smiles, peering into the goblet. "I would like it very much if you stayed at the palace a little while longer," she says sweetly. "You were away too long the last time. If you'd come home sooner,

I wouldn't have had to work so tirelessly to replenish my supply. You know how I hate to see you in pain."

By the wicked gleam in her eye as she removes the full goblet and places it on the table, I know that statement can't be further from the truth.

She takes a key from the table and removes the first cuff from Titus's wrist. His body gives a violent jerk as the remaining chain takes the brunt of his limp body. When she removes the second chain, he falls to his knees with a resounding *thud*, his face pressed to the stone.

He groans, bloody skin pulled taut over his muscles as he attempts to lift himself off the ground.

Calantha rolls her eyes. "I expect to see you back here in three days," she says, taking the goblet with her as she slips through the door to the cell, pausing halfway to look down at Titus's broken body with utter contempt. "Enjoy your wedding."

The door closes behind her, and Titus collapses in a heap on the floor.

The first sob is quiet, excruciating. The second breaks me.

I squeeze through the gap, nearly throwing myself at him. I land beside him, my hand outstretched as if to touch him, but from this close, I see just how mangled his flesh looks, the cuts deep enough to expose sinew and bone.

"Titus?" I say gently, my voice shaking.

With an unexpected burst of strength, he whirls, scrambling onto his back, his teeth bared in a snarl, eyes glowing gold. But something akin to shame passes over his expression, and his bottom lip trembles as he fights to hold back another sob.

"Aster?" The sound cracks. Splinters. Shatters. Panic flares in his eyes, blue eating away at the gold. "Get out of here!" He drags himself to his feet, his jaw clenched so tightly I fear he'll break it. "Go! Before—before she—" He glances at the door, his expression somewhat hysterical—wild and vicious and animalistic in his fear.

"I'm not leaving without you!" I say, meeting him where he stands. I reach out to cup his cheek, but he flinches. "Titus, please. Come with me. Let me help you."

He bites his lip, shaking his head, his eyes glassy with tears. "You can't be here."

"I *am* here," I say firmly, taking him by the hand. "I have you," I add, prompting him to meet my gaze. "I'm not letting you go."

He looks as if he might snarl at me again—might snap at me with those vicious teeth. Might rip my heart from my chest and feast on it in front of me. But then his shoulders sag, and he nods, allowing me to lead him to the gap in the wall.

He hisses through gritted teeth as he squeezes along the passage, the stone grating against his open wounds.

"I'm sorry," I say over and over again. "Just a little farther. We're almost there."

When we finally emerge into Hildegarde's cavern, Titus stumbles, and I'm barely fast enough to wedge myself underneath him, catching his weight as he plunges into the shallow pool. His head slumps on my shoulder, and I know that it's only because the water aids me that I'm able to keep us both above the surface.

"We need to get help," I say, watching as the water turns crimson all around us.

Too much blood. He's losing too much blood.

"I'll bring Will—"

"No," he rasps, his chest rattling with every breath. "Not—here. Up—stairs."

"I can't carry you," I insist. "We'll never make it. If I just go—"

"Don't"—he heaves, his body shuddering—"let—go."

He tightens his heavy hold on me, and I grit my teeth, determined.

"Never," I say, pulling him closer.

I send a quick prayer to the Stars, petitioning them for strength, and drag him through the water, to the edge of the pool.

He curses, hauling himself onto the rocky bank.

I grab him under the arms, pulling him to his feet. "I'm sorry," I say. "I'm sorry."

"Not—your fault," he murmurs, a cord in his neck bulging as I bolster him beneath his shoulder, cringing at the whimper that escapes his lips. I lead him to the staircase, my forehead slick with sweat.

The first couple of steps are the hardest. Halfway up, he stumbles forward, catching himself on the jagged stone with a low howl of agony. From that point on, it's as if something shifts, and he insists on clawing his way forward, stone by stone. By the time we reach the top, he slams his hand against the wall, renewed vigor in his voice as he hums the words, *"Adonoc verash melor."*

He teeters backward, and I think for a moment we're both going to plummet to our deaths, but when the ceiling opens up, revealing my room, Titus lunges forward, scrabbling into the suite on all fours.

His eyes roll to the back of his head as he collapses onto my rug.

He doesn't move.

CHAPTER THIRTY-THREE

Blood sprays the stone as Will slams his fist against the wall.

"You said—" Will spits, his voice rough, uneven. Unhinged. "You said she'd stopped."

"William, please." Titus sighs. "I'm quite all right."

I can't help but stare at him, sitting up in my bed, the wounds that only an hour ago gushed blood onto my sheets now healed, three thick pink scars amid the myriad of white lesions the only indication they ever existed. Will mended Titus's flesh, but the loss of blood was evident in his pale face, his sluggish movements. I left his side only long enough to change from my bloodstained undergarment into a pair of trousers and a linen shirt, but I haven't moved from the edge of the bed since, my hand hovering near his, close enough to touch.

"No, you're not *quite all right*." Will runs his hands through his hair, his palms stained red, even after washing Titus's blood from his skin. "If I hadn't been here—if I'd been even a minute too late—"

"You weren't," Titus says calmly. He shakes his head, eyes shut tight. "She just—she cut too deep."

"Too deep?" Will's eyes flare—a flash of gold light illuminating his face. "You should have told me. You should have said something—"

"So you could what?" Titus rolls his eyes. "Charm her into giving up her little habit?"

"I told you the last time," Will says, his voice lethally quiet. "The next time she laid a hand on you, I would tear her arms from her body."

Titus frowns, his nonchalant expression faltering as he meets Will's vengeful stare. "I appreciate the sentiment, brother, but I'm afraid not even that would curb her addiction."

"Addiction?" The word slips out of my mouth like a bitter poison.

Titus and Will both look at me then, as if they forgot I was in the room. From the moment Titus gained consciousness, Will alternated between scolding him and promising violence on Queen Calantha.

"Why would your mother do this to you?" I ask, angling myself toward Titus, noticing out of the corner of my eye the way Will calculates the proximity of my hand to his friend's.

Titus scowls, but his eyes soften. "Calantha is not my mother." He takes a deep breath—winces. "My father had my mother executed just after I was born. He married Calantha to fix his... mistake."

My jaw goes slack. "Mistake?"

Will slumps on the opposite side of the bed, pinching the bridge of his nose between his forefinger and thumb. "Titus's mother was human," he says. "A servant in this very castle."

I look between the two of them, feeling as if time has altogether stopped.

I start, "You're—"

"A halfling?" Titus finishes, his cracked lips tilted, the ghost of a smirk. "Aside from a life of piracy, it looks as if we finally have something else in common."

I shake my head, my eyes burning with unshed tears. "That's why Calantha was...why she—" I try to speak, but tears clog my throat, and I have to look away from him, the image of his blood-smeared face in the dungeons seared into my memory. "Your blood—you're part human. So the *Manan*...she harvests your *Manan*? Oh, Maker of All—" My breath hitches on a sob, thinking about every time I saw Calantha touch Titus—the way he tensed. Every time it looked as if it pained him to sit down, to put any pressure on his back. How many times has she done this? How long has he endured this kind of torture?

His fingertips brush mine. "Forgive me, love," he says, and I meet his gaze. "You shouldn't have had to see that."

"She saved your life," Will says, his voice even for the first time since he burst through my door and found Titus unconscious on the rug. He runs his hand over the two puncture marks in the bedding, where my daggers tore feathers from the mattress, a glint of amusement in his gaze that would feel entirely out of place if I hadn't seen that look in his eyes a dozen times. If it weren't for Titus, recovering from the brink of death between us, I would have been the one scolding *Will* for daring to lock me in my room when I could have been of help.

Then again, if I had gone with Will, Titus might have bled out in that cell. Alone.

"It wouldn't be the first time," Titus says, his smile somewhat pained.

I open my mouth to ask him what he means, but the servants' door opens, and Killian sweeps into the room, followed by—

"Mother?"

"I came as soon as I heard," Mother says as Killian shuts the door behind them. Her gaze lands, almost immediately, on Titus's hand, clasped tightly in mine.

I didn't even realize I grabbed his hand, but his thumb brushes my knuckles, and my heartbeat slows, if only a little. Still, guilt gnaws at my chest, and when I glance at Will, I find him staring at our clasped hands. Though his taciturn expression gives nothing away, I note the hurt in his gaze—the resignation. I know I should pull my hand away, but I don't—*can't*, as if some invisible force binds me to Titus in this moment, too powerful to resist.

"Hello, Grace," Titus says, smiling slightly. "How nice of you to visit."

Mother's brow quirks, a motherly look of disapproval, tempered only by genuine concern as she examines the scars on Titus's chest. "Killian said you had new information concerning the princess," she says, glancing at Killian, smoking a cigar in the armchair in front of the fireplace, looking as if he bears the weight of the world on his shoulders. "He said it was urgent."

Titus grimaces. "Calantha confirmed it, Grace. She confirmed what I've been trying to tell you all along. *Taunted* me with it."

Mother and Killian share a wary look. Will buries his face in his hands.

"Titus," Mother starts, her voice steady, "we've been over this. What you're asking us to do—"

"I'm asking you to listen to me!" Titus shouts, his face turning red, his eyes pleading. For a moment, I'm reminded of one of the last conversations Owen had with Mother, when he begged her to search for the Red Island. He said something so similar then. *If only you would listen to me!*

By the wounded look on Mother's face, she remembers, too.

"I *am* listening," Mother says, regaining her composure in the blink of an eye. "We've checked Princess Leonora time and time again. She shows no signs of possession—"

"It's her!" This time, he grips my hand, clutching it tight as if to keep himself from springing out of the bed. "It's Morana! Of course you wouldn't see the usual signs—"

The usual signs. As Titus and Mother argue, my gut twists, and I realize what I've been too blind to see before. While Will once told me that Underlings despise sugar, Leo eagerly partook in the plate of sweets the day we met in the Queen's Court. And Will told me once that Underlings hate flowers, but Leo walked willingly through the garden of Bloodroses and seemed serene in the Crystal Atrium. Eliza, however, always declines dessert. She fled from the Bloodrose garden, and she looked as if she were about to jump out of her skin in the Crystal Atrium earlier this evening. Still, something more glaring than the peculiarities of Eliza's personality was right in front of me all along, hanging from Eliza's neck, taunting me with the truth: The Changeling had transformed into a bat—the same bat that represents the crest of House Cooper.

"It's Eliza," I say, the words tumbling out before I've fully come to the realization, but the moment I say it, Will's head whips in my direction, his eyes wide, and Titus jerks his hand away from mine, looking at me as if I just slapped him. But, hearing it aloud, I know it's true, even if I wish with all my heart that it wasn't. I stand, facing Mother, my chin held high. "It's her—Morana has possessed Eliza Cooper. She's been right under our noses all this time. She, Flynn, and Gabriel—the three of them were spying for the Guild of Shadows."

"Flynn?" Titus gawks at me as if I've just sprouted a second head. "Don't tell me you believe all that rubbish about their allegiance to the Underlings?"

My chest squeezes at the hurt in his gaze, but we're almost out of time, and no matter the pain it might cause him to hear the truth, I finally see what I didn't before. "Eliza killed Eva Mercer. It was Gabriel who attacked me at the train station. And tonight…" I hesitate, glancing at Mother and Killian, knowing that what I'm about to say will change everything. "Tonight, Flynn tried to kill me."

I can't bring myself to look at Titus, focusing on Will instead, now on his feet, pacing the room again.

"How did I not see it!" Will's voice breaks as he runs his hands over his face, through his hair. He turns to Titus then, his expression crestfallen. "Aster's right. Eliza…she never was quite the same after the death of their parents. I wanted to believe the rumors were false, but…"

"It's Eliza," I say again, feeling the weight of the words as they tumble out of my mouth, forming a blade in my grasp, condemning Eliza Cooper to death. "And now she's missing. She's gone and…"

It's as if the blade I fashioned for Eliza is now turned on me, threatening to spill blood. Because if Eliza is gone, then Morana has fled, and with her, our chances of obtaining a cure for Will have vanished. And with Eva dead, the Order won't have access to the trade routes needed to infiltrate Castle Grim tomorrow.

The invisible blade twists, and all my hope—every lingering belief that we can still find a way to save Will, to expose Morana and defeat the king of the Eerie in one fell swoop—dies with a final, gasping breath.

Killian's eyes narrow, and Mother takes a step toward me, but Titus is already standing, gripping my arms with such ferocity I never could have guessed he was on the brink of death only a short while ago.

"Where is he?" he demands, his grip firm, almost painful. "Where is Flynn?" He lets me go, turning on Will, wincing as he hobbles toward him. "Gabriel—"

Will catches him by the arm just as he stumbles, guiding him back to the edge of the bed. His voice is soft when he answers, "Flynn's dead." He glances up at me, his lips pressed tight, before adding, "Gabriel's missing. He must have fled after Eliza...." His throat bobs on a swallow, and he shakes his head, as if he can't bear to say what Eliza did, even if it isn't truly Eliza but Morana acting through her.

Emotions flash across Titus's face—rage, disbelief, sadness—before his shoulders slouch, and he lets out a small sob.

"I thought," he says through gritted teeth, "Calantha said—" He looks up at Will, his expression twisted, tormented. "The cure...I was so sure Morana possessed Leo, I—" He chokes on the words. "We're too late."

Too late because tomorrow night, Will is doomed to begin his transformation into a Shifter.

"Maybe not." Mother's voice is quiet, her gaze fixed on the doors to my balcony, as if she were trying to spot something in the distance. "Morana clearly hasn't found what she's looking for, and I don't believe she'll leave Castle Grim without it. We should expect her to make an appearance at the wedding tomorrow. Gabriel as well." She pivots, looking at Killian, Will, and Titus in turn, and with all the authority of a captain, says, "Send word to the Order. Tell them that plans have changed."

Mother's measured stare meets mine. "Will Princess Leonora stand with us?"

I try to swallow, but my mouth is too dry. I see Titus look at me out of the corner of my eye, his gaze narrowing. "She will," I say, even though, as Mother and the others clear out of my room, hurrying down the passage to warn the Order of the Coopers' treachery, I still don't know if I can convince Leo that Titus isn't compelled.

Because, after tonight—after learning of Eliza, Flynn, and Gabriel's betrayal—I can't be sure of anything.

Trust no one, Killian said to me only hours ago in the Crystal Atrium. And I see it in his eyes as he walks past, following Will through the servants' door—see that same warning flickering in his gaze.

Trust no one.

Not even myself.

Chapter Thirty-Four

Water laps at my ankles where I sit on the bank of the pond in Hildegarde's secret cavern. It's hard to believe that a few hours ago I brought Titus back here, broken and bleeding. That before, I was willing to go with the Shifter who cursed me, if it meant keeping my family safe. That he was dead now—Flynn is dead—by Will's hand. And that Eliza has been here all along—that *she* was possessed by Morana, not Leo—and we didn't capture her before it was too late.

I didn't see what was right in front of me. And now I've not only failed Will, I've let the Order down—let my family down. I've failed Owen again.

I've failed them all, just as I failed Father.

Rage boils my blood, and I long for battle—for the chance to expel this bitter hatred with my blade. But there's no one left to blame—no one left to hate—but myself.

It was my responsibility to identify Morana—to discover whom she possessed and expose her. Instead, I befriended her. I let my guard down with Eliza, Flynn, and Gabriel—I was so desperate for friendship, I overlooked every warning sign. I was so unwilling to trust Titus, but I put my faith in three strangers without reservation, and now, Will is going to pay for my mistakes with his life.

My chest aches as I run my fingers over the surface of the medallion, tracing the familiar grooves—the skull and crossed daggers. Tomorrow, though I don't see how, the Order will carry out its attack on Castle Grim. And if I can't convince Leo that Titus isn't compelled before they say their vows, she plans to kill him.

All this time, Leo thought he was sneaking off to the dungeons to harvest human blood. But now that I know he was held captive by his stepmother—that he endured the same torture as the humans and Myths that occupied the dungeons alongside him—it shouldn't be too difficult to tell Leo she was wrong. That Titus is a victim himself. That by marrying him tomorrow, the two of them will be able to lower the wards to Castle Grim, allowing the Order to launch its assault. That tomorrow, the exchanging of their vows will mark the beginning of the end of six hundred years of war and hatred. And perhaps with their combined magic, Titus and Leo could be strong enough to perform the ritual needed to force Morana to take her corporeal form. We could still cure Will before he begins his transformation.

But if I'm wrong, and Titus *is* compelled...

"Thought I might find you here," Titus says, his quiet voice so low I almost think I've imagined it. I turn to find him leaning against the wall at the bottom of the staircase, one hand tucked casually in his pocket. Will healed him, but I can tell by the tension in his shoulders that the pain lingers, and I wonder if that's a result of the many years of torture—if even after the wounds mend, the ache never truly leaves.

"The sun will be up in a few hours," I tell him, slipping the chain of the medallion back over my head. "I didn't see the point in sleeping."

He nods slowly as he removes his coat, his gaze fixed on the sea, spanning out beyond the mouth of the cave. "I was thinking the same thing." He casts his coat to the floor. "Actually, I considered taking that swim we discussed." He rolls up the sleeves of his wrinkled black shirt, revealing a host of tattoos, and I'm drawn to one in particular—the tattoo of the moth that covers a scar made by teeth.

My teeth. My moth tattoo.

He offers a lopsided grin, but it doesn't meet his eyes. "Care to join me?"

"You're going swimming in that?" I scoff, gesturing at his clothes.

He smirks then, his eyes flashing with mischief, and pulls his shirt over his head.

For a moment, it's all I can do not to stare at his chest—at the scars, at the ink scattered across his skin.

"See something you like?"

I roll my eyes, fighting the blush that creeps into my cheeks. "Nothing I haven't seen before."

It's true, but for some reason, when he was wounded in my bedroom, I didn't look at him the way I look at him in this moment. And he certainly didn't look at me the way he does now, as I shimmy out of my trousers and pull my shirt over my head, standing before him in a silk camisole and a pair of ruffled bloomers.

"What's the matter?" I cock my head, a teasing grin playing on my lips. "Were you expecting something else?"

A crease forms between his brows, his teeth clenched as he runs his hands over his face, through his hair, sending blond strands tumbling into his eyes.

He laughs.

For a split second, I want to throw myself into the ocean and never resurface, wishing I didn't leave my daggers in my room upstairs. "I hate you," I mutter, crossing my arms over my chest, feeling more exposed than I ever have in my entire life.

But he crosses the distance between us in a few strides, his hand raised as if to cup my jaw, but his fingers hover in midair, a breath away from touching. His eyes search mine as he smiles softly, dropping his hand. "If only that were true." He chuckles again, but his gaze intensifies, pinning me to the spot, making it difficult to breathe. "Forgive me—it's only that I had the fleeting thought that you'd be armed to the teeth with daggers and pistols." His lips quiver, as if fighting back another bout of laughter, but his expression turns serious, his voice somewhat thick when he murmurs, "It's nice to see *you*, Aster."

I blink, unable to form words. Unable to think clearly—rationally.

And then I shove him into the water.

When his head breaks the surface a moment later, I think he might die of laughter. But I have only a moment to feel smug before he grabs me by my calves and pulls me into the water with him.

"What are you—" Water fills my mouth, and I sputter, coughing.

"What?" He cocks his head, mocking me. "Were you expecting something else?"

I shove at his chest as his arms tighten around me, pulling me closer, but I can't help laughing with him as we drift out from the mouth of the cave and into the sea. Real, genuine laughter that leaves me gasping for breath.

I allow myself to look at him—really look at him. His eyes, crinkled with joy, his open mouth. The shake of his shoulders. His head thrown back in abandon. Purely joyful. Wholly himself.

Titus.

Suddenly, he falls quiet, his gaze roving my face as he lifts a hand, his thumb stroking my cheek. "What is it, love?"

I didn't feel the tear slip from my eye until he smears it across my skin. I want to tell him about what Leo said, but if there's even a small possibility that she's right, I can't afford to expose her.

Even if it means I will lose him.

"I don't know what's going to happen today," I tell him, using the truth to mask the lie. "I'm afraid."

He frowns, tucking a strand of wet hair behind my ear. "I am, too," he whispers, his voice strained, as if it costs him something to admit it. "But we still have a little time before the sun comes up." He looks up at the tapestry of stars twinkling overhead. "It's still night," he says, meeting my gaze once more. "I think we've earned a few hours to just be, aye?"

To just be—I almost laugh at the simplicity of it.

Titus and Aster.

Not Titus the prince. Not Captain Shade the vigilante. Not Aster the pirate, the maid, the lady, the rebel, or the knight.

Just Titus and Aster.

"I want to show you something," he says, drifting slowly away from me, his hands still lingering on the small of my back. "Do you trust me?"

I quirk a brow. "I don't know if I should answer that?"

He barks another laugh. "Follow me."

He dives below the surface before I can say a word.

Gently, he tugs my ankle.

I hesitate. Already, my power rises within me. Just treading the water feels like too much of a risk. If I go under, if I lose control...

He tickles my foot, and I kick, my heel colliding with his face.

He surfaces, choking on his childish cackles, and I realize I never want him to stop laughing—proud that I'm the one to bring this side out of him.

"Aster," he says, cupping my face in his hands, his blond hair dappled silver in the moonlight. "Trust me."

When he dives below the surface once more, I take a deep breath and follow.

Instantly, the magic in my veins warms my blood, making me feel almost feverish. I know I should continue my descent into the dark—should follow Titus's moonlit silhouette as he dives deeper, but...I fall still, my hair floating around me, feeling as if nothing else exists here. No wars or curses. No fear. No death.

It should always be this way. I could *make it* this way. I could drown them all—I could spin the seas to my will and command the waves to sweep Castle Grim into the ocean. I could flood the Eerie with my rage, washing away both Underlings and Nightweavers alike.

I need only think it.

And I almost do.

I almost forget myself. Forget my family. Forget Will.

But Titus takes me by the hand, and I remember his laughter. I remember his eyes, as blue as the ocean. I remember it all.

We swim, side by side, until it feels like my lungs might burst. But just as I tug on his wrist, signaling I need air, I notice a faint outline of blue light radiating from a stone structure below.

He guides me down toward the structure, which reminds me of Hildegarde's Folly—the same domed roof and stone pillars, hidden deep beneath the waves. The blue light pulses, glowing like luminescent vines encasing the underwater folly, brighter as we draw near it, as if it senses our presence.

The instant our feet touch the stone floor, we enter a bubble of air, the floor now dry. All around us, the sea is calm, and beyond the stone pillars of the structure, fish dart past, illuminated by the blue glow. In the center of the structure is the statue of a woman wearing a winged crown, her sword pointed at the ground, a goblet raised to the sky.

"What is this place?" I ask, panting for breath.

I glance at Titus to find him watching me, his eyes glittering with awe.

"Another one of Hildegarde's hiding places," he tells me, a grin tugging at the corner of his lip. "Enchanted so that only those who have entered the cavern we've just come from can find it."

I run my hand along the stone blade, staring up at the woman, an ache forming in my throat.

"It's her, isn't it?" I ask quietly. "Hildegarde."

He nods, strands of wet blond hair stuck to his face. "Aye, it's her."

I reach for my medallion where it hangs between my collarbones, clutching it tight. "Have you seen it?" I glance at him sidelong, my brow furrowed. "The Red Island. Have you been there?"

He shakes his head. "No, love. I'm afraid I'm what you might consider a security risk."

I frown, my stomach twisting into knots. Because of his stepmother, I realize. Because of the torture.

A thread of terror winds through me. Calantha had drained Titus of his blood, weakening him to the point of near-death. "If Morana makes an appearance tomorrow," I say slowly, "you won't be powerful enough to perform the ritual, will you?"

Titus's jaw clenches even as he smirks, shrugs. "I could always rip out a few dozen hearts to get my strength up."

A few days ago, I might have believed him. But now…

I take a step toward him. "What about my blood?"

He takes a step back, shaking his head. "Not an option."

"Why not?" I press. "You've said it yourself—my blood has power. You could feed—"

"No!" he shouts, his lip curled. He inhales a sharp breath, and I think I can feel his heart pounding in his chest as his gaze dips to my throat, and he swallows as if it were suddenly painful. Quietly, he says, "You don't know what you're offering."

"I know exactly what I'm offering. For Will's sake—"

"For Will's sake, I will never ever let myself come close to even tasting your blood." A shadow passes over Titus's face, a honey-gold light sparking in his eyes. Then he smiles, flashing his teeth in a roguish grin. "You don't need to worry about me, love. I'll be ready for Morana, and you"—he points at the medallion hanging from my neck—"can take a nice, long honeymoon to the Red Island, wherever that may be."

Heat flares in my cheeks, my mouth gaping slightly.

He must regret the words the instant he says them, because his face pales, and he looks at the statue once more, his expression nettled.

Honeymoon. Did Will tell him he proposed?

Did he tell him I didn't give him an answer?

I clear my throat, attempting to pretend I hadn't offered Titus my blood, and he hadn't thrown my potential engagement in my face. "So, you really don't know how to find the Red Island, then?"

He rubs his chin, his brow furrowed. "It's best I don't."

I nod, looking up at the depiction of Hildegarde once more—her triumphant expression immortalized in stone. "But my mother knows. She knew, and she pretended she didn't." I almost kick myself for saying the words aloud, because while my mother lied to me about the Red Island, Titus kept plenty of secrets for her.

Titus's fists clench at his sides. "Aster," he says softly, but this time he doesn't try to explain, and I'm glad. The last thing I want to do is spend the rest of the night arguing with him.

"The sun will rise soon," I say. "We agreed to just *be*, right?"

He sighs, his face falling. "I don't know what I was thinking bringing you here," he says, pinching the bridge of his nose. "I just—I reasoned it could be my last chance—"

I close the distance between us, placing a hand on his cheek, and his eyes widen, his lips parting on a shaky breath.

"Thank you for showing me," I say.

He dips his head, my fingertips skimming his jaw. Tenderly, he whispers, "You're the only person I've ever wanted to share this place with."

His secret. His hiding place. His escape.

"I trust you, Aster."

He leans in, and I almost allow myself to want—to truly just be.

But tomorrow, he'll be married. Tomorrow, we go to war. Tomorrow, Will begins his transformation. Tomorrow, everything changes.

Everything.

I force myself to say, "We should head back." Force myself to pull away, my heart caught in my throat. Force myself to put distance between us once more, to let my hand fall from his cheek.

"Of course," he says, blinking as if to clear a haze that momentarily clouded his eyes. "We should head back," he echoes, every word punctuated with something akin to agony.

By the time we reach the cavern, the moon descends slowly toward the horizon. Titus and I lie on our backs on the cave floor, still gasping for breath after our swim home turned into more of a competition than either of us intended.

"You're quite fast," Titus says between pants. "I'm impressed."

"And you're rather slow," I say, wincing from the stitch in my side. "If Margaret had known Captain Shade was such a poor swimmer, it might have changed the way she felt."

He snorts a laugh. "Your sister would be pleased to know Captain Shade is a *fantastic* swimmer—second only to Aster Oberon, of course."

I smile, and it feels natural. Easy. "Was that a compliment?"

"Was it?"

I roll onto my side, facing him. "You said something nice."

He turns to face me, a challenge in his eyes. "I say nice things all the time."

"Not to me."

"*Only* to you."

There's a long moment of silence—too long—in which we both can't seem to look away.

"Aster?" he says finally.

I yawn, my eyelids growing heavy. "Titus?"

His lip quirks, but his eyes are full of sadness. "Will you tell me goodbye? Before you leave?"

I reach out, covering his hand with mine. "I'm not going anywhere."

He lifts our clasped hands, placing a chaste kiss on my knuckles, his eyes drifting shut.

He remains like that for so long, his lips merely an inch from my hand, and I don't move—don't risk waking him if he's fallen asleep—but as I feel my own body begin to relax, feel my mind wandering, I whisper, for reasons I can't begin to understand, "What was her name?" I hope he understands the question I'm asking—feeling as if he'll know I mean his mother, the woman his father executed to hide his own shame.

He doesn't answer, and I close my eyes, savoring this moment with him—my hand in his, our clothes drenched from the sea, the briny scent clinging to our hair, our skin.

"Mina," he murmurs. "Mina Avery."

Chapter Thirty-Five

When I wake in my bed, Titus is still here, asleep in the blue armchair in front of the fireplace, the early-morning sun dappling his golden hair with apricot light. He must have carried me up the stairs after I fell asleep, but I drifted off into such a pleasant, dreamless slumber I didn't stir.

Carefully, I tiptoe out of my bed and start for my wardrobe, but I stop short, my breath catching. A shimmering blue gown hangs from the door, glittering in the sunlight like my beloved ocean.

"It took the dressmaker a couple of days to get the dye just perfect," Titus says, his voice rough from sleep.

I turn to find him already on his feet, and though Will healed his wounds, he winces as he stretches his arms over his head.

"Well?" he says, motioning for me to step behind the screen on the far side of the room. "Go ahead, try it on."

I hesitate, my bottom lip caught between my teeth. There's so much I want to say to him, but I can't seem to find the words. In a few hours, he'll be married, and if the Order succeeds in overthrowing the Crown, Titus will be king. He'll be free—free of his father's control that forces him to act as the Reaper, free of his stepmother's cruelty that demands he endure unspeakable torture. But if Morana truly has fled Castle Grim...without a cure, when the sun drops below the horizon, Will begins his transformation into a Shifter.

I can see in Titus's eyes that he's thinking the same thing—that no matter what happens today, if Will turns...we're not done. We will have no choice but to go after Morana—to find her and force her to give us the cure. However long it takes, we'll have to keep working together. Only, I'm not sure what that looks like after today. Will Leo join us on our quest? Will the Order offer its support? Will my siblings remain on land to help Mother and the Order fight in the coming war, or will they come with me, unable to resist the pull of the sea?

I think of the *Starchaser* gliding over open waters, Titus at the helm as we set out to defeat the queen of Underlings, and shame twists my gut.

How can I so easily picture a future without Will, even if that future is because of him?

I hurry to duck behind the screen, gown in tow, if only to tear myself away from Titus's gaze. My thoughts spiral as I dress, but all thoughts of Underlings and curses and weddings dissipate when I realize I can't clasp the gown on my own.

Holding the gown together as best I can, I step out from behind the screen, intent on asking Titus to fetch Margaret, but the moment I catch sight of myself in the mirror, I can't seem to form a coherent sentence. And as Titus closes the distance between us in a few long, almost urgent strides, his gaze roving the length of my gown, my gut twists for an entirely different reason.

It took the dressmaker a couple of days to get the dye just perfect.

"Why this color?" I ask, my voice thick, heart racing as I meet his stare.

The subtle spark of delight in his eyes reminds me of warm, summer days spent at sea. "May I?" He inclines his head, indicating the gown, and I nod. He takes a step toward me, closer now than before. "It's my favorite color." His arms wrap around me, his hands finding the clasps with ease as he brings his mouth to my ear to whisper, "The color of the ocean." He hooks each clasp, moving higher and higher, his every touch like a spark of electricity as his fingers work against my spine. When he reaches the last clasp, his fingers skim the exposed skin of my shoulder blades, sending a shiver through me. "The color of your eyes."

He draws away slowly, and it's as if I can feel his heartbeat pounding in tandem with my own.

"You told me it was your favorite color, too," he says, "the night I found you."

My mouth goes dry. The night he—Captain Shade—saved me from the *Deathwail*. Vague memories of him asking me questions, trying to make conversation with me in my feverish state, bubble at the surface of my mind but never fully form.

He remembered. After all this time, he remembered something as insignificant as my favorite color.

"*'Not just any blue,'* you told me," Titus says, a grin tugging at his lips. "It's *'the color of the sea at dusk, when the sun is just about to set—right before the stars twinkle into being.'*" He backs away, opening the door to the servants' passage. "You spoke a lot of nonsense that night, but that..." He shakes his head as he enters the passageway. "That was poetry."

He reaches for the stone handle, and my stomach lurches, as if there were an invisible string pulling me toward him.

"Wait!" I say, my voice choked. "Titus—"

He brings a finger to his lips. "Whatever it is you're going to say, tell me tonight." As he pulls the door closed, he pauses, his lips quirking. "Save me a dance, will you?"

Before I can give him an answer, the stone door seals the passageway, leaving me standing alone. I turn, staring at myself in the mirror—at my eyes, a deep sapphire shade of blue.

I fold onto the armchair, my fingers grazing the blue fabric, and my heart skips a beat. I'm back on my feet in an instant, tears pricking my eyes as I take in the suite, decorated with the same brilliant blue as my gown.

The stone door creaks, and I whirl, expecting to see Titus—thinking that, for some reason, he came back, ready to hear what I was about to say—but instead, Margaret is there, jaw agape.

"Well, all right then," she says, eyes widening as she takes in my gown. "I can work with this."

A firm knock at the door interrupts the steady rhythm of my footsteps as I pace the length of my chambers.

"Come in," I call out, stopping to check my reflection once more in the full-length mirror, running my hands over the sapphire-blue gown as if I could smooth out my feelings.

The door closes, and I lock eyes with Will over my shoulder, his lips parted slightly on a breath.

"What do you think?" I ask quietly, turning to face him.

His gaze roves the length of my gown, a crease forming between his brows. "Aster, I—" He shakes his head—laughs. "I'm afraid I lack the words to describe what it is I'm thinking at this moment."

A blush creeps up my neck, into my cheeks, but the sensation is short-lived as I note the dark circles around his eyes, his pallid skin. In less than a heartbeat, I close the gap between us, my hands on his face, my fingers stroking his cheeks.

"Will," I say, checking that the door to my suite remains shut. "About last night—"

"I'm not giving up," he assures me, his hands settling naturally on my waist, firm and gentle. "I never truly thought that Leo was possessed. If Morana really is here, she'll show herself today, and then—then I'll do whatever I must. I've already spoken to Titus about keeping me chained up so that—so that I don't hurt you or anyone else—at least until we can find another cure and—"

"Will," I repeat, softer. "I meant about…"

A faint flush of pink colors his cheeks. "Oh."

"Oh?"

His throat bobs. "Aster," he says, his voice strained, "it was wrong of me to ask when I did—*how* I did." He must read the hurt in my expression, because he quickly shakes his head, his eyes widening slightly. "No, no, not because—" He clenches his jaw, his hands flexing at my hips. "Not because I regret asking. I meant every word, and I…I would very much like to know your thoughts. It's only that—well, I think it might be best if you wait to tell me your answer. In fact, I must insist that you wait until you're *ready* to answer."

He says it as if we have all the time in the world. As if, should Eliza not make an appearance at the wedding—should we fail to obtain the cure from Morana before sundown—come tomorrow, he won't have turned into a Shifter, and I can still give him my answer.

He eyes me cautiously, his shoulders tense, as if he were anticipating a blow. "Please?"

Please. There was a time when I would have answered without a second thought. But now, after everything that's happened…

I hesitate.

My thoughts drift to Titus. He's infuriating, confusing, manipulative. But I can't shake the memory of his laughter. Can't forget the way it felt to be held by him. Can't stop thinking about his lips pressed to my knuckles, even though I know that after today, it doesn't matter. He's going to be married. And whatever it is I might feel for him… he doesn't feel the same way. He can't. He *shouldn't*. I know, without a doubt, he cares about Will too much to stand in his way.

Everything about Titus is complicated, but Will has finally made his feelings for me clear. So, for the first time in months, I don't think about the consequences of my actions. I grab his lapels, rising onto my tiptoes and—

The instant our lips meet, it's as if honey flows through my veins, thick and sweet, slowing time while somehow quickening my pulse to a feverish tempo. He pulls me closer, one hand coming up to cup my face as if I were made of glass, the other digging into my hip with barely contained strength. His mouth parts, and he half-growls, half-groans as he deepens the kiss.

Breathlessly, passionately, he murmurs against my lips, "My undoing."

I throw my arms around his neck, forgetting, if only for a moment, what awaits us just beyond the door to my suite.

Until the guard knocks, breaking the spell Will's words cast over me.

Will hisses through his teeth, his nose brushing mine. He clears his throat, takes a deep breath, and places one final, tender kiss on my forehead.

"The plan is still on," he whispers, almost reluctantly, prompting me to meet his gaze once more. "The Order will attack Castle Grim today, just after Titus and the princess exchange their vows."

"But how? Eva was supposed to ensure the ships could pass. If she's dead—"

"I don't know all the details," he says. "Apparently, no one does. Your mother has kept us all in the dark. All I know is that we're to be ready. At her signal, she asked that you and I make our way as quickly as possible to the harbor. There'll be a boat waiting to take us to the fleet."

I wince inwardly at the sting that comes from finding out something my mother could have told me herself, and nod along to what he says. "What about the others? I'm not leaving here without Charlie and Lewis."

"Neither is your mother," Will assures me. "Everyone has been given their own escape route. We're all to meet at the fleet. No one is getting left behind." He tilts my chin, searching my gaze. "I promise."

I nod again, unease twisting my stomach into knots.

Another knock.

Will sighs, his thumb stroking my cheek. "Aren't you going to tell me how handsome I look?" he murmurs, a grin playing on his lips. "It is my birthday, after all."

I trace the gilded thread that lines the lapels of his formal scarlet jacket. The rich shade of red brings out the paleness of his skin, and I know that beneath his clothes, the cursed wound festers, green lesions pulsing.

"You do," I say, choking on the lump in my throat. I meet his gaze, forcing a smile. "You look really nice."

He chuckles, capturing my hand in his and tucking it under his arm. "Really nice," he echoes, leading me to the door of my suite. He knocks once, signaling for the guards to open it, and guides me into the hall. "I'll try not to let that go to my head," he says, smiling as if I've just crowned him king of the Known World.

"The princess is not to be disturbed," the guard says, blocking the door that leads to Leo's chambers.

"I just need to speak with her," I insist through gritted teeth, wishing I could unsheathe the daggers at either hip and rephrase my request with the sharp end of a blade. "To congratulate her. It will only take a moment."

"Miss—"

"*Dame*," I correct him, my eyes narrowed.

The guard's swallow is audible. "Forgive me, Dame—"

"Oberon," Will finishes for him, adjusting his cuffs with an indolent air. "It's a matter of utmost importance. Let her inside."

"But—"

Will fixes him with a look that leaves the guard fumbling to open the door. He remains with the guards, but I rush inside.

"Leo, I—"

I take a step back as Queen Calantha turns to face me, a sweet smile on her bloodred lips. Behind her, Leo gives the slightest shake of her head, her eyes screaming at me to turn around, to flee.

"Dame Oberon," Calantha says, her head cocked as she appraises my gown, "what a lovely surprise."

"Your Majesty," I say, dipping low in a curtsy. "Pardon me for intruding."

"Nonsense." Calantha waves her hand, and her long scarlet nails catch the light, glistening like fresh blood. "I was just leaving."

I rise, my skirt still gathered in my fists, as Calantha breezes past me. The instant the door closes behind her, I start for Leo, but—

She flinches, and I halt.

I take a step toward her.

She takes a step back.

"Is everything all right?" I ask, noting the way Leo's hand trembles as she struggles to light the pipe perched between her fingers.

"Fine," Leo answers, nodding vigorously. She flicks the lighter again and again, but it never sparks. "You should go. The wedding is starting soon and—"

"Leo," I say slowly, reaching out to take the lighter from her. "You can talk to me. Tell me what's the matter? Is it the queen? Did she—"

"No, no." Leo shuts her eyes tight, shaking her head. "I'm just…" When she opens her eyes again, her expression is pleading. "I can't do this. I can't hurt him."

My shoulders sag with relief as the lighter ignites.

"That's what I've come to tell you." I light the end of the pipe tucked between her lips, and she puffs a cloud of smoke. "Titus isn't compelled."

A wrinkle deepens between her brows. "How do you know?"

I glance over my shoulder to where the queen exited only moments before. There isn't time to explain everything that's happened, and I feel strange at the prospect of revealing the torture Titus has endured at the hands of his stepmother.

"I'll explain everything," I tell Leo. "But for now, I need you to trust me. There is..." I hesitate, thinking about Flynn, lying dead under the bridge, and Eliza and Gabriel, still missing. *Your mother has kept us all in the dark*, Will said. "There's a plan. We need your help."

"We?" Leo's voice is small, but some of that familiar steely determination returns to her gaze. "What plan?"

I tug at my glove, revealing the tattoo of the winged dagger. "We want the same things, Leo. If you help us—if you help *me*—we can make a difference. For humans and for Nightweavers."

She nods slowly, her brow furrowed. "What do you need me to do?"

Chapter Thirty-Six

The throne room looks nothing like it did the day I swore an oath to become a Bloodknight.

Once, I thought the size and opulence of Bludgrave Manor's ballroom was beyond compare. But as I enter the massive, domed room, its floor-to-ceiling windows and open double doors leading out onto terraces that overlook both the city of Jade and the ocean beyond, I realize the Castors' ballroom could fit inside Castle Grim's throne room at least a dozen times.

As Will escorts me through the open double doors, down the plush ivory carpet that separates the hundreds of pews brought in for the occasion, I note the elaborate vases overflowing with white roses and hundreds of cream-colored candelabras scattered about the room. Aside from the crimson flag bearing the crest of House Anteres, the black flag bearing the scarlet sun of the Eerie, and the orange flag of Hellion, adorned with a golden stag hanging above the dais, the décor is as white as pure snow, colored only by the soft coral light of the setting sun.

Annie waves at me from the front row, alongside her parents and Killian in his formal military uniform. I meet Henry's gaze across the room, and he offers me a pained, somewhat apologetic smile.

I smile back. I'm convinced what he said to me the other night was a direct result of the sorrowsnap in his system. After this is all over, I'll find a way to walk with him through his grief, whatever it takes. If there's ever a time he feels as if he's stumbling through the dark shadows of his past, then I will meet him in that darkness. We'll escape the *Deathwail* together, this time, even if only in our minds.

Somehow, that thought gives me the courage I need to hold my head high as Will escorts me down the aisle. This time, when every head turns to find me, I don't cower. I meet the stares of the wedding guests, made up mostly of nobility, with a confidence I wasn't sure I possessed before today.

I'm not giving up. Will seemed convinced this wasn't the end—that we could still find a cure. That whatever my mother has planned for today, we are going to make it out of this alive. We can have a future.

Together.

I just have to make it through the next few hours.

"...missing," a woman whispers, and I catch the word as I pass. "Probably fled just after their sister murdered Lady Mercer."

My stomach sours, and I slow my pace.

"Shame," another woman replies. "The Cooper men were rather..."

"Hattie!" A third woman swats her friend's arm. "It's bad enough they didn't cancel the wedding."

"Did you really think they would?" the first woman asks.

"Murder is hardly a reason to postpone an alliance between the kingdoms."

We're almost out of earshot when the third woman adds, "Well, if that wasn't a reason, I heard Eva's daughters went missing last night, as well." She adds excitedly, "I think those two Bloodknights have them somewhere. Suppose they're going to ransom—"

A trumpet sounds, signaling for everyone to take their seats. We reach the front row, and I find my place between Will and Annie just as the orchestra begins to play.

I survey the throne room, overflowing with Bloodknights, League soldiers, and palace guards stationed in clusters at every exit. Dispersed among them are human servants, and I scan their faces, searching for Margaret, or Jack, or—

Mother stands near the terrace on the far side of the room. She whispers something in Sybil's ear, and the maid dips her head once in acknowledgment. I will Mother to look at me, but she never even glances my way. Instead, I follow her gaze to the entrance, where Titus stands in the open doorway, wearing a suit that gives him the appearance of the night sky incarnate.

The scarlet embroidery of his lapels shimmers like rubies as he saunters down the aisle with feline grace, his tousled blond hair tumbling into his eyes when he lifts his chin, staring straight ahead, as if there is no one else in this room.

Except for me.

Our gazes meet as if he knows exactly where I am, and in one moment, one look, I feel everything his eyes convey—sorrow, despair, defeat.

I force myself to look away. *A political alliance*, I tell myself. That's all this marriage is—a means of winning the battle to end the war before it can truly begin. It doesn't mean he loves her. It doesn't mean she loves him.

But the look in his eyes...I can't help but feel like this represents something different for Titus.

When he takes his place next to the officiant atop the dais, he turns on his heel and our eyes meet once more.

My lips part, my own emotions warring within me—emotions I can't define. Especially not now, on the day he's to be wed.

This time, he looks away, down the aisle, and Will lightly taps my arm, signaling for me to stand along with the rest of the crowd.

Making her way toward Titus, Leo glides down the aisle like a star given flesh. The gossamer fabric of her long, billowing skirt glitters with thousands of tiny crystals in a mesmerizing display that leaves the entire room gasping in awe. Diamonds adorn her dark hair, her face dusted with shimmering powder that conceals the dark circles under her eyes and gives her an ethereal glow not of this realm.

I see the moment their gazes meet, see the small, hesitant smile on her lips. But he doesn't react—doesn't even pretend to play the part of an adoring fiancé. Not as he did last night in the Crystal Atrium.

No—today, he looks as if he'd rather drive a blade through Leo's heart.

I cut a glance at the king and queen to find Calantha watching Titus carefully, a hint of a smirk tugging at her bloodred lips. Calix watches Leo, however, his false smile like that of a proud father-in-law—a triumphant king. Almost as if he senses me watching, Calix turns his stare on me, and for a split second, I think I see something like fear in his eyes, as if someone other than the bloodthirsty king of the Eerie were looking at me, an unmistakable plea for help woven into the very fiber of his skin.

Calantha places a hand on his arm as Leo nears the dais, drawing his attention away from me, and I feel as if I imagined the shift in him—the terror in his eyes. The desperation.

Titus's expression is unreadable as he takes Leo's hands in his, his voice quiet as the officiant guides them through their vows.

"I do," Titus says, a muscle in his jaw twitching.

My heart beats faster. I glance to my right, searching for Mother, but she and Sybil are nowhere to be found, as if they vanished.

"I do," Leo echoes, her voice soft, her gaze fixed on their clasped hands.

I fidget in my seat, and Will's hand brushes mine. I fight the urge to pull away from him. After today, it won't matter, so I allow him to twine our fingers together even as I feel the heat of the stares from nearby nobility.

Despite everything, my heart flutters with the possibility of being with Will—of sharing a life with him—that we don't have to keep secret. Maybe my confusion about my feelings for Will has been because of the threat of treason hanging over our heads. Maybe without the secrets we're forced to keep, we could be truly happy together....

"It is my honor to pronounce you husband and wife," the officiant concludes. "You may now kiss the—"

BOOM.

The first explosion rocks the castle with such force it throws me from my seat onto the marble floor. I brace my head between my hands as a second explosion rattles my skull, my ears ringing. Something heavy buries me beneath its crushing weight, and I open my eyes to see both Henry and Will have covered my body with theirs, shielding me.

"Now!" Will shouts, grabbing my arm and hauling me to my feet as Henry gathers himself, hands outstretched as if ready to defend us at a moment's notice. "Aster, come! We have to hurry!"

Somewhat dazed, I search the throne room once more for Mother, though I know it's futile—if she's still here, it will be impossible to find her in the chaos. The wedding guests scream, attempting to flee the throne room, but something blocks their path. Over the ringing in my ears, I barely make out the sound of the Gore's laughter—hardly register the blood that spills onto the marble floor as the Bloodknights form a circle around the king and queen. A League soldier is tossed into the air above the crowd, his legs ripped from his body, and I catch a glimpse of the Gore blocking the double doors.

It all happens so fast I can't make sense of what I'm seeing.

To my left, a single vessel launches an assault on Castle Grim, emerging from the cloud of smoke and mist, its cannons blazing with orange light as another explosion causes the chandeliers to tremble overhead.

Not thousands. Not a fleet. Only one ship.

The *Starchaser*.

My vision comes into focus, throwing Titus into sharp relief against the backdrop of the sea, lying unconscious on the ground beside Leo. But at the very moment I move toward them, away from Will and Henry, red smoke fills the throne room.

I stumble, alone in the haze. Nearby, Will and Henry both shout, calling for me, but the smoke disorients me. No matter what, I can't seem to reach them.

"Aster Oberon," comes a feminine voice, a soft purr that somehow rises over the din of chaos. "You didn't really think we would let you get away again?"

I whirl, attempting to locate the voice, but it sounds as if it comes from all around. Slowly, I slip my hands in my pockets, grab the hilts of my daggers, and take a deep breath.

"You're free to try to stop me," I say, my voice steady even as my blood pounds a fierce rhythm in my ears.

"That's the spirit."

Calantha emerges from the smoke, her eyes like two wells of black ink. *We.* Of course, not only has the king sided with the Underlings, but the queen herself is a Shifter. I knew she was evil, but I would never have guessed she was a member of Morana's Guild of Shadows.

"*Aster Oberon, the Shadowslayer,*" she says with mock reverence. The queen's atroxis wends between her legs, its eight insectoid eyes smoldering red. She laughs, melodic and sickly sweet. "Yet, you hardly seem dangerous. I've often wondered if the rumors about your fierce skill in battle were even true. You *are* a pirate, aren't you?"

I twirl my daggers. "Would you like to find out?"

Calantha's bloodred lips twist, her smile eager. She holds out her arms, as if to bow, but as she pulls her hands back together, thin streams of blood converge from out of the cloud of red smoke surrounding us. She twists her fingers in the air, forming the blood into a scarlet sword. Beside her, the atroxis grows to the size of a hog, its tusks like four wicked knives.

Calantha swings the blade in a smooth arc, cocks her head. "Shall we?"

The atroxis leaps, its claw-tipped paws outstretched, surprisingly fast.

But I'm faster.

I dodge, using the momentum I gain to lunge for Calantha.

She narrowly avoids my strike, lashing out with her own weapon. I twist, sidestepping the blade, but the blood transforms midair into a whip, thrashing my arm.

I hiss, my teeth gritting against the sting as Calantha draws my blood from the fresh wound, using it to transform her scarlet weapon into a longer whip. I'm quick to regain my footing, pushing through the pain, but the atroxis barrels into me, sending me careening backward, knocking my daggers from my grasp.

Pinning me on my back, the creature swipes at my face, claws ripping through my flesh. Its mouth opens, putrid breath roiling my stomach as it gnashes its teeth at me, but I grab the atroxis by its beastly jaws before it can bite. A furious scream bursts from my chest as I push the creature off, scrambling back onto my feet.

Again, Calantha draws my blood, adding barbs to the crimson whip.

She smiles as the atroxis rubs against her leg, purring. "I have to admit," Calantha says with a low sigh. "I thought this would be more of a challenge."

I spit at her feet, roll my shoulders. "And here I thought you were taking it easy on me."

The atroxis crouches, as if preparing to spring, when something darts between my feet, drawing the creature's attention away. Calantha's eyes narrow on the tiny brown mouse as it scurries past, and the atroxis leaps, chasing after it.

"Come back here, you useless mongrel!" Calantha hisses, her lip curling into a snarl.

I attempt to seize my opportunity to grab my daggers, but Calantha strikes, her whip inches from my outstretched hand.

"You're nothing without a blade, *pirate*," Calantha says with a sneer.

"A few days ago, I might have agreed with you," I say, and I can't help the grin that tugs at my lips. Because somewhere beneath the screaming and the shouting comes another sound, like waves crashing against the rocks that surround Castle Grim. I focus on the hum of the water in the blood, listening to its unique song as I feel my power thrumming inside me, begging to sing along.

Calantha's eyes narrow, her manic laughter now as grating as a Gore's. She lashes out again, the barbed end of her whip like a rod of crimson lightning flashing across the sky, aimed for my face.

But it stops a breath away from my nose.

Calantha makes a choking noise, her eyes wide, as my hands close around the whip, unharmed. She curses as I take hold of the weapon, pulling the liquid from her grasp.

I fashion the blood into two cutlasses.

The liquid feels like an extension of my own hands, buzzing in my grasp with an addictive energy I've never felt before. I perform a mock curtsy, delighted at Calantha's horrified expression. She stumbles backward. "Abomination!" she cries as she turns, fleeing into the cloud of red smoke.

My magic latches onto the scarlet cutlasses in my grasp, desperate for more—more blood, more power. The notes that moments ago resonated with my heart now feel unbalanced. Still, I can't bring myself to let go of the unnatural weapons.

More. More. More—

"Aster!" Will's voice is rough, cutting through the haze.

Blood splashes my dress as the weapons lose their shape.

Will.

Quickly, I kneel, collecting my daggers and chasing after Will's voice. I emerge from the smoke a moment later to find Will near the dais, and I watch as a Gore evaporates with one fatal strike from Will's Elysian blade.

The smoke has begun to clear, and I see them—Titus and Leo—lying only a few feet away, unconscious.

Unconscious, not dead.

Please, don't be dead.

When Will sees where my gaze has landed, he grabs me, desperate, as if he fears I might slip from his fingers. "Quickly, my darling, we have to—"

I wrest myself free of his grasp and throw myself at Titus. "Help me!" I cry, looking over my shoulder at Will, who doesn't move. I grab the front of Titus's jacket, attempting to drag him, but his body jerks with a spasm and he coughs, sitting upright, our faces only inches apart.

"Aster?" he chokes out, searching my gaze. "You stayed."

"Yes," I say, tightening my grip on his jacket, attempting to pull him to his feet, but he doesn't budge. "I'm not leaving here without you!"

He smiles, his eyes glassy, his hand cupping my cheek. Despite the chaos that rages all around us, despite the way Will lurches toward me, my name on his lips, I allow myself to lean into Titus's touch, allow myself to savor the caress of his fingertips as they graze my jaw.

When the dagger pierces my stomach, his hand shifts to the back of my neck, pulling me close to whisper in my ear, "I hoped you might say that."

Chapter Thirty-Seven

Titus removes the dagger and stands in one smooth, fluid motion, allowing my body to fall at his feet. Blood pours from between my fingers as I attempt to stanch the flow, my jaw gaping to fit a scream that never fully forms.

My vision blurs as I watch Titus wipe the dagger clean on his pantleg, cool and indifferent despite the screams, the cannon fire, the Gore laughter, as if none of it has anything to do with him.

Leo places a hand on his shoulder, peering down at me, saying something I can't hear. She smiles, speaking softly, calmly, her expression blithely innocent. "You should have listened to your gut, pirate," Leo says, glancing at the gaping wound in my stomach, a mock pout on her lips. "I tried to tell you Titus was compelled," she adds with a shrug. "But you just couldn't believe that your little prince could truly be...monstrous. Or that the sweet, human-loving princess—the girl you were so quick to trust, to defend—could be possessed by the queen of Underlings."

Titus smirks.

He crouches in front of me, twirling the dagger, and over his shoulder I see Will on his knees, grasping at his throat, his face turning blue. Nearby, Lord Bludgrave and Lady Isabelle fight side by side against a handful of Gores, while Killian and Henry attempt to shield Annie from the attack. Mother, my siblings—I can't find them anywhere. Can't—

"They're not coming," Titus says, his head cocked as he watches me struggle to breathe, eyes narrowed as if he were a beast studying his prey. "There is no fleet, Aster. There never was."

"It's time," Leo—no, *Morana*—croons, running her fingers through Titus's hair. "Go on," she adds, jerking her chin in the direction of the king and queen, who kneel before Leo, eyes fixed on the floor. "The king is of no further use to me."

Titus watches me for a moment longer, brow furrowed, before standing. Calantha looks up as Titus makes his way down the steps of the dais, a cruel slant to her bloodred lips. "Finally," she says as she looks past him to Leo. "May I, my queen?"

Leo dips her head, and Calantha stands, stretching, as if some great burden has been lifted from her shoulders.

"You have been loyal to me since your youth," Morana says to Calantha. "Your service will not go unrewarded."

Calantha's lip curls with disgust as she cuts a glance at her husband. "No longer having to pretend he's the one ruling this kingdom will be reward enough."

Leo's mouth twists, a sadistic smirk. "While that may be true," Morana says, "you have fulfilled your pledge to me by delivering the prince into my hand." She gestures at the throne. "The royal halfling will do my bidding, and you will rule the Eerie in my name." She turns to face the king again, his face blank. "I think it might be sweet if we give Calix the chance to say his goodbyes, don't you agree?"

Calantha laughs as she perches on the arm of the throne. "As you wish, my queen."

Instantly, as if coming awake, Calix raises his head, looking around the room in a panic. His eyes dart from Titus to Calantha to Leo to me, his mouth gaping in horror.

He appears so... *young*. Boyish. As if he were merely a child.

"What have you—" He searches the throne room, tears streaking his face. "Mina?" he cries. "What have you done with her? What have you done with—with Mina—"

Titus's shoulders tense at the mention of his mother's name, but then Leo is there at his side, her hand on his forearm, whispering in his ear.

Calix looks at Calantha, then me, and it's as if he pieces something together, his eyes wide.

"She—she compelled me—" he stammers, looking back at Calantha. He looks up at Titus then, choking on a sob. "My son! Oh, Mina, forgive—"

In one fluid motion, Titus slashes the king's throat.

Calix stares at me, grasping at the thin seam of red that opens, gushing blood down the front of his jacket. He cuts his eyes at Titus only once before they roll to the back of his head and he falls face-first in a pool of blood, his crown toppling from his head.

Calantha claps as Titus crouches, lifting the bloody crown and placing it atop his blond hair. It sits askew, beads of scarlet dripping down his face as he stands once more. He smirks, pointing his dagger at Will, who fights for breath, held captive by Leo's magic.

Merely twenty feet away, a barricade of Gores block Lord Bludgrave and Lady Isabelle from reaching me—it seems as if every time they cut one down, two more take its place—and Killian stands over Henry, bleeding out on the floor, his left leg hanging on by a few stubborn tendons. Sybil appears, taking Annie by the arm, and I hear Killian shout, his voice ragged, "...to the ship!"

My eyes meet Will's, and I don't know why I expect to see some glimpse of hope there, because all I find is terror.

"S-stop," I manage to gasp, unable to recognize the sound of my own voice. "L-let him—g-go—"

Titus's smirk broadens to a vicious grin. "You should have left when you had the chance," he says to me, slowly making his way back onto the dais. He kneels at my side, lifting the medallion out of my pocket, placing the chain around my neck. He squints, his mouth pressed tight as his fingers trace the symbol of the skull and crossed daggers, but Leo places her hand on his shoulder, clearing her throat, and he gets to his feet, stepping away to allow her access to me.

Leo smiles, her eyes glowing red. *"Finally."* The voice that speaks is no longer Leo's—coarse, like smoke, and somehow powerful and all-consuming, as if she were a storm wrapped in flesh, her every word like the low growl of thunder as she says, *"You have something that belongs to me."*

Black spots edge my vision, my breath coming in ragged gasps. With one hand I press against the wound in my stomach, and with the other I reach for one of my daggers, but Titus steps on my fingers, shattering the bones with an efficient *snap*. I cry out in pain, blinded by white light.

I barely make out the shape of Leo as she grabs my arm, wresting my hand from my stomach, and slides the leather bracelet from my wrist. She tosses it aside with a scoff. "*Pitiful sorcery.* Did you think your little trinket would protect you from *me*?" She leans in, her face inches from mine as she traces my jaw with a long, decaying nail. The sharp tip punctures my skin, drawing blood, but I'm numb to the prick of pain. *"If they'd only told you the truth about who you really are, you might have had the means to save yourself. To save them all."*

She grips my chin, painfully tight, her nails digging into my flesh. *"He had his chance,"* she says, examining my face with idle curiosity. *"I let him have his fun. But I've waited six hundred years for this—I won't waste another second playing his games."*

I know she's referring to the Shifter who bit me as a child—to Flynn. But I can barely focus my thoughts as I watch Leo lift the dagger, crackling with purple lightning.

"Come with me to Havok," she says, her voice like a silken whisper, soft and cool. *"You need only say the word, and I'll release Titus. You can save him, Aster. He'll finally be free."*

I think of Father's compass, tucked safely in my pocket. *There is still time to chase another star.* If I go with Morana now, there's no guarantee she'll free Titus. But if I refuse—if I fight—there's still time to save him myself. To cure Will and free Owen.

She doesn't want me dead, I think. *She wants me to be compliant.*

But I will not be silenced.

"Rot in Havok," I say through gritted teeth.

Leo's eyes flash, a bright scarlet light that burns hotter than any fire.

I think I might have been wrong—that Morana might kill me right here, right now—but as Leo drives the dagger toward my shoulder, it's as if some invisible force grabs her wrist, forcing her to halt midstrike, as if the True King reached down from his heavenly realm and commanded her to be still.

But then, I see Leo's red eyes go wide. See blood dribble from her lips as she coughs, the dagger clattering to the floor beside her.

I feel as if I'm dreaming when my vision focuses, briefly, on Mother, standing where I'm certain she wasn't just seconds before, withdrawing a sword made of Elysian Iron from Leo's back.

Calantha shrieks, springing from her seat on the throne.

Everything seems to slow as Will—free of Leo's hold on him—lurches for me.

Another explosion rips a hole in the throne room, and the ceiling crumbles overhead, chunks of stone plummeting to the marble floor, taking out the barrier of Gores that hindered the Castors' escape and blocking Calantha from view. Titus stumbles back a step, removing his foot from my hand.

"You get Henry!" Will shouts at Mother, his eyes glowing gold. "I've got her!"

Lady Isabelle and Killian hoist Henry into the air. Mother hesitates, looking from Will to Titus to me. She appears as if she's about to take another step toward us, but something gives her pause.

"Help them!" Will roars, gathering me into his arms. I can feel his magic prodding at the wound in my stomach, attempting to stitch me back together, and a pitiful wail escapes through my clenched teeth as my broken fingers straighten out. I know it takes everything within him to resist the blood—*my* blood—noticing the way his nostrils flare, the muscles in his jaw rippling.

Mother nods, just once, before turning to cut through the remaining Underlings, clearing a path for Lady Isabelle and Killian.

Hope flares in my chest. *They're going to make it out of here alive.*

But I know, judging by the deep rasp of Will's voice when he groans, "You—you're bleeding—*Aster*—" that if we don't get out of here soon, Will might not be able to stop himself from ripping into my throat.

He stumbles to the left, where Sybil and Annie stand between us and Will's family, blocking our escape. For a moment, I think Sybil might be frozen with fear, but when Lord Bludgrave attempts to grab Annie's hand, Sybil takes a step back and, in a flash of steel, draws a dagger from her apron.

Annie throws off Sybil's grip, retreating onto the dais, a wreath of shadows encircling her black ringlets like a crown. Her eyes glow red as she tilts her head to the side, a sinister grin tugging at her lips.

Horror, sharper than the pain, pierces me like a knife.

Mother's Elysian Iron blade expelled Morana from Leo, but it appears as if the Underling queen has chosen a new host: Annie.

Her sharp trill of laughter sends a shiver down my spine.

"*He tried to tell you, didn't he?*" Morana's voice slithers out of Annie's mouth, a vile, living thing snaking through the air all around us.

"Go!" Lord Bludgrave shouts at Will and me, taking a step toward Sybil, his hands raised, engulfed in flames. "Leave, while you—"

Lord Bludgrave staggers, looking down at the shard of glass protruding from his chest. He coughs, thick crimson blood splattering the marble before he falls, his wide, vacant eyes fixed on me.

She's doomed, boy, he once told Will. *You can't save her.*

Owen appears behind him, two fingers outstretched, as if he used his affinity to levitate the jagged piece of glass that stabbed Lord Bludgrave through the heart.

I think I hear Lady Isabelle scream, but a moment later, Will and I are surrounded by Bloodknights, their weapons all pointed in our direction.

"I've been dying to try that," Owen says as he steps over Lord Bludgrave's body, joining Annie on the dais.

Seizing the momentary distraction, Titus tackles Will from behind, knocking me from Will's grasp, and I land in a heap beside Leo, watching through a haze of smoke as Titus lands blow after blow to Will's face.

"He—" Leo wheezes, her voice so soft, so small, I think I've imagined it. But when I crane my neck to look at her, I notice the faint rise and fall of her chest. She's still in there—the *real* Leo—clinging to life. "He's—*good*—" She whimpers, her body twitching as she stretches a hand toward me.

I attempt to reach for her, my fingers outstretched, but pain radiates from my abdomen through my limbs, and I fall short of her grasp.

"Glad he—found you—" Leo manages to say, her voice a dull gurgle. "Trusts…"

Her head lolls to the side, eyes vacant.

Gone.

I watch from the ground, my vision skewed, as Annie brings her fingers to her mouth and whistles, shrill and piercing. A moment later, a large, hairless wolf soars through the broken window on black webbed wings like that of a bat—unlike any Myth I've ever seen in Elsie's books.

Owen helps Annie onto the creature's back, then makes to climb up after her—hesitates.

"What about her?" he asks, his expression neutral as he cuts a glance at me. "We've come all this way—"

"*This form is too weak!*" Annie hisses, causing Owen to wince. *"We must go, now!"*

Sybil bows, and as she kneels, she transforms—her hair shorter, turning a dark shade of purple, her eyes glowing red. She looks at once ten years older, her frail body now lean with muscle. She smiles up at Annie, and I realize that's not Sybil—it's a Shifter. She might have always been a Shifter, and no one ever knew. We knew Morana had an accomplice, but I would have never expected Sybil.

You've become far too trusting for your own good, Owen said to me that night on the train. He was right. I trusted all the wrong people, and now, I'm going to pay for it with my life.

"Go, my queen," she says. "I will ensure their safe passage to your kingdom."

The *Starchaser* launches another cannonball at the castle, and the floor trembles underfoot as the wolfish Myth carries Owen and Annie out of the throne room, vanishing into the mist.

Titus saunters onto the dais then, two Bloodknights stepping out of formation to stand at his side. He takes his seat on his father's throne, staring at the bloody pool where the king lies dead.

My head swims as I try to make out his features—try to see him—but darkness edges my vision, and he sounds so far away, so unlike himself when he speaks, that I can't be sure what he says. Still, my mind attempts to latch onto the words, even as the world implodes around me.

"Take them to the dungeons."

Chapter Thirty-Eight

I wake to the sound of my own screams.

Pain slices through me. My head pounds, my vision blurs as I attempt to open my eyes. I blink, wincing at the light of the torches lining the aisle between the iron cells, struggling to make out my surroundings in the flickering glow. I shudder at the chill even as sweat rolls down my neck, my spine, my legs. It's too bright. Too dark. Too hot. Too cold.

I can't feel my hands. I kick, feeling for purchase on solid ground, but my feet dangle an inch from the stone floor. Chains rattle as I squirm.

"Billie, listen to me."

Eliza's voice warbles nearby, but my head is too heavy to lift, my neck too stiff to turn and see what direction her voice is coming from.

A low, menacing growl is the only answer.

And it comes from my cell.

"Look at me," Eliza pleads. "You don't have to do this. Just—just look at me, please."

Squelch. Crack.

The choked whimper comes from my left, and I cut my eyes in the direction of the sound, gasping at the ache that lances through my skull at even the slightest movement.

Cold horror floods my veins.

Will crouches over the limp, starved body of a woman, cradling her close to his chest as he rips into her throat. Blood coats his face in layers that have long since dried under the spray of fresh, bright red from his latest victim.

Beside him, a pile of eight corpses lies in a tangled heap of shredded remains.

As if he senses me staring, his head jerks up, his gilded eyes shining bright enough to light the cell. He cocks his head, licks his lips. His gaze roves from my head to my feet, his entire body preternaturally still.

"Billie, stop," Eliza whispers, and I see her then, chained to the floor of the adjacent cell, her hands gripping the iron bars. "It's Aster," she says. "You don't want to hurt her, do you?"

Will sniffs, his nostrils flaring. His tongue darts between his teeth, snakelike.

In a flash, he discards the woman's corpse and lunges for me.

I jolt, shutting my eyes tight to brace myself against his assault, but there's a loud *snap*, followed by the deep rumble of Will's snarl. I have the faintest thought that he's broken my neck, and for a moment, I consider giving in to the agony that pulses, bone-deep—consider giving up. Letting go. Accepting my fate. But when I open my eyes, I find that something stopped Will just before he could reach me. His hands grasp at the air, his fingertips grazing my flank, but the iron collar around his throat pulls tight. He snaps his jaws, his teeth clacking together, his eyes bulging.

The glow of his iris shifts from gold to red.

"Will?" I croak, my hoarse voice barely a whisper.

"Yes, *Will*."

The cell door creaks as Titus enters, followed by a Bloodknight.

Titus doesn't even spare me a glance as he makes his way to the table to my right, arranged with various knives and crude tools—the same weapons Calantha implemented in his torture. Between us, the stream cuts through the cavern, feeding into the canal that divides the cells.

I try to speak to the water—try to bend it to my will—but there is no song to be sung. No voice to be heard, as if the sea has gone silent.

"Now, Aster," Titus says, running his hands over the handles of various weapons. "Now you see him for what he truly is." He turns, pointing at Will with the dagger he's selected—a weapon similar to the dagger Flynn possessed, crackling with cursed green energy. "A bloodthirsty monster."

My head throbs as I look between Will and Titus, my mind racing. "Stop," I plead, struggling to get the words out, "this—isn't you. You've been—compelled!"

Titus smirks. "Oh, you finally noticed?" He jerks his chin, and as if obeying the silent command, the Bloodknight grabs Will's arms, forcing him to kneel. Titus crosses the cell, squatting in front of Will, the edge of his blade pressed to his cheek. There's a grotesque sizzle as the cursed energy burns Will's flesh. "It's about time. You know, your brother paid me a visit the night he appeared to you on the train," Titus says, watching the blood bubble to the surface of Will's skin with rapt interest. "He's quite clever, that Owen. I see where you get your violent streak. He compelled me to send word once we reached Ink Haven, accusing Winona Congreve of siding with the rebellion." He tuts. "Poor, wretched little thing."

My stomach roils. Titus was compelled the night I slept in his bed aboard the train, and I didn't know. He was forced by his father to become the Reaper, forced by his stepmother to submit himself for her depraved collection of his blood, forced by Owen to betray his friends. All this time, he was compelled to act against his own will, and I didn't see it. I was so focused on finding a cure for Will, on overthrowing the Crown, that I overlooked what was happening right under my nose. How could I have been so blind?

"Oh, come now; no need for sad faces. There's nothing you could have done. Besides, Owen's compulsion was only temporary. For all his power, his brief imposition on my will was merely a test—an exercise meant only to give Morana an idea of how difficult it would be to compel me for longer stretches of time. It wasn't until I returned to Castle Grim that Morana called to me herself. She showed me what true power looked like." He runs a hand over the front of his jacket, smoothing the creases. "Enough power to overthrow those who might have tried to subdue me." His expression shifts at his own words, his brow furrowing, jaw clenched. But he shakes his head, flashing his teeth in a venomous smile as he peers over Will's shoulder at the pile of corpses, and the torchlight casts the crown atop his head in a fiery golden light. "Enough power to take what is rightfully mine."

My chest aches, my heart throbbing painfully against my sternum. "When?" I manage to choke out.

"Just after the parade," Titus says, tilting his head, his eyes narrowing. "I had no memory of the compulsion until after we'd said our vows, but..." He clucks his tongue. "I *was* certain Leo was possessed. Tried to tell you even. But, no—you were so convinced it wasn't her. Even when Calantha confirmed my suspicions, you insisted it was Eliza that Morana had possessed."

He laughs, the sound cruel and cold. He purses his lips in a mock pout. "Poor, innocent Eliza. Though, I suppose you can't shoulder all the blame. *He*"—Titus points his dagger at Will—"couldn't fathom that his best mate might actually be right. We are best mates, aren't we, William?" His head swings in Will's direction, his eyes narrowed. "Do you want to tell her what I told you all those years ago? How I confided in my *best mate* about the girl I couldn't stop thinking about?" He grits his teeth, his jaw tight. "How, after the night I finally saw her again, after I rescued her from the *Deathwail*—after I held her in my arms, after I had to let her go—that if our paths ever crossed again, I could only pray she might see past the monster I've been forced to become?"

His words are like a wave, crashing over me, condemning me to the depths. If what he's saying is true... Will knew Titus cared for me long before the day he took me from the *Lightbringer*, and Will still chose to... *romance* me during the weeks we grew close at Bludgrave Manor. Will kissed me, knowing Titus spent years waiting—hoping for the chance to see me again.

Will hisses, his eyes glowing bright red as he strains against the iron band around his throat—Elysian Iron, I realize, noting the way the dark metal appears to undulate with iridescent shades of blue, purple, and green. Even in this state, does he understand what Titus has said? If he could speak...would he defend himself? Could he?

And still, Titus is compelled—he could be lying.

He *must* be lying.

Titus sighs, running a hand through his hair. "But that's all in the past, hmm?" Titus twirls his dagger. "This could have been painless, Aster. But you just don't know when to stop fighting."

He turns toward me, fixated on my throat—on the scar that stretches from ear to ear. "We're to set sail for the Burning Lands, and on to Morana's lair in Havok—I'm sorry, William, I'm afraid it looks as if you won't be joining us—but first, Queen Morana asked that I carve that fight from you by whatever means necessary."

Slowly, almost reluctantly, Titus meets my gaze for the first time since he entered the dungeons.

Something flashes in his eyes—recognition, horror, desperation. His dagger clatters to the stone floor. His lips part, his hands fisted at his sides. But his mask slips back into place, all easy charm and sinister humor, and he smirks.

"So, tell me, Aster," he croons, his hand coming up to clutch my jaw. He whispers, his hot breath caressing the shell of my ear, "how much suffering will you endure?"

"Rot in Havok," I spit, wheezing at the stitch of pain that cleaves my abdomen in two.

He chuckles, the sound deep and rich. "This is going to be fun," he murmurs, his lips brushing the exposed column of my throat. "Maybe I'll even take you up on your offer." His tongue caresses the sensitive skin where my pulse jumps, frantic. "Just a taste, perhaps? I promise I'll try to be gentle." He strokes my cheek, smearing my tears under the calloused pad of his thumb. "You—"

His shoulders tense.

He draws back, a crease forming between his brows as he stares at the path of his thumb. Again, that flash of raw emotion, like lightning illuminating the night sky. Somehow, I'm getting through to him. His throat bobs, and he meets my gaze once more, searching my eyes. Softly, almost as if he were caught in a daze, he whispers, "Don't cry, love."

"Titus?" His name escapes me on a breath, my voice cracking.

He jerks his hand away as if my skin burned him, his mouth twisting into a scowl. "Enough!" Gilded light rims the blue of his eyes as he picks up the dagger once more. He fishes the band of braided leather from his pocket, tosses my bracelet at my feet. "There's nothing stopping me from breaking the enchantment once and for all. And once the venom reaches your heart, you'll come with me to Morana's throne willingly, and I will have accomplished what your brother first failed to do that night on Reckoning Day. You'll have no other choice."

He moves at an unnatural speed, the tip of the dagger poised over my chest. He presses it deeper, his angle precise, the cursed energy searing my flesh. I'm deaf to my own screams, my jaw gaping as bile burns my throat.

Agony consumes me.

I *feel* the enchantment fracture. Feel the magic dispersed, like shards of glass scattered in the air around me. Feel the Shifter's venom pump through my veins. Feel my heart stutter—stop—start again.

Feel him twist the knife.

Memories flood my mind—memories of Titus, hanging from the same chains now used to bind me. Images of his bloody, broken body in a heap on the floor. The way he looked at me just last night, as we lay beside each other, listening to the waves lapping at the mouth of the cave, his hand in mine.

I have only one breath—only enough air in my lungs to speak just once—and even though it nearly kills me, I force myself to meet his gaze, my dry, cracked lips splitting open when I choke on the words, "I trust you, Titus."

It's as if an invisible string pulls taut—a thread I didn't know connected us, but that feels like it's been here all along, woven into the very fiber of my skin. Titus's heartbeat fills the air like music, as familiar as the voice of the sea. Titus gasps, his eyes darting from the blade to my face to the Bloodknight holding Will captive on the floor.

"Aster?"

I don't have time to think about how broken he sounds—how terrified he appears as he scrambles back, shaking his head, a wild look in his eyes.

Everything happens so fast. The Bloodknight knocks Will unconscious with a swift yet powerful fist to the back of his head. Then the Bloodknight unlocks the collar around his neck and turns to face Titus, the collar dangling from his gauntlet.

"Do it," Titus says. "Now, Gabriel!"

Gabriel?

The Bloodknight—Gabriel—doesn't hesitate, locking the iron band around Titus's throat. Quickly, Gabriel opens Eliza's cell, helping his sister to her feet, before returning to me. He holds me up as he unlocks the chains that bind my wrists, and when the second fetter opens, he catches me in his arms. I don't question Gabriel and Eliza's allegiance, especially now that I know I was wrong about Morana possessing Eliza. Hazily, I wonder if I was wrong about Flynn, too—if somehow he was framed as well. But in this moment, all I focus on is a way out of the dungeons.

"The tunnel," I groan. I will my arm to move, but it hangs limp and lifeless at my side. "The—water. Follow—"

Gabriel hoists Will's unconscious form over his right shoulder with supernatural strength. Eliza places a hand on the cave wall, near the crack in the stone.

"It's too narrow," she says. "We won't fit!"

"Gabriel," Titus grits out. "Command the stone!"

Eliza whirls on him, her eyes bright. "It's not that simple! He could cause a collapse—we could be trapped—"

"Just do it!" Titus shouts, his teeth clenched. "Now!"

Gabriel throws me over his left shoulder, albeit more gently than he holds Will. I stare directly at Titus, his jaw clenched as tears streak his face.

"Not—leaving here—without you!" I gasp, my chest spasming with every word. I can't leave him with Calantha, to be tortured and used. I *won't*.

"Yes, you are." Titus nods as if to assure me everything is going to be all right. He reaches for me, but quickly balls his hands into fists at his side. "This won't last," he says. "You're not safe with me."

The ground trembles as Gabriel stretches out his hands, his red gauntlets vibrating as he forces the gap to widen, allowing Eliza to slip through the crack.

Titus holds my gaze, and it's as if everything else fades away, until it's only him and me. "I told you to live, Aster. Not just survive—*really live*. You can't do that if you stay here." He smiles even as tears drip from his nose, his chin. "This is goodbye, love."

I want to scream at him, but I'm too weak to even cry. "Broke the—compulsion—once," I manage to say, my throat burning with the effort. "Can break it—again."

Gabriel grunts, and the stone parts enough for him to enter. The last I see of Titus is his blue eyes, glassy with tears, as Gabriel carries me away, disappearing through the crack.

A fresh jolt of panic courses through me at the sound of soldiers shouting, their boots pounding the stone as they race toward our cellblock.

"Hurry!" Eliza's footsteps splash as she races down the tunnel.

We're almost there—I can hear the waves, can taste the salty air.

But we're not alone.

In the distance, the soldiers' boots splash in the stream as they chase us down the tunnel.

"Quickly now!" Eliza shouts, clambering into a boat tied to the stone at the mouth of the cave.

Gabriel deposits Will and me into the boat and grabs the oars. He and Eliza row us out to sea, and through the dark spots edging my vision, I see we're surrounded—that the castle is encircled by the Eerie's naval fleet, hundreds of ships staggered in formation around the island. We're hidden now, behind the jagged cliffs, but in a moment, they'll see us.

Eliza closes her eyes, lifting her hands.

"Keep rowing," she says. "I'll manipulate the light. I can't hold it for long, but it should give us enough time to reach them."

I'm too weak to question her—too weak to do anything but lie there, next to Will, laboring for breath. The minutes blur. I know the moment we reach the Eerie's fleet, because Gabriel takes a deep breath, and he and Eliza fall eerily silent. It feels as if we're caught between the hulls of their ships for an eternity. Distantly, I hear the shouts of the crew members high above. I close my eyes, bracing for the moment when Eliza's magic fails, and they spot us.

Waiting.

I must faint, because when the jolly boat creaks, and my stomach lurches at the sensation of being lifted out of the water, fresh panic jolts me out of my feverish slumber.

"She's burning up," Eliza murmurs, placing the back of her hand on my forehead. "If she dies, the transformation will be complete. If I can—"

Her words slur, and my vision undulates as Gabriel picks me up, passing me to someone aboard the ship.

"It's her!" someone shouts. "It's Aster! Quick, Marge—"

I blink up at Charlie, but he's too busy barking orders to notice my mouth part. I attempt to speak, but I can't find my voice.

The stars streak across the sky as Charlie carries me from the deck into a room, the warm golden light illuminating his face as he places me on a table. Eliza hovers over me, along with Margaret, the two of them speaking to each other at a dizzying speed.

A red skeletal mask appears in my peripheral vision. It's all I can do to glance in his direction, and I feel as if I'm dreaming at the sight of him. How can Captain Shade be here, now, when we left Titus behind at Castle Grim?

"You're safe now, Aster," the man says, removing the mask.

I'm dead, I think. I must be dead.

"We're going home," the man says, the brim of Captain Shade's red tricorn hat casting shadows over his familiar face as he bends down to place a kiss on my forehead. "We're all going home."

PART THREE

AWAKENING

Chapter Thirty-Nine

Sunlight prods at my eyelids. I blink, my temples throbbing from the effort to lift my head. Squinting through bleary eyes, I'm met with a modest room made entirely of wood. At first, I think I must be aboard the *Starchaser*, but everything is perfectly still, aside from the occasional gust of wind. From where I lie on a large, cushioned bed in the center of the room, in a pool of warm light that floods in from the window opposite me, a familiar, glittering stretch of blue fades into the horizon.

Chirp.

A bird lands on my windowsill, startling me. It's unlike any bird I've ever seen before. Unlike anything I might have seen in the Eerie. Its feathers are green and red and gold, its beak long and curved. It cocks its head at me, squawks.

I look down at my white cotton gown—at the band of braided

leather on my wrist. Eliza or Gabriel must have recovered it from the dungeons before we fled.

Instinctively, I reach for the medallion hanging around my neck, rubbing my thumb over the skull and crossed daggers as if to soothe myself. As if to ease the soreness in my rib cage or the ache behind my eyes. Someone has healed my wounds. There are no marks, no scars from the wedding. But I feel what they couldn't mend with bonewielder magic and human medicine.

Father's compass! I scan the room for any sign of the tiny golden trinket, but it's nowhere to be found.

I swing my legs over the side of the bed, wincing at the pain that burns in my chest, pumping through my veins with every beat of my heart. Gripping the bedpost, I attempt to stand, only to collapse onto the edge of my mattress, panting for breath. I bite my lip to stifle a wail as I try again, but just as I gather the strength to take a step, my legs give way beneath me and I fall to the wooden floor, my face colliding with a loud *smack*.

Instantly, the door to my room swings open, and Charlie and Lewis rush inside. They haul me to my feet, depositing me on the bed once more, both talking over each other as they fuss about my cheek.

"—bleeding again—"

"—definitely going to bruise—"

"—told you she would try—"

I grab them both by their shirt collars and pull them toward me, throwing an arm around each of their necks. They tense—I can practically feel them looking at each other over my shoulder—before returning the embrace, squeezing me tight.

"You're okay," I say weakly, my voice hoarse from disuse. I draw back to look at them both, wanting to be certain they're really here and not just a cruel trick of my mind—another nightmare waiting to devour me. Fear grips my heart. "Will? Is he—"

"He's alive, and he's here," Charlie assures me, but something about the way he cuts a glance at Lewis sends a chill down my spine. "Sort of."

My heart leaps into my throat, but before panic overwhelms me, Lewis continues.

"He hasn't turned into a Shifter," he says. "It's as if his transformation was...suspended somehow. But, Aster..." He hesitates. "He's ill. He won't come ashore. He insists on staying aboard the *Starchaser*."

I think of the last time I saw Will—the pile of corpses, the way he tried to attack me, lost to his bloodlust as the Shifter curse weakened his resolve—and something in my chest splinters, piercing my heart.

"I need to see him." I try to get to my feet, but Lewis seizes my wrist, his grip gentle but firm.

"You can," Lewis says, cutting a glance at Charlie, who scowls, shaking his head slightly. "Just...not yet."

I want to argue—want to insist they take me to see him this instant—but another, more immediate question takes precedence. "How did you escape?" I ask, looking between the two of them, searching for any sign of injury, but they appear strong—healthy in a way I haven't seen them in a long time. Maybe ever.

"It's all thanks to the *Starchaser*'s crew," Lewis says, plopping down beside me on the edge of the bed. "When Titus lowered the wards, it wasn't just Underlings that were able to enter Castle Grim." I wince at the mention of Titus working for Morana, but

Lewis doesn't seem to notice. "The suggestion of the Order's fleet was a distraction, and when Eva Mercer was killed, it worked to our advantage because Morana's forces thought the Order had called off the invasion. But they didn't expect the *Starchaser*—weren't even looking for it. Our people stormed the gates during the attack and got us out of there, guns blazing. It was incredible."

Our people. I know they mean pirates—*humans*—but the words puncture something inside me.

"I have to tell you—" I start, but Lewis cuts me off with a wave.

"We know about Mother," he says, his brow quirked.

"Halflings." Charlie snorts a laugh. "Surely, someone could have come up with a better name for a half-human, half-Nightweaver offspring."

I blink at them, stunned at how quickly they've adjusted to this discovery. "Mother told you?"

Charlie nods, his brows pinched. "She said we might never access our affinities. Something about repressed magic." He shrugs. "How can you miss something you never knew you had, hmm?"

My heart aches for them when I think about my connection to the water. I can't imagine never feeling that pull, never hearing the song of the sea as I do now, growing louder, calling out to me....

"Where are we?" I ask.

Their faces brighten, and they share a knowing smile.

Lewis answers, "Why don't you see for yourself?"

My brothers bolster me, half-walking, half-dragging me to the open window. I look down, through the canopy of leaves, at a beach where Elsie and Albert splash in the shallow water, along with a few other children I don't recognize. Nearby, Margaret and Jack stroll hand in hand, walking barefoot in the sand. Margaret turns, shouting something over her shoulder, and Jack waves as if to beckon someone.

Henry limps toward them, dragging his left leg slightly.

Relief nearly knocks me off my feet, and if it weren't for Charlie and Lewis, I might collapse again, overwhelmed at the sight of a harbor to the east, where hundreds of ships make port, an entire fleet flying a crimson flag embroidered with a silver eight-point star. Owen used to tell me stories about what paradise might look like, but I could have never imagined anything this beautiful. From my window, I can see where this room had been built into boughs high above the ground, along with dozens of offshoots of rooms—some smaller, some much, much larger—in all directions, all tucked into the gnarled branches of this massive, ancient tree.

"Is this..."

"Welcome home, Aster Oberon."

Gripping Charlie's and Lewis's arms, I turn to see a beautiful woman standing in the open doorway, a golden crown adorned with seashells and precious gemstones atop her long, dirty-blond waves. Everything about her is graceful and relaxed, from her hair to her posture to her simple blue silk gown, the loose silhouette and draping sleeves different from anything I might have worn at Castle Grim. She grins at me, her tanned, freckled face beaming, and her kind eyes remind me in an instant of Father and Owen.

"My name is Orella," she says, her grin broadening to a full, joyful smile. "Orella Oberon."

"Father's little sister," Charlie adds with a grin.

Orella laughs, the sound as warm and beautiful as she. "I've been waiting a very long time to meet you, Aster."

I stare at her, my mouth gaping. Mother and Father never

spoke of their lives before us—never spoke of their siblings. For all we knew, our parents had no family.

Sympathy flickers in Orella's eyes, but her smile remains as she gestures at the open window, at the white sandy beach and sparkling, sunlit waves. "Welcome to the Red Island."

CHAPTER FORTY

"Az, slow down!" Charlie urges as he and Lewis flank me, ready to catch me if I were to trip and fall. But I feel stronger than I have in days—weeks—as I follow Orella through the humid maze of staircases, rope bridges, and wooden hallways of the Palace of Pearls. Or, as Orella refers to it simply and lovingly, the Pearl.

"When you first arrived two days ago, you were very ill," Orella tells me, slowing her pace to match mine.

"How long was I...?" I glance at Lewis, and he frowns.

"The wedding was three weeks ago," he says. Hesitates. "You've been...unstable."

Three weeks. Panic flares in my chest.

"Shouldn't I have...am I—"

"You have not turned," Orella says slowly, carefully. "Your curse is unlike any other. The venom should have already transformed you into a Shifter—the moment the enchantment broke and the venom infected your blood, you should have succumbed to the fever. But it's as if something is...interfering. I sense the presence of Underling magic—a force that seems to *speak* to the venom." She shakes her head, her expression perplexed. "The same can be said for your friend, William. He, too, has managed to stave off the transformation, though we don't know how."

My heart pounds against my sternum, my mouth suddenly dry. "The Shifter who bit me as a child," I say. "He said he could control the venom."

But Flynn is dead. Which confirms what I suspected in the dungeons: Flynn was framed. The Shifter who bit me is still alive.

But that doesn't explain why Will hasn't turned. Could the Shifter have something to do with Will's curse, too? Could he be keeping Will alive for some reason?

"What can we do?" I ask.

Orella casts a sidelong glance in my direction, hesitating, and my stomach clenches. "I've done all I can to form a new enchantment around your heart and buy you more time," she says. "But my magic is not strong enough to break the curse."

"You're a—" I shake my head, suddenly dizzy, and Lewis places a steadying hand on my elbow. "You're a Sorceress?"

The corner of Orella's lip kicks up, a familiar smirk that reminds me of Margaret. "*We* come from a long line of Sorcerers and Sorceresses." Her mouth twists, a sad expression that clashes with her lovely, cheerful face. "If it weren't for your father's magic, you might not have survived the initial fever."

"My—" I trip over the hem of my white gown and stumble a few steps before Charlie grabs my arm.

I try to grasp at a splintered, fever-drenched memory of a red skeletal mask and a man's voice telling me I'm safe, but I can't seem to grab hold of it.

My mouth works, struggling to form words, when a muffled voice at the end of the bridge gives me pause.

Laughter, full and rich, sends my mind into a whirl.

And then I'm racing toward the sound of his voice. I don't slow down, not even as I throw myself at the double doors, stumbling into the warm, sunlit parlor, my vision blurring as I attempt to survey the room and its inhabitants.

I thought I imagined him—thought the vision of him dressed in the scarlet garb of Captain Shade was a result of my injuries, but…

"Father?" I cover my mouth to hold back a sob as he enfolds me in his arms. I inhale the scent of fresh bread, cinnamon, and vanilla, as if he spent all morning baking in the kitchen, his dark apron dusted with flour. The salty sea brine clings to his loose linen shirt, his skin tanned. He looks nothing like he did the last time I saw him at Bludgrave Manor, the night he drove a blade through his own heart. He looks healthy, and happy, and…

"How?" I draw back, my fists clenched tightly around his shirt, afraid I might let go and this will have all been a dream.

Father smiles, but sadness twists his lips. "I had a little help."

I catch a glimpse of Killian over Father's shoulder. He leans against the fireplace mantel, brows pinched as he puffs on a cigar.

"You!" I say, storming past Father. I rip the cigar from Killian's hand and stomp it underfoot.

"That was a rather fine rug," Killian remarks dryly, giving me an expectant look—the kind that says, *Go on, have at it.*

And I do.

"You let me believe he was dead! That we couldn't recover his body from the fire!"

"Aster." Mother's soft voice comes from behind. I whirl to find her sitting on one of the two velvet sofas, her expression pitying. "You mustn't blame Killian. He was following orders."

My lip curls. "*Your* orders?" I bark a laugh, and in the corner of my eye, Charlie winces. "Of course, I should have known! This is all your doing!"

Mother sits up straighter, but I don't miss the exhaustion that seems to weigh on her shoulders as she smooths her yellow brocade coat. "Your father was compelled. He would have killed you had he not chosen to sacrifice himself. He trusted that Killian might be able to save his life, and he *did*."

I shake my head, staring at Father—at the scar peeking out from his half-buttoned shirt where the blade pierced his chest. "I watched you die."

"Yes," Killian says, his voice gentle. "His heart had to stop for the compulsion to break. As soon as I could, I used my magic to repair the organ. The moment you were gone, I knew I had to get Philip out of there." He takes another cigar from his jacket pocket, lights it. "Luckily," Killian goes on, cutting his eyes to the right side of the room, "I have some friends who are rather adept at staying hidden."

I was too distracted—my focus solely on Father when I entered the parlor—but now I see the cervitaur I met the night I joined the Order of Hildegarde, her long mossy-green hair shimmering in the sunlight. She smiles at me, bowing deeply, and to her left, the dwarf—*Grendwin*, I think—follows suit. To Elatha's right, the bespectacled badger, Tollith, gives me a shy wave, and Bronmir, the faun, dips his head respectfully.

"They hid Philip until you disembarked the *Starchaser* and he was able to come aboard," Killian says. "I stayed close by, keeping an eye on things at home through Liv."

As if summoned, Liv pokes her head out of Killian's pocket and blows me a kiss, her musical laughter like the tinkling of the tiniest, clearest bells. I think about what Killian said on Holy Winter's Eve—about his *sources*—and I realize the pixie must have been spying on me longer than I even suspected. I quirk a brow at her, and she sinks back into her hiding place.

"Why keep it a secret?" I ask, turning to look at Father—wanting to hear it from him. "And why were you dressed as Captain Shade?"

The air shifts, and Grendwin clears his throat.

"Your Majesties," he says. "I'll take my leave."

Majesties?

"You're quite all right, Grendwin." Father chuckles, and I catch the way he glances at Mother, a mischievous smile tugging at the corners of his lips, before he looks at me once more, his expression somber. He lifts the medallion from my neck, running his fingers over the skull and crossed daggers. "My mother gave this to me when I was just a boy. She used to tell me stories from a time before the Fall—stories of a legendary hero known as Malachi Shade." He pauses, his brow furrowed. "I created the identity of Captain Shade as a means of spying for the Order just after Owen was born. When I met Titus, I passed the mantel on to him, along with Hildegarde's maps of Castle Grim. Taught him the magic needed to access her many hideaways. He's been acting as Captain Shade ever since."

The room spins, and I stumble backward a step.

"We never meant to hide the truth from you forever," Father says, taking me by the hand and guiding me to the sofa, where I sit between him and Mother, my skin itchy and hot and altogether uncomfortable. "We only hoped that when the time came, you might be able to understand the choices we made to protect you and your brothers and sisters."

"What choices?" I ask slowly, my heart pounding painfully against my rib cage.

Mother just shakes her head. "Morana has been watching you, Aster. Listening to your conversations. There is a...connection between the two of you."

I get to my feet, my head throbbing. I think about the Shifter—how he said we shared a connection, one that allowed him to influence my feelings, both emotional and physical. He was capable of that kind of control because *his* venom surged through my veins, but Morana... "Connected how?"

Mother sighs. "I couldn't tell you before. We can't be certain who is spying for Morana. It could be anyone. I thought it would be safe to tell you the truth once we'd come home, but—"

"*Home*," I echo, looking up to find Father watching me carefully, hesitantly. I remember what Mother said just after I learned she was Dawnrender—about the heir of Hildegarde having received a portion of the Lightbringer's power. And how Morana came after me at the wedding—not to turn me into a Shifter, but to *take back* something that belonged to her. My vision swims, and it feels like the floor shifts beneath me. "But if the Red Island is our home...If she"—I cut a glance at Orella, perched on the opposite sofa, her crown glittering in the sunlight—"is our aunt—your sister, an Oberon—a *queen*—then..."

"The descendants of Hildegarde have guarded this island and its secrets since Hildegarde used the True King's power to form it out of the sea," Orella says, her big, round eyes kinder even than Father's. "The power is passed on from generation to generation—from firstborn to firstborn, transferred at the time of their birth."

Orella hesitates, and Father clears his throat.

"I was the firstborn child—"

"And rightful king," Orella adds, as if scolding her brother.

The ghost of a grin touches his lips. "Until I abdicated the throne to a far better choice," he says with a pointed look at Orella.

"When Owen was born," Mother says, her voice quieter than I've ever heard it, "the power went to him."

Father's expression darkens, his eyes glazed with memory. "Until the night you were bitten."

Mother covers my hand with both of hers. "You were too weak to survive it on your own," she says, her voice choked with tears. "You were only a child. Even with the enchantment..."

"No one survives the fever," Father says, his brows pinched. "You needed the True King's power—the power of the Lightbringer."

Owen's power.

"It had happened only once in the history of the Lightbringer that a living heir could transfer their power to another," Orella says. "That was four hundred years ago, and it killed the heir who surrendered their power."

Father nods, his mouth pressed in a tight line. "We didn't even ask," he says. "We wouldn't have known how. Owen just...knew what to do."

"He lived," Mother says, her gaze searching my face. She

reaches up, her calloused fingers caressing the bruise on my cheek, her touch unnaturally warm. "And so did you."

I move so suddenly I feel as if I might faint, searching for the exit, but Charlie is there to steady me, his hands on my shoulders.

I turn, facing Mother and Father, their faces golden as they beam up at me, and it feels wrong. Everything feels wrong.

"All this time," I say, shaking my head. "It was... *me?*"

Father's expression is solemn, his voice reverent when he says, "The power is yours, Aster. You are the living heir of Hildegarde."

Chapter Forty-One

"I'm what?" I sway, but Lewis and Charlie steady me.

"Well, *we're* princes," Lewis says, wriggling his eyebrows. "Truthfully, I always knew I was meant for a life of royalty."

"She just found out she's a princess *and* possesses unfathomable power," Charlie says, shooting him a disapproving glance. "Must everything be about you?"

Lewis opens his mouth to say something else, but the double doors open behind us, and two women in dark tricorn hats enter the parlor. The pirates skirt around my brothers and me and bow first to Orella before kneeling on the rug in front of Mother.

"We're sorry to interrupt," the first starts.

"But we have the information you requested," the second finishes.

Mother dips her head, and her expression shifts from that of my mother to that of the captain—to that of Dawnrender. "Very well," she says, and the two pirates rise.

My eyes narrow on the two women—their raven hair so black it's almost blue.

Mother looks at me, gestures at the pirates. "You remember Clemson and Davina Mercer?"

Clemson and Davina turn to face me, each dropping to one knee, their heads bowed.

"*Dawnrender* has spies everywhere," Lewis whispers in my ear.

"Just wait until you hear about the chauffeur," Charlie adds. "Old Boris has been in Mother's pocket since before we arrived at Bludgrave."

Clemson looks up, her expression genuine. "I believe we got off on the wrong foot," she says.

"We're sorry to have stepped on any toes, Your Highness," Davina adds with enough sincerity that I can hardly reconcile this version of her with the giggling courtier I've come to despise.

My head spins. "I need to sit down."

"You can sit in the war room," Mother says, getting to her feet. "There's much to discuss, and I'd hate for you to be late for the party," she adds, a small smile on her lips. "It's being held in our family's honor, after all."

"We expected you to sleep through it," Lewis says with a grimace. "But it's the thought that counts, right?"

"She's awake!"

"I can't believe she's really here!"

The walk from the parlor to the war room is a blur of bowing servants and excited whispers. If it weren't for Charlie and Lewis guiding me down the halls, I might never have reached the armchair waiting for me in the large treehouse they call the "war room." Even after I've taken my seat, my head pounds and my chest aches, but at the very least, my vision has stopped spinning.

Mother and Father stand side by side at the head of the table, flanked by Killian and Orella, who I notice more than once casting sidelong glances at each other. Lewis keeps looking over his shoulder at the doorway, and Charlie leans on the back of my chair, crunching on something he's stashed in his pocket. The four Myths—Tollith, Elatha, Bronmir, and Grendwin—keep to the opposite end of the table, and Clemson and Davina fill the gap, somewhat unrecognizable in their matching leather frock coats.

The two sisters waste no time debriefing the room, and for a moment, I wish I was back in my bed, before I knew I was a princess—or an heir, for that matter.

"He's used his knowledge of the Dire to navigate through most of our defenses," Clemson says, dragging her finger over the map.

"You're lucky you managed to avoid him for as long as you did," Davina adds with a pointed look at Mother. "He must have been right on your tail."

I lurch forward in my seat, my pulse leaping into my throat. "Titus?" I ask, searching their faces for any indication that he's all right. "Is he—" I stop short when I realize the room has gone eerily still, as if everyone is bracing for impact. I look to my right, where Lewis refuses to meet my gaze.

"We've lost four ships to the Reaper in the past week," Clemson says bitterly. "Good people."

I stand, imploring Mother to look at me, but her eyes are fixed on the map in front of her. "He's been compelled!" I insist. "We can help him. If we capture him, we can—"

"Aster," Father says softly, shaking his head. "He's been compelled by Morana herself. The only way to break that compulsion would be if Titus consumed a drop of her blood—blood from her *corporeal* form."

A drop of Morana's blood—the same cure I was searching for to save me and Will. We can still do this. I look between Father and Mother. "Then we need to find Morana."

"It's not that simple—" Killian starts, but I ignore him.

"Use me," I say, gripping the edge of the table, the room spinning once more. A sharp pain splits my skull, and I press the heel of my palm to my forehead. "You were already looking for her—at Castle Grim. You said she was after something that would give her the strength to find the heir, but that wasn't true, was it? You knew she had already found the heir...." I choke on the lump in my throat as the reality of what I've just said pierces my heart like a blade. "You knew she was after *me*."

Oh.

Oh *Stars*...

"You were using me as bait?" I stagger backward a step, my heart hammering. I was more than willing to lure Morana out with my blood when I thought it would help us obtain the cure for Will, but knowing now that Morana wanted me for a different reason, and my mother knew, all this time...

Mother winces, and I almost think she might—for the first time in my life—second-guess herself. But then she lifts her chin, injecting authority into her posture once more. "In order for Morana to have reclaimed the power of the Lightbringer, she would have had to take her corporeal form, which she hasn't done outside of her own realm in centuries. She wanted to take you to the Burning Lands, but we never would have let that happen."

She grimaces, the lines around her eyes softening. "Underlings crave despair—they feed on your fear, your doubt, your confusion. Morana was toying with you, feasting on your sorrows, but we knew from the beginning that she never intended on killing you there, at Castle Grim."

"If you would have told me"—I shake my head, blood pounding in my ears—"I could have done something! I could have—"

"Morana fooled us all," Mother says, her own frustration evident in the way she clenches her fists, her jaw tight. "We knew she was near, but we didn't know that she had possessed Leo, nor that she had compelled Titus. We suspected that she was somehow working with Queen Calantha—perhaps even possessed her—until all signs pointed to Eliza. Still, we had a plan: Leo and Titus would marry, they'd bring down the wards, and our forces would attack and take control of the Eerie before Morana could reveal herself through Eliza and make her move. Before Morana could do *anything* to harm you or take you away." Mother's gaze softens as she looks at me. "Of course, we know now that we had it all wrong."

"Leo *told* me Titus was compelled," I admit, hot, angry tears pricking my eyes. "But I thought it was another one of Morana's tricks—that she was just feeding misinformation somehow, trying to turn Leo and Titus against each other to get in the way of the Order's plans at the wedding. I should have listened. If I had—"

"Morana knew that you wouldn't," Mother says gently. "She

used your... *friendship* with the prince to torment you." Her gaze searches mine, and I think she might have said more if we were alone. Suddenly, I'm glad to be surrounded by Order members, even if the looks my brothers give me make me want to elbow them both in their ribs.

I'm thankful when Killian clears his throat, diverting the attention to himself. "Morana's magic is stronger than we could have ever anticipated—it leaves no trace," he says, scratching his jaw. "Even if you had shared your suspicions that Titus was compelled, there would have been no way to prove it."

Mother exhales a heavy, slow breath, her eyes narrowed at the maps laid out on the table before her. "Regardless, we should have guessed that she would want to tie herself to Titus's magic through a marriage bond with Leo," she says. "But by compelling him, even now that the princess is dead and their marriage bond is broken, Morana still has control of his mind—a contingency we never accounted for. It's clear to us now that by using Titus, she planned to take control of the Eerie, all while convincing you that the only way to save him was to go with her to the Burning Lands, a willing sacrifice."

Sweat slicks the back of my neck.

A willing sacrifice.

"The Shifter who bit me as a child—he tried to get me to go with him of my own accord," I say. "Do you think he could be the exiled general? Could it have all been a ruse to bring me to Morana himself and regain favor with his queen?"

Creases line Mother's forehead as her brows pinch, and she shakes her head. "It's possible. But when Flynn—"

"I came as soon as I heard!" Eliza pants, bursting into the room, but when her wild eyes find me, her teeth worry her bottom lip. Whatever it is she wants to say, I don't give her the opportunity.

I'm on my feet in an instant, starting toward her. Lewis tenses as I lift my arms, as if he considers blocking my path.

I throw my arms around Eliza as she squeaks out a small sob, and she returns my embrace without hesitation.

"I'm sorry," we both say, hugging each other tighter.

"For what?" we ask in tandem.

"I thought you were possessed," I admit, shame strangling my voice.

Eliza's sniffle turns into a choked laugh as she draws back, wiping tears from my face with the hem of her sleeve. "Now, now," she says. "That's not your fault. I should have been more forthright with you. Perhaps I could have dispelled some of the rumors before things got out of hand."

"I shouldn't have assumed—"

"Please, Aster," Eliza says, patting my hand, "anyone would have. *I* would have!" She turns then, facing the table, her chin held high. "Flynn is not a Changeling, not a Shifter, and he is certainly not an Underling general." There's a threatening edge to Eliza's voice, and I don't miss the way Lewis reaches out, twining his fingers with hers. "He was compelled, just like Titus."

"We know," Mother starts, and for a brief moment, her tone shifts from that of the pirate captain to that of a caring, sympathetic parent. "We're sorry we believed you and your brothers were guilty of—"

"No, you don't understand!" Eliza says, slicing her hand through the air. "It's more than just Flynn's compulsion. Yes, my brothers and I were framed, but I *saw* who killed Eva. I watched him do it!" She cuts an uneasy glance at me. "Owen Oberon killed Eva."

"Eliza, please," Killian says softly, pinching the bridge of his nose. "Now is not the time—"

"No, I believe her," I say, my voice rough, burning my throat with every word. I face Mother, my chest tight. "How long have you known? How long have you known that Owen was alive? That he was working for the Guild of Shadows?"

A chill sweeps through the room, the only sound that of Killian's lighter as he ignites the tip of his cigar.

"What is she talking about?" Charlie says, stepping up to stand beside me.

"Owen is—" Lewis scrubs his hand over his face. He looks at Eliza, who gives a subtle shake of her head, her expression apologetic.

"Is he alive?" Charlie demands, his voice thick with emotion. "Is my brother *alive*?"

Mother nods, her mouth pressed tight. "Not in the way you might think," she says gently. "He is a Shifter now."

Lewis lets out a small, choked noise. Charlie curses as he storms away from the table, slamming his fist into the wooden plank of the wall.

Father places a gentle hand on Charlie's shoulder as he begins to weep.

Mother watches, her expression torn, before fixing a stern look on me. "I've known about Owen since Reckoning Day," she admits, her mouth pressed tight.

Lewis attempts to stifle a sob, but when Eliza gathers him in her arms, and he falls apart, I want to fall apart, too. But when I look at my parents and see that they look just as defeated as I feel, my grief gives way to rage.

Mother's throat bobs, but she straightens her spine, regaining her composure. "I never wanted to keep this a secret from you all, but I did it for the good of everyone," she says, as if still trying to convince herself she did the right thing. "The Order couldn't let Morana, Owen, or any Underling know we were onto them. And although some of our suspicions were wrong, we still acted when it mattered most."

Mother withdraws a compass from her pocket, places it on the table in front of her.

Father's compass—*my* compass.

"Gabriel took it from you as you were escorted to the dungeons," she says, cutting a glance at Eliza, her expression grateful.

"I don't understand," I say, my gaze narrowing on the small golden trinket. "What does Father's compass have to do with any of this?"

Mother and Father share a look.

"No one has ever been able to locate the entrance to Morana's kingdom," Mother says. "Her lair has been obscured by the fire and shadow of the Burning Lands, so no one has come close to finding it. But the sword that expelled Morana from Leonora's body was enchanted—spelled in a way so that the magic attached itself to Morana's soul, giving us the means to track her with this," she adds, tapping the lid of the compass, etched with Father's handwriting. "But for the spell to work, we needed the enchanted compass close by when the sword made contact with Morana's host. This linked the two enchantments and enabled us to track Morana."

I try to catch Father's eye, but he stares at the compass, his expression nettled. "That's why you gave it to me," I say. "Because you knew Morana would come for me."

Mother nods, her expression solemn. "Now," she says, "for the first time in six hundred years, we can attack Morana where she least expects it—in her own kingdom, where she believes she's safe. Our Sorcerers can perform a ritual to bind her in her corporeal form and bring her here, where you will be able to take back the full power of the Lightbringer. With Morana defeated, we could turn the tide of the war. You could eradicate the Underling threat—once and for all. And with just a drop of Morana's blood, we could break Titus's compulsion. We could save Will from his curse." She pauses, drops her voice an octave. "We could set Owen free."

My hands brush my hips, itching for the familiar hilts of my daggers as I look around the room. "Why are we still here?"

The four Myths shift uneasily, and Killian sighs, running a hand through his hair. He scowls, casting a glance at Mother, who watches Father whispering quietly to Charlie, his hands on my brother's shoulders. To my right, Eliza murmurs something in Lewis's ear, and I turn to see Lewis staring blankly at the map in front of him.

"It's not that simple." Killian clears his throat, his brow furrowed. "This kind of attack—it takes time. Planning."

"What about Will?" I ask, and a muscle in Killian's jaw twitches, but he doesn't answer. I look at Mother, feeling that wild, vicious beast clawing at my chest. I think of Owen, forced to serve Morana, and Will—he might have survived the initial fever, but I can't be certain how long he'll be able to stave it off. "Titus doesn't have time!" I insist. "What if Morana—what if she—"

"Aster," Mother says calmly. "We have plans to leave one week from today."

"Why not now? Why not—"

"Aster!" she repeats, firmer this time. "The Shifter who bit you is still alive. Orella believes you haven't succumbed to your curse because he's manipulating it somehow—manipulating *you*. We need to focus on keeping you well. If something were to happen to you now—"

"I'm going!" I say through gritted teeth. "I refuse to stay here while you risk your lives—"

"No," Father says quietly, and I whirl to face him, tears stinging my cheeks. "Listen to your mother, Aster. You will stay here, where Orella can continue using her magic to keep you alive long enough for us to get the cure. That's an order."

I look to Killian. I don't know why I expect him to speak up, to take my side, but he doesn't even meet my eye. No one will. The realization grabs hold of my throat, cutting off my supply of air, until the room is spinning in earnest. They didn't listen to Owen. Or Titus. They're not going to listen to me.

Father reaches out to grasp my shoulder, but I shove past him, through the doorway, leaving the room without looking back.

Chapter Forty-Two

The colorful bird perches on my window. I sit in a wooden rocking chair with my legs underneath me, and Dinah, Killian's bloodhound, lies curled up at my feet, sleeping soundly. I bask in the final apricot rays of sunlight, watching as the waves crash against the white sandy beaches down below. My chest aches knowing that somewhere, out there, Titus is looking for me. That after spending a lifetime being forced to act with such cruelty by his parents, he's been compelled to kill the very people he's fought to protect. And I'm stuck here, only steps away from a fleet of ships, and I'm still not free to go where I please. Because if I could, I would have already commissioned a crew and set sail for the Burning Lands.

Somehow, I know that if the roles were reversed, Titus would do the same. If it meant freeing me from Morana's compulsion, he wouldn't take no for an answer. He'd storm the gates of Morana's kingdom and wouldn't leave until he procured a drop of her blood. For Will, and for me. That's just who he is.

Despite everything I think about him—his arrogance, his violent nature—I am certain of this: Titus is not what he's been forced to become. He is not the Reaper. Not a puppet for Morana to control. He's the boy who endured unspeakable torture, to keep others from suffering his same fate. The boy who dedicated his life to saving children from cannibal ships and feeding starving pirate clans—the very people who would have hated him if they knew he was a Nightweaver prince. The boy who risked his own life—his own freedom—every time he put on the mask of Captain Shade, but did it anyway, because it meant others might be freed.

Leo knew this. She used her final breath to tell me so. And I believe her.

Titus *is* good. Now, I must be good enough to save him. Brave enough. Fearless enough. Fast enough.

I will not let them take him.

And still, what he said to me in the dungeons—what he said about Will. What Titus said about *his own feelings for me* ...

I shake my head, attempting to clear my thoughts. I can't focus on that now. Not when he needs my help. Not when I can't be sure what he said was even true and not just a product of Morana's compulsion.

Margaret came to check on me an hour ago, to see if I wanted anything for supper. I didn't. She tried to persuade me to eat something before the party tonight, but I don't seem to have much of an appetite. An aftereffect of the fever, perhaps. Or maybe I just can't bring myself to eat when I know Will is suffering from an unspeakable hunger that cannot be slaked by roast chicken or apple pie. I told her I was saving room for the buffet that was prepared in honor of my family's return.

A half-truth.

The party doesn't start until twilight. If it weren't for my siblings, I would stay here in my room, angry at my parents, at myself, at the world. But when Margaret sat on the edge of my bed, she didn't even get a word out before she started sobbing. I knew instantly that Charlie or Lewis or possibly both told her the news about Owen. "Why?" she asked, and I knew she was asking me the same way I asked Father and Mother about keeping Owen's survival—his involvement with the Guild of Shadows, his part to play in the events that took place at the Reckoning Day ball—a secret. But like Mother and Father must have known, I realize my answer will not satisfy.

Because I didn't want you to hate him, I think. I wonder if Mother and Father feel the same way. Not even Charlie and Lewis know about Owen's involvement in Father's would-be death. That he was the one to compel Father. And maybe it's because I want to protect him that I don't want them to know. Not when there's still a chance he can be saved.

Despite how I feel about attending the party, I am determined not to withdraw from my siblings. Not this time. Not after the months I spent isolated at Bludgrave, unaware that Margaret was struggling with adjusting to our new life just as much as I was. Not after the days I spent at Castle Grim, determined to fix everything on my own. Whatever happens next, we will face it together. All of us.

There's a soft knock at my door. I consider staying silent,

hoping whoever it is will move along, but then I think about Elsie or Albert standing on the other side of the door, and I can't bring myself to turn them away.

"Come in."

Father brings a tray of fresh fruit and cheese and sets it on my bedside. Dinah sniffs the air, and Father tosses her a chunk of apple.

"You need your strength," Father says quietly, leaning against the rugged frame of my window. I expect the colorful bird to fly away, but when Father reaches out to stroke its wings, it doesn't even startle.

"I don't see why it matters," I say, my eyes narrowed on the bough of the tree just outside my window, the sunset illuminating its leaves with a pinkish glow. "You're not going to let me come with you."

Father looks out at the ocean. "We should have told you," he says. "We planned to, we just..." He clenches his jaw. "We couldn't."

I want to scream at him. I want to tell him it isn't fair—that none of it is fair. If they hadn't kept us away from the Red Island, none of this would have happened. I would never have been bitten. Owen wouldn't have been turned into a Shifter. I want to tell him that it's all their fault for lying to us.

"There's still so much your mother and I want to tell you," Father says, and I can see him watching me out of the corner of my eye. "About why we left. About..." He sighs. "About everything."

"But you can't," I say. "Because of this... *connection* between Morana and me?"

He frowns. "I'm afraid so."

I stand, careful to avoid stepping on Dinah. "I have to get ready."

He nods slowly, accepting my obvious dismissal. "Of course," he says, scratching Dinah between the ears as she stretches, preparing to follow me to my bathing chambers. Father turns to leave, but he pauses in my doorway, his back to me. "This was my room, you know." He pats the weathered frame. "The wood was taken from the wreck of the *Sunseeker*—my father's ship."

I know I'm supposed to be angry with him, but I've never heard him mention his father—my grandfather—and I can't help but ask, "What happened?"

His shoulders sag. "My mother's ship was caught in a tempest near the borders of the Dire. My father came to her aid. She made it home." He runs his hand over the grooves of the wood. "He didn't."

There's a tight feeling in my chest that I've come to know intimately as grief. But in this case, it feels hollow, because how can I grieve for people I've never met? People whose names I don't even know?

"I was only Albert's age when he died. For so long, I was angry with him for leaving us too soon," Father says, and I think about him at eleven years old, forced to bear the heavy burden of the crown. "It wasn't until I met your mother that I understood why he'd done it."

Many times, my siblings and I asked Mother and Father to tell us the story of how they met. Each time, they'd come up with a fantastical tale—one that almost always included them having been enemies who couldn't help falling in love. Once, it was that they were locked in battle, fighting for enemy clans, when a sea serpent attacked and they were forced to vanquish the Myth together. Another time, Father claimed Mother stowed away on his ship, and when he woke to her knife at his throat, he blurted out a marriage proposal right then, and Mother laughed so hard she cried.

"It's tradition, here, that when you propose marriage, you're to present your bride-to-be with a set of pearls that can be found only near the Red Island," Father says, glancing over his shoulder to look at me. "When I asked your mother to marry me, I gave her the pearls you wore at the Reckoning Day ball."

My heart sinks. "I lost them that night." I swallow around the lump in my throat. "I don't know how. I was wearing them when Owen attacked me, and when I finally woke up, they were gone. If I had known—"

"I know," he says, his kind eyes crinkling around the edges as he smiles. "It was the sight of those pearls that night that broke the compulsion, if only for a minute. And I realized what my father must have known when he went after my mother in that storm."

Tears spring to my eyes, and I want to run to him—to throw myself in his arms and bury my face in his shirt like I might have when I was a little girl and I still believed he could solve any problem I was facing—but I don't move. "What was that?"

He looks around the room, at the wood that no doubt holds so many memories for him—some painful, some happy, I'm sure. "Love is always worth the risk."

CHAPTER FORTY-THREE

When Bellaflor arrives to find me languishing in a towel, curled in a fetal position on my bed, I've hardly had a moment to register her presence before she pulls me into her embrace, and I begin to cry.

"There, there," the woman says, rubbing small circles on my back.

I can't figure out what it is about her that makes me feel this comfortable, but when my sobs have subsided enough for Bellaflor to be heard over my sniffling, she takes my hand in hers and says, "I knew you wouldn't remember me. So many of your memories were lost after you were bitten."

"Lost?" I rasp. I thought perhaps Mother used magic to alter my mind, just as Will suppressed Annie's and Lord Bludgrave's memories. "Why?"

Bellaflor tucks a strand of hair behind my ear. "Before the

enchantment could protect your heart, the curse had a chance to eat away at your happiest memories."

I think about how I didn't remember meeting Titus.... Could that have truly been one of my happiest memories?

"Why didn't I remember being bitten, then?"

Bellaflor grimaces. "It was such a painful experience," she says slowly, shaking her head. "Our mind has its own ways of protecting us from things we'd rather not remember."

I nod, even as tears spill onto my cheeks. The realization that it wasn't magic suppressing my memory—it was only because the memory was just too painful to relive—makes it that much worse, somehow.

"What about Owen?" I ask. "Wouldn't he remember saving me? And my siblings... wouldn't they have known I was bitten?"

She winces. "Your brothers and sisters weren't there when the Shifter attacked. Only Owen. He'd followed your father ashore, and you'd chased after him. If you hadn't..."

If I hadn't, I would never have been cursed. Owen would still be the heir of Hildegarde.

"When he transferred the power of the Lightbringer to you," she says, "he woke with no knowledge of the Shifter's attack or what followed. Your parents thought it might be better that way—never knowing he'd had the power to begin with, or that he'd been the reason you were attacked in the first place."

Even though I wish I didn't agree with the way my parents kept yet another secret from us both, I understand. I remember what Will said to me the day we observed Father's burial rites. *Sometimes, people keep secrets for reasons we could only understand if we found ourselves in their position.*

I think about how I didn't tell Margaret or the others about Owen's role in Father's death. Mother and Father wouldn't have wanted Owen to blame himself for leading me ashore, even if he *did* give up the power of the Lightbringer to save my life.

Bellaflor works quickly, braiding my hair in a crown atop my head and applying a light, rosy sheen of powder to my cheeks to detract from my sickly appearance. All the while, she tells me her story. How she knew Father since he was a child, and when we were children, she sailed with us aboard the *Lightbringer*, taking care of my siblings and me when Mother and Father were acting on Order directives. I remember, now, how my older siblings had faint recollections of an elderly woman who sailed with us for a time but went ashore one day along the Cutthroat Coast and never returned. I learn from a teary-eyed Bellaflor that Mother asked her to keep an eye on Titus and that she spent years in servitude at Castle Grim, watching over both him and Will.

"Have you seen Will?" I ask as she pulls my coat over my shoulders.

She nods, a crease forming between her brows. "Poor dear. He insists on staying locked up in that brig; he's so frightened."

It's as if I've taken a blow to the chest, knocking the wind from my lungs. I open my mouth, but before I can ask anything else, Bellaflor takes me by the arm and turns me so that I'm facing the cheval mirror in the corner of my room.

"Oh!" I gasp, taking a step closer to my reflection, wanting to get a better look at the details of my coat. The simple trousers, linen shirt, and boots are a welcome reprieve from complicated gowns, and I'm delighted to find that I have full range of motion. But the coat...

Sapphire blue, the color of the sea just before the sun sets, that falls to my knees, thick and warm to protect against the cold nights at sea, sturdy enough to provide some protection against a blade but lightweight enough to allow me to move deftly and with accuracy. Gold and silver threads embroider the collar, sleeves, and trim, and the entire surface of the fabric is embellished with stars that appear to glitter, twinkling with every movement as if infused with *Manan*.

"He kept this one aboard the *Starchaser*," Bellaflor says, smiling wistfully. "Just in case."

"Titus found this?" I ask, running my hands over the soft material, like velvet to the touch.

Her eyes twinkle with adoration. "He had it made, just for you. He was very specific about what he thought you might like."

I know I should say something, but all I can do is stare at the coat. At the details Titus chose simply because he thought I'd like them. "It's beautiful," I finally manage to choke out. "Did you... you made all my gowns, didn't you?"

Bellaflor grins, her expression softening. "They were all his ideas," she says. "I just brought them to life."

A knot forms in my stomach. Each gown he chose, every article of clothing—he put so much thought into the fabrics, the designs.... It's hard to picture him describing such beautiful dresses to his "Auntie Bella," but I can almost see his face—see his broad smile, his glittering eyes—and my heart splinters into a thousand pieces.

Before I can even begin to put them all back together, there's a knock at the door, and Bellaflor opens it to receive Orella.

The queen—my *aunt*, a concept I'm not sure I'll ever get used to—wears a gown made of gold silk, her face bare, body free of jewelry but for the crown of gilded seashells atop her wavy hair.

She smiles sadly, but her eyes sparkle with mischief. "I thought we could walk together."

Bellaflor gives me a kiss on the cheek, still fussing over me even as I follow Orella into the hall.

"She never changes," Orella says, grinning as she leads us out onto the bridge that separates the wing of the Pearl that houses my room and the main structure of the palace. Behind the palace, clustered among the branches, the lights of Ember twinkle like the stars strewn about a dark green sky. The city goes on for miles, spread out through the jungle, thinning as it reaches the mountain—the volcano Orella calls "Samael."

Orella pauses, leaning leisurely on the ropes, staring out at the ocean beyond. The canopy isn't as thick here, allowing us a breathtaking view of the beach, where crowds have already begun to gather for the party beneath a dusky lavender sky. Among them, Elsie and Albert race barefoot, weaving between groups clustered together in conversation and diving under buffet tables. I spot Lewis balancing a skewer of fruit on his nose near the dessert table, and I smile at the way Eliza claps for him, head thrown back as she laughs with abandon. Charlie lingers nearby, chatting with a member of the *Starchaser*'s crew—I think her name was Nadine—and when she looks away to answer someone's call, Charlie takes a long draught of his wine and smooths his hair, nervously adjusting his shirtsleeves. Margaret and Jack walk hand in hand as the tide laps at their feet, wholly absorbed in each other's presence, as if they were the only two people on the entire island. Meanwhile,

Henry sits at one of the long banquet tables, kicking the sand with his newly repaired leg, his expression dour as he watches them strolling along.

"That's a beautiful coat." Orella glances at me, her smile exuding warmth. "Where did you get it?"

My stomach twists, and I shrug, attempting to appear unaffected. "It was a gift."

She nods, brows raised. Her expression reminds me of the look Margaret gives me when she knows there's more to a story than I'm letting on. "Quite the gift."

I run my hands over the fabric, tracing the pattern of a star on my sleeve. "It's not like that," I say, a blush creeping into my cheeks.

"Oh, right," she says with a wink. "Of course."

"I mean it!" I protest, but even I don't think I sound convincing.

Orella laughs, holding her hands up in mock surrender. "I believe you!"

But by the look she gives me, I know that isn't true. And when I give an uneasy chuckle, she nudges me with her shoulder.

She says, her voice soft, "I'm guessing it wasn't a gift from that boy who's locked himself up in the brig of the *Starchaser*, then?"

I grip the rope, staring out at the sea, my chest hollow. "No," I say quietly. "It wasn't."

Orella nods slowly. "Would you rather he'd given it to you instead?"

"I—" A breeze rustles the leaves, and I pull the coat tighter around me. Quietly, I say, "I don't know."

I cut a glance at her, expecting to see judgment in her eyes, but

I follow her gaze to where Killian sits next to Dinah in the sand, watching the last semicircle of amber light dip below the horizon. I don't know why I didn't think of it before, but it's as if seeing the look of barely subdued longing on Orella's face reminds me of the night Killian told me the Red Island was real—the night he gave me my daggers. He said then that a family rescued him, and I know now that he and Father have been friends since they were teenagers, but...

"You and Killian?" I ask. I regret saying this almost immediately, but Orella just grins, her eyes glassy with tears.

"I think," she says, "that as your aunt, I'm supposed to give you advice when it comes to matters of the heart." She rolls her eyes, sticks out her tongue, and we share a brief laugh before her expression turns serious. She faces me, taking both my hands in hers. "If you're ever lucky enough to find someone who looks at you like you breathed life into the heavens themselves, whatever you do, Aster, don't let them go."

A pang of grief seizes my chest. "You waited for him? All this time?"

She tilts her head, and a tear slips onto her cheek. "There's no one else like him," she says.

I squeeze her hands. "It's not too late," I tell her. "To be happy."

"To chase another star," she says, nodding slowly. Gently, she pats my face before looping her arm through mine and starting down the bridge once more. She laughs, but it sounds more like an attempt to mask the quiet sob that chokes her voice. "I'm supposed to give *you* advice, remember?"

I take another bite of the stewed goat meat, chewing slowly.

As I savor the bite, I glance about the party, at the crowd gathered among the torches and the lanterns strewn from the branches of the trees across the beach, illuminating smiling faces huddled near buffet tables boasting platters overflowing with fruits and meats I've never seen, let alone tasted. Whisked away by her adoring public the moment we arrived, Orella stands nearby, chatting with a group of dignitaries—fleet delegates, captains, quartermasters. Watching her from behind the roast pig, Killian smokes his cigar, his eyes filled to the brim with that same intense longing I saw from the pirate queen, decidedly unconcerned with whatever Clemson and Davina are telling him, though it seems, even from here, to be of utmost importance.

It's only when Father comes along, giving Clemson and Davina their leave, that Killian pulls his attention from Orella. He claps Father on the shoulder, and a moment later, the two of them are snickering like two teenage boys. My heart twists when I think about Will and Titus. Can things ever be the same between them? It's not like Titus chose to be compelled—it isn't Titus's fault, no more than Will's Shifter curse is his. But still, the things Titus said, the things he did... even if Will can forget, I'm not sure Titus will be able to forgive himself.

And if what Titus said about Will is true...

The food suddenly tastes like ash in my mouth, and I'm considering making the trek back to my room when a smattering of applause draws my attention to the water.

Jack kneels before Margaret, a small velvet box in his hands. Margaret covers her face, and for a moment Jack looks as if he's about to faint, but then Margaret nods, tackling him to the sand. I spot my parents on the outskirts of the crowd, their hands clasped, faces beaming. Elsie squeals, jumping up and down. Albert rolls his eyes, but when Charlie and Lewis rush Jack, hoisting him onto their shoulders, my little brother chases after them, whooping and cheering.

I'm on my feet then, starting toward Margaret, when I notice Henry leaving the scene, heading down the beach in the opposite direction. In the few seconds I pause to watch him go, my sister is overtaken by a small group of women, all giggling and admiring the pearls from Jack. I'm torn, caught up in the excitement of Jack's proposal, wanting nothing more than to throw myself into their midst and bask in their joy. This is what I'm fighting for—moments like these. But as I watch Henry trekking down the beach alone, I'm reminded that this isn't over yet. *Soon*, I promise myself as I jog to catch up with him. Soon, I can be happy, too.

"Party's that way," I say, panting to catch my breath.

"You shouldn't exert yourself like that," he mutters, cutting a glance at me, his face drawn.

I snort a laugh. "Not you, too."

He scoffs, shaking his head, his black curls dappled silver by the moonlight. "You really don't get it."

I don't know what I thought was going to happen when I chased after him—that perhaps we'd clear the air after our conversation in the tunnels at Castle Grim. Instead, I snap, "Get what?"

He stops, turns to face me. "You're always trying to fix everything on your own! You think it's your responsibility to protect everyone. To make sure everyone else is happy, and safe, and—" He groans, a muscle in his jaw feathering, but when our eyes meet, his gaze is soft, his voice gentle. "Who takes care of *you*, Aster?"

I blink, stunned. "Henry—"

He laughs, running his hands over his face. "I'm not offering," he says, giving me a somewhat comical look. "And I'm—" He grinds his jaw. "I'm not going anywhere, either. But, it's as if I see her everywhere I look." He glances across the beach, at Margaret, and I realize he must be thinking of Dorothy—of how, in another life, he might have watched her beaming after *his* proposal. "I just don't know what to feel."

I frown, taking his hand in both of mine. "Give it time," I say. "But, Henry, if you don't stop with the sorrowsnap—"

"I *have* stopped," he says, covering our clasped fingers with his other hand. His teeth worry his bottom lip, and he looks everywhere but at me. He adds quietly, "Your sister helped me through the withdrawals, while we were aboard the *Starchaser*."

"O-oh?" I stutter, my eyes widening before I can school my expression into something less...surprised.

He raises his brows at me, a familiar, teasing smirk curling his lip. "This is what I'm talking about," he says. "You could drop dead any minute and defect to the Underlings and you're worried about *my* destructive habits."

"Stop being destructive, and I won't have to worry."

He gives me a dull look. "I'll try," he drawls. "If you promise to *rest*."

I start to pull away, but his grip is unyielding.

"I *will* rest," I assure him, "after—"

Just then, someone calls out, "Aster!" and I turn to find Orella waving at me from across the beach, where the commotion that followed Jack's proposal has passed, the crowd dispersed, my siblings nowhere to be seen.

"You'd better go," Henry says, squeezing my hands before releasing me.

I rise onto my tiptoes, placing a quick kiss on his cheek. "You're a prize, Henry Castor."

He rolls his eyes, but his smile is full and genuine. "And you're a princess among thieves, Aster Oberon."

I make a rude gesture behind my back as I walk away, and his laughter follows me down the beach. Once again, his laughter fills me with hope. We survived the *Deathwail*. We can survive this, too.

Orella loops her arm through mine and leads me toward the harbor.

"Smile," she says without moving her lips, as she waves at her people gathered near a stall selling wood-carved icons and bracelets made of braided leather. "We don't have long before they wonder where we've gone."

Instantly, her words send my mind into a whirl, my heartbeat kicking into a gallop. But I do as she says and plaster on a smile, speaking through my teeth when I whisper, "Am I in trouble?"

"Not as much trouble as I'm going to be in," she whispers back, her pace increasing.

The sounds of the party fade beneath the crash of the waves as we make our way down the dock, toward the *Starchaser*. Orella moves quickly, stopping only once we've reached the gangplank, and even then, she looks over her shoulder before taking something from the pocket of her gown.

"I had an opportunity, once, to choose my own path," she tells me, pressing the fabric-wrapped parcel into my palms, closing my fingers around the small disc-shaped object and covering my hand with hers. "I didn't take it."

She withdraws her hands from mine, and I unwrap the parcel, revealing the compass etched with my father's handwriting. I gape at her. "But—why—"

"You would have tried to take it, anyway," she says with a knowing look.

My eyes narrow suspiciously. "How do you know that?"

She smiles, caressing my cheek with the back of her hand. "Because it's something your father would have done."

I look down at the compass, then at the *Starchaser* behind me, before throwing my arms around her. She hugs me tight, stroking my hair.

"I wish—" My voice cracks, and I press my lips together to barricade the sob that threatens to slip out. *I wish I could have known you my whole life*, I want to say.

She seems to understand, because she draws back, pushing a few loose strands of hair out of my face. "We'll have plenty of time to get to know each other when you get home."

I blink, wiping the tears from my eyes before they can fall in earnest, and take a deep breath. "I can't crew a ship by myself."

She nods slowly, a mischievous grin tugging at her lips. "Go. Talk to him," she says, jerking her chin in the direction of the brig. "Let me handle the rest."

Chapter Forty-Four

My heart pounds against my rib cage as I climb down the steps that lead to the brig. I woke only this morning, but it's been three weeks for Will. Three weeks since he began his transformation. Three weeks since he was betrayed by his best friend. Three weeks since we barely escaped Castle Grim with our lives.

I steel myself as I step into the guttering lantern light. I'm not sure what I expect to find, but when I see him slumped against the bars of his cell, his hair wet, as if he's bathed recently, an untouched plate piled high with food beside him, my knees threaten to buckle. I note the collar of Elysian Iron clamped around his neck, and my stomach flips.

"Will?"

His eyes fling wide, and his head snaps up in that animalistic way it did in the dungeons that night. I brace myself for him to lunge, taking a step back from the cell, but when he sees me, his expression twists, full of anguish. He doesn't move from his place on the floor, but his voice is strained, and it seems as if it takes every ounce of self-control to stay seated, his hands flexing at his side.

"Gabriel told me you were awake," he grits out. His throat bobs, and tears streak his face even as he clenches his jaw. "You need to go, Aster. Please. It's not...safe."

Please. At the sound of his voice, I throw caution to the wind, stepping up to the bars of his cell, close enough that if he wanted to, he could easily grab hold of me. I unwrap the compass. It glints in the lantern light, reflecting the flames in its polished brass surface. "This compass will lead us to Havok," I explain, telling him as quickly as possible everything I heard in the war room. All the while he watches me, his brows knit, eyes narrowed. "It's not over," I tell him. "If we can get a drop of her blood—"

"Aster." He sighs, shaking his head.

"Don't," I say, shoving the compass back into my pocket. "Don't give up. You can't."

"It's too late." He winces as he shifts slightly, as if he were about to stand but decided against it. He clutches at his stomach, where I can only imagine the gruesome wound has festered, eating away at his flesh. "I'm dying. I don't have long, and then—"

"Stop!" I shout, gripping the iron bars, needing something solid to cling to. "I don't know why you didn't turn on Holy Winter's Day, but here you are! You're still alive. If you want to give up, fine. But I won't let her use Annie like this. She—" My voice catches, and hot, angry tears burn my cheeks. "She's still in there, Will, and you know it. We...we have to set her free."

I know my words have met their mark when Will's jaw goes

slack, his eyes glazed—haunted by memories of his time spent on the battlefield. I know he's thinking about the troop of soldiers he was forced to execute, banishing the Sylks that possessed them. *They're still them when they die*, he told me then. I don't know what Morana plans to do while in possession of her body, but Annie deserves to be at peace. To go out on her own terms.

Will nods slowly. "When do we leave?"

Relief and fear flood me in equal measure. "As soon as possible." I don't tell him we don't have a crew just yet, because I don't want him to doubt that we can actually pull this off. "I just need to check on a few things," I tell him, making the climb abovedeck before he can say anything to change my mind.

When I emerge onto the main deck, I expect to find Orella waiting for me, but she's already gone. In the distance, the lights of Ember flicker, warm and inviting, the sweet scent of coconut bread and grilled pineapple wafting toward me. The faint music from the party, accompanied by the lulling cadence of the waves, almost causes me to falter. I take the compass out of my pocket, turning it over in my hands, thinking, vaguely, that it feels heavier than it had before. Here, on this island, is everything I've ever wanted. Freedom. Safety. Family. But knowing that Owen isn't here to share in our victory makes it feel hollow. Even if he were here, even if I could manage to rescue him from Morana's kingdom...

There's still someone else who would be missing.

I peer over the taffrail, down the empty docks. How long did Orella expect me to wait while she gathered a crew and provisions? Mother and Father will discover I've gone soon, and then it will be too late. If they suspect I've left—that I've taken the compass—they won't let me out of their sight.

"Going somewhere?"

I whirl at the sound of Jack's voice and find him tangled up in the rigging. I didn't notice him before—it's too dark to make out much of anything—but as I scan the ship, the moonlight illuminates their figures as they step out of the shadows and into the silver light.

"What?" Charlie calls from where he stands behind the helm. "Did you really think we'd let you run off and claim all the glory for yourself?"

"Not a chance," Lewis says from behind me. He grins, eyes twinkling with mischief, but beneath his carefree facade, there's a steely determination in his gaze—an anger I know all too well. "He's our brother, too," he adds, his voice steady. "No matter what he's done, we're going to bring him back. All of us."

All of us?

"Orella thought you could use some friends," Eliza says, crossing the deck to stand beside Lewis.

Behind them I spot Margaret instructing Henry how to hoist the sail. The luff rope jams and he runs his hands over his face, clearly frustrated, but Margaret doesn't lose her cool, her tone patient as she helps him correct his mistake. He looks up at her as she speaks, but she doesn't seem to notice as his gaze takes in every detail of her face. When his eyes land, finally, on her pearl earrings, he grimaces, focusing once more on the task at hand.

"Well, Miss Oberon?" comes another, familiar voice from across the deck. I squint in the darkness, attempting to make out his face in the shadows. Tall, tan, he wears a plain black shirt, his dark trousers tucked into a pair of scuffed boots. It must be a trick of the light, but as he draws near his ears appear...tapered. As if they end in sharp, curved points. I try to place his voice—rough and quiet—but then I note the two bloodred swords sheathed at his hips, and my heart leaps into my throat.

"Gabriel?" I give him a shove before throwing my arms around his neck.

"Not what you were expecting?" he asks as he draws back, the ghost of a grin on his lips, and I'm struck by the resemblance between him and his identical twin.

I touch the tip of his ear, confirming what I thought I saw—the tapered points. Gabriel isn't a Nightweaver. And he isn't human, either. "You're a Myth!"

"An elf," Eliza says, folding her arms over her chest. "Most elves joined with Underlings centuries ago."

Gabriel's jaw tightens. "Those of us who didn't were shunned by the other Myths, forced to hide because of our...similarities with the Shifters."

"Similarities?" I ask, looking between Eliza and Gabriel.

Eliza nods slowly, casting a hesitant glance at Lewis. "Elves can shape-shift as well." She wriggles her nose, and it's as if a veil is lifted. Eliza's ears taper to sharp points, just like Gabriel's.

"But you're a Nightweaver?" Lewis asks, his face a mixture of awe and confusion.

Eliza ducks her head, uncharacteristically bashful as she peers up at him through thick lashes. "We manipulate *Manan* like the Nightweavers," she says.

My heart stutters in my chest, and I sway. "So Flynn truly *wasn't* a Shifter?"

Eliza's expression turns grim, her eyes brimming with tears as she looks at Gabriel, who dips his head as if to reassure her. I note the weight of grief that settles on her shoulders, and guilt and gratitude overwhelm me in equal measure as I watch the two of them silently communicate. They've just lost their brother, and yet, they're going to help me and my siblings save ours.

"No," she answers quietly, her brow furrowed. "The Cooper family *was* slaughtered—even the children. But Flynn, Gabriel, and I took their places. We allowed the rumor of our allegiance to the Guild of Shadows to spread because we wanted the nobility to fear us." She looks at Lewis then, cringing slightly. "Well? Say something."

But Lewis doesn't say anything. Instead, he takes her face in his hands, caressing the tapered point of her ears as he presses his lips to hers. They break apart when Charlie shouts an order, but not without another smattering of kisses and whispered promises.

As they join the others in preparing the ship to sail, Gabriel flicks a glance at the compass in my hands.

There is still time to chase another star.

"What say you, Captain?" Gabriel asks.

"Captain?" I ask.

He grins. "We took a vote."

A swell of emotions balloons in my chest. I think of Will in the brig, clinging to life. Owen, forced into Morana's service. Annie, held captive by Morana's possession. And Titus... this is the only way to break his compulsion. I can free them all.

I can free myself.

I look around at my siblings, my friends. I could be leading them all to their deaths—or worse. And yet, they're trusting me to lead them anyway.

I think of what Father said: *Love is always worth the risk*. We're all here because of someone we love.

I look to the stars above, and for the first time, I feel as if someone is looking down at me—watching me. *Seeing* me. Could Mother have been right? Does the True King have a plan for me? A purpose to fulfill? All this time, the power of the Lightbringer has flowed through my veins. I am Hildegarde's heir, a child of the sea.

I will not be shaken. I will not falter. And I will not be silenced.

I lift the lid of the compass and the needle spins wildly before pointing west, toward Dread. "Set a course for the Burning Lands."

Acknowledgments

To God be the glory! It will take an eternity to thank Him for gifting me grace at my lowest, and for His peace that goes beyond all understanding. I wouldn't be here, doing what I love, if it weren't for Him.

To my mom, who always makes sure my writing candle is stocked (IYKYK) and who lets me ask her a million questions (often the same questions over and over again), and to my dad, who keeps the coffee poured and would hand-sell copies of my books to a squirrel if they had opposable thumbs, thank you. Thank you for believing in me and for never letting me give up on my dreams.

To my beloved husband and best friend, Harrison, who loves me even when I'm on deadline, thank you for never letting me forget why I started doing this in the first place. Thank you for standing beside me, for holding my hand through the tough times, and for celebrating all the wins—big and small—along the way.

To my siblings, Rachel, Josh, and MJ... There, I said your names. Reply to my text messages in a timely manner and next time, I might even thank you for inspiring all the best parts of the Oberon siblings. Maybe.

To my agents, Peter and Gwen, and the entire team at UTA, thank you for being my literary cupids, and for making me feel like I *can* do this writing thing when all I want to do is bang my head on my keyboard. And to Ciara and the team at Curtis Brown, thank you for all the restful nights of sleep I've got knowing I'm in such capable hands.

To my publishers, Megan Tingley and Jackie Engel, and to my dream team at Little, Brown Books for Young Readers, thank you for believing in Aster's story, and for the love and care you've shown not only to this book but to me. I feel incredibly fortunate to work with a group of people as talented as they are kind. To Alexandra Hightower, my lovely editor, Amanda Gaglione, and the entire editorial team, thank you for all you've done to help me shape this story into something legible. Thank you to Patricia Alvarado, Jen Graham, Karina Granda, and Elena Aguirre Uranga for designing and producing this gorgeous book, to Colin Verdi for once again blowing my mind with a cover I wish I could live inside, and to Srdjan Vidakovic for bringing this world to life with a map that at one time only existed in my dreams. Thank you to Emilie Polster, Andie Divelbiss, Savannah Kennelly, and Christie Michel, for championing *Starchaser* near and far, and to my extraordinary publicist, Hannah Klein, for brightening my day every time I see your name in my inbox.

Thank you, Katie Sinfield, Nina Douglas, Chessanie Vincent,

and all the folks in the UK for everything you've done for *Starchaser*. Planning my trip to London as we speak!

Thank you, Ashlee, for loving me through every awkward phase and sending me videos of your live reactions to this story. You keep me going. Thank you, Christin, for every encouraging voice message and for being the best thing to come from my time on the internet since Neopets. Thank you, Emilio, for being excited about every piece of news, even if Harrison's already told you first, and for not holding me to those WrestleMania tickets too harshly. One day.

Thank you, Nikkita Bell, Emmory Jarman, Logan Karlie, Elora Cook, and Nicole Reeves, for being the best bunch of writers I know, and even better friends.

A very special thank-you to Julie Hays for being one of the first to believe in my story, and for being my friend.

Thank you, of course, to my dogs, Archie and Merlin, for making my office a cozy, happy place and not just the place I go to check my email and bang my head on my keyboard.

Last, but certainly not least, thank YOU, dear reader! None of this would be possible without your love, support, and most importantly, your friendship. Thank you for believing in me when I didn't believe in myself, for not letting me give up, and for making my wildest dreams come true.

And to you, the dreamer: Keep chasing those stars.

Jeremiah 29:11

Kayla Pavao

R. M. GRAY

lives in Texas with her husband and two giant dogs, where she enjoys writing stories about pirates, magic, mystery, and all things fantastical. A self-proclaimed expert at whistling and a dedicated collector of lightsabers, she spends her days drinking too much Earl Grey tea, rewatching old cartoons, and thinking up new ways to break readers' hearts. She is the author of *Nightweaver*. She invites you to visit her online at rmgraybooks.com or @rmgrayauthor.